ONLY THINGS

Also from Brad Carter

THE BIG MAN OF BARLOW
(DIS)COMFORT FOOD
SATURDAY NIGHT OF THE LIVING DEAD

ONLY THINGS

BRAD CARTER

POST MORTEM PRESS
CINCINNATI

Copyright © 2015 Brad Carter

All rights reserved.

Post Mortem Press - Cincinnati, OH

www.postmortem-press.com

All characters appearing in this work are fictitious. Any resemblance to real persons, living or dead, is purely coincidental.

No part of this book may be reproduced in any form or by any electronic or mechanical means including information storage and retrieval systems, without permission in writing from the author. The only exception is by a reviewer, who may quote short excerpts in a review.

FIRST EDITION

Printed in the United States of America
ISBN: 978-0692309780
Library of Congress Control Number: 2014956910

*For all those who have stood by me through it all.
You know who you are.
You know how I feel.
Now let's get this show on the road....*

A house is just a place to keep your stuff while you go out and get more stuff.
--George Carlin

Prologue: The Full Moon Effect

Nights with a full moon were always the worst. Dr. Potts had worked in five different ERs in three different states, and nothing could convince her that there wasn't something about a full moon that drove people to extremes. Even in a quiet town like Fayetteville—well, quiet as far as university towns went—it had been a night for the books. Some frat boys had gotten the idea that giving their new pledges Budweiser enemas was a suitable hazing ritual. Now there were three rooms occupied by groaning man children in Greek letter t-shirts. A brawl in the parking lot behind a Dickson Street bar had sent four people in with lacerations and broken bones all around.

All that before the two apparent suicide attempts had shown up within minutes of one another. Yes sir, it was one for the books.

Dr. Potts ducked into the room where the first suicidal kid was sleeping it off. He'd swallowed down a couple big bottles of Tylenol, and would have been circling the drain if his roommate hadn't come back from a party early. They'd pumped the kid's stomach then filled him up with activated charcoal. He'd stay overnight then sit for a psych workup. The standard thing. She resisted the urge to flip through the kid's chart. The nurses here were good, and the last thing she wanted was for them to think she was second-guessing their work.

She went to the neighboring room where the other attempted suicide was also spending time in dreamland. This one was female, a few years older than her neighbor. She'd taken a handful of her prescribed antidepressants with a glass of vodka. Then she'd gotten into a hot bath and slashed both wrists. But she'd left the water running, and it leaked into the downstairs apartment. Her annoyed neighbor—who just so happened to be the landlord—found her and called 911. Dr. Potts moved to her bedside and watched the young woman sleep for a minute. She left the chart alone.

"Pretty one, isn't she?" One of the nurses, Kayla, had drifted in silently to go through the hourly vitals-checking ritual. "You'd think it would be the awkward, nerdy ones, right? Seems like it's always these pretty girls that end up trying to kill themselves."

Dr. Potts knew that she should hush that kind of talk. Some of these young nurses lost all sense of propriety during the overnight. But she'd been thinking the same thing herself, and besides, she didn't have it in her to play the harsh taskmaster.

"It does make me wonder," Dr. Potts said. "I guess that's just the mother in me."

"Tara's, let's see, is she fourteen now?" Kayla asked.

"Fifteen last month, and already talking about needing a car."

Kayla sighed wistfully. "They grow up so fast."

Dr. Potts cut her a sideways look. Kayla couldn't have been more than three years out of school. She was closer in age to Tara than she was to Dr. Potts. What the hell could she possibly know about it? Give a kid—and Kayla was still very much a kid—a bit of responsibility and she takes it as license to spit out a world-weary routine. Like she knew anything about the world.

Dr. Potts shook her head. Where the hell had that come from? She'd never thought of herself as having a short fuse. Maybe the full moon was getting to her too. Or maybe it was her new shoes. They looked fantastic, but they were pinchy as hell. Whatever it was that had her so irritable, she told herself to shrug it off. It was just the beginning of what looked to be a long night.

She told Kayla to keep up the good work and left the room.

The screaming started three hours later.

Dr. Potts was in the staff lounge, picking at a Lean Cuisine and leafing through an Avon catalog someone had left on the table. It was one of those rare breaks in which she had the entire room to herself, and she meant to savor it. She was reading about a new selection of flavored lip gloss and had her forkful of angel hair pasta with Alfredo sauce halfway to her mouth when she heard it.

After two decades working in Emergency Rooms and Trauma wards, Dr. Potts had heard plenty of screaming and yelling. Once, when she was working in Little Rock, some idiot high on sherm decided he was Jesus Christ and started trying to perform forcible baptisms in the men's bathroom urinals. There'd been plenty of screaming then. But this was different. There was a crazed edge to it that made her wince and broke her arms out in goosebumps.

She dropped her fork and ran out of the lounge, pinchy shoes be damned.

It wasn't hard to find the source of the racket. Nurses were buzzing in and out of the room as Dr. Potts made it around the corner.

Good gravy, it was that female attempted suicide making that noise? What the heck was that about?

Dr. Potts' heart felt like it was racing toward tachycardia as she charged into the room. She barked out an order to start pushing haloperidol, and was relieved to see that Kayla was already drawing up the syringe, per standing protocol. Maybe that kid wasn't so bad after all. The kid on the bed, however, looked pretty darn bad. She was twisted up in the sheet and blanket, thrashing around as she screamed. Her eyes were rolled back so far that only the whites were visible. Foamy spit ran out of both sides of her mouth. Her neck was swollen. It looked like a snake swallowing a particularly obese rodent. Amazingly, all the drool and the swelling didn't stop her shrieking.

And it wasn't just screams, either. Between the wordless shrieks, she spat out an endless stream of nonsense: *Something was crawling into her, she insisted. Something was laying its eggs in her. Something horrible that only she could see was attacking her.*

Kayla had given up trying to inject the haloperidol. The patient was too agitated for her to get a clear target. She pushed it into the IV port instead, and soon enough the young woman stopped her thrashing and raving. The swelling in her neck went down too, like a balloon deflating.

Dr. Potts had just enough time to sigh and wipe her forehead with the back of her hand before the other attempted suicide, the young man who'd taken all the acetaminophen, started wailing. It seemed that something was trying to crawl inside him as well. At least that's what he screamed before his voice dissolved into guttural choking sounds. Dr. Potts didn't even have to tell Kayla to get more haloperidol. The nurse was already out the door, leading the charge.

As Dr. Potts followed, she caught a quick glimpse of the night sky through the window at the end of the hall. The big full moon stared back at her.

18 Years Later
Chapter One: Percy

Percy killed his golf cart's engine and clambered off the vehicle. The keys clipped to his belt jingled when he walked. Besides the crickets and tree frogs, that soft metallic tinkling was the night's only sound. He cast the beam of his Maglite up and down the central driveway. Not so much as a stray cat lurking in the shadows. He glanced down at his watch. 11:30 and all was well at the Edgewood U-Stor-It.

This wasn't hard, not even compared to working at the Burger Stop. Patrol the perimeter. Check the locks. Make sure there weren't no high school kids drinking, smoking pot, or screwing between the storage units. But for Percy Flannigan, it was thirsty work. Summer nights in Arkansas never really cooled off; they just got less hot. Even riding around on the golf cart brought out the sweat.

Two and a half hours into his shift and it was time for a break.

He let himself into the guardhouse, that cramped shack that he referred to as "HQ," and paused at the little keypad just inside the door to punch in his code to turn off the alarm. He panicked for a moment halfway through the four digits, but then he remembered the last two numbers and made it with seconds to spare. He breathed out a sigh and pushed his cap back off his forehead.

"There's a co-cola in that cooler with my name on it," he said to no one in particular.

Most people thought the night watchman gig was a shitty job, and Percy knew it. He was slow, but he wasn't stupid. He knew it was a shitty job because the manager trusted him to do it. Not many people looked at him as someone they could put a lot of faith in to do a job and not screw it up somehow. The folks at Burger Stop hadn't seen fit to offer him advancement, not even after three years of working the prep station without a single day out sick. And that time when he nearly hacked off his finger chopping onions? Did he turn around and sue the shit out of them the way some people would have? Not at all. Suing folks was for pussies. And though the jock assholes in high school had been fond of calling him Pussy Flannigan, he was not about to let a few little stitches get him into some lawsuit.

Once upon a time it would have gotten him down, knowing that the only reason he had a job was that it was too simple to fuck up. But no more. Percy had turned over a new leaf, developed what he thought of as a philosophy for life. And that philosophy was "just go with the flow."

Last year he'd watched his Uncle Mike have a heart attack. They'd been enjoying a football game, and Mike had laid big money on the Razorbacks to pull an upset. Of course, that upset started looking less and less likely as the game went on, and Uncle Mike had just blown a gasket right there on the couch, spilling Budweiser and peanuts all over the floor. Percy had decided on the spot that he wouldn't let that happen to himself. Then again, it wasn't just stress that got Uncle Mike. The man had been fat as the Goodyear blimp.

Percy took a seat in a cushioned swivel chair and threw his feet up on the desk. There was a little TV up there, and he found an episode of *Law and Order*. His heart sank a bit when he realized that it was past the good part where the cops busted heads and kicked in doors and interrogated the criminals. It was into the second half, the boring shit with lawyers and judges. That stuff rarely made a lick of sense to Percy, and when it did, it was still boring as Sunday school. Even worse, it seemed like half the time they just let the bad guys go for some reason. Oh well. There was probably another episode coming on, and he could watch the good part of that one before it was time to make his rounds again.

At half past midnight it was time to check the premises, and Percy decided he'd do this one on foot. Too much riding around in that golf cart and he'd be fat as Uncle Mike. He strapped on what he thought of as his utility belt, checking that keys, flashlight, pepper spray, and pocket knife were all present and accounted for. And of course there was also the snub-nosed .38 that he was not supposed to carry but did anyway. Pepper spray was okay, but if it ever came time to really throw down, he didn't want to be caught with nothing but an aerosol can between him and the bad guys. He tugged the bill of his cap down on his forehead and left HQ.

The Edgewood U-Stor-It wasn't a large place. There were forty units total, arranged in neat little rows. The whole place was surrounded by a ten-foot fence topped with barbed wire. Add in the fact that there was twenty-four hour on-site security, bolstered by video cameras, and the good people of Edgewood, Arkansas felt mostly secure storing their extra stuff at the facility. The units stayed full; sometimes there was even a waiting list. And at night, Percy was in charge of it all. It was a shitty job, but it did carry a certain amount of responsibility.

He strolled around the perimeter, playing the beam of his flashlight up and down the fence as he went. No apparent breaches in the chain link. No bits of torn clothing on the barbed wire. The backs of all the units appeared secure. He turned the corner and headed down the first alley between the units. He was nearly to the end of the line when he heard a sound behind him. Faint rattling followed by muted thumps. Like something banging on one of the unit doors from inside. A slow sweep of the Maglite turned up nothing, and Percy was about to chalk it up to one of the many stray cats that prowled the surrounding woods when that noise kicked up again, louder this time.

What in the holy hell?

The sound was coming from Unit 9; Percy could tell that much just walking back down the alley. When he lit it up with his flashlight, he could even see the door shiver, as if something was thrown up against it from the inside. Then there was a sound—a scream almost—that seemed human. He cocked his head to one side and listened. There it was again. He'd be damned if that wasn't someone—a woman or maybe a child—hollering away inside that locked unit.

"*Jeee-zus* Christ," he whispered, picking up his pace as he went back down the alley.

He'd seen *Silence of the Lambs* and all those serial killer pictures. He knew the kind of sick shit people used their storage units for. But damn it, didn't that always happen in places up north or out west, the big cities? There were perverts in Edgewood, no doubt about that. Percy knew perverts were everywhere. But that kind, the Hannibal Lecter-Jeffrey Dahmer type, in Edgewood? No way.

"Hold on in there!" He put his hand on his .38 as he ran, finding a bit of courage and reassurance by touching the textured pistol grip.

The key to HQ seemed to be hiding on his keyring, and his fingers fumbled and shook as he separated it out from the others. The little alarm pad beeped at him when he opened the door, and he found that the code was completely gone from his brain. He stood in the doorway, spitting out every cuss word in his vocabulary.

"Hell with it!" He tugged the bolt cutters off the tool rack on the wall. "It's go time!"

He kicked the door open and jumped out into the muggy night air. His breathing fast and ragged, his heart hammering, he ran at an all-out sprint around the corner and down the alley toward Unit 9. By the time he skidded to a halt, he was so jacked up on adrenaline that he thought he might be able to rip through the padlock with his bare hands. He clamped the business end of the bolt cutters down on the lock and snapped it off.

All right. This is it.

He tossed aside the bolt cutters, kicked the broken lock out of the door, and drew his gun. He used his foot to send the overhead door rocketing up its track and entered the dark space with his flashlight in one hand and his piece in the other.

"Ma'am, do not be alarmed." Percy tried to get as much calm authority in his voice as possible. "I'm security officer Percy Flannigan, and I'm here to help."

He took a deep breath and played his flashlight beam across the room. There were stacks of boxes piled up all over, but it didn't look like there was much else. Percy called out again and got no response.

Various scenarios played out in his head. The victim was so shocked by hours of torture at the pervert killer's hands that she was frightened of any man's voice. Maybe he should soften his tone next time he spoke. Or maybe she'd been hollering because she was bleeding to death behind all the boxes. Or maybe—and Percy checked to make sure the gun's safety was off as he considered this one—the killer was back there with her, his hand clamped over her mouth to silence her screams.

Percy swallowed. He took a few tentative steps into the unit, shining his light behind each pile of boxes as he went. Nothing. No damsel in distress. No crazy-eyed murderer. He pressed on further into the dark interior. His nose started to itch, but he didn't dare scratch it. Lower his guard just to scratch his nose? Forget it. He was slow, but he wasn't stupid.

"All right," he said, fighting to keep his voice steady. "Whoever's in here, I'm giving you a five count to come from behind them boxes with your hands up. I'm armed and well within my rights to fire on you."

8 | ONLY THINGS

He actually had no idea about his legal standing at that moment, but he liked the sound of those words coming out of his mouth. They were ones he'd practiced over and over in his head during the slow hours of his night shift, always dreaming, but never really expecting, he'd have the chance to actually use them. Scared as he was, he got a charge out of it. He thumbed the hammer back on his gun, enjoying the good, solid sound it made. It put some weight behind his words, showed he wasn't fucking around.

He didn't get an answer. He didn't expect he would. Whoever was in here was hiding in the back corner, he figured. Back there behind where the boxes were stacked highest, where it was darkest. He halfway expected his boots to squelch into a pool of blood. But the ground remained dry as he edged forward. He didn't bother calling out again. He'd made it clear that he was armed and willing to fire. There was nothing else that needed to be said. He took one last calming breath and sprang around the wall of boxes.

The woman standing there smiled at him. Percy's breath exploded out of him with a little yelp.

"*Jeee-zus* Christ, lady! I nearly shot you." Percy lowered his gun. "Just what are you doing in here anyway?"

She didn't say anything, just went right on smiling.

Now that he no longer felt like his heart might explode, Percy examined the woman a little closer. The alarm back at HQ would have the police out here soon, and he should know just who he was dealing with when he gave his statement. She was older than him, but still a looker. She had long, dark hair that framed her pale face. She was slender, and the black dress she wore hung loosely on her shoulders.

"You gonna say something, lady?" Percy was getting annoyed. He didn't expect her to blurt out her life story, but a little gratitude for getting her out of this trap wouldn't have been out of order. "Like, why in the hell were you locked up in here? You couldn't have locked it from the outside, so someone had to put you in here, right?"

She remained silent, but she took a step forward.

"Why don't you just sit tight? The police are on their way on account of the alarm going off. I expect maybe you'll want to talk to them."

She took another step. Then another. She was close to Percy now, close enough that she could have reached out one of her long, thin arms and touched him. That thought—of this pale smiling woman touching him—made him queasy. There was something about her that just wasn't right. It was her eyes. She was close enough now that Percy could see them in the Maglite glow. Her pupils had dilated so far that her eyes were entirely black.

That explains it. She's on something, some kind of drug.

"Now, how about we just wait for them to get here?" Percy's took two quick backward steps. He pressed up against the boxes behind him. "Tell you what, you just stay right where you are."

She didn't take his suggestion. She walked another step forward.

Percy raised his gun. "That's far enough. I think it's best if you just stay put."

The smile fell away from her face. Her lips pressed into a thin line. Those black eyes—they didn't even blink, Percy realized—stared right at him. The gun trembled in Percy's hand.

"Please, lady," he whimpered.

The air in the unit—still and stale when he'd entered—had gone cold. He clenched his teeth, afraid that his jaws would chatter.

Her thin lips peeled back in an impossibly wide grimace that split her face from ear to ear. The Maglite beam flashed across a mouth that was impossibly full of teeth, rows of jagged and irregular teeth on either side of two massive incisors.

Jeee-zus Christ, like a rat!

"Mine. It's all mine," she spat.

Percy pressed back against the boxes behind him. He pressed harder, feeling the pile scoot back a bit.

The box atop the stack wobbled and then fell. It bounced off Percy's head and slammed into the floor, the contents—glass by the sound of it—spilled out onto the floor and shattered. Percy risked a downward glance. Water ran out of the open flaps of the cardboard box. A dusting of thin glass fragments had exploded out around his feet. And there were tiny flecks of white in it…

Snow globes, like Grandma always had out at Christmas time.

The rat-faced lady screeched like a scalded beast. She sprang forward, her long fingers with their pointed nails outstretched. Percy fired, the gun's recoil jerking his arm into the air. He fell, bringing down the entire stack of boxes. The sudden movement jarred the flashlight of out his hand, and the room went dark. Sprawled on the floor, he raised the gun, clutching it in both hands the way his Uncle Mike had taught him at the firing range, and fired again. It was like firing into a cloud. The muzzle flash illuminated the woman's enraged features which didn't even twitch as the bullets whizzed through her. At this range, the gun should have opened her right up, but as far as Percy could tell, she wasn't even scratched. He fired again and again. The chamber clicked empty, but he went on pulling the trigger.

The woman fell on him. He braced himself for impact, but she landed with no more weight than a damp mist. Those long fingers, their touch like clammy air, wound themselves around his neck. She lowered her face closer and closer, until her cheek rested against Percy's own.

"All mine," she whispered.

The hands around Percy's neck solidified until they were hard and cold, the nails razor sharp icicles that tore into his throat.

Percy Flannigan, Security Officer of the Edgewood U-Stor-It, lay there on the cold, wet floor in Unit 9. He gurgled out the last of his life as he stared into the pitch black eyes of the rat-faced woman who chanted in her grating voice that the contents of the unit belonged to her and her alone.

Chapter Two: Chris

The dreary night suited Chris Clanton just fine. The grey sky threatening a storm matched his mood. He wanted lightning to split the heavens. He wanted the clouds to unleash a downpour. Maybe a good rain could wash away the stink that clung to everything around him.

He tuned the car's radio to a station playing soothing classical music. The soft sounds did little to calm his jangled nerves. The more he tried not to think of his rage and embarrassment after being served with a restraining order in front of everyone at work, the more the memory came back. It stung like a wasps' nest set loose in his brain. That was it, the last straw. Even the whiskey, gulped from the now mostly empty half-pint bottle in the glove compartment, couldn't take his mind off the fact that Julian—*Chris' own brother*—had convinced the police department to issue Chris a restraining order. Being drunk did not change the fact that Chris was no longer allowed within a hundred yards of the house on Buchanan Street. Within a hundred yards of the house where he grew up. Within a hundred yards of his ungrateful younger brother.

The light turned green, and Chris made a left onto University Avenue. Rain spattered against the windshield. It was coming down too slow to leave the wipers on the lowest setting, but the drops were too big to leave them turned off. This was all that those storm clouds could deliver, a faint piddling? It was just another annoyance at the end of a day that had been nothing but a long string of annoyances, culminating in that smirking process server bustling into the stacks where Chris was shelving a cart load of books.

"Chris Clanton?" he'd asked, even though Chris' nametag was hanging right there in plain sight.

Chris had carefully shelved a weighty tome of gluten-free dessert recipes and straightened the rest of the books before looking at the little man. "Yes, how may I help you?"

"Legal notice served." The man had smiled and snapped the envelope into Chris' hand then tipped an invisible hat and walked away.

Chris replayed the scene in his head as he drove past the parking lot of his apartment complex. He couldn't go home yet, not when this whirlwind of anger and shame was tearing its way through his grey matter. The thought of facing the blank walls of his one bedroom apartment while eating a plastic microwaved dinner was just too much. So he drove on, leaning over the seat to retrieve the whiskey from the glove compartment.

As he drank, he replayed the day's torment in his mind. It hadn't stopped with the issuance of the restraining order. His supervisor, Effie Landeros, that miserable dike, had chosen that day to dream up problems with Chris' work performance. Apparently, he was lagging behind the other workers when it came to shelving books. Never mind that Chris' sections were neat and impeccably ordered while other sections might as well have been maintained by a pack of wild dogs. No, in Effie's view, he needed to step up the speed.

Try to stay on task, she'd said. As if Chris was just strolling through the stacks aimlessly, waiting for the next opportunity to step into the employee restroom and jack off. *Let's just give it a little more gas, okay, Chris?*

And like a meek little lamb, he'd nodded, said he'd try his best, and slunk out of the office.

More drops spattered the windshield, and he thumbed the wipers on and off. The whiskey burned his throat, but it was a good feeling. He deserved to burn. He deserved it for quietly folding that restraining order and slipping it into his pocket. He deserved it for not telling Effie that she was a stupid bitch for criticizing the performance of her best worker. Most of all, he deserved it for not driving over to the house on Buchanan street and strangling Julian to death. Chris caught a glimpse of his reflection in the rearview mirror and sneered.

He drove on through downtown Little Rock, up and down narrow One Way streets, looking for a suitable hell to wallow in.

The bar was called Rock Town Tavern, and it stank of old cigarette smoke and stale beer. Although the city had banned indoor smoking several years ago, the smell still hovered in the air like a ghost. The bartender might have once been a pretty woman, but her skin was past the point of no return on the journey from bronze tan to wrinkled leather. Gravity and time had pulled stretch marks like a topographic map across the breasts that her low-cut sleeveless blouse revealed. On the whole, the place was disgusting, and that suited Chris just fine.

"What are you drinking, sugar?" the bartender asked, giving Chris a perfectly nauseating look at her cleavage as she leaned over the bar and snapped down a cardboard coaster.

Chris ordered a beer and recoiled as she smiled, revealing front teeth that looked to have been cleaned with a hammer and chisel. While he waited for his drink, Chris examined the bottles behind the bar. They were arranged on the shelf with no attention to organization. Vodkas mingled with whiskeys. Tequilas snugged up against the rums. The bottles were turned this way and that, some with their labels turned completely to the back. Disgusting. No order whatsoever. How could this woman work this way?

"You look like you got a lot on your mind." She placed the frosted mug of beer in front of him.

"Nice goddamn observational skills."

She got the message loud and clear, and found something to do at the opposite end of the bar.

A hand tapped Chris' shoulder. "Shouldn't be too hard on her, man."

The owner of the hand sat two stools down. He scooted one stool closer, bringing his drink with him. He was a stubble-faced drunk who looked to be pushing seventy, but was probably short of that by a couple decades. Chris could imagine this fine fellow stumbling into the Rock Town Tavern as soon as the doors opened, eager to get the first few drinks in him so his hands would stop shaking. For all Chris knew, this was one of the homeless men who stumbled in and out of the library during the day, in search of a public restroom to foul.

"I just don't feel much like talking," Chris said, hoping this idiot would figure out that his advice wasn't welcome.

"Her boyfriend did that to her mouth." The conversationalist gestured to his own front teeth, which were a dingy yellow. "He was a real rough customer, a wanna-be Hell's Angel type, you know. Whopped her across the face with a baseball bat. He's in the penitentiary now, but you just watch, soon as he's out, she'll take him back. It's sad."

Chris looked down the bar at the woman, watching her wipe up spilled beer with a rag. Her eyes darted over in Chris' direction and then quickly away. She let her lank dark brown hair fall in front of her face. Maybe it was the alcohol, but Chris regretted the way he'd snapped at her.

"Belinda, I'm ready to settle up and get home." Chris' new friend rose from his stool and placed some crumpled bills on the bar.

"See you later, Mr. Drymon." Belinda waved at the man, who gave Chris one last pointed look then stumbled out the door.

Chris resisted the urge to pick up the bills and straighten them. Instead, he watched Belinda as she walked back toward him, slipping the rag into her back pocket. He looked over his left shoulder then his right. They were alone. He glanced at his watch. It was nearly midnight. On a Wednesday. He'd been so wrapped up in his anger that he'd driven around for hours without even noticing.

Belinda looked over at the crumpled bills that Mr. Drymon had left for her. Then she looked at Chris. She hesitated for a moment then came closer.

"Look, I'm sorry I snapped at you earlier," Chris said. "It's just that I've....well...."

"Got a lot on your mind?" Belinda smiled a bit, but took care not to show her ruined teeth.

"Yeah. It's been one hell of a day."

"Tell me about it," she said.

Chris nodded and took a long swallow of his beer.

Belinda propped her elbows on the bar. "I didn't mean that just as an expression. Tell me about your day. I'm a bartender. We're sort of required to listen to people's hard luck stories. And besides, I don't know if you've noticed, but it's a slow night in here. Kind of stupid to be the only ones here and not talk."

Chris looked around again. "Yeah, I wondered about that. No bouncer."

"Ricky went home sick an hour ago. Said he could call one of the other guys, but I told him not to bother." She stepped back and poured herself a beer. "So spill it, Mr. Serious. What's got you so down?"

"My name's Chris. And I'll tell you one tragic story if you really want to hear it."

They left the Rock Town Tavern an hour later, having closed up the place early. The rain had finally stopped messing around. It hammered down with a vengeance. They laughed as they ran unsteadily through the downpour to the parking lot. After putting away a few rounds, they'd decided to go back to Belinda's place for a few more. Maybe they'd chosen her place because it was she who hesitantly put forth the idea. Or maybe it was just because her house was closer. Chris really couldn't remember. He wasn't accustomed to drinking so much, and his head was foggy.

He slipped into his car, frowning at the water that puddled on the floorboards. He looked out the window and watched Belinda open the door to her own car. She drove a beat to hell Honda with missing hubcaps. Chris fired up his car's engine. He followed the twin beacons of the Honda's taillights onto the road.

Chris couldn't account for his actions. He didn't consider himself a social person. He'd never picked up a woman in a bar before, not even during college. But there was something about Belinda that had made him open up, in spite of her appearance. He considered that it could be *because* she wasn't beautiful that he was able to speak to her so directly. There was no pressure, no intimidation. She was lucky to have him speak to her in such confidence. Her eyes positively lit up when he'd begun to unload his troubles. That was the word she'd used: unload.

"Chris, you look like you need to vent," she'd said, helping herself to another drink. "I'm listening. Go ahead and unload."

And unload he had. He'd started with his shitty day at the library, working backwards from his meeting with Effie to his encounter with the process server, perfectly aware of how the latter made him appear unstable. But Belinda had only nodded sympathetically.

"How'd things get so bad between you and your brother?" she'd asked.

Chris had laughed, but there was no humor in it. There was nothing funny about the situation. "If you are a fan of sad stories, I have a classic."

The Sad Tale of Christopher Clanton (which is how Chris thought of it when, in moments of despair or anger, he narrated the events in his mind) began when Chris was a child. It reached a new depth of tragedy five years ago, when his father passed away.

Vernon Clanton had been a big man in ways beyond his large stature. He possessed a booming baritone voice that he put to use in the First Nazarene Church choir and in court as a defense attorney for Roth, Morgan, and Clanton Law Firm. He wore double breasted suits and cowboy boots. Whenever he was out of court, he covered his bald spot with a grey Stetson. He was a fan of strong men like General Patton and

John Wayne. Should the boys suffer a minor lapse in discipline, Vernon used a stern lecture to bring them back in line. Should the lapse be more severe, he brought them back in line with a generous application of his belt to their backsides. Usually, a few licks would suffice. Sometimes, it took quite more than that to drive the point home. Had he been over-indulging in Wild Turkey—his strong drink of choice—that application of the belt could stretch on for half an hour.

"So he beat you?" Belinda asked. She'd come from behind the bar to sit on the stool next to Chris. They were sitting close enough that their knees touched, but just barely. "That's awful. Where was your mother in all this? Did he beat her too?"

"I don't know for sure, but I suspect he did. But the beatings stopped after Mom was gone. What came after, I almost preferred the belt." Chris looked down at his drink. "My mom died when I was seven years old. It was a memorable scene. We were having a birthday party for my little brother. I was seven, so that would have made him four that day. Had a big, three-layer strawberry cake. Lots of presents, because Julian was the baby of the family, you know. Anyway, there were the four of us at the dinner table, all of us laughing and carrying on. Julian asked Mom to help him blow out the candles, and she took a deep breath, making a big deal out of it, clowning around so we'd laugh. Then her eyes rolled back in her head and she fell out on the table, face-first into that strawberry cake."

"Good Lord," Belinda said.

"Massive stroke. Dead by the time the ambulance got there." Chris used a paper napkin to wipe up the drops of condensation that had rolled off his glass onto the surface of the bar. Without thinking, he did the same for the drops that had come off Belinda's glass.

She put her hand on Chris' knee.

"Dad changed after that," Chris said. He considered Belinda's hand. The nails were well kept and manicured, possibly professionally. Chris liked that, the attention to detail. Strange that a woman so ugly had such nice hands.

"Well, that's understandable, his wife dying like that." Belinda gave his knee a brief squeeze.

"It started subtly. I guess even earthquakes and forest fires start that way." Chris had no idea if this was true or not, but he liked the analogy. "He kept all of Mom's things exactly the way they were when she passed

Brad Carter | 17

on. Her clothes, jewelry. Even all her makeup and perfume bottles. All the shampoo and lotion and scented soaps that she liked."

"I guess that's not so strange," Belinda said.

"But that was just the beginning. Dad began to buy new things for her, things she would have liked. You know, the way a husband who works long hours will try to make it up to his wife by bringing her home a bottle of perfume or some new earrings. He started doing that. Mom liked clothes from Ann Taylor, so once or twice a week, Dad would come home with a box from that store. Mom liked perfume that came in decorative bottles, so a lot of that came into the house too."

"What did he do with it?"

Chris sipped his drink. He felt loose and warm. "Nothing. He came into the house and placed the box on the counter or on the stairs or wherever he felt like putting it down, and there it stayed. I didn't dare touch that stuff, and I made sure Julian didn't either. Dad had calmed down quite a bit in Mom's absence, but there was an instability about him that told me he could still blow up. Partly that was because he was drinking more and more. It seemed like he was coming home with a new bottle of whiskey every night. A new bottle of whiskey and some little gift for Mom."

Belinda sighed. "That's so sad."

"Well, the slope from sad to crazy was a slippery one for Vernon Clanton." Chris knew the bitterness in his voice wasn't appropriate for the conversation, but he let it creep in all the same. "He picked up an Avon catalogue from one of the girls at the office and ordered just about everything in it. Then it was Mary Kay. Tupperware got their claws into him as well, although I can't imagine how. He discovered those late night infomercials and the home shopping networks. There were packages coming to the house just about every day. I was just a kid, but I knew it was weird what Dad was doing."

Chris went on, enumerating his father's purchases, describing the piles of junk that accumulated in every spare corner, on every shelf, in every closet. The house on Buchanan Street was by no means a small place, but it filled right up. There were six bedrooms, and by the time little Julian was in school, all three of the spares had been packed with Vernon's purchases. Even the bathrooms were a riot of clutter.

"I began to have nightmares about being buried alive," Chris said. "I was only ten years old and having nightmares about being buried alive. I'm no child psychologist, but I know that's not normal or healthy."

Belinda went over to the front door and turned off the neon Open sign. She refreshed their drinks then sat back down. Chris wished Belinda would put her hand back on his leg. He could still feel the warmth where her palm had rested.

Chris smiled. *So this is what it's like. This is how you're supposed to react to these things.*

"All those boxes and packages, I bet they piled right up," Belinda said.

"It was a nightmare. I wasn't the type of kid who had a lot of friends, so I didn't really have much of a handle on how most people lived, but I had an idea that our house was very different from the ones the other kids lived in."

Belinda returned her hand to Chris' thigh. "You poor thing."

"Thank you," Chris said, not sure what exactly he was grateful for. "I vowed that as soon as I could, I'd be out of there, away from the mess. It was Julian that I was worried about. By that time, he'd already started mimicking Dad's behavior. He couldn't throw anything away. Coloring books that had every page filled in. Dried up scraps of modeling clay. Broken toys. None of it could be thrown away without Julian dissolving into hysterical fits. And getting him stirred up meant pushing Dad into one of his rages, so I quit trying after a while."

He told Belinda how he'd watched helplessly as his brother and father spiraled into what could only be described as a type of madness. It was a madness that had driven Chris from the house at the first opportunity. It was a madness that ultimately snuffed out Vernon Clanton's life, the old man coughing and wheezing his last breath in that dusty, moldy landfill that was his bedroom. And it was a madness that still drove a wedge between Chris and Julian.

"When Dad died, he left the house and a good portion of the estate to Julian," Chris said to his glass of whiskey. "I wasn't left out or anything like that. There was money…to be blunt, I don't really even have to hold down a job. But the house…the place where we grew up…where our mother died…just seeing it so filthy and cluttered, it just kills me."

"Can't you talk to your brother about it?" Belinda edged forward on her stool, getting closer and closer to Chris.

He shook his head. "I've tried. I've talked and talked and talked. Julian just smiles and reminds me that I was off in Fayetteville, going to college and then working at the library, while he was the one taking care of Dad. And that's true, but he doesn't understand that no matter how much I would have liked to help, I just…*I couldn't.*"

"What about, you know, like, codes or neighborhood regulations? Can't you at least get them to make your brother take better care of the house?"

"Vernon Clanton may be dead, but his friends and connections live on. Even if someone found out about the house and filed a complaint with the code enforcement office, there's a long line of judges and attorneys who'd make it disappear. Dad was friends with everybody. Or at least he was before he quit working altogether and shut himself up in the house with all the things he'd accumulated."

"That's so sad." Belinda's eyes were wet with sympathy.

"And Julian, he just dropped out of school and stayed home with Dad, making the problem worse. The two of them, letting the filth and clutter just pile up." Chris stopped there, afraid of the strange emotions churning like a whirlpool inside him.

Belinda refilled his glass.

It had been the sympathetic look in Belinda's eyes, Chris decided as he followed her car. That was what had drawn him in. Those big brown eyes full of tears and sympathy. Then again, maybe the whiskey had impaired and finally drowned his judgment. There was no arguing his lack of sobriety. He had trouble keeping the car on the narrow roads Belinda was leading him down. She lived in one of those rundown neighborhoods on the south side of the interstate, the kind of place Chris never thought he'd visit.

He wondered if maybe Belinda was even drunker than he was, that she'd gotten lost trying to drive home. The turns she made without using her signal seemed so random. Chris was thankful for his car's GPS system. If not for that, he might never find his way back home after…

After what, Chris? Just what are you planning to do?

At long last Belinda turned into a narrow, barely paved driveway. Chris parked behind the rust bucket Honda and climbed out of his car, wondering as he followed Belinda into her house if his car would still have its hubcaps after…

After what, Chris?

Her house was dark, but Belinda didn't turn on any lights. The same stale aura of cigarette smoke that Chris noticed in the Rock Town Tavern was present here, but this time it was muted by soft, feminine smells: perfume, fabric softener, and the cheap, cloying aroma of scented candles. Belinda pulled him inside. She slammed the door shut and nearly tackled him. She was all over him, running her hands up and down his back, pressing her mouth against his, thrusting her wet tongue into his mouth. Chris recoiled a bit—just a bit—and then gave into it. His sudden hunger overcame his usual revulsion at such intimate contact. He knew that their saliva mingled and traveled as they kissed, and while such a thought might normally make him faint with disgust, he did not pull away. He twined his fingers into her tangled hair and pressed her face closer. He let his own tongue slip between her lipstick-coated lips, between her jagged, broken teeth.

This is it, Chris. You deserve this.

Belinda led him through the cave-dark interior, taking him by the hand, guiding him through a narrow hallway to her bedroom. The smell of cheap perfume was stronger in here. Belinda dragged him along. She dropped his hand and hooked her fingers behind his belt. Chris felt her knuckles press against his erection as she pulled. He stumbled once, and Belinda gave him a gentle push. He toppled over onto a bed, bouncing as he landed on the squeaky springs.

"The lights..." Chris gasped as Belinda climbed atop him, the bedsprings announcing her arrival.

"No, it'll be better in the dark."

Her breath was hot, moist in Chris' ear as she whispered. It made him squirm a bit beneath her. What followed seemed to Chris to be something of a wrestling match as they struggled out of their clothes. Although the only light in the room filtered around the edges of the curtains in the small window to the left of the bed, Chris' eyes were beginning to adjust. He could discern Belinda's curvy outline, and when he looked down, the circus tent of his underwear, pushed aloft by the steady, building pressure he could feel in his member. He felt Belinda grasp him...

Dear God....

The explosion was instantaneous and seemed to go on forever. Even through his shame and revulsion, Chris moaned and writhed with pleasure.

Belinda laughed, her voice husky. "Wow, that was quick."

"I'm sorry, it's been so long," Chris lied. In truth, this had never happened. He'd never allowed things to go this far.

Belinda rolled off him. "It's okay, honey. We have all night. Let me go wipe all this off me, and we'll try again."

"I'm just out of practice." The lie made Chris' face burn.

"We'll practice some more," Belinda said, climbing out of bed. "Just give me a sec."

Chris listened to her muted footfalls as she crossed the bedroom. She clicked on the bathroom light as she pulled the door closed. He lay there, listening to a blast of water splash into the bathroom sink. Then the toilet flushed and the bathroom door swung open. Chris had to blink furiously to make his eyes adjust as the light spilled out into the bedroom.

"Ready to try again, baby?" She leaned against the door frame, her back arched and legs spread slightly, to give Chris a better view of her intimate parts. What Chris saw did nothing to rouse his member for another go-around. The feeling that rushed over him was something like buyer's remorse mixed with guilt and revulsion. He was tempted to flee from the room, but he was paralyzed.

This was the creature he'd confessed his life's anguish to? This was the creature poised to take his virginity? Chris tasted bile in the back of his throat. The semen on his thighs and belly felt cold, clammy.

"Like what you see?" Belinda traced a finger between her heavy breasts.

Chris moaned, and she must have taken this to be an expression of sexual yearning. She ran her hands over her stretch-marked and sagging body, pinching her nipples, and toying with her thick mound of pubic hair. When Chris finally tore his eyes away from the hideous spectacle and glanced around the room, what he saw brought the bile up with renewed vigor.

Each corner of the room was heaped with unorganized piles of stuffed animals. Teddy bears mostly, but Chris also saw monkeys, puppies, kittens, tigers, even frogs among the tangled masses. The closet doors were open, and the clothes within were hanging askew from their hangers above a riot of shoes. He heaved himself up on his elbows to get a better look at the wreckage around him. Dirty laundry was strewn here and there, underwear and socks and shirts wadded up and thrown about carelessly. There was a dresser, atop which were scattered tubes of lipstick and vials of perfume, nail polish, and mascara. A tube of lotion leaked a congealing line of fluid down the side of the dresser. Chris groaned again. Although he could not see the kitchen, his imagination conjured up snapshots of the horrors that were surely waiting there: a sink heaped with dishes crusted with food, a countertop littered with wadded up fast food wrappers, a trashcan overflowing with empty beer cans dribbling warm backwash onto the sticky linoleum, a refrigerator filled with out of date food items and moss-covered leftovers. He imagined a living room carpet so stained that its original color could no longer be determined. A coffee table buried in old newspapers, unopened mail, and cigarette butts.

While Chris' mind reeled with these nightmare images, Belinda left the bathroom doorway and advanced on the bed like a perfumed predator. She slithered onto the bed and pushed Chris back down on his back then slipped between his legs.

"Let's see if we can't breathe some life back into our friend down here," she said, her mouth hovering above his penis.

The nightmare wave that had been growing to Tsunami proportions in Chris' mind crested and then broke as he watched her mouth open as she descended upon him.

"No!" he screamed, his hands springing into action. He grabbed two fistfuls of her hair and wrenched her head away.

He perceived the next few horrible seconds in a detached manner, as if he were watching them played out in slow motion across a television screen. He saw a look of shocked bewilderment cloud Belinda's features. He saw his own face contort in anger and disgust. And he saw the muscles in his arms and shoulders strain as he twisted her head until her neck broke. He watched until the job was more than done and Belinda's chin rested between her shoulder blades.

Chapter Three: George

The phone buzzed and vibrated on the nightstand, ripping George out of dreamless sleep. He awoke in confusion, staring at the unfamiliar surroundings. He rubbed his eyes and remembered that he wasn't in the old house anymore. He was in the new place, in Barlow. And the right side of the bed was empty because Kathy was dead.

"All right, all right, all right, damn it," he stammered, groping for the phone. It was an ancient model. He'd refused to upgrade for the past few years, despite the fact that the provider kept offering him freebies. Those smart phones looked to be a pain in the ass. Kathy used to call his flip phone his "dumb phone."

"Hello?" he said, putting the phone to his ear.

"I apologize for the lateness of the hour, but I need to speak with George Young."

The voice was crisp and professional, but the accent was pure Arkansas. George was going to have to get re-acquainted with that. All those years away from the south, and he'd lost most of his own accent, or at least he thought so.

He popped on the bedside lamp. "This is George Young. What can I do for you?"

"Mr. Young, this is Constable Ray McFettridge up in Edgewood. I believe you have a storage unit rented out at the U-Stor-It here in town."

The fog of sleep was mostly gone, but George had no idea where this was going. "Yes, I do. There's no such facility in Barlow, so I had to take my business to Edgewood. Can you tell me why you're asking?"

"Mr. Young, there's been a…well, an incident. I've called Sheriff Wilson and he's on his way up from Barlow as we speak. We'd both be grateful if you could see your way clear to making the trip also."

"Right now?" George looked at the alarm clock. "It's almost two in the morning."

"Yessir, I realize what time it is, and I promise you I wouldn't be asking if it wasn't real important. Now I can radio Sheriff Wilson and have him turn back and pick you up if you like."

"No, that's okay. I prefer to drive myself."

"Thank you for your attention in this matter."

George snapped his phone shut, enjoying that turn of phrase. It was as if the constable was asking him to please not park so far from the curb rather than issuing some mysterious summons to the storage facility in the next town over. The old George would have told the officer to wait just a damn minute, to start explaining just what the hell was going on. But that George had died along with Kathy, and the new George was a bit more easygoing. This house—this *brand new* house—was not going to devolve into what the house in Wisconsin had become in the last decade of his marriage to Kathy. This was a second chance at life for him, and though it had arrived in his sixth decade, as he rounded third and was heading for home, he was determined to see it through.

He picked out a pair of comfortable jeans and a t-shirt he'd bought at Batch Bakehouse, his favorite bakery back in Madison. He stomped into a broken-in pair of sneakers and stepped into the bathroom to give himself a final once-over. Back all those years ago, when they made *Speak Softly, Lover* into that movie with Robert Redford playing occult detective Ben McCauley, George's friends would tell him that it was a wonderful coincidence. According to those generous souls, George and Redford favored one another. George had always played at modesty, shaking his head and telling them he didn't know what they were talking about. But the truth was, there was some resemblance.

George brushed his teeth, splashed a little cold water on his face, and decided that he looked presentable enough for the local law enforcement.

They met him at the front gate of the Edgewood U-Stor-It, two cops probably doing their best to look like their TV counterparts as they sipped coffee from Styrofoam cups and leaned against their vehicles. These two were a study in opposites. The sheriff wore his full uniform—hat included—and looked impossibly young for such a post. He was a gangly scarecrow, who looked like he might take flight if the wind kicked up. The Edgewood Constable didn't wear any kind of uniform, and he looked to be a few decades the sheriff's senior. He had a badge hanging from a chain around his neck, but apart from that, looked like he was a construction foreman on a break from the job site.

It was the short, stout construction worker constable who offered his hand first.

"Ray McFettridge." His hand was calloused, his grip crushing. "I believe we spoke on the phone."

George tried not to wince as he dropped his hand back to his side. "That's right."

The scarecrow nodded a curt greeting but didn't shake on it. "Tate Wilson, Gayler County Sheriff's Department. Sorry to get you up at this hour."

"No problem, really. Tell you the truth, I'd just gone to bed a couple hours ago. I got sucked into one of those *Law and Order* marathons," George said. "They start the next episode as soon as the credits roll on the one before. Pulls you right in before you can grab the remote."

"All the same…" McFettridge shrugged. He looked down at his hand and rubbed his fingers across his thumb, as if stroking some invisible fabric. There was a look on the constable's face that George couldn't quite read, something like consternation mixed with dyspepsia. Like the man was suffering indigestion from a chili dog he couldn't remember eating.

"All the same, a crime has taken place," the sheriff finished.

"Yeah," George said. "About that…you gentlemen feel like cluing me in to what's going on here? I figure it's theft, right? Just between you and me, I'm almost relieved. I'd have liked to have been able to get a little money out of it, but really, I just want to get rid…"

He stopped talking when he caught the look the two officers were giving one another.

The sheriff cleared his throat. "Mr. Young, it's not theft."

The constable jumped in. "There's an alarm system here at the facility, same as there is at many of the businesses in Edgewood. I know this because I sold it to the owners. McFettridge Security Systems. My company 'til I sold it off a few years back."

"Law enforcement more profitable?" George asked.

He shook his head. "The constable job is my semi-retirement. Most people don't know the post ain't much more than a security guard for the town. Something bigger than a bar fight or a car accident pops up, about all I can do is hold down the fort until the county sheriff's office can respond."

"And here's the sheriff. So, I take it this is bigger than a break-in or some vandalism." George had a sinking feeling in his belly.

"You're right on that count." McFettridge cleared his throat and looked to the sheriff.

"I was on night duty. Don't have to do it, but I like to lead by example," the sheriff said.

George forced a smile. He was all for good leadership in his civil servants, but he wished Stan and Ollie would just spit it out. The finer points of police procedure were great on an episode of *Law and Order*, but out here they were just dragging down the narrative.

"I admit that I wasn't in a hurry to respond," McFettridge said. "The night watchman here—Percy Flannigan—was a bit slow on the uptake. One of the reasons he has the job, doesn't mind picking up minimum wage working nights. There's an alarm pad in that little guard station, and Percy just couldn't get the hang of it. God knows why the owners even wanted it there in the first place."

"I guess because your old outfit put the hard sell on them," the sheriff said, smiling.

The constable leveled a sharp look at the younger man. "It ain't really the time for jokes. Now you know I got all kinds of respect for the office, but I don't need to hear that kind of shit right now. Percy's aunt, the only family he had left, she's with the coroner, crying her eyes out while they fit the boy for a toe tag."

The sheriff looked suitably chastened. "Yeah, you're right."

The sinking feeling in George's stomach expanded to engulf his whole being. "Did you say someone was killed here?"

McFettridge seemed to realize he'd let the cat out of the bag. He gave the sheriff a different kind of look, one that told him it was time for the full-time peace officer to take over.

"When Constable McFetteridge arrived on the scene, he found Percy Flannigan deceased. The evidence seemed to suggest homicide."

George groaned inwardly. Sheriff Tate Wilson was one of *those*, a cop who overcompensated for the popular perception of police officers as donut chewing lunkheads by using as much jargon as possible.

"We established a perimeter and ascertained that there were no imminent threats in the area. We notified next of kin, and had the body removed to the coroner's office pending positive identification," the sheriff continued.

Brad Carter | 27

"We all know it was Percy. Hell, you went to high school with the boy," McFettridge snapped at the scarecrow with the badge.

The sheriff continued undeterred. "The scene has been closed until the state crime lab can get evidence technicians down here from Little Rock. They should arrive in a couple hours."

George held up a hand. "I'm sorry, I still don't see what this has to do with me."

The sheriff took a sip from his cup of coffee. "Sir, the deceased was found in a storage unit rented in your name."

They had questions. Of course they did. Cops loved their questions. Even someone who'd had limited interactions with police officers, someone like George Young, knew that. And that made him nervous. He didn't get the feeling these two had it in their heads that he was a suspect, at least they didn't come on that way. Or maybe that's just what they wanted him to think. Probably he'd just been watching too much *Law and Order*. The cops on that show were full of guile, devious, the kind of characters that George would have put in one of his novels back in those halcyon days before the muse turned tail and ran. These two weren't in that league. Tate Wilson came off like he was still a bit shocked they allowed him to carry a badge and an actual *real* gun *with bullets and everything*. And Ray McFettridge looked like he'd rather be just about anywhere else, the way he kept fiddling with the badge around his neck. McFettridge didn't even wear a firearm that George could see. Maybe he kept it in the car.

They crowded into the little guard house. The two officers let George take the only chair while they half-sat, half-leaned on the desk. George didn't care for the arrangement one bit. They loomed over him, and it made even the small talk they started with carry the full weight of interrogation.

"Seems to me that most people, if they get famous, they leave Arkansas without ever looking back," McFettridge said.

"I wouldn't say I'm famous." George smiled up at the constable. "I'll bet the young sheriff here has no idea who I am."

"Guilty as charged." The sheriff put up his hands apologetically.

"He wrote that movie about the guy marries a younger woman. Thing is, he's living in this house he got by being a gigolo. The older woman's ghost doesn't care for that arrangement at all." McFettridge looked at the sheriff to see if any of that registered. When the sheriff shook his head, the constable went on. "Well, it's sort of slow at first, but the last fifteen minutes or so are scary as shit. I'm not kidding you either. It's got Robert Redford in it."

George shifted around in his seat to look at the sheriff. "It's called *Speak Softly, Lover*. And I didn't write the movie. I wrote the novel they adapted for the screenplay."

"Well, I'll be damned. A real star in our midst."

George couldn't tell if the sheriff was being genuine or not. He decided to take the comment at face value and nodded his thanks.

"So, I'll start by asking the obvious question," the sheriff said, dropping his smile for an all-business stare. "Did you know Percy Flannigan?"

George thought about asking if he should have an attorney present, but against his instinct decided to play along. He sipped at the can of soda he'd taken from the refrigerator. He'd have preferred coffee but that wasn't on offer. There'd been a couple cans of beer stashed in the back of the fridge, behind the remnants of someone's brown bag lunch. His breath caught in his throat as he reached around them for the Mountain Dew.

He wondered if the cops were observant enough to pick up on his reaction. Maybe the constable. He had the look of a man who'd done some drinking in his time, and George knew that old axiom of drunks and convicts: it took one to know one.

"Mr. Young?" the sheriff prompted. "Did you know the deceased?"

"Oh, sorry. This whole thing has been a little sudden. Of course I didn't know the man," he said. "I've only been in Barlow for a week. I stopped here before I even went to the house. I unloaded my boxes into that unit, slapped a padlock on it, and planned on forgetting about it for a while. You know, I just wanted to get settled in."

"You got a place over on Bradshaw. Nice neighborhood," the sheriff said. "Got me a place a couple blocks over."

"It's a nice place." George didn't know what else to say.

"And why did you move to Barlow?" The sheriff nodded at McFettridge. "The constable here says you're some big shot writer. This ain't exactly a literary hotspot. Seems a little funny, you ask me."

George knew he was guilty of forming snap judgments about cops and that at least some of these judgments had to be wrong just by the

Brad Carter | 29

law of averages. But this jumped-up *kid* wasn't doing much to contradict those judgments.

"I'm not sure I care for the tone of the question, but I'll answer it anyhow. I moved to Barlow because I grew up here. In Arkansas, I mean. After Kathy…after my wife died, I needed a change of scenery. This place just seemed right. I saw that Bigfoot movie they made here, and I thought it looked like a quirky little town." That was half of the truth anyway. The other half was that Little Rock and Madison were too much a part of his old life. They held too many memories of his drinking days. In Barlow, his sobriety stood a fighting chance. And then, who knew what could happen. Maybe he could do some writing.

The sheriff plowed straight on ahead with his questions. "And what about the contents of the unit? What all do you have in there?"

Now it was George's turn to inject a little venom into his tone. "I'm sure an upstanding law enforcement officer such as yourself would have searched those boxes as soon as he established a perimeter on the crime scene." That last bit was pure *Law and Order*, and George felt a little silly even as the words left his mouth.

The sheriff snorted. "None of it looked valuable."

"Some of it is. Some of that stuff is highly collectible." George nearly winced. Kathy's words coming out of his mouth like a reflex.

"Looked mostly like a bunch of things from flea markets and garage sales. There were a bunch of boxes had nothing but snow globes in there. Boxes of little stuffed animals, action figures, all kinds of toys. You have kids, Mr. Young?"

"I do not."

"There seemed to be a lot of children's toys in there. But you say you never had any kids?"

"I say it because it's the truth."

The sheriff nodded like he'd just scored a point. "So you just have a lot of that sort of stuff. Doll clothes and teddy bears and whatnot."

"Most of it belonged to my wife." In fact, all of it belonged to Kathy. Every last bobble and trinket was something she'd dragged into their house. But George would be damned if he was going to trot out that tale for the sheriff.

"She one of those people that just couldn't help herself around a flea market? Had to buy every little thing caught her eye?" The sheriff was needling him now.

"You have no right," George said.

"Bet she hauled stuff into the house by the truckload. Tell me I'm wrong."

That brought the constable to his feet. "Tate, goddamn it, that was way over the line." He turned to George and made an apologetic motion, patting the air in front of him. "Sir, we appreciate your time. We'll do our best to see that none of your belongings are harmed during the investigation, and we'll have your storage unit back in order as soon as possible."

George got up from the chair. He gave the sheriff a look that he hoped carried the full weight of his contempt. "Amazing that people voted you into office. Most politicians have at least some rudimentary social grace."

George shouldered past the two officers and headed for the door.

"I'm not a politician," the sheriff said to George's back. "I'm a peace officer."

"You're a fucking asshole," George said as he walked out into the night.

He half-expected the door to fly open behind him, spilling Sheriff Tate Wilson out in hot pursuit. George doubted many people spoke that way to his face, but he believed that plenty did it behind his back. Just what in the hell had brought that last bit on, anyway? There had been a wicked, vicious gleam in the sheriff's eye when he questioned George about Kathy's collections. Was that some sort of interrogation tactic George wasn't aware of? Had he missed that episode of *Law and Order*?

He glanced over his shoulder at the guard house. Maybe he'd get away from this encounter without getting beaten like an old, white Rodney King. He slid behind the wheel of his sensible Chevy Impala, eager to get back to his new house, that clean, uncluttered space where he could get a good night's sleep. But he knew that the possibility of sleep was slim.

A dead man lying there among Kathy's things…

He swallowed drily and drove on.

Brad Carter | 31

Chapter Four: The Killer

Chris didn't know what to do. He sat on the bed and watched Belinda's still body. It wasn't at all like the dead bodies he'd seen in movies. Her eyes didn't flutter peacefully closed. They remained wide open, staring at him. Her tongue lolled out of her mouth. He shuddered and looked away.

Now that the woman was no longer intent on molesting him, Chris could take better stock of his surroundings. The mess that he saw around him made him reluctant to leave the relative safety of the bed. The carpet—those patches that were actually visible through the islands of dirty clothes and wadded up tissues—looked as if it had never known a vacuum cleaner. Chris' toes curled as he contemplated walking across it. Although he still wore his socks, he'd discarded his shoes in the hallway. How much of a barrier was the thin fabric of socks?

"How can you live like this?" he asked Belinda's wide-eyed, gape-mouthed corpse. "You know, it was just bad luck for you, Belinda. You picked the wrong Clanton boy. Julian would have looked at this mess and fallen in love."

He laughed, wincing first at the harsh, unstable sound of his laughter and again as he swung his legs over the side of the bed and his feet made contact with the filthy floor. He tiptoed into the bathroom. The mess in here was equally disgusting. There was tile on the floor, but the grout had long since gone black. The sink, counter, and mirror were flecked with bits of dried toothpaste. He urinated into a toilet that probably hadn't been cleaned in years. There was a damp washcloth on the counter. He assumed Belinda had used this to wipe the semen from her hands. He groaned at the mental image.

His clothes were scattered at the bedside, and he avoided looking too much at Belinda as he dressed. The thought of their abbreviated sex act nauseated him. He'd always viewed sex with a mixture of curiosity and revulsion. Now, he could only muster up revulsion at the thought of mingled fluids and groping, sweaty hands.

"Sorry about this, Belinda. I really am," he muttered as he zipped his pants. "This never should have happened, only I was so angry at Julian. And drunk too. But this puts it in perspective. I think maybe I'll be able to talk sense to him now."

Belinda stared back at him with glazed eyes. Her mouth hung open in a silent scream. Chris backed away from the bed.

"I guess this is goodbye," he said as he walked out of the room and down the hallway, stepping into his sneakers without untying them first.

Half an hour later, Chris was back in his tiny apartment. He stood beneath a scalding hot shower, furiously scrubbing his skin with a rough washcloth. As the elation of the whiskey and the sexual climax had given way to the nauseating sensation of being covered in filth and dirt of every stripe, the full horror of what had taken place had dawned on him. He'd broken so many of his personal taboos in the last few hours that he felt the need to recite them like a perverse litany as he scrubbed. He paid special attention to his genitals, washing and re-washing until the skin was red, raw, and stinging. Again and again, his mind conjured up images of Belinda's hideous mouth—all that whorish makeup, all those teeth in need of an orthodontist's attention—descending on his penis, her eyes gleaming like those of a jackal hovering over a carcass.

He showered until there was no hot water left then dried with a clean towel and dressed in a pair of loose shorts and a white t-shirt. He walked to the front room of the apartment and peered out the window. There was no SWAT team poised to kick in his door. There was no swarm of police cars flashing blue and red lights in the parking lot. Not yet anyway. But Chris knew that those things were in the cards for him. He'd killed someone tonight, and he hadn't been particularly careful about it. His car had been parked in front of her house the whole time. He'd left traces of himself all over that—*filthy, disgusting, unhygienic*—house. The bed sheets were by now crusty with his semen. His hair, skin cells, all the flaky, dead detritus that the human body shed near constantly, it was all over that hovel.

Standing there in his spartan apartment, Chris probed his conscience like a boxer touching his split lip. What he found during this examination surprised him.

Try as he might, he could conjure up no remorse for killing Belinda. Oh, there was remorse for the act itself, regret that he might now have

Brad Carter | 33

to face the consequences for what he'd done. But the only emotion that the actual murder brought out was a sort of perverse satisfaction.

No, not perverse. You want it to be perverse because that it is what you feel would be appropriate. But it is not what you actually feel.

The pride he felt was that of a soldier who fires the first shot in a just war. Belinda, sympathetic though she seemed, could never have understood Chris' true plight. Sure, she might have sympathized with his complicated family life, but she could never understand the simple truths that drove him. Because, if he knew anything, Chris Clanton knew this: eventually, chaos would consume the universe and obliterate all life. This wasn't some silly idea he had gotten from an internet chat room. It wasn't some conspiracy theory he'd picked up on a late night HAM radio broadcast. No, it was a fact borne out by the laws of thermodynamics. Entropy increases. Chaos swells. The only weapon for combating this total breakdown of the universe was humanity's capacity to impose order on its surroundings. That was what separated man from the lower animals. Not a talent for speech and abstract thought, not the capacity for empathy, and certainly not artistic inclination, but the ability to fight back the encroaching chaos of the universe. Order, cleanliness, organization, these were the only things standing between humanity and a complete breakdown. People like Julian and Belinda didn't just represent a distasteful blot on their neighborhoods; they were an actual threat to the species, to the world itself.

When the police showed up at Chris' doorstep, they wouldn't be aware that he'd struck a blow for their side, if not exactly for law, at least for order. They wouldn't see a man who had the best interests of humanity at heart. They'd only see a murderer, and one who was possibly a pervert, at that. There was a tragedy here, yes indeed. But that tragedy wasn't Belinda's death. No, the tragic outcome of tonight's events was that Chris wouldn't be allowed to fight on behalf of humanity once incarcerated.

He stood at the window and waited, considering the ways in which his life had led to this point.

Chris had meant for his time at the University of Arkansas to be an escape from the ever-escalating insanity of the house on Buchanan Street. He'd envisioned a time in which he could breathe easy and sleep through the night without nightmares and the creeping feeling of the walls closing in on him. He'd lose himself in academics—for which he'd always had a love and ability—and the simple life of a student. He'd applied himself in high school and had won enough scholarships to be free from employment, and he'd enrolled in a full eighteen hours of classes. Surely what awaited him was a period of respite from the hell his life in Little Rock had become.

He should have known. There is no escaping chaos.

His roommate was Mark Dixon, a jocular country boy from south Arkansas. The university had randomly assigned them to live together, and although the prospect of living with a stranger made Chris uneasy, he was resolved to make it work. And for a short time, Chris and Mark got along nicely. They seemed to agree to make the best of their situation, realizing that they had divergent interests and would never be friends, but remaining civil enough that their living arrangements would be tolerable. Soon, however, cracks appeared in the foundation.

After two weeks of classes, Mark had exhausted his supply of clothes and was forced to do laundry. Chris did his own laundry twice a week and barely had enough to justify the trip to the bowels of Yocum Hall. But when Mark took up his bulging laundry bag and a fistful of quarters, Chris gathered up his own mostly empty bag and joined him. He thought it would be a nice gesture, one that would maintain civil relations with his roommate.

His roommate's method of laundry horrified Chris. Mark shoved clothes—without even the pretense of sorting—into a washing machine until it was nearly impossible to close the lid. He repeated the process three times, pouring unmeasured glugs of liquid detergent into each machine. Chris was so stunned by the display that he stood there frozen, watching the spectacle. Towels, shirts, pants, socks: all of it went into the same machine. Mark shoved quarters into the coin slots, set the machines to a heavy cycle of cold water, and smiled, dusting his hands together dramatically, as if proud of a job well done.

"Forget to bring quarters?" Mark asked.

Chris shook himself out of his trance as Mark thrust a few dollars' worth of coins at him.

"What are roommates for, huh?" he grinned magnanimously. "Listen, I'm going to run over to the dining hall, get some lunch. See if I can't scare up some trouble."

"You're just going to leave your clothes in the washing machine?" Chris tried to keep the incredulity in his voice to a minimum. "They'll just be sitting there wet until you get back."

He thought of mold and mildew and all sorts of insidious, creeping filth laying spores all over the clothes. They'd be a petri dish by the time they made it to the dryer.

Mark shrugged, already halfway out the door. "Just a couple hours. Maybe three, tops."

"Do you want me to put your stuff in the dryer for you?"

"Dude, I think you're an okay roomie and everything, but don't go handling my fucking underwear," Mark said as he banged through the door.

Chris carefully separated his color and whites. Although there were hardly enough clothes to justify the two loads, he pushed the quarters in, measured out the detergent, and started the machines. He felt better when there was no dirty laundry on his side of the room anyway. He sat down at one of the sorting and folding tables and flipped through a textbook. But he couldn't study. The three overloaded washing machines kept pulling his attention away from his work.

He could take it no more.

He snapped his textbook shut and sprang into action. He paused the cycle on all three machines and began removing armloads of sopping wet, soapy clothes. Separating them was quite a chore in their soggy state, but Chris began to breathe easier as he worked. There were enough colors for the three machines already on the cold cycle. The socks, underwear, and towels could have probably fit in one machine, but Chris felt better when towels were washed completely separate from clothes. In fact, when left to his own devices, he'd often wash towels two, even three times. But this time, one good hot cycle would have to suffice.

All told, when he'd finished setting the laundry to rights, he had seven machines in use. Good thing that Saturday mornings were slow laundry days in the dorm. Chris was sure he'd wilt under the scrutiny and toe-tapping of other residents waiting for their turn with the machines.

He was poised to begin studying once more when something on the floor between two of the washing machines caught his eye. Some clothing had dropped in the narrow space between the washers while Chris transferred wet clothes from one machine to another. He cursed himself for his carelessness as he groped between the two whooshing machines. At last his outstretched fingers snagged the fallen garment, and he tugged his arm free. He shook out the damp article of clothing and examined it. A pair of Mark's underwear, white boxer shorts emblazoned with a pattern of snorting, stampeding Razorbacks.

In those days, Chris still believed in the concept of fate, and events in his life had convinced him that fate was a cruel force. And it was fate, college freshman Chris believed, that caused Mark to reenter the laundry room at that exact moment.

"Hey, I locked myself out of the room again," he said as he barged in. "You got your key? I'll bring it…."

He stood frozen in the doorway, watching as Chris held aloft a dripping pair of underwear.

"What the fuck, man?" Mark crossed the room in a series of quick, angry strides and snatched the boxer shorts away. "You're in here playing around with my fucking underwear?"

"I was just trying to help…" The words stuck in Chris' throat. How could he possibly explain? What explanation would be satisfactory? He lowered his head. His face burned with shame.

"I knew you were a weirdo, always emptying the trashcan and sweeping the floor a million times a day, but this is over the goddamn line," Mark thundered. "You're one fucked up little dude, you know that?"

Chris kept his head down, just as he had when his father had been in a belt-swinging mood. Saying anything at this point, no matter how apologetic, would only make things worse. Better to keep his silence, curse his fate, and take his beating, if it came to that.

Mark gave Chris a sharp shove against the washing machine. "I'm going to the RA. See if I can't get me a new roommate, one that's not some underwear-sniffing faggot."

Chris made a hasty exit, abandoning his clothes and his textbook.

When the sun broke over the horizon, spilling orange-yellow light over Little Rock, Chris was still standing at the window, waiting for the inevitable end. He could feel chaos closing in on him, the fingers of entropy gripping tighter and tighter around his throat. He steeled himself for the horrors to come.

Chapter Five: The Caretaker

Myrna Wilson brought home three boxes of things from the Rosebud Flea Market. Although she'd often left the flea market with twice as many boxes, Myrna considered it a successful Saturday morning. The angel figurines she'd bought were particularly nice. They had a beautiful warmth to them that had called out to her from the seller's table.

Now came the tough part. Myrna pulled her Crown Victoria into the driveway and sat in the car for a moment, admiring the little ceramic cherubs in their boxes on the passenger seat, each diapered and chubby-cheeked little angel swaddled carefully in bubble wrap and arranged just so. She looked at those smiling faces peering through their plastic shrouds and sighed with contentment. Another box contained some cute decorative bottles with foreign words painted on the sides. And the final box contained nothing but Mason jars full of buttons, assorted and mismatched buttons she'd bought on a whim.

The man at the button booth had been so nice. He'd introduced himself as George (no last name, just George). She'd looked over his meager offerings, searching for things she might add to her collections. He had jars full of buttons, nothing else. Myrna had purchased all he had on offer.

"I've never seen you here before," she'd said as George made change from a zippered bank bag. "Do you just sell buttons?"

He'd smiled at her then, and she decided that she liked his smile. It was warm, kind, and maybe a bit sad. It was a nice smile.

"You haven't seen me here before, because I've never been here before. I'm new in town. And to answer your other question, I have plenty more than just buttons to sell. I have a metric ton of treasures that I promised to find a good home for. Only there was a bit of a problem with my storage unit on Wednesday night. But I'm told I'll be able to get back there next week."

When he mentioned his storage unit, that kind smile faltered a bit. He looked for a moment like a man who'd been enjoying a particularly tasty apple only to discover that he'd bitten into a worm. Then his face cleared, and the soft smile made a comeback.

38 | ONLY THINGS

"So you'll be here next Saturday?" Myrna asked, perhaps a bit hopefully.

"Every Saturday until my stock runs out, which won't be anytime soon, I'm afraid. I have a great many treasures in that storage unit."

Sitting there behind the wheel of her car, Myrna considered the box of buttons with apprehension. She'd never bought buttons before, and she wondered briefly if this morning's button-buying frenzy signified the beginning of a new collection. This possibility both excited and horrified her. Were more things calling out to her now? She climbed out of the car, pushing this thought away. She gathered up her three parcels, and went inside.

Walking through the house had more in common with a carefully plotted expedition than it did with a simple stroll through a few rooms. Getting through the foyer to the stairs meant negotiating a shifting foundation of bags of clothes, stacks of magazines, piles of stuffed animals. The stairs themselves were no picnic either. They were heaped with other stacks and piles, and finding a path required consideration as careful as that of a mountain climber with no safety line selecting hand holds on the sheer face of a cliff. But Myrna was familiar with this treacherous expanse, and with the plodding determination that carried her through each ascent, she made her way to the house's second story.

"We'll find a place for you up here," Myrna assured the boxes she clutched under each arm. "Don't you worry."

She checked Henry's old study first but found the door wedged firmly shut. Even after she put her full weight against it, the door wouldn't budge more than an inch. This irritated her no end. Of course, she knew what had happened. She'd been too sloppy with her arrangements, tossing things in without a thought for the structural stability and then slamming the door behind her. One too many additions to the stacks, one too many door slams, and then an avalanche that barricaded the door, sealing the barrier between her and some of her collections. When this happened with Dale's room, she had been forced to take the door off the hinges. The collections within had spilled into the hall when she removed the door. Today, she just didn't have the energy for that type of work.

Myrna sighed and walked the narrow path to her own bedroom. She stacked the three new boxes on her dresser. She kicked aside the piles of clothes that all but obscured the carpet and sat down heavily on her bed.

She looked around at the mounds of things and felt a sick twinge. Already the collections had so filled the kitchen that she was reduced to cooking all her meals in the microwave and eating them while sitting on the couch in the TV room. The collections had long ago taken over the garage and the living room. Her sons' old rooms were packed. And now her bedroom had begun to gradually fill. Depending on how well-stocked the garage sales were over the rest of the summer, the bedroom could be unlivable before the year was out.

Myrna lay down on the bed, drawing her legs up and squeezed her eyes shut. A lone tear escaped and slid slowly down her cheek.

She heard the bedroom door squeal open on its unoiled hinges. Light footsteps whispered across the carpet. She drew herself up more as bedsprings squeaked and the bed shifted a bit. She felt a familiar presence, that secret presence that had troubled and consoled her in the seven months since her "spell."

"No, you're not here," Myrna said. "You're not real, no matter how much I want you to be. It's just not possible."

The voice was soft, comforting, familiar. "Mom, that's no way to talk. You know I can't stand to see you crying like this."

"Then why do you never stay?" She sniffed. "You come and go. I don't see you for weeks at a time."

"I wish I *could* stay, Mom. It's not that easy. I don't really understand it myself. But I always come back don't I? Because I love you."

Myrna smiled through her slow tears. "I love you too, Dale."

"We all love you, Mom." A hand, insubstantial and feather-soft, caressed a tear from her cheek.

"I know, son. I just can't believe that you're real, that any of you are real."

Her dead son's voice was closer, so close she could feel his breath. "But none of that matters. We believe in you. You're our caretaker."

Myrna let the gentle voice whisper her to sleep.

She'd begun acquiring things a little over a decade ago, after her husband slipped into the great beyond, his ticket to heaven punched by a second heart attack. Her need to purchase and store was only made more insistent by the death of her baby boy Dale three years later. And now that her older son Tate had been elected to a second term as the sheriff of Gayler County, there wasn't much to occupy her time. No husband to cook for, no sons to look after, only the flea market and the Saturday garage sales. And the ghosts.

Myrna had experienced what she referred to as "a spell" last year around Thanksgiving. She'd been doing some wishful thinking, hoping that she might get the downstairs clear enough to invite Tate over for turkey and dressing rather than imposing herself on him. A mother should be able to cook for her son, if only once a year. And to do that, to be able to allow Tate into her house without him being overcome with shame and horror at the state of the place, she had to clear out the first floor of the house.

With that self-imposed ultimatum in mind, she'd started cleaning with a fury the week before the holiday. She'd done what passed for housecleaning these days, anyhow: moving her collections from one place to another. She started before sunrise, putting away the breakfast dishes and then getting down to the business of hauling things upstairs. Progress was slow at first, but by the time she'd taken a break for lunch, Myrna had cleared most of the front hallway and a good portion of the living room. There was a light at the end of the tunnel.

But her triumph was short lived.

She'd started vacuuming the living room after lunch, working the machine over carpet that hadn't had a good cleaning since she'd gotten the news that Dale had been taken from her by something called an IED in Fallujah. But the carpet was so laden with dust that the vacuum bag filled to bursting in no time flat. She'd had to go to the Walmart for more bags.

Then, on the way home, she saw that Barlow Presbyterian was having another rummage sale. These were Myrna's true weakness: rummage sales, garage sales, flea markets, estate sales, thrift stores, and consignment shops. Brand new stuff didn't speak to her soul like the worn-in and gently marred things that filled the stalls at the Rosebud Flea Market did. These things—used, secondhand things—were different. Many of these things hadn't just been used, they'd been *loved*. At estate sales especially, she found things that she could tell had been important to their owners. She could tell just by touching them, by running her fingers over them, that these were not just physical objects. These things *had meaning*. They weren't useless crap, the way her son Tate said they were. No, they were treasures that needed to be preserved. They called out to her with voices that were so real that she almost believed they

Brad Carter | 41

were audible to other people. The things she bought were one step away from ending up in the landfill. She was their one shot at preservation.

And on that day, driving home from Walmart with her vacuum cleaner bags long forgotten in the trunk of the car, she found so many items with that special aura of meaning that the space she'd cleared in the living room was soon occupied with new additions. At Barlow Presbyterian she'd dropped fifty bucks on clothes and purses and shoes. Then, she'd spotted a yard sale, where she discovered a set of Nancy Drew books that practically screamed at her to be purchased and a pile of Matchbox cars that sang a lonely song until she scooped them up. And before she could even make it to her car, she was forced to double back and buy the ceramic miniatures she'd almost passed up.

The morning's progress was undone by one burst of shopping. Thanksgiving plans would just have to be canceled. Tate would understand. They'd have the big meal at his place again.

She drove home feeling light as a feather, and she hummed a happy tune as she carried her parcels into the house. So the house wasn't exactly spotless. There were worse things in the world to worry about than a little clutter.

She started up the stairs, clutching a box of newly purchased items in one hand and the handrail in the other. Her mind was already occupied with compiling a grocery list for Thanksgiving supper at Tate's house—the boy never had much beyond frozen pizza and Frosted Flakes. She didn't have the spare mental energy to use on making it up the stairs.

Later, after the calamity had passed and she'd had time to reflect, she'd swear herself a promise to never again make that perilous ascent with anything less than full focus. Some lessons could only be learned the hard way.

She'd been going along at a pretty good clip. Two steps up—thinking, *sage, French fried onions*—two more—thinking *will Tate have canned green beans?*—two more—thinking *pumpkin pie filling, pecans*—two more steps…

Her foot slipped on a magazine, a stack of junk mail, something. Instead of tossing the box of stuff to the side and using both hands to catch herself, Myrna's instinct told her to clutch the box to her breast. Her feet slipped, one to each side, throwing her center of gravity straight back. Waves of vertigo swept over her, and at last she dropped the box as she teetered on the edge of the stair. Her grip on the bannister slipped, and she pinwheeled her arms madly.

She plummeted backwards. The stairs *thump-thump-thumped* beneath her back painfully, as she slid down to the floor below, where she slammed into a haphazard pile of boxes. Her head smacked against the rigid corner of one of the boxes hard enough to make her ears ring. Her eyes opened wide as she watched the box—labeled "books," but really, its contents could have been anything—atop the stack teeter precariously and then fall. She turned her face away, preparing for the bone-smashing impact....

...that never came.

She lay there with her eyes shut tight, panting as her pulse thrummed away like an over-revved engine. Lord only knew how long she remained there, motionless and confused. A minute? Two? An hour? Her sense of time seemed to have been knocked out of her along with her equilibrium. Her mind offered up a menu of the horrors that might await her: a hospital visit to repair a broken hip, a long period of recovery in a wheelchair or walker, an invasion of her home by caregivers who would cluck their tongues and make condescending remarks about her collections.

Tears threatened the corners of her eyes as she mulled the terrible possibilities. Ears ringing, head pounding, and the rest of her body a grab bag of aches and pains, Myrna didn't dare move. She felt sleepy. Maybe if she could just rest, get her thoughts in order...

And then she was lifted from the floor and carried up the stairs by someone much more sure-footed than her. She opened her eyes and saw through vision still hazy the face of her rescuer. He was indistinct, as if tucked away in shadows. She stared at the smiling face as recognition cut through the layers of her woozy confusion. Even though he was hidden in half darkness, Myrna swore that her rescuer had the face of her son Dale. But that was impossible. Her baby boy had died on the hot sands of Iraq, along with the other boys who'd been riding in the truck when it rolled across that homemade landmine. Yet, there he was. Washed out and grey, but her baby Dale all the same.

He spoke to her as he laid her on her bed, but her ears were still ringing too loudly for her to hear what he said. He reached a hand out of his shadow and placed it on her forehead. The touch was so light, it was almost imperceptible, but that simple caress was enough to make Myrna feel warm and secure. At last the ringing in her ears began to subside. If she forced herself to concentrate, she could hear Dale's voice.

"…and you've saved us, Mom, by taking care of the things we loved in life. You've kept our memories alive. You've kept *us* alive," Dale said.

When Myrna spoke, her voice came out soft and raspy. "Who, son? Who have I saved?"

Dale stepped back from the bed and swept his hand around at the room, like saying *voila*.

From the corners heaped with stuffed animals and dolls, from the shelves groaning with knick knacks and paperback novels, from the boxes stuffed with comic books, from the plastic grocery bags packed with mismatched clothing, other shadowy forms emerged. The hazy figures flowed in and out of the shadows that shrouded them. Myrna found it difficult to determine just how many there were.

"Who are you?" Myrna managed through her confusion.

Dale stepped back over to the bed. He sat down, and Myrna was surprised that this ghost of her son had enough weight to make the mattress springs creak. "They can't speak, Mom. Not to you anyway. I can hear them, but it's like listening to echoes underwater. Unclear and sort of far-off."

"But who?"

"Shades of those who've died but were not ready for…well, for what comes next. Limbo, I guess you could call it. The big waiting room. They hung onto the things they loved in life and were able to avoid the waiting room's pull. These things that they loved, so many of them are in this house, in your collections. It's really pretty cool if you think about it, Mom. Not many people can see us, I don't think."

Dale sounded so calm, so reasonable, as he explained these concepts that Myrna didn't even think to doubt him. And when he told her that it was cool, well, he was just her little boy again. He'd been the wide-eyed, enthusiastic son, a balance to Tate's serious-minded nature. She loved both of them, of course, but it had always been hard to be affectionate with Tate. He was so guarded, so studious and almost detached. But Dale, her baby, he'd been easy to hug, always willing to talk, to share. When that explosion in Iraq took him, it surely took a piece of Myrna too. But now here he was, if not alive at least *present*. And all because she'd kept his things—all of the toys and comic books and Little League uniforms—that he'd loved in life.

"That's right," Dale said, as if reading her thoughts. "These others are seen and not heard because you only have some of their things. You might only have one or two items that belonged to them. But you can see me and hear me and feel my touch because you kept everything that was mine. Just about everything I owned is in this house."

"Tate wanted me to get rid of so much, said it wasn't healthy to hold on."

"My big brother. He knows a lot, but he doesn't know everything."

That brought a smile to her face, but even smiling took so much effort. She was so tired. "Dale, no one will believe me if I tell them about this. They'll say I hit my head too hard on that floor. They'll think I'm crazy."

He nodded. "Probably."

"But you're here, son. That's all that matters to me, whether you're real or not." She blinked slowly, and each time it took more effort to open her eyes.

"Mom, you really need to rest now. You had a pretty big scare back there, and you'll feel better after you get some sleep." Dale leaned down, and his light, barely-there lips brushed her cheek then her forehead.

Although Myrna wanted to stay awake and talk to her son, her body was so heavy with exhaustion that she felt paralyzed. When she blinked this time, she let her eyes stay closed.

She awoke hours later, the soft orange-yellow light of autumn dusk spilling through the blinds. She propped herself up on her elbows and looked around the cluttered room for any sign of her younger son, wanting to see him again now that her head had cleared. She called and called, her voice growing more desperate with each repetition of his name. Her calls went unanswered, and she sunk back into bed.

Chapter Six: Chris

The Fulbright Branch Library was surviving somehow without Chris' close attention to detail. At least that was what Effie told him when he called in sick for the third day in a row. Chris expressed his deep concern about missing so much work, but Effie acted like it was no big deal. She told him that somehow they'd manage, even without him there. He hung up the phone before realizing that she'd been speaking sarcastically.

Bitch. If you only knew what I was capable of...

He shook his head. There was something wrong with him. Something inside him had broken Wednesday night when he'd dispatched Belinda. It was as if there'd been an abscess in his brain, festering and swelling all his life, and it had finally burst. He knew that he should feel guilty, consumed with regret, but that simply wasn't the case. Even the fear of being arrested had begun to fade. Her body was discovered Thursday night—it was on the local news—but there had been no swarm of police cars in the parking lot of the apartment complex. It occurred to Chris that there was some cosmic force out there protecting him. Not a god necessarily—he believed in none of that superstitious claptrap—but some sort of anti-chaos entity that recognized what he'd done as an act for the benefit of all humankind.

Somehow, deep down, he'd always known he was meant for something great, but he'd never been able to determine what this higher calling might be. But now, the clouds were parting. Plans and ideas were forming in his mind. They were still in their infancy for the most part, but one thing was clear: restraining order or no, the time had come for the Clanton brothers to have a conversation.

Today was a day for accomplishing things.

He ate a massive breakfast: three scrambled eggs, five strips of bacon, two slices of toast, a tall glass of orange juice, and an entire pot of strong black coffee. After breakfast he brushed his teeth, setting the timer he kept by the sink for a full ten minutes. As was his Saturday custom, he indulged in a hot, soapy enema, relishing the sensation of his body being cleansed from within. He lingered in the shower, scrubbing, lathering, rinsing, repeating, until he was clean from his scalp to the soles of his feet. He dressed in a pair of khaki slacks and a baby blue polo shirt. Then it was time for one final round of grooming. Standing in front of the bathroom mirror, he plastered his hair down with gel, slicking it back in his usual manner. He examined each nostril for any stray hairs and was both satisfied and disappointed to find none. At last, it was time to start the day.

The house on Buchanan Street looked perfectly habitable from the outside. Vernon had kept a groundskeeper on permanent retainer, a man who made a weekly pilgrimage to the house to keep the landscaping neatly trimmed. He also painted and repaired the exterior as necessary. Julian must have continued to employ the man. Chris stepped out of his car and noticed that not only was the yard evenly mown, but the grass along the driveway had been meticulously edged. The neighbors would never know that the interior of the house was a riot of clutter and filth of every stripe. Chris sneered as he ascended the steps to the wide front porch. His palms were already slick with sweat and itching at the thought of the mess that lay beyond that front door. His mouth went dry at the thought of the bacteria-choked air within.

He rang the bell, mildly surprised that it still worked. He waited for a minute then rang it again. And again.

Julian finally answered. He was dressed in a t-shirt and plaid pajama pants, his feet jammed into a pair of fuzzy slippers. "Guess you didn't get the memo about a restraining order being more than just a polite suggestion," he said.

"Don't be so ridiculous. You know that wasn't necessary." Chris tried to keep his voice even. He wiped his palms on his pants. "I just want to have a civil conversation."

Julian gave him a look, squinting at him like he was a scientific specimen. "Okay, but the minute you start acting crazy, you have to leave. And just for a little bit. I got things to do today, and I can't have you monopolizing my time."

Chris wanted to shake his brother violently. What could he possibly have to do today? Julian hardly left the house. He had groceries delivered, for crying out loud.

"You promise?" Julian asked.

Chris wiped his hands again. "Do I what?"

"Promise not to act the fool if I let you in here. We don't want a repeat of last time, do we? So, before I let you in, I want to hear you promise."

"Sure. I promise."

Julian eyed him suspiciously then opened the door. "I was just fixing some breakfast. You can have some coffee, but the bacon and eggs are all mine."

"Thanks, but I already ate."

And I'd sooner starve than eat food prepared in this house.

The first thing that Chris noticed as he stepped inside was the smell: a wet, rotten stench of old food, older paper, and mildew. The detritus of years of senseless acquisition was heaped high in every direction. Julian picked his way through it with the assured balance of a Sherpa ascending Everest. Chris traversed less nimbly. He took stock of the strata of trash as he went. Like a paleontologist examining the fossil record in layers of rock, Chris could read the history of the house by studying the piles of useless junk.

The bottom layers, so compressed they were now just barely visible, revealed the beginnings of Vernon's madness: clothing boxes containing dresses purchased for a dead woman, parcels stained with dried remnants of ointments and lotions purchased from Avon or Mary Kay. Further up in the strata, Julian's sickness made its presence known: comic books, discarded boxes from action figures, worn-out paperback books, broken toys, deflated basketballs, and half-assembled model cars and airplanes. And then there was the paper: years of newspapers, magazines, shopping circulars, and junk mail. Pizza boxes like exhumed coffins, full of fossilized crusts like bleached bones in their cardboard sarcophagi. Plastic containers crusted with the remnants of microwaved meals.

Flies buzzed lazily through the air, the result of generations grown fat and content with the easy feasts they enjoyed in the house.

Chris congratulated himself for making it through the front room without vomiting, having a panic attack, or both. He followed Julian down the short hallway to the kitchen, walking with exaggerated caution over the shifting piles of paper.

The kitchen could have been a training ground for people looking to enter the field of hazardous materials disposal. The smell in the air could have been simple food spoilage and decay, but then again, it could have been the gaseous emissions of some rare and invincible strain of bacteria that festered in the puddles of spilled food on the floors and countertops.

Smoke billowed from the stovetop. What looked to be an entire package of bacon blazed away in a skillet. Some of the strips were blackened, while others curled up their pink ends above the tangle.

Chris waved his hands in front of his face, coughing. "You're going to set off the smoke alarm."

Julian turned from his work at the stove. He tapped his forehead with a greasy spatula. "Way ahead of you, boss. I took those goddamn things out of the house. Every time I cooked bacon, they started squawking loud enough to wake the dead."

Chris bit his tongue. His brother was not only crazy, he was suicidal.

In a strange, roundabout way, Chris pitied him. This madness wasn't his fault. It arose from the chaos that surrounded him, the chaos that their father had given a foothold. He was no more to blame for his condition than a doctor who picked up a flesh-eating bacterium while doing charity work in some African hellhole. Only it was so sad that Julian was far beyond redemption. He'd long ago ceased to even register the chaos. Now he reveled in it.

Chris watched in horror as Julian took two eggs from the overstuffed refrigerator and cracked them into the skillet with the coiled mass of bacon. More smoke poured out as Julian stabbed the mess with his spatula. At last he seemed satisfied, and slid the greasy pile onto a paper plate. There was an open bag of white bread next to the stove, and he pulled out two slices. After a cursory examination revealed spots of mold, he tossed the bread over his shoulder. He repeated the process three times until he found two slices that met his standards. He pressed the bread down on his plate of bacon and eggs, then poured coffee from a stained pot into a cup and motioned for Chris to follow him to the next room.

Like a lot of the old and overpriced houses in the neighborhood, this one had a breakfast nook with a skylight overhead. The yellow rays of sunshine only served to highlight the mess. The little table was buried in unopened mail and old newspapers. It also appeared that Julian took many of his meals here, as a great many crusty paper plates and plastic forks were among the detritus. The table had four chairs set around it, but only one of them was clear. Julian sat down in this one and immediately attacked his food. Chris had to move a stack of aged phone books and catalogs just to have a place to sit.

"So what was it you had to talk to me about that was important enough for you to violate a court order?" Julian asked around a mouthful of food. "You'd think the son of a respected attorney would know better than to go flipping his middle finger at the law."

Normally a reference to their father would bring out the argumentative side in Chris, but he let it slide this time. This was too important to be petty. And he knew that Julian was just firing a shot across his bow anyway, trying to needle him into a blow-up.

"I wanted you to know that I'm sorry for the things I said last time," Chris said, trying to fight down the disgust as he watched his brother eat. "You see, I've been thinking about things."

Julian laughed. Chunks of food flew from his mouth. "You've had a fucking revelation, have you? Well, let's hear it. I could use some entertainment."

Blood thundered in Chris' ears. It was hard enough fighting back the rising panic that just being in this filth brought on, but adding his brother's addle-brained wit to the mix was sheer torture. "Yes, well, I met someone the other night. And we had a good time…"

"You finally get laid? Mingle some bodily fluids?"

"…and we had a good time just talking. She really got me thinking about a lot of things, like your situation…our situation…"

"So you're saying that you didn't get laid after all?"

"Julian, none of this is your fault." Chris waved a hand around at the mess. "None of it was really even Dad's fault. He was vulnerable after Mom died, and there are forces out there that prey on the vulnerable. I don't know why they didn't get to me. Maybe I was stronger or…"

"Goddamn it, didn't I tell you that if you were going to come in here, you couldn't start acting crazy?" Julian shoved his plate away. It slid off a stack of newspapers, spilling the contents on the floor. He didn't seem to care or even notice. "Now you start in about mystical forces and all that bullshit, ruining my breakfast. Just what is wrong with you, anyway?"

Chris sat there in the wobbly chair, his feet planted on the sticky floor, seething.

What is wrong with me? Have you looked around at this mess? Smelled the rancid atmosphere?

"Chaos seeps in, Julian. I wouldn't expect that you'd notice it, because it's insidious. It grew up around you, so you didn't panic. You acclimated slowly, became inured…"

Julian slammed his fist down on the table. A paper avalanche spilled more trash onto the floor. "Goddamn it, I'm warning you! I don't want to hear this crap again. Why do you think I had you served with those papers? The house is mine. You don't get any say in how I keep it, so just deal with it. You get your monthly check from the trust. You should be grateful you even get that, the way you treated Dad."

Chris' pulse redlined like a race car's engine. "It's made you this way, Julian. It's not your fault. There are so many people that it's hurt, driven crazy."

"That's really funny, Chris. It's goddamn hilarious, you sitting there calling *me* crazy."

"You're like an addict, and that's your disease talking. That's the chaos, the entropy. It's twisting your perceptions." Chris' voice quavered, betraying the storm that was kicking up inside him.

"Let me tell you a story, Chris. Put this whole goddamn thing in perspective for you. Then you can get your crazy ass out of here and consider that restraining order in force." Julian took a long drink of his coffee. "Dad used to worry about you, after you went off to college. He said that you were fragile. I think what he meant is you were unstable, like mentally."

"So says the shut-in who lives in filth." Cold fury sluiced through Chris.

"I'm going to let that one go just so I can get on with the story." Julian pulled a pack of cigarettes from the pocket of his pajamas. He poked a cigarette into the corner of his mouth and shuffled piles of paper around on the table until he found a lighter.

"You do that in here, with all this paper lying around?" Chris asked, watching his brother light up.

"Yeah, and I haven't burned the place down yet. Not everyone is scared of his own shadow like you are. Now quit interrupting so goddamn much." Julian blew smoke in Chris' direction. "Like I said, Dad worried about you. Christmas had come and gone, and we hadn't even heard from you, much less seen you." Julian tipped his chair back, leaning against the wall. "So when your second semester rolled around, I took a trip up to the old U of A to pay you a visit. I knew I was probably the last person you wanted to see, but I told Dad I'd look in on you, make sure you were okay. And since I'm a loyal son, unlike others I could name…"

Chris ground his teeth together, his jaw muscles bunched so tight that they felt like they might tear through his skin. "No, that's not right. You're twisting this all around. I *couldn't* come home."

"Anyhow, I borrowed the car, made the drive, and tried to check in on you. I knew your room number from the return address on the one letter you'd written. The girl at the front desk, she was so nice. She let me in, even though it was against the rules. After all, I was the concerned brother. You'd missed Christmas, and the family was worried about you. How could she say no to that?"

Chris remembered that lonesome holiday. He'd been packing his bags, dreading the trip home, when he was overcome by what could only be described as a panic attack. He'd gone to the student housing office and begged to be added to the roster of students remaining on campus. The secretary had taken pity on him. She must have sensed his desperation. Ashamed, he hadn't even called home.

"So I get up there and knock on your door. Of course, you're nowhere to be found." Julian shook his head with mock dramatic sadness. "But your roommate, a really fun guy named Mark Dixon, was more than willing to chat with me." Julian's eyes sparkled. He was enjoying this more and more. "After he told me about your fondness for other men's underwear...he didn't say if you sniffed it or not....well, after that, he told me about the Trashcan Game. Said his friends found it hilarious."

The Trashcan Game, as Mark was fond of calling it, involved Mark and his friends tormenting Chris after they'd been out drinking. They'd barge into the room, joking loudly and stinking like they'd bathed in cheap beer and marijuana smoke. Invariably they'd have with them a bag of greasy, pungent food from a fast food restaurant. Once they'd had their fill of burgers or tacos, they'd toss the remains into the waste basket that stood in the corner of the room. And then they'd sit back and watch Chris squirm.

"Old Mark said that you were usually asleep when they got in," Julian continued. "Or at least you were pretending to sleep. He said sometimes you could make it a full five minutes before you got up and emptied the trashcan into the trash chute out in the hallway. If you'd been too much of a prick during the week, he said they might pour a little beer on the floor and watch you run for the mop."

It was true. To this day, Chris couldn't stand to have food waste in his apartment when he went to bed. Mark had discovered this aversion by accident one night, and whenever the occasion arose, he used it for entertainment. Every Friday and Saturday night, when he'd laid down his head, Chris wondered if he would get a good night's sleep or spend the late night hours emptying the trashcan or mopping up spilled beer while a group of jackasses brayed their drunken laughter at him.

"That told me all I needed to know about you, Chris. Not that you were some neat freak weirdo. I'd known that for a while. The way you kept your bedroom, with the bed made military style and shoes all lined up neatly in your closet." Julian stabbed out his cigarette on the table then thumped the dead butt right at Chris. It missed him, falling to the floor. "I mean, I *always* knew you were an uptight, pompous, neat freak. *That* wasn't what surprised me. What surprised me was how much of a cowardly pussy you were. I mean, your father was Vernon Clanton, a guy that wasn't afraid of murderers and rapists and thieves, and here you are letting these rednecks make a spectacle out of you. And that's why I didn't come visit you in your new room. I was too goddamn disappointed. I drove back home and told Dad you were fine, that you'd just been hitting the books a little too hard. I didn't tell him that you'd gotten even worse."

It wasn't just Chris' hands that were sweating now. He could feel cold perspiration pooling under his armpits. Sitting there stock still, he felt a droplet detach itself from his neck and slide down his back. "You wouldn't have done a single thing differently," he said from between clenched teeth.

"You're wrong. I'd have slept through it like a baby. I don't give a shit if there's a half eaten burrito in the trashcan, Chris, and I'll tell you why. Because it just *does not matter!* There's no goddamn cosmic chaos or mysterious force of entropy bearing down on you and making you into a nervous, sweaty wreck. It's just something you've dreamed up. Christ, you're so wound up you can't even get laid." Julian lit another cigarette. He folded his hands behind his head and puffed away triumphantly. "You want to believe that I need your help. That living like this is some sort of torture being inflicted on me by unseen forces. But the truth is—and I want you to listen, really *listen* to me when I say this—I live this way because I like it. I'm comfortable this way. Dad was comfortable this way. That's all there is to it."

Brad Carter | 53

"Dad was miserable. He spent the last two decades of his life unraveling right in front of us."

"That's certainly one opinion, and it's one that I don't share."

"It's not my opinion. It's a fact. The man was disturbed. Mom's death changed him, and not for the better. You were too young to see it for what it was." Chris took a deep breath, trying to calm down. "Look around you. Surely you don't believe this is normal. This is not something that people in their right minds do, not unless they're being acted upon by some outside force, something invisible and inexorable."

"Those five dollar words are poetic, but they're still bullshit. You think I'd be better off spending my days perfectly aligning my shoes, scrubbing the kitchen counter, and giving myself enemas?" He giggled at that last bit, making a face of exaggerated surprise. "Oh yeah, Mark knew all about that too. He found your little bag and hose kit. He figured going through your stuff was okay, because, after all, you did sniff the man's underwear."

Chris leapt over the table, scattering paper, bits of food, and trash. The two brothers toppled to the floor, smashing Julian's rickety chair beneath them. They flailed at one another, bellowing and snarling. Chris straddled Julian's waist and smashed a fist into his face. The impact jarred him from knuckles to elbow. He winced at the warm, wet sensation of blood on his hand. Julian screamed in pain, spraying Chris' face with blood and thick saliva. Chris jerked back, wiping furiously at his face. Julian's hand came up holding one of the splintered chair legs. He swung it at Chris' head, catching him with a sidelong blow that split his scalp. The impact caused Julian to lose his grip on the piece of wood, and it flew across the room. He grabbed a fistful of his spilled breakfast and smeared the congealing mess into Chris' face.

Hot blood and tepid grease filled Chris' eyes. He shoved himself backward, scrubbing at his face and only succeeding in opening the cuts along his scalp even further. Blood and bacon fat mixed into a stinging slurry. The coldness in his belly had given way to a boiling heat. Vomit tickled the back of his throat.

"You're fucking crazy!" Julian screamed. He sprang up from the floor, brandishing another piece of the chair. He dealt Chris a sharp kick to the ribs. He drew back his foot again and sent an overfilled ashtray spinning into Chris' face. Ashes and cigarette butts showered him.

Blind panic consumed Chris. He experienced the pain from the kick as a sort of afterthought. His true source of agony was the slop covering his face. Bits of limp bacon, wet eggs, and stained cigarette butts adhered to him. Each second that went by was another that his pores clogged with the stinking mess. And that was to say nothing of the fact that he lay on that sticky, debris-covered floor. The thin layers of his clothing were all that separated him from that surface. The skin on his ass and legs crawled. His scrotum wrinkled and shrank. His imagination ran riot, conjuring up a thousand different infections that could be tunneling their way into his flesh, setting up a refugee camp of boils and suppuration that would rupture and spill. He imagined his socks soaking in the pus, his shoes gradually filling. His shirt clung to his back, sticky with sweat and filth. His stomach rebelled. His massive breakfast spewed out of his mouth and soaked his shirt.

And as he convulsed with nausea and panic, he became aware that he was shrieking hysterically, his voice shrill and crazed. He spat out dire warnings about the encroaching entropy that threatened the earth, but to his own ears, it sounded like incoherent screams.

Chris wasn't sure how he'd left the house and driven back to his apartment. His mind must have folded up on itself in shock. Or perhaps his subconscious had already locked the images away as fodder for future nightmares, events that were too arduous to be experienced in present time lest his sanity snap away altogether. He came back to consciousness in the shower, where he was busily engaged, for the second time that day, in scouring his flesh. When he finally emerged into the steam-choked room, his skin was raw, and he smeared antibiotic ointment over every inch of himself, exhausting his supply of three extra-large tubes of the stuff.

He crawled into his bed, pulled the sheets up to his chin, and trembled.

His theory about the repressed memories coming back to him as nightmares proved correct. No sooner had he fallen asleep than the events of his final moments in the house on Buchanan Street came back to him with horrible clarity.

In his dreams, Chris hovered above his body, drifting along the ceiling as he watched the events below. He saw himself slumped over, dry-heaving until he was nearly whiplashed. He watched as Julian disappeared into the kitchen, leaving him sprawled on the floor, shuddering and moaning. Then Julian strolled back into the room, whistling a happy tune. His arms were loaded with containers of food that he'd taken from the refrigerator. He swept an arm across the table, clearing a surface onto which he dropped the containers.

"Think of this as radical therapy, Chris," Julian said. "Maybe someday, you'll even thank me for it, although I doubt it. You've never been the grateful type."

Even asleep, Chris' mind recoiled in disgust. But the nightmare would not allow him to look away, and he could not wake himself up. He watched as Julian selected an ancient carton of Chinese take-out, the contents of which were so fuzzed with mold that it was impossible to tell what they once were. Julian upended the carton over Chris' prone body. Next was a bulging plastic bottle of milk, which came out lumpy and nearly yellow as it rained down on his face. Julian giggled as he pelted him with fossilized pizza crusts and scraps of slimy sandwich meat. The torture continued until Chris was covered with all manner of rotten foodstuffs and clotted condiments. Julian found more ashtrays and dusted him with their contents. At last, he seemed to tire of the humiliation and dragged Chris like an overstuffed laundry sack to the front porch. He ducked back into the house and reemerged moments later with a bucket of cold water, which he upended over Chris, shocking him back into a dazed state of semi-consciousness.

"And next time you think about coming over here, you just remember what that restraining order means," Julian said as Chris blinked slowly, looking around as if he were an astronaut crash-landed on an alien world. "It means you're not welcome here."

Chris watched through his unblinking dream-eyes as his body stood up and walked zombie-like across the lawn toward his car.

He awoke screaming.

And for a moment, another memory danced across his semiconscious mind. Through his terror, he recalled waking in a hospital bed, screaming in pain. The memory flared brightly for an instant and then fizzled away to nothingness.

Chapter Seven: George

George stood on tiptoe and peered over the partition into the adjacent booth. He looked down at Luanne Samples, who was busy filing her nails and humming the theme to *Jeopardy*. Her table was covered in an assortment of paperback books with shiny raised type proclaiming titles like *To Ravish His Maiden Fair* and *Taken by the Sheik*.

"Business good today?" George wondered idly if any of his old paperbacks were buried in the boxes behind her. He was never surprised to see a used copy of *Speak Softly, Lover* or *The Haunting of Harlow Manor* at a secondhand bookstore or a flea market. But the more he looked over Luanne's stock, the more doubtful he became. She didn't seem to have much outside of bodice-rippers.

Luanne looked up and smiled. "I guess I can't complain, Mr. George. Some lady bought the entire *Vampires Seeking Werewolves* series earlier. But I don't really aim for the big money. I just try to get enough to buy more books."

"Bet you've sold some of your pictures, though," George suggested, pointing to the stacks of 8x10s piled up alongside the books.

Luanne nodded enthusiastically. "Sure have. There are a lot of fans of that movie. I get compliments on my acting all the time."

"I'm not a bit surprised."

This was only George's second Saturday as a seller at the Rosebud Flea Market, but he'd been brought up to speed on just about every facet of flea market gossip by Luanne, Barlow's resident aspiring movie star and lover of paperback romance novels. The woman was a fount of information. George suspected that he was either cursed or lucky to have a stall next to hers, and only time would tell which was the case. At the moment, George was leaning toward the latter. He figured that learning the local ways of Barlow might be a chore, but with the buxom Ms. Samples on his side, he might be up to speed before the day was over.

Luanne split the rent on a booth at the Rosebud Flea Market with her coworkers Maria and Arlene, the stylish triumvirate that presided over the town's best salon, Primp 'n Perm. The first Saturday of each month, Maria dealt in old vinyl LPs and battered cassettes as well as old t-shirts she'd embellished with tie-dye or sequins or both. Arlene took the Sunday afternoons, selling homemade candles after church. The candles weren't big sellers, but Luanne suspected that her friend had something going on with Presley Wood, the guy with the ponytail that sold comic books and old movie posters. The last time Luanne had been to Arlene's apartment, she'd seen a videotape of some movie called *Graveyard Rampage* on the coffee table, and Luanne knew that Arlene was no fan of monster movies. Luanne told most of this to George in one breath.

She also explained how she arrived early each second and third Saturday to sell her old paperback romance novels, as well as autographed publicity shots from her appearance in the film *The Big Man of Barlow*. These 8x10s were brisk sellers due largely to the fact that she made her short appearance in the film almost completely naked, and the pictures reflected that. She made a few gestures to modesty, covering the nipples in the photos with shiny pennies. Husbands and boyfriends dragged along to the flea market on a Saturday morning could find solace in those pictures, which Luanne dutifully autographed.

"Do you know that lady who bought my buttons?" George asked. He'd come out of his booth to stand in front of Luanne's table. He raised his hand even with his shoulder. "She was about this tall. Had the saddest blue eyes. She picked up each jar of buttons and ran her fingers over them with her eyes closed, like she was a blind woman reading Braille print. There was something about her…"

He shook his head as he remembered the spark that had passed between him and the blue-eyed woman. It had been like an arc of static electricity discharge followed by a split second of weightlessness, like being in a roller coaster as it plunges over a steep drop. Not entirely unpleasant, but a little disorienting.

"Well, duh. That's only Tate Wilson's momma. You know, he's the sheriff." Luanne held her hand at arm's length to admire her manicure work. "Myrna Wilson, that's her name. She comes in all the time. I saw her over there making moony eyes at you. It was cute."

"That woman gave birth to that wretched little shit of a sheriff?"

"Wretched little shit? I see you've met him." She leaned over and whispered conspiratorially, "Myrna's such a sweetheart. She worries about everyone's feelings. She even bought some stuff from Crazy Annie."

Luanne's booth was sandwiched between George's on her left and Crazy Annie's on the right. Crazy Annie—this was the only way that Luanne referred to her, even when she introduced George to her—was a wild-eyed woman who sold sweaters and blankets made from cat hair. According to Luanne, she was suspicious of all people, especially pretty women, which George imagined put her at constant odds with Luanne. Cruel fate (or perhaps just a flea market manager with a sense of humor) kept the two women in close proximity. George thought that even slow days at this flea market could be entertaining. Surrounded by characters like these, he shouldn't have much trouble getting back to writing.

"I hear you talking about me, you slut!" Crazy Annie blurted from her cat-hair handicrafts booth.

"Oh, pipe down, Annie. Nobody's talking about you," Luanne snapped.

Annie went on muttering.

"We had a nice conversation," George said to Luanne.

Luanne's nose scrunched up, her brow creased. "I didn't think anyone could have a conversation with Annie."

"I can still hear you! Slut!" Annie screeched.

"No, I mean I had a nice conversation with this woman who bought all the buttons," George said. "She had a kind way about her, gentle. Pretty much the polar opposite of…well, of most of the women I've had in my life. And there was a moment where I…felt something, a connection. I could tell by her eyes that she felt it too."

"Oh, that's so sweet! But I think she's a little off. You know, Tate doesn't talk much about her, but when he lets something slip, it's always about how she's a little nutty. Not that she didn't come by it honestly. Tate's little brother Dale got blown up over there in the Middle East, and it probably did something to her, made her a little strange. But not like Crazy Annie. Myrna's just a little…off. I think."

Annie stomped around to the front of Luanne's booth. She wore a fuzzy white sweater—one of her own creations—that emphasized the throbbing red anger in her face. She was a tall, flat-chested woman with pinched features, and standing there with her hands planted on her hips, she looked primed to explode.

"I've had about enough of you," Annie spat, jabbing a long finger at Luanne. "And that filth you sell…it's nothing but pornography."

Brad Carter | 59

"This is literature." Luanne tapped a nearby paperback.

George smiled, stepping back so that he could take in the whole spectacle.

Annie stamped a foot. "I'm talking about those indecent pictures, the ones from that horrible movie. What sort of woman sells pictures of her bosoms? A filthy Jezebel, that's who." Annie turned her glare to George. "Sir, you should be ashamed of yourself. Consorting with the likes of this Jezebel. Her boyfriend is in and out of jail all the time, she sells naked pictures of herself in a public market, and she gave my niece Darla a belly button ring at that salon of hers."

George rolled his eyes as Annie stomped back to her booth. He winked at Luanne. "I like those pictures you sell. Think I'll buy one, have it framed. My walls are pretty bare over at my new place."

"Thank you, Mr. George. I'm glad to see there's someone in this town appreciates art."

"Now, this Myrna Wilson…" George made vague gestures.

Luanne nodded. "She's available, if that's what you're asking. A widow."

"Well, that's good to know."

Although had Luanne asked, he wasn't sure he'd be able to articulate why it was a good thing that Myrna was available. She was pretty enough, although not like Kathy. His late wife was nearly two decades his junior, and despite her condition at the end, had been beautiful in a way that made George self-conscious in those rare instances of reflective sobriety. But there was something about Myrna that George couldn't articulate. If he were to sit down and try to describe the attraction through a character in a novel or short story, he'd inevitably end up pacing the floor, scratching his chin while he waited for a lightning bolt of inspiration to strike.

"You might think twice about asking her out," Luanne said.

"What? I don't think I'm quite…"

"Not that you wouldn't be a cute couple and all that. But you'd have to deal with Tate. From the sound of it, you've already had a run-in with him, and he's not really the forgiving type. He's made up his mind about you, there's not much you're going to be able to do to change it."

There was an unfamiliar pickup truck parked on the street in front of George's house when he returned home from the flea market. It was an older model Ford, liberally coated with dirt road grit and grime. George pulled into the driveway, parked his car, and made his way to the front porch. The owner of the unfamiliar truck turned out to have a familiar face and handshake.

"Afternoon, Mr. Young," Constable McFettridge said, crushing George's fingers in his calloused grip. "I'm sorry to drop in unannounced like this, but if you're not too busy, I thought we might have a word."

"Yeah, sure." George jammed the key into the front door. He made an after-you motion to the constable and opened the door. "I didn't see your official car out there, so I didn't know who was waiting for me up here on the porch."

McFettridge removed his sunglasses. "Oh, I'm not here in any official capacity. Barlow's out of my jurisdiction, anyway. But I'm pretty strict about keeping the mileage down on the car. The constable position is always up for the chopping block when times get tight, and I don't want to give Mr. Taxpayer any excuse to swing the axe."

George could guess the reason for the visit had to do with the storage unit and that dead security guard. He didn't imagine that McFettridge was here to ask him to join the local bowling league.

"Have a seat. Can I get you something to drink?" George asked. "I have some bottled water. Can't get used to the taste of what comes out of the tap down here. There's some root beer and orange juice. Or I could make coffee."

McFettridge sat down on the couch. "I'm fine."

"Think I'll have a root beer." George went into the kitchen and got a cold bottle of IBC from the refrigerator. He twisted the cap and took a long drink as he went back around the corner into the living room. He took a seat on his new easy chair and placed his bottle atop a coaster on the little table between him and the constable.

"Not much furniture in here," McFettridge said. "Everything looks new."

"That's because it is all new. And I don't have much because I don't need much." George tried to keep his tone from getting peevish. But all this small talk wasn't building any suspense, it that was what it was supposed to do. It was just annoying him.

"Men our age, we tend to accumulate things. A guy like you, a writer who made a bit of money in his time, I figure would have something more to show for it in the way of material goods." McFettridge's words may have been circumspect, but his expression was anything but. He fixed his eyes right on George and kept them there. "You got a TV, this here couch, a new La-Z-Boy, a little coffee table, and a lamp. Looks like a table and a couple chairs there in the kitchen. So unless you've got the bedrooms upstairs packed up to the ceiling, I'd say you just don't got that much."

"The upstairs is about the same as the downstairs, furniture-wise. I'd give you the full tour, but I'm pretty eager for you to get to the point, to be perfectly honest."

"Have I done something to get on your bad side?" McFettridge asked. "I ain't Tate Wilson, looking to intimidate you. Not all peace officers start their day wondering how many constitutional rights they can violate before lunch."

George smiled at that one. "Okay, it looks like you got me sized up."

"Uh huh, and let's test that theory a little bit further, see if I got you pegged as well as I think. How long you been on the wagon?"

George's smile disappeared. "Excuse me?"

"I'm sure you've figured out that it takes one to know one. If it makes you feel any better, I can tell you I've been riding that wagon for some years now myself, give or take a few slips here and there. I sure as hell ain't making any judgments."

"A little over a year. Ever since my wife died. After her funeral, I went on a bender that landed me in the hospital, and I knew that I could stop drinking or join my wife real damn soon. So I dried out and moved to Barlow." George shrugged. That was the short version of it, and the one he felt comfortable telling the constable. "I figured if I was going to make a new start, here was as good a place as any. Quiet enough that I could get some writing done anyway."

It wasn't a lie, not entirely. He wasn't quite sure why he'd chosen Barlow. There was something that seemed right about it, though. Something about returning to his home state after the last twenty years of darkness appealed to the writer in him. If he'd been writing himself as a character, this was how he'd plot this chapter of his life. Like the charged feeling he'd gotten in Myrna Wilson's presence, he couldn't quite articulate his reason for picking this place out of all the others in Arkansas.

"Well, I guess I'll come to the point." The constable shifted around a bit on the couch. "And once again, I'd like to stress that I'm not here in any official capacity. I expect that if Sheriff Wilson knew I was here, he'd read me the riot act before trying to have me removed from my post."

George raised an eyebrow. "He could do that?"

"He'd damn sure try. Would he succeed? Maybe, maybe not. I guess it would be up to the registered voters of Edgewood. But he'd sure as hell be a thorn in my side for a good long while, and I do my best to avoid those. So, this is just two guys talking, okay?"

George took a long drink of his soda. It wasn't beer, but it would have to do. "I think I can handle that."

"You're going to get a call from the sheriff's department in a couple days, letting you know that you're free to use your storage unit again. State crime lab couldn't turn up a bit of evidence. Wilson's plenty pissed, mostly at himself. He knows he acted like an ass during that interview. Now, if it turns out you're involved, he'll have to work twice as hard to get a decent word out of you." He raised a hand to silence George's objection. "Look, I *know* you're not involved. Not unless you're some sort of super villain with the power of invisibility."

George shook his head. "Why do I get the feeling that you're not making jokes here?"

"Because I ain't. Remember me saying that I knew Percy Flannigan's people? I'm the one who got to tell his Aunt Lori that the only kin she had left was dead. Wasn't a damn thing funny about it." He leveled that cop stare at George to signal how serious he was. "The reason I asked you if you were one of the X-Men or something like that is because there was a surveillance camera over that storage unit. We reviewed hours and hours of footage, and no one ever went into that unit before Percy, and afterwards, no one came out. That's why we opened all the boxes, in case the killer was a midget and packed himself up while he waited to make his getaway. Sounds ridiculous, but bullshit theories are all we could come up with."

"That doesn't make any sense..." George's throat had gone dry, and even a sweet swig of rapidly warming IBC didn't do much to change that.

"You're right on that count. But the reason I'm here telling you all this is that I needed to look you in the eyes when I asked you if you knew anything about the how or why this was done to Percy." He leaned forward, propping his elbows on his knees. "So, Mr. Young, is there anything you want to tell me?"

George also leaned forward. "I promise you that I don't have the first clue who killed that young man or why."

McFettridge nodded and sat back. "Like I said, I *know* you didn't have nothing to do with it. But I had to ask. A thing like this, well, we don't get much of it in Gayler County. We got our share of problems, with the meth and all the shit that goes along with that. We've even had a couple of murders last year, but they were straight-up meth killings, open and shut type deals. This Flannigan thing is stuff for Columbo and Perry Mason, not Tate Wilson. He knows that he's got a narrow window for solving it before the state police step in. Hell, as weird as this one looks, might be a case for the FBI."

George thought this was all very compelling, much like an episode of his beloved *Law and Order*, but he failed to see just how it involved him. Well, other than the young man who met his demise in a storage unit full of George's property.

McFettridge seemed to read his mind. "Guess you'd like to know what this has to do with you."

"I was thinking something along those lines," George said.

McFettridge looked down at his lap, suddenly intent on picking at a loose thread hanging off his jeans. "I made the trip all the way down here to ask you something. Now that I'm here, it almost seems too stupid to even say out loud."

"Oh, this sounds like it could be interesting."

"I thought you might have some insight into the case."

George was too taken aback to formulate a response. He settled for looking perplexed.

"Well, I may look like an ignorant redneck, but I read," McFettridge said. "I read *Speak Softly, Lover* and *The Haunting of Harlow Manor*. I even read the ones that didn't get made into movies, like *Eyes of Damnation* and *The Specter Remains*. Back then, I was real interested in ghost stories, and I thought your novels were really some of the best."

George made *Aw, shucks* gestures. These days, he was amazed when anyone remembered his books, much less praised them. Back in the seventies, he'd lapped up accolades without savoring them, and years later, found that he couldn't even remember the taste. People knew the film version of *Speak Softly, Lover* because Robert Redford played Ben McCauley. And they remembered the film version of *The Haunting of Harlow Manor* because it had foreshadowed some of the tricks that Tobe Hooper brought out in *Poltergeist*. But rarely did they remember the books on which those films were based. And though his other novels had enjoyed modest success on the backs of those first two, each of them had sold fewer copies than the one before, until, at last, George found himself without publisher or agent. Only *Speak Softly, Lover* and *The Haunting of Harlow Manor* were even in print these days.

"Bet you hear that kind of thing all the time," the constable said.

"You'd be surprised how rarely I hear it. But how does having authored some ghost stories—and thank you again for reading them—how does that qualify me for having some insight into this case?"

"Come on, Mr. Young. You know what I'm asking."

"You can call me George, by the way. Anyone who remembers *Eyes of Damnation* might as well be on a first name basis with me." George finished his root beer and went to the kitchen for another. He called out over his shoulder, "But I really don't know where you're going with this, unless you actually think there's some supernatural element at work, and because I'm a writer who did a bunch of supernatural novels thirty years ago, I can help you."

When George got back to his recliner, he saw that McFettridge wasn't laughing.

"Guess you figured me out," McFettridge said.

George nearly spewed root beer through his nose. "You can't be serious."

"I couldn't be more serious, Mr. Young."

"George."

"I couldn't be more serious, *George*." McFettridge's cop stare seemed to dare George to laugh again. "Or are you going to offer up some better explanation about how a soft-headed but able-bodied young man gets his throat torn out in a storage unit without the surveillance camera catching anyone other than Percy getting near it."

"Look," George said. "Just because I wrote about that stuff doesn't mean I believe in it."

"Hell, I'm not sure I do, either. But I've turned it over in my mind. I've turned it over and over again, and I can't come up with anything else that fits. You come up with some natural explanation, I'd love to hear it. Might make me feel less crazy for considering this stuff."

George mulled that over for a moment. "You realize what you're asking me boils down to something like this: if this were a book I was writing, where would it go from here? That's not what I'd call real police work. No offense."

"None taken. Lots of folks are quick to remind me that I'm not the real police, anyhow." McFettridge stood, rubbing his hands together. "You think about what I said. Just give it a little time to play around in your head, see if anything shakes loose. Or just laugh your ass off about the superstitious redneck constable. Whatever you do, though, don't tell Tate Wilson I was here. I hope I can count on you for that."

"I'm known for my discretion," George said, walking him to the door.

The constable hesitated, one foot out of the house, one in. "I really thought you might be a believer. You certainly write like one."

George looked the constable over, reevaluating the man, attempting to square the small town lawman with the believer in the supernatural. "You really believe in that stuff, constable? The supernatural and all that?"

"Let's just say I've had some experiences that have left me open-minded. Best leave it at that, though. Not that you look like the type for telling tales out of school, but I'm an elected official. Wouldn't do me much good at the polls if word got out that I was into ghosts and such."

"Understood."

McFettridge treated him to another bone-crunching handshake. "Nice talking to you, George."

"Maybe we'll do it again sometime. Shoot the shit over a couple of root beers," George said.

"Might just take you up on that. You get any ideas, any insights, you give me a call, okay?"

"That's a promise."

Chapter Eight: The Dreamer

Myrna slipped easily into the world of dreams.

Since childhood, she'd been a great dreamer, just as likely to spend her nights in an enchanted world as a landscape of horrors. The nightmares had troubled her parents enough that they sought the help of a doctor, who assured them that some night terrors were completely normal for a child, and that they would decrease over time and eventually stop altogether. The nighttime disturbances, in which young Myrna would scream and cry nearly inconsolably, eventually did decrease, at least as far as her parents knew. The truth was that the nightmares continued, at least a couple per month, but Myrna learned over time to tolerate them.

As she fell asleep to the hushed tones of Dale's voice, she found herself thrust into a nightmare. She was in a dark, enclosed space. The air was stifling, oppressive. That claustrophobic sensation alone was uncomfortable, but it was compounded by the eerie feeling that someone was watching her. Myrna reached out her hands and moved about in the total darkness like a blind woman. The walls in here were shaky and irregular, like she'd been thrown into a maze.

No, not walls. Something else.

She paused, running her fingers over one of the surfaces in front of her. The material was rigid, yet not so hard that it could be wood or cinderblock. There were seams, corners…something peeling away from the surface, something sticky to the touch…

Cardboard boxes. The sticky stuff was packing tape that had come loose.

Experience with nightmares told her that inaction would only prolong the dream. If she wanted to wake up, to escape, she'd have to press forward and see the dream to its completion. Experience also told her that there was something waiting for her in the darkness, a monster or some other horror, and she resigned herself to this. But it didn't make going forward any easier. It was always terrifying. No amount of preparation could change that. So she steeled herself as best she could, drawing in a deep breath and shuffling through the maze of boxes with her hands outstretched. Her face felt hot, her body sweaty. The close air made breathing a chore. Then, there was a break in the darkness. She noticed it out of the corner of her eye as she groped her way around a wobbling box tower.

It was dark grey fog, hovering near the floor. Wispy trails drifted off the main body, like a cloud gradually dispersing in the night sky. She stepped into it and felt immediately chilled. Foggy tendrils snaked up her legs, wrapping themselves around ankles, her calves, her thighs. They encircled her waist like a belt made of damp early morning mist. As she watched the progress of the grey substance, she became aware of a gentle yet insistent pulling. The stuff was urging her forward, guiding her toward its source. The more Myrna resisted, the stronger the pull became. She gave in, letting herself be taken toward whatever waited around the corner.

There was no slobbering maniac wielding an axe. There was no scaly monster baring its mouthful of fangs. What waited in the cardboard alcove was only a woman, her body so wrapped in the grey fog that her features were indistinct. But Myrna could see her outline well enough. She was tall and slender, with dark hair that hung loose around her shoulders.

The grey woman tilted her head to one side, observing Myrna. She swept an arm out of the gloom that wrapped around her. "This is mine," she hissed.

Myrna nodded. "I never said it wasn't."

She tried to take a step backward, but the misty tendrils held her fast. They wrapped tighter around her legs and waist, cinching about her like a too-small pair of pants. The distance between her and the shadowy woman shortened, and Myrna couldn't tell whether she had been pulled forward or the woman had simply drifted closer.

Myrna could see the woman's face much clearer now. Her features were mangled so severely that she hardly appeared human anymore. Her mouth was twisted into what looked to be a permanent scowl, the lips stretched in an impossibly long line that went nearly ear to ear. Her nose looked to have been shattered and then shoved back into her face, leaving the nostrils as two holes in her face. Her jaw was thrust forward, accentuating both of these features so much that the woman's face was dominated by what Myrna thought of as a snout.

The grey woman's long arms reached out to Myrna, brandishing thin fingers that tapered into pointed claws. "Mine!" she screamed, her voice drilling into Myrna's eardrums.

Myrna awoke to the sound of breaking glass. The sound knifed through her post-nightmare disorientation, and she sat bolt upright in bed. She rubbed her eyes and looked around. She'd slept the day away, and the yellow rays of the summer sunset were streaming through the cracks in the blinds. The house was quiet, almost eerily so. It was an old house, built right after the Second World War, when it looked like business would boom loudly and forever, even in a place like Barlow. And like most old houses, it came with its own soundtrack of creaks and groans as the foundation settled and floorboards and joists became crotchety in their old age. That soundtrack had gone silent as Myrna sat in her bed, blinking away the nightmare and searching for the source of the noise that had awakened her. She swung her legs out of bed and got up.

It didn't take long to discover what had made the noise. The jars of buttons lay shattered just outside the bathroom. They'd been reduced to a scattered mixture of broken glass and mismatched buttons of all shapes, sizes, and colors.

Myrna stood over them, biting her lip. She could have sworn she put them on the big dresser across the room. She also could have sworn they'd still been in boxes, packed up with wads of newspaper. She looked over her shoulder. There were the boxes on the dresser, all right, but they'd been opened, the newspaper unwrapped.

Who knows? Maybe I did put them on the bathroom counter. Sure, I put stuff down all over the place, forget where I put it.

She nodded. That was it. She'd unwrapped the jars of buttons, carried them into the bathroom, and set them on the counter, too close to the edge apparently. She'd forgotten it, because she'd had another of her spells. Those jars must have been teetering on the edge of the counter. The house must have settled a bit, just enough to send them over the edge. The jars shattered on the tiles and landed out here in the doorway.

Only, why were there no pieces of glass or buttons on the bathroom floor? The arrangement of the broken mess looked more like it had been thrown across the room with some force. And when Myrna squinted and examined the wall, there *did* seem to be a small knick that hadn't been there before.

No, it's an old house, and there are cracks and dings everywhere. That crack in the ceiling plaster in the dining room, it gets a little longer and a little more jagged every day. The buttons fell off the counter. The only one here to do any throwing of jars was me, and unless I was sleepwalking…okay, that's a possibility too.

Myrna retrieved the empty boxes from the dresser and began sorting through the mess. She put glass shards in one box, buttons in the other. Such a mess for a few jars of buttons! But at least it took her mind off the horrible possibility that her spells were getting worse. She knew that she'd…slipped….over the last few years. She wasn't so far gone that she could look around her own house and not think there was a problem. She *knew* that this nonstop accumulation of things was not normal. But she *felt* there was no other way for her to live. She *knew* that her baby boy Dale was dead and gone. But she *felt* his presence was as real as if he'd never enlisted, never been deployed to that desert hellhole. Myrna Wilson may not have had any post-high school education, but she was no idiot. Her situation was far from ideal. All the signs pointed to an ever-increasing mental illness, possibly brought on by…

By what? A brain tumor?

Myrna paused in her work. She'd watched reruns of *ER* and the show with that mean-spirited Dr. House. And yes, while those were most assuredly fiction, she knew that there was some medical fact backing up those stories, and most of them said that a brain tumor was a death sentence. When foul-mouthed Dr. House had worked his way through a dozen wrong theories, and it turned out that the real answer was that his patient had a brain tumor, there was always some tearful bedside scene, usually set to some mopey music. And if the patient did live through the brain surgery, there was always some lasting damage that made the patient miserable. Like just last week, there was one about a man who had a brain tumor taken out, and when he woke up, he didn't know his wife and children. It was terrible. Myrna had cried.

No, if it was a brain tumor, she'd just let it be. Fifty-four seemed an awful young age for this to happen to her, but that was life. Things didn't work out the way you wanted them to sometimes. She hadn't planned on being pregnant at seventeen and married less than a year later. She hadn't planned on being a widow. That was just life. Besides—and this was a terrible thing to think, which is why she avoided it most of the time—losing that brain tumor would mean never getting to see Dale again. And real or not, she had come to value his brief and sporadic visits. Lord knew Tate was never so understanding or sympathetic. He had too much of his father in him.

She did the best she could getting all the glass out of the carpet. It was tedious work, and some little bits of glass inevitably remained, buried deep in the pile, but getting the vacuum cleaner upstairs was too big a job for this late in the day. She found a spare bathmat in the bathroom closet and slapped it down where the glass had been. She transferred the shoebox full of loose buttons to the bookshelf, wedging it in beside an incomplete set of encyclopedias and a glass jug containing a miniature model ship.

"Now you stay put this time," she said, shaking a finger at the box and forcing strained laughter into her voice.

She picked her way carefully down the stairs, one hand gripping the bannister, the other thrown out beside her for balance. After the Thanksgiving Incident, she'd done her best to keep too much loose paper off the stairs, but time had softened her resolve, and the staircase was again growing treacherous. She made a mental note to clear a better path on the stairs. But she knew, even as she resolved to do it, she never would.

Chapter Nine: The Good Son

Tate Wilson worked at least one Saturday each month. He required all the deputies to do so, and, just as he told George Young, he was a firm believer in leading by example. He didn't mind. Saturday mornings in Gayler County were quiet. By the time the night shift came on, there'd be action: domestic disturbances at the trailer court or the Blue Mountain View apartment complex, fights inside or outside the Dixie Tavern over in Crystal Falls, DWI arrests up and down Military Road and Highway 218, meth heads racing cars down the dirt roads between Barlow and Edgewood, and who knows what else. But Saturday mornings were all youth soccer, lawn mowing, fishing trips, and dog walking. And garage sales and flea markets, damn them all.

Over the last ten years, flea markets and garage sales had earned a special place on Sheriff Tate Wilson's shit list, right there with all the smartass out of towners who flocked to Barlow hoping to see the Sasquatch. Tourist revenue be damned, those idiots were nothing but trouble. Ever since that stupid movie came out, he could count on several carloads of true believers traipsing through the woods each good-weather Saturday. Of course, once they found out that their chances of actually seeing the Big Man of Barlow were down around absolute zero, they'd get into drinking or public fornication or both. Then their tourist money got spent twice: first on their hotel and food, and then on bail bonds and court fees.

Tate wheeled the cruiser into Maple Oaks (and wondered, as he did each time he came to his mother's neighborhood, what kind of moron named the subdivision), and hooked a left onto Biscayne Boulevard. He sighed, seeing that the driveway was empty. There were only two explanations for the absence of his mother's Crown Vic: that she'd finally cleaned out the garage or she'd given into her addiction and headed over to the Rosebud Flea Market. Since the former explanation was about as likely as Tate scoring with each member of the Swedish Bikini team, he stomped on the brakes, pulled a U-turn, and headed toward the west end

72 | ONLY THINGS

of town, where that monstrous barn full of curios, keepsakes, and collectibles squatted like a giant, ugly toad.

No doubt his mother was inside, throwing away good money on second-hand junk. He wondered if he could extricate her without causing a scene. He was certain she'd gone on one of her buying binges. He'd been trying to raise her all morning on her cell phone, but each call had gone straight to voicemail.

The radio squawked a burst of static. Shelly Sisco's nasal voice broke through. "Sheriff, you need to get over to Big Savers. Looks like there's some kids fighting in the parking lot."

Tate gritted his teeth. "Shelly, can't you get someone else? I'm clear across town."

"Both Ewell and George are already out at the fairgrounds. Some other kids were popping off fireworks out there. Busy Saturday."

"A regular crime wave. I'll get right on it."

Tate pulled another U-turn and headed back toward downtown Barlow. He flipped on the rack lights and put the hammer down, squealing his tires as made the turn into the parking lot of the Big Savers grocery store. His sudden appearance scattered the small audience that had sprouted around the two combatants.

Tate didn't have the heart to put the bracelets on a couple of kids with bad haircuts and worse attitudes. And since there were no broken bones or dislodged teeth, Tate just gave the two proud peacocks a stern lecture and sent them on their way. He was sure they'd just end up punching it out in the park or over in front of the old Casa del Fuego building, but hell, Tate figured, boys will be boys. Besides, he had bigger fish to fry. The Flannigan thing wasn't going to solve itself. He reckoned that he had another week, ten days at the outside, before the state police swooped in. And he didn't have shit for leads except for George Young. The whole thing was a big dead end.

He hit the radio. "Shelly, the Big Savers riot has been dispersed. No casualties and no arrests."

"Okay, boss. We can all breathe easier."

He drove back through town, cruising easy and waving to the sparse downtown foot traffic. The Big Man Sasquatch Shop was still hanging on, as were Grouchies and the Pancake Hut. He'd heard rumors that one of the big national coffee chains was going to put in next to the old Lyman's Furniture store. Maybe downtown Barlow could hang on for another decade. Edgewood up north had the motel trade locked down,

Brad Carter | 73

being closer to the interstate and all. But Crystal Falls to the south was on its last legs now that the water park was closed, and Deacon to the northeast was practically dead, its school already consolidated with Edgewood.

But this was Tate's jurisdiction, what he privately referred to as his beat, and he'd be damned if he would skip out to a bigger department.

The radio squawked again. "Boss, it looks like there's a situation up at the Sunrise Inn on I-30. Two naked males and one naked female running around the complex."

Tate sighed. "I'll turn around and get over that way. See can you raise Constable McFettridge and get him out there. Might need some backup if three of them's tear-assing around there."

"I'll get right on it, boss."

Another U-Turn with the lights going full blast. Looked to Tate like it might be one of those days. He made a mental note to check if there was going to be a full moon that night and gunned the engine.

His prediction about it being a day for the books proved to be spot-on. After he'd nabbed the gang of streakers, with a little help from a bemused Constable McFettridge, Tate had to deal with some of his beloved Bigfoot hunters taking some time out from their scientific pursuits to get down and dirty on the edge of Grouse Lake Park. Seemed like the concept of free love had finally made its way to Gayler County. Next, it was shoplifters at the Big Savers, which brought him back across town for a second time. And so on. The one upside was that it made his shift go by in a few blinks of the eye. He'd even had to eat his lunch—a couple of hot dogs and a milkshake from the Tastee Freezee—behind the wheel of his cruiser. By the time he got a chance to swing back by his mother's place, his shift had not only ended, but gone into overtime.

His mother's car was back in the driveway, and Tate pulled the cruiser in next to it. He popped a couple Tums into his mouth and chomped them down as he got out of the car. Not only were the hot dogs deciding to bark, the dread he felt at visiting with his mother also stirred up his belly.

He rapped sharply on the front door. "It's me, Mom. Open up."

There was a noise on the other side of the door like a small avalanche: a rapid series of thumps, a crunching and crinkling of paper. The door opened just enough to admit Myrna Wilson onto the porch.

Tate could hear the TV. She'd been watching that stupid doctor show, the one with the smart-assed doctor played by the British actor who talked like an American. Tate didn't like it. That doctor was the type that would be a pleasure to hit with the Taser a couple times, see if that got him talking in a more respectful tone to his patients.

"Good evening, son." Myrna stood on tiptoe to give him a hug.

Tate broke away, looking down at his mother. "I came by this morning. Your car was gone."

"Oh, I had a couple errands to run."

"I bet. Where'd you go?"

Her smile faltered. "Oh, here and there. Nowhere in particular. Saturday doesn't feel right unless I run a few errands."

"The flea market?"

"Well…"

"Mom, we've talked and talked about this…" Tate wondered how many times these words had come out of his mouth. "You can't keep buying all that junk."

"Oh, it's not junk. They're all collectibles. These things were once important to people. They have value."

Tate crossed his arms across his chest. "It's crap, Mom. It's crap that's taken over your house. You won't even invite me in anymore. I can't even come visit you in the house I grew up in. That ain't right, and you know it."

"I just need to tidy up a bit. Housework is just a little overwhelming lately. Listen, we could go to the Pancake Hut for dinner. How's that sound? We could talk about Luanne."

"Mom, Luanne is still living with that no-account boyfriend of hers." Tate regretted ever telling his mother about Luanne Samples. Although he hadn't entirely given up on the idea that Luanne might one day come to her senses, Tate didn't like his mother bringing it up every chance she got. He put the conversation back into safe territory. "I tried calling you all morning and it went straight to voicemail."

"I mislaid my cell phone again," she said. "I'm so forgetful these days."

Tate's posture softened, and he let his arms drop to his sides. "All right, Mom. But look, please try to go through some of your collections. Last time you let me in there, you had stuff piled all over the living room and the kitchen. You don't get a handle on it soon, you'll have that mess upstairs too."

Brad Carter | 75

Myrna nodded vigorously. "I just need a little motivation."

A burst of static came from the radio on Tate's shoulder. "Boss, this is Shelly, come back."

Tate grunted. "Look, Mom, I got to go back to work. I'll come by after my shift, if it ever ends, take you out for coffee and pie, all right?"

"That would be great!" She sounded like a kid glad to be dismissed from the principal's office.

"But we're going to have a talk about all the mess in that house. It ain't right, you keeping me out the house I grew up in."

He hugged his mother one more time and trotted back to the cruiser. He hit the radio and asked Shelly what was so all-fired important. Shelly came back and told him that Mavis Kilgore was outside someone's trailer, hollering that she knew that young lady inside had been ogling her girlfriend.

"Shelly, I thought Mavis only got violent after midnight," he said into his radio. "And who'd want to ogle Becky Dusenberry anyhow?"

"I'm sure I don't know," Shelly replied.

"This is what comes of all those alternative lifestyles. Maybe being that way flips some switch in your head."

"I'm sure I don't know about that either, boss."

Tate instantly regretted the comment. He'd had his suspicions about Shelly's preferences for a while now. She wasn't hard on the eyes, Tate supposed, but she was somehow too much like one of the guys. She watched NASCAR and had last year taken fourth place at the bass fishing tournament in Maumelle. But unlike the rest of the anglers at that tournament, Shelly sported a rack second only to the one that Luanne Samples paraded around town. It sure was a head-scratcher.

"You there, boss?" Shelly prompted.

"I'm right on it, Shelly."

He flipped the rack lights on and headed for the trailer park, his thoughts tangled up with Shelly and Luanne and the mess in his mother's house. Tate hadn't been allowed into the house for some time, and his mother had the locks changed so that he couldn't sneak in while she was away. Tate supposed he could have broken in easily enough, but he didn't have the heart for that. And in a way, he was just too afraid of what he might find if he did break in. There was no telling how much junk she'd accumulated in the last year. Tate shook his head to clear out the confusion. He even tried a breathing exercise he'd read about in *Men's*

Health. Neither action had any effect. He settled for popping a couple more antacid tablets.

Tate *did* take his mother to the Pancake Hut that night, but the topic of her collections was only discussed briefly, despite earlier promises. Myrna Wilson could steer a conversation any way she chose, the same way an Olympic skier navigates a difficult track. They started off discussing how Myrna should sort through her collections and maybe sell some stuff or even donate it to the Goodwill store, but before Tate knew it, they were onto different subjects.

It wasn't until he was driving home that Tate realized how skillfully she had avoided the topic. He cursed and smacked the steering wheel with his palm. But he told himself that he'd try again next Saturday. After all, how much crap could the woman buy in one week?

The clock on the dashboard said that it was nearly ten. Good Lord, he'd nearly worked a double. And just as he'd suspected, the moon overhead was indeed a full one. He firmly adhered to the theory, shared by cops and ER doctors everywhere, that the full moon did something to people, made them crazy.

He took the cruiser back to the station and picked up his own truck. Finally time to call it a day.

It was all the coffee he'd had alongside his slice of lemon ice box pie. That's what Tate told himself as he paced around the living room. All that caffeine was why couldn't sit still, not even to watch a rerun of *Saturday Night Live* that he hadn't caught on the first go around. Instead, he marched around the living room, squeezing a tennis ball and occasionally pausing to throw it against the wall and catch it on the rebound. His mind kept ping-ponging back and forth between his mother's out of control clutter problem and the Flannigan case. The first problem was just as unsolvable as the second, it seemed. He threw the ball against the wall too hard and missed it as it rocketed back at him. It bounced into the kitchen.

He followed the tennis ball over to the refrigerator and got himself a can of light beer. Maybe a couple cold ones would clarify things in his mind. He drank the first can down in a few long gulps, and when it yielded no great revelations, he opened a second.

If Mom didn't let him in the house soon, he could always have Judge Crawford swear him out a search warrant. The old man owed him a favor for burying his granddaughter's DWI.

Tate shook his head. He wasn't executing a search warrant for his own mother. Not yet anyway. He turned his attention to the other problem: how a man gets himself killed in a locked room that no one has been in or out of for nearly seventy-two hours. There was no one in that storage unit before Percy Flannigan went in. And no one came out after. So, what the hell happened?

He rinsed his beer can out and shot it into the recycle bin with its partner. He hesitated with his hand on the refrigerator door. He rarely allowed himself more than two. But he figured he'd earned it.

As much as he wanted it to grant him some sort of insight—the way that British doctor that his mother loved always had those huge epiphanies—all the alcohol was doing was making him go in the same circles he'd been going in for the last few days. Worse, it wasn't calming him down one bit. He squeezed the tennis ball and stomped around some more. He kept coming back to George Young. There was something about him that wasn't right. McFettridge acted like the guy was hot shit because he wrote some books, but that didn't cut any mustard with Tate. As far as he was concerned, this Young character was involved. He *had* to be.

Tate was out on the sidewalk, headed toward Bradshaw Street before he'd even thought it through. Knowing that Young was living right around the corner had been gnawing at him, so he figured he'd take a spin around the block, get a look at the guy's house. Nothing wrong with that. He didn't need a warrant to walk past someone's house.

He turned left at the end of Johnson and headed down Bradshaw. This was a fairly new neighborhood, but the houses on Bradshaw were actually brand new, as in "never been occupied." They went up when it looked like the faucet factory might expand, bringing in new employees. But then a new factory went up in Conway instead of an expansion to the one in Barlow. Most of the brand new houses were empty, some of them unfinished. That meant Young didn't have a lot of neighbors around to observe him. If someone was into something shady, he might appreciate the privacy.

"Speak of the devil," Tate said as he neared the house.

78 | ONLY THINGS

Young was still awake. In fact, he was sitting on his front porch, rocking back and forth in one of those wicker chairs. Tate figured if he could see Young that the old guy could see him. Turning back now would just look strange.

"Little late for a walk," Young called out.

Tate tried to look casual. He didn't feel like he was doing a very good job of it. "Guess I could say that it's also late to be sitting on your porch rocking chair too."

"The air conditioner's broken. I forgot how hot it gets down here."

"It's the humidity that does it to people," Tate said.

"You walk over here to talk about the weather?"

Tate had been walking slowly up the driveway and now he was close enough to see that the old guy was smirking at him. It was the kind of smile worn by folks who didn't believe the duly elected Sheriff of Gayler County was a real cop. It was the kind of smile that Tate loved to see disappear when he unhooked the bracelets from his belt or whipped out the pepper spray. On Young's face, maybe it was the look of someone who was hiding something and didn't think Tate was smart enough to ferret it out.

"I was just out for a stroll. And, well, I knew you lived over here, so I thought I'd take a look." Tate had one leg on the stairs leading up to the porch. He propped his elbows on his knee and threw Young's smartass grin right back at him.

"And now you've gotten a look at my palatial dwellings. I'd offer you the grand tour, but I'm not sure it's the proper hour for receiving guests."

Tate nodded. So this was how it was going to be. Might as well let him have it then. "You know, Mr. Young, I ran your name through a few databases. Don't look surprised. We have the internet down here, too. Pretty interesting stuff there, about how your wife passed away recently. She was younger than you, wasn't she?"

"You think that's interesting?"

"Something about those circumstances might be considered suspicious," Tate said. "Especially when one looks at how much money went right into your bank account upon her death."

"If you looked into the report, you'd know that I wasn't even in the house when Kathy…"

"Just like you weren't anywhere near that storage locker when poor Percy met his untimely end. I know, I know." Tate stood up, raised his

Brad Carter | 79

hands. "There's more than one way to be mixed up in bad business, Mr. Young. All kinds of ways to get yourself into trouble."

"Sheriff, you have worn out your welcome." Young got out of his rocking chair. "Next time you want to visit this property, I'll expect you to have a search warrant in good order."

"That's the way you want it, that's the way we'll do it."

Young went into the house, slamming the door behind him.

Tate stood up and began the walk back home. Maybe one more beer wouldn't hurt.

Chapter Ten: The Hunter

There were different looks people got in their eyes when faced with a garage sale or a flea market. Some couldn't wait to get away, bored stiff by the prospect of looking through someone else's junk. Their eyes glazed over, maybe glimmering with a bit of disdain. Dragged there by spouses or significant others, they suffered with varying degrees of patience. Others were intrigued, hoping to find a rare treasure among all the useless trash. These people's eyes were fierce, focused. Still others seemed to nearly weep with joy at the opportunity to acquire things cheaply, no matter how broken, used, or marred these things were. This last group made pilgrimages early on Saturday mornings, scouring the streets for driveways and carports strewn with cast-off crap to be had at bargain prices. These people threw themselves into each sale with crazed avidity, purchasing all manner of bric-a-brac until their vehicles were heavy-laden and their wallets empty.

It was this last group that interested Chris. They had a twitchy, almost giddy way of handling the objects they purchased. Their smiles—blissful and detached—reminded him of Julian. And thinking of Julian made his blood boil.

Following their confrontation, Chris had lain in bed for days, emerging only to go to the toilet and to call in sick to work. He was tormented by nightmares and by the constant urge to stand for hours beneath a scalding shower. He could do nothing about the nightmares. They came to him each time he fell asleep. And he was forced to resist the urge to bathe, as his frantic showering on Saturday had left his skin rubbed so raw that it was broken in large swaths across his body. He'd bled onto his clothing and his bed, waking up glued to the sheets with dried blood.

Finally, on Wednesday night, he'd left his bed. Weak with thirst and hunger, he stumbled into the kitchen. He drank down two tall glasses of water while he prepared a meal of canned chicken soup and toast.

He ate slowly, his stomach threatening rebellion at first but gradually calming as he went. By the time he was done, he felt stronger, refreshed. The humiliation he'd suffered at his brother's hands still stung fiercely, but Chris resolved as he ate his toast to not only survive but see his suffering avenged.

He rose well before sunrise on Saturday morning, feeling invigorated. He'd come to a decision. Action would be taken against the forces of chaos. He wasn't quite sure what this action would entail, but he knew that it was time that he carried it out. Standing under the shower—not so hot this time as his skin was still healing—he felt like he was poised on the cusp of great things. People around him couldn't see it now, but soon they would know that Chris Clanton was a great man. The humiliation he'd suffered at the hands of his brother would have broken a lesser man. But Chris had survived and come out stronger, like steel forged with white hot fire.

The donut shop on Rodney Parham wasn't the best spot for breakfast, but it was owned by a Lebanese family who kept the place spotless. Chris admired that quality. He was the lone customer at that early hour. He ate a donut while circling ads in the Classifieds section of the *Arkansas Democrat-Gazette*. Garage sales, estate sales, moving sales…there were so many of the damnable things. There was so much to do.

The old hippies were at the third garage sale Chris visited. He zeroed in on them once he got a look at the delirium that pawing over the useless junk roused in them. They looked positively gleeful. Each of them carried a large cardboard box into which they put their purchases: mismatched clothes, battered books, a set of wind chimes, old VHS tapes, a plastic Jack o' Lantern, rolled up posters, and other assorted trash. When he drifted close, Chris could practically smell the anticipation wafting off their skin. Their incessant chattering fascinated him in some morbid way. It was like being unable to look away from the spectacle of a monkey masturbating in a zoo cage.

"Oh, this would be perfect for the living room," the woman cooed, lifting yet another set of wind chimes.

The man, nearly drooling his approval, nodded. He lifted his own newest find, an incomplete set of steak knives. "These are dull right now, but I can get them sharpened up. Don't know if we'll use them all that much since we quit eating meat, but at two bucks, I can't pass them up."

"You boys and your toys!" the woman squealed.

They went on like that, giggling as they inspected a stack of jigsaw puzzles. Chris wanted to scream that each of those puzzles was missing pieces or mismatched. The pressure of holding back made his head hurt, and he eased off, pretending to look through a milk crate of old vinyl LPs while he watched the hippies. They were both short, squat types and wore old cutoff blue jeans. Their fingers, the ones that caressed the items on sale, had dirty nails, like they'd been digging in the garden and hadn't bothered to wash their hands. Chris' skin crawled.

When they'd finally finished shopping, they took their selections to the garage, where the owners of the home were making change out of a zippered bank bag. The totals were ridiculously low. The people running the sale knew the things they were selling were mostly worthless. They just couldn't bear to consign them to the depths of the landfill without giving these vultures a chance to take the choicest bits. In a way, he supposed the sellers were just as complicit in aiding the chaos as those buying the useless junk by the box load. They were collaborators of a sort, and he hoped they would see the error of their ways.

To blend in, he scooped up a random paperback book and handed over a dime. The people with the bank bag thanked him and smiled. Chris wanted to tell them that the book would never enter his apartment. He'd toss it into the dumpster as soon as he got home. Instead, he just returned their smiles and muttered some inanity.

The hippies drove a beat up cargo van, which was plastered in layers of bumper stickers promoting various political causes. Greenpeace. Amnesty International. People for the Ethical Treatment of Animals. Earth First. The cliché was so tired that it made Chris laugh. Here were these two dirty agents of chaos, proudly advertising numerous ecological causes while driving a van that belched black smoke every time it came to a stop.

Was that irony? Chris watched smoke pump out of the van's tailpipe as it sat idling at an intersection. He decided that it *was* irony, and rich, at that.

It wasn't hard to follow them, not even in the crosstown Saturday morning traffic. Their vehicle was the very definition of conspicuous. Chris discovered that he could hang back as many as three, four cars and still see the mammoth van. Even when some ridiculous SUV insinuated itself between them, he could keep track of the van by following the vehicle's emissions.

He followed them from yard sale to estate sale to church rummage sale. At each site, the bulbous pair pored over the wares on display, each of them making enough selections to fill a cardboard box. In the space

Brad Carter | 83

of a few hours, they'd purchased enough to stage their own yard sale. But Chris had no illusions that this pair was going to let go of any of these new possessions.

They proceeded in that manner until early afternoon. Then Chris followed them to the packed-to-the-rafters hovel that they called a home. They lived outside the city limits in one of those little towns that would soon be swallowed up by Little Rock as the city pushed west. The house looked like it was one step away from being condemned. Situated in a patch of overgrown weeds and rusting machinery, the building was a mass of peeling paint and termite-eaten wood. Chris pulled his car into the abandoned gas station across the road and watched the couple unload their new acquisitions.

Chris returned at midnight. Something about that hour just felt right for this kind of work. He parked his car behind the derelict gas station and stepped out into the muggy night air. Mosquitoes sang in his ears, and he swatted them away absently. His attention was fixed on the house across the road. The windows were mostly covered, and the little light that spilled out gave the objects in the yard a sinister cast. The rusted machinery—the old washer and dryer, the wrecked lawn mowers—crouched like fallen gargoyles among the weeds. They glared at Chris, and he glared back.

He advanced on his objective, crossing the street in measured strides. An unfamiliar sensation had come over him, a pleasantly detached feeling. He found that his feet were marching forward almost of their own accord. It was as if he'd handed over the controls of his body to some unseen force. And because Chris knew what this unseen force intended, he smiled. He felt serene as he walked through the cluttered front lawn and knocked on the front door.

The door opened, and Chris found himself face to face with the man he'd followed all day. The sweet odor of marijuana smoke and the wet stink of mildew assaulted Chris' nose with equal force.

"Hello, young man. What can I do for you?" The man was shirtless, and his torso sported a coat of curly grey hair. His belly hung down over a pair of flower-patterned shorts, the only garment he wore.

"My car broke down." Chris pointed over his shoulder. "That gas station looks like it's closed, and I really need to get home. My phone's dead, and I have no idea where I am."

"Been there before!" The man laughed, his double chin wobbling. "Well, brother, I tell you what. We don't have a phone, but you're welcome to come in and sit for a while. Me and Moonflower roll out early on Sunday morning to catch the yard sales, and we can give you a ride back into town then. We're not in much shape to drive at the present time, if you know what I mean."

Chris smiled. "That'd be great."

The man held out a pudgy hand. "Name's Jubilee. People call me Jube."

Jubilee and Moonflower. Some people deserve everything that's coming to them.

Chris shook hands. "I'm Chris."

"Come on in and take a load off, Chris." Jube swept his arm expansively, as if he was ushering his guest into Buckingham Palace.

The room was crowded and hot. An enormous couch, lumpy and patched here and there with silver duct tape, dominated one wall. Floor-to-ceiling shelves lined the other walls, crammed with books and papers and fuzzy with dust. Wind chimes hung from the ceiling at irregular intervals. Their tinkling and jangling provided the room with its own soundtrack as they were stirred by the wind of an oscillating fan that whirred away in one corner. Moonflower was seated in the middle of the floor, her bulk supported by two beanbag chairs. On her lap was a shoebox full of sunglasses.

"Babe, this is Chris," Jube said. "He's going to hang out for a while."

She held up the shoebox. "Twenty cents apiece at the St. Raphael rummage sale last Saturday. Can you believe it?"

"Sounds like a steal." Chris looked around. To his left was a kitchen, and the bit he could see through the doorway was predictably disgusting. The stovetop was coated in grease and surrounded by open cans. He couldn't see the sink, but he imagined it was packed full of dirty dishes. A hallway to the right of the kitchen led to the rest of the house, and also served as a playpen for a trio of obese cats who half-heartedly wrestled on the dirty carpet.

"Sit yourself down, my friend." Jube plopped down on the couch. He reached between the cushions and produced a blue glass bong and a cigar box. "Had to stash my stuff down there, in case you were the pigs knocking on the door."

"How did you know that I wasn't a police officer?" Chris asked, equally amused and disgusted as he watched Jube studiously readying his bong for use.

"You're dressed too nice."

"What?"

By the time Chris asked, Jube had the bong bubbling away and was sucking down what seemed like a dozen lungfuls of pungent smoke. Moonflower answered for him.

"A cop comes to this place, he wants to blend in. He'll be wearing a brand new Grateful Dead shirt or some tie-dye he bought at Walmart." She put on a pair of horn-rimmed sunglasses and tossed her mane of lank grey hair about, giggling. "Cops always try to blend in and fail. But you're dressed just like some ordinary guy, so we figure you're okay."

Jube exhaled a stinking cloud into the softly tinkling wind chimes overhead. "What the hell were you doing way out here anyway? Since the gas station went belly-up, we don't really get traffic."

Chris tried his best to look sheepish. "I was at a party and had a few drinks. I think I got turned around."

His hosts laughed. Moonflower pulled off the horn rims and tossed them over to Chris. "These are more your style, Buddy Holly!"

The glasses bounced into Chris' lap, and he set them on the arm of the couch. He winced as his fingers brushed the frayed, stained fabric. "This is quite a place you have here. Lots of interesting stuff."

The words felt forced, wrong. He wanted to scream at them that it was wrong to live this way, that they were dragging humanity down a road that ended in madness and death. He wanted to tell them that entropy, that great cosmic chaos, was coming, and they were putting out a welcome mat for it.

"Can you believe every bit of this stuff came from rummage sales and that sort of thing?" Moonflower beamed proudly as she selected a pair of wraparound shades that would have looked more at home on the face of a NASCAR driver than an obese hippie. "People just get rid of stuff. They want everything to be new, new, new."

Jube blew out another cloud. "We can live like royalty just on our disability checks because we don't expect everything to be bright and shiny. Well, there might just be a little money coming in from my herbal enterprise."

"Speaking of which, where are your manners, Jube?" Moonflower pulled off her race car shades. "We have a guest and all you can do is Bogart the bong."

"No thanks," Chris said. "I think I've had all I can handle tonight."

"Well, pass it over here then." Moonflower snapped her fingers.

86 | ONLY THINGS

Chris stood, doing his best to suppress a shudder as he watched Moonflower press the bong to her lips. "I don't suppose I can use the bathroom?" he asked.

Jube pointed to the hallway. "First door on the left."

The cats stopped their play to eye Chris suspiciously as he passed. One of them took a tentative swipe at him, and he pulled back his foot to deliver a kick but then stopped himself. The cat was just a dumb beast. It wasn't at fault for the state of the house.

He stepped into the bathroom. It was cluttered and unsanitary. There were two sinks, and both of them were crusted with soap scum and bits of hair. Damp and stinking hand towels were scattered across the counter. Behind him was a tub sporting a dark ring about its circumference. An acrid chemical smell stung his nostrils. This was the cats' restroom as well. Hard blackish-brown turds lay scattershot all over the floor.

Chris looked into the mirror, studying his reflection in the pitted and cloudy surface. He wondered if he was truly ready to do what had to be done. What if he was wrong? What if these people could be saved? He thought of Belinda, slumped at the end of the bed, her head twisted around backwards. And he thought of Julian.

His resolve stiffened.

The cats seemed to sense his intentions, and they scattered as he emerged from the bathroom.

Moonflower and Jube were both laughing when he reentered the living room. They'd finished smoking and had raided the kitchen for snacks. Jube spooned up globs of chocolate ice cream from the container in his lap. Little brown spatters covered his hairy chest. Moonflower ate handfuls of cheese flavored crackers, the crumbs flying from her lips as she giggled.

Jube smiled broadly. "You were gone so long, we thought you fell in."

"I was just thinking," Chris said.

"I find I do my best thinking in that room, too."

Moonflower threw a handful of crackers at Jube. "You men are so gross."

Chris strolled around the room, dodging the wind chimes and looking at the bookshelves. He pretended to be interested in the titles while he gathered his thoughts. "It occurs to me that you two might just understand what it is that I was thinking about back there. What I've been thinking about for most of my life, really."

Brad Carter | 87

Jube set his ice cream aside. "All right, my friend, let's get into it. Let's get heavy."

Chris took a deep breath. "I believe—and science as well as most religions back me up on this—that the universe is ruled by two opposing forces."

Jube nodded sagely. "Good and evil. The eternal struggle."

"Not quite, Jube."

Moonflower lobbed another volley of crackers at him. "Jube, you dope. It's light and dark. Everyone knows that."

"Sorry, Moonflower, but that's not it either." Chris leaned against the bookshelf. "Chaos and order. Entropy and design. Filth and cleanliness. Discord and procedure. Different sides of the same coin, and each of them fighting to rule the universe."

"This takes me back to college. Our bull sessions could go all night in those days," Jube said. He had the bong out again. "Tell me more about this philosophy, my friend. Expound. Edify. Elucidate."

Chris looked into the hanging garden of wind chimes. "It's funny you mention college, Jube, because that's where I was when this came to me. It was a revelation, you might say. I think I always knew on some level, but it was during college that I had this….this flash of inspiration, in which it all became clear to me. I saw that life and intelligence arose out of chaos, the chance result of billions upon billions of interactions. It was a beautiful idea, that a swirling cosmic chaos could birth something so elegantly ordered. Chaos, quite by accident, birthed order. And as is the case with all things, the superior form arose from the inferior. It was evolution on a cosmic scale, this emergence of order."

He didn't mention that this flash of insight came on the heels of a suicide attempt. There were some matters that should always remain private. A simple matter of falsified contact information had kept the incident a secret from his father and brother. As the years had passed, Chris had locked the whole business away inside him. It had been a shameful, cowardly act. But the wisdom he'd gained had made it worth the pain.

"Order," Chris repeated. "Glorious and perfect order."

Jube exhaled a long stream of smoke. "That's a far-out way to look at it."

Chris held up a hand. "But the birth of order didn't vanquish the chaos. It's still out there, fighting its way back to supremacy. And unfortunately, it will eventually win. You see, entropy is still the natural state of things. It increases. That's a law of thermodynamics, that in any system, entropy increases. It builds and builds."

"Until what?" Jube asked.

"Total disorder. A return to the primordial chaos from which the universe arose."

"And it's unavoidable?"

"Sadly, yes." Chris paused, letting that sink in. "But it can be delayed, perhaps even indefinitely."

"How?"

"By maintaining order. Our species may have arisen as a result of chaos—as did the entire universe, I suppose—but that doesn't mean we have to give in to that base instinct. Cleanliness, order, design, organization, procedure…these are not just concepts for good living. They are also weapons for combating a cosmic force capable of consuming not just life on this planet but the very fabric of the universe and reality as we know it." Like some cheap-suited preacher, he was gesticulating wildly and sweating as he spoke. "As we clean and organize, we stave off the destruction of mankind. Don't you see?"

They stared at him blankly for a moment.

Moonflower broke the silence. "Yeah, that's a fancy theory, but I don't really believe it. Life is messy." She tossed a handful of crackers into the air to illustrate her point. "And messy is fun."

"My friend, you make a convincing argument," Jube said, fixing his dilated-pupil gaze on Chris. "But I have to agree with my woman. Life is messy. Nature is beautiful, but it sure ain't clean. You just have to accept that. Get down in the mud and love your Mother Earth. Get in touch with that primal instinct you're talking against. Just might be you'll like how it feels."

Chris sighed. "I was afraid you'd say that. But to tell you the truth, I'm also a bit relieved that you did. It makes what I have to do so much easier."

Some of the wind chimes hanging from the ceiling were delicate glass structures. Others were hollow wooden pipes. But the one Chris tugged loose from its fellows was made of thick metal and nearly a foot and a half long. It had a smooth, solid feel as he hefted it.

"I have dreamed about this day for so long," he said, gazing down at the weapon in his hand.

His first swing caught Moonflower on the back of her head. The sunglasses she'd been wearing and the mouthful of crackers she'd been chewing both shot across the room. Chris brought the chime back down, like a tennis player's backhand shot. It slammed into her mouth, smashing her teeth. A choking, gurgling noise came out of her as she slumped over. Blood poured onto the floor. She lay there twitching.

The reality of what just happened seemed to finally dawn on Jube, and he struggled to lift his bulk from the low-slung couch. Before he could manage to get to his feet, Chris whipped the chime into his jaw. The fat man lifted up with the force of the blow and then sprawled back onto the couch. Chris planted his feet and took his time lining up his next shot. He brought the chime down with all his strength, hitting Jube on the side of his head, just above his ear. The blow left a divot in Jube's skull so big that his eye bulged from its socket. Chris pounded away until the eyeball completely dislodged and hung on Jube's cheek.

Chris stood over the couch, breathing heavily as he admired his handiwork.

Something wrapped around his ankle, and he nearly jumped. He looked down and saw that Moonflower had crawled across the room and was now clutching at his leg. Her mouth lolled open, revealing the extent of the damage done to her teeth.

"This is for the good of humanity," Chris said as he jerked his leg away. "I don't expect you to understand."

He brought the piece of metal down on her head again and again until her scalp was a pulpy, sticky mess.

He stood there, looking over the bodies while his pulse wound down to a normal rate. It didn't seem right to leave them like that. Their remains, exhausted of the potential to usher in more chaos, were still a part of the general disorder of the area. Flesh and blood clutter. No, the job was not done yet. He bit his lip and considered his options. There had to be some way to dispose of the mess, to banish the disorder these two agents of chaos had created.

When the idea came to him, he nearly laughed aloud. There *was* a method for stripping away filth and chaos, of returning things to their natural state so that order, glorious order, could be imposed upon them.

The fire wasn't raging out of control when Chris drove away, but there were yellow flames climbing up the curtains and flashing in the windows. He'd knocked over the shelves full of books and used them as kindling. The dry, yellowed pages had gone up quickly, filling the room with thin streams of smoke. He'd left the front door open as he walked away from the house. The cats had bounded out into the night.

Chris watched in his rearview mirror until the house was out of view. He imagined that by the time morning came, the house would be reduced to a smoking ruin, ready to be bulldozed away. Perhaps the fire would spread across the road and also consume the abandoned gas station.

As he drove, he became aware of the pressure of his erection against his pants. He forced himself to concentrate on the road, willing his organ to wilt. Unbidden, his mind returned to each detail of the act: the righteous fury he'd felt as he made his case, the satisfying impact of metal upon skull, the cleansing heat of the fire. His arousal persisted.

A cold shower calmed him somewhat, finally forcing him back to a flaccid state without the necessity of an emission. He slipped into bed and snapped off the bedside lamp. The adrenaline high finally began to taper off. Exhaustion crept into his muscles, and he closed his eyes.

In his dreams, Chris saw himself as a hard-jawed warrior with a flowing mane of blonde hair. He was mounted atop a horse of pure white and wore gleaming armor. A flaming sword was clutched in one hand, a polished shield in the other. The horse beneath him pranced with anticipation, and Chris held his sword aloft, brandishing it at the dragon that whipped through the blackened sky overhead. It was the dragon whose name was Chaos, and Chris was all that stood between the universe and the destruction that Chaos would bring.

"Come down and face me!" he roared at the beast.

It flashed its fiery fangs as it hurtled down from the clouds.

They joined in fierce battle. Chris lashed out with his burning blade. He blocked blasts of the dragon's smoldering breath with his shield. His glorious blonde hair was singed and blackened, but he fought on, feinting, parrying, and thrusting. The beast named Chaos attacked him with razor claws and serrated fangs that tore away Chris' armor and cut his flesh. He hacked with his blade, his mouth foaming with fury. But then he swung too hard, and his momentum twisted him to one side as the beast slipped outside the blade's downward arc. Chris' side was exposed, and the beast took advantage. Its jaws snapped onto him, sinking razor-sharp teeth into his ribs.

The agony was white-hot intense, and Chris cried out as the beast shook him back and forth in its jaws. In its triumphant throes, the dragon did not see the fury that still blazed in Chris' eyes, even as his life pumped out of multiple puncture wounds in thick red gouts.

He twisted in the dragon's mouth, driving the teeth even deeper into his body but also getting a clear shot at the beast's throat. With all of his remaining strength, he hefted his flaming sword and plunged it into the dragon's throat. The creature's jaws opened, dropping Chris. It howled in pain, staggering backwards and swiping with its claws at the blade lodged in its throat. The dragon fell to the ground, thrashing its limbs, beating its wings. These movements only served to make the blood gush from the wound Chris had struck. He saw in the beast's black eyes the dawning realization of imminent death. Chris smiled woozily. It seemed that he would at least live long enough to watch his nemesis die first.

At last the dragon was still. Its heavy corpse lay in a tangle of limbs, oozing blood. Chris slumped back onto the ground and looked up at the sky. The clouds parted, revealing a deep blue expanse brightened by the rays of the sun. In the distance, he heard the cheering of a crowd of billions. They applauded his last heroic stand, and as the life passed out of his body, Chris smiled.

His spirit detached itself from his corpse and floated bodiless into the sky, filled with a sense of tranquility that he'd never known in life. It was as if his every particle had at once relaxed. Upward, upward he drifted, leaving behind his wrecked and ravaged flesh. He left the planet's atmosphere, coming to a gentle stop above the green and blue sphere of Earth. And he watched in awe as the planet remade itself into an image of orderly precision, the continents shifting and reforming until they were of uniform size and shape, their coastlines smooth and joined by perfect right angles. The weather patterns dispersed, patches of clouds now distributed evenly across the globe. The once raging oceans were placid blue-green expanses surrounding each square landmass…

…Chris woke as he climaxed. He groaned with simultaneous pleasure and disgust as warm semen squired onto his thighs, gluing his underwear to his skin. He lay there, panting, relishing the dream but also knowing that he'd have to shower and change the sheets before he could sleep again.

Chapter Eleven: Ray

It was past four in the morning on a Sunday, and Ray couldn't sleep. There was nothing unusual in that. He was a borderline insomniac even years ago, during that period of his life when he seemed to be doing his best to drink himself into a coma. Although he'd cleaned up his act, the sleepless nights had, if anything, just gotten worse. But the insomnia wasn't what made him consider crawling back inside the bottle. What got that old urge all fired up again was this Percy Flannigan business, and what he feared it signified.

He flip-flopped around in bed, only succeeding in getting himself more riled up and tangled in the sheets. He gave it five more minutes before conceding defeat. There was no sense in going back to sleep anyhow. The early service at Edgewood Baptist would start in a few hours, and he'd be expected to put in his weekly appearance. Not that he went in for any of that stuff. The constable job was an elected office, however, and that required a man to keep up certain appearances. Since Edgewood Baptist was the biggest church in town, he figured it was the best place for him to throw in his lot. And the early service didn't just appeal to his insomnia. There was another service following, which meant that the preacher couldn't rattle on indefinitely. And since Ray was always up at that hour, it was easier to just get it over with.

His lack of Baptist zeal wasn't the only thing Ray had to keep hidden. His family history was also something he kept quiet. If the office of constable was more desirable, he might have worried that some ambitious challenger would do some digging and uncover just what kind of family business his mother and his aunts had run. But Ray had run unopposed in three straight elections. Most youngsters with the law enforcement fire in their bellies went down to Barlow to suffer under Tate Wilson's tutelage or tried for the state police. Fact was, most youngsters with any kind of fire in their bellies usually just got the hell out of Gayler County. And Ray didn't blame them one bit. There'd been a time when he was eager to flee the confines of small town Arkansas, sure that he'd find the meaning of life out there in the wide world. What

Brad Carter | 93

he'd found was a drinking problem and dwindling career prospects. And so here he was, back in Gayler County. Full circle. Or some such shit.

He put on his slippers and went to the kitchen to start the coffee pot. It'd be another hour before the newspaper thumped against the front door, and there wasn't anything worth a damn on TV this early. Nothing for a man to do but sit with his thoughts and look out the back door at the darkness.

And on this particular morning, his thoughts turned to his mother and her two sisters, Jolene and Ellen, all three deceased. If they were still around, would he pick up the phone and ask for their input? If he was honest with himself—and really, what other way was there to be at such an early hour—he'd admit that he could use their help. But they were gone, and what remained of his family was long estranged.

Still, he wondered…

The church service was mercifully short. The preacher thundered away about heaven, hell, sin, and all the usual topics, but not so forcefully that it disturbed Ray's meditation on more pressing concerns. He suspected that Brother Gibson was holding back, using this early sermon as a warm-up for the big show later on. And that was just fine with Ray. Too much of that fire and brimstone bullshit made his head hurt. When the benediction ended, he sneaked a look at his watch and was glad to discover that only one hour of his life had been donated to Edgewood Baptist.

He ran a gauntlet of handshakes on the way to the parking lot. A few folks wondered aloud to him about the progress the sheriff's department was making with Percy's murder. Ray told them the honest truth, which was that he expected it to be handed over to the state police sometime during the week. The sheriff's department—down three full time positions since the last budget was passed—just didn't have the manpower.

He smiled his best smile and played the dutiful elected official, but he was glad to be on his way. Church wasn't anywhere on his list of favorite places to be, and he just wanted to get home and enjoy his day off.

"Free at last," he told his reflection in the rearview mirror as he pulled out of the parking lot. The classic rock station he liked was playing Bachman Turner Overdrive, and he couldn't help but smile when "Roll on Down the Highway" was cranked up.

His joy was short lived, however, and his hopes for a day of rest and relaxation went down in flames when he neared his house and saw Tate Wilson's truck in the driveway.

"Of course he's here. Damn it!" Ray beat his fist on the steering wheel. He snapped off the radio. He didn't want to have one of his favorite songs poisoned by his disappointment.

Ray opened a couple cans of Coke and brought them out onto the porch. The sheriff accepted his without getting up from his chair and nodded his thanks. Ray took the other chair, and both men sipped their drinks as they looked out at the gravel and dirt stretch that served as the road.

"Skipping out on Sunday services today?" Ray asked.

Wilson shook his head. "I go to the early service. With another service coming up, you sort of know how long the preacher is going to take."

Ray had to laugh at that one. Seemed maybe he wasn't the only lawman with a low tolerance for hellfire and brimstone. "Okay, so you've been saved for the time being. What brings you out here on your day off?"

The sheriff took his time, drinking his Coke and watching a wild turkey trundle out of the woods across the road. Ray wondered if he should repeat the question.

"What's your impression of George Young?" Wilson finally asked.

"I think his early books are among the best of their kind. It's a real shame they've fallen out of favor, but I guess most people want a horror story to have lots of blood and guts."

Wilson scooted his chair around until he was looking right at Ray. "I don't mean what is your critical take on his books. He could be Louis L'Amour himself and it wouldn't make a difference to me. What's your opinion of the man?"

"I couldn't really say." This was, if not an outright lie, at least a half-truth. Ray had plenty of opinions about George Young. He just wasn't willing to share them with Wilson.

"Really?" Wilson made an exaggerated face that Ray supposed was meant to convey shock. Mostly, it looked like the sheriff had just crapped his britches. "He's mixed up in this Flannigan case, I just know it. He was acting all kinds of suspicious out at the U-Stor-It, for one thing."

"You were pretty hard on him. Digging at his wife like that."

Brad Carter | 95

"Guy moves down here, a big shot writer who just inherited a ton of money from his dead wife, and suddenly a dead body pops up in the storage unit he rented. You don't think he's part of it?"

Ray took his time answering, spelling it out the way he would for a stubborn child. "Not unless he's mastered the art of invisibility."

"I didn't say he *did* it. Not all by himself anyway." Tate was getting antsy, fidgeting around in his chair, tapping his foot. "But there's something wrong about him."

Ray took a drink and put a hand to his mouth to cover his belch. "Sheriff, I'd like to tell you something, but I want to be real clear up front that I don't want you to take it the wrong way. So do you mind if I speak a bit freely right now?"

"I ain't your boss, Ray."

But by the way he said it, Ray could tell that the sheriff clearly believed he was superior in plenty of unofficial ways. That was okay. Wilson was young and full of shit, and he'd learn some hard lessons soon enough. Ray knew all about how life had a way of teaching you lessons.

"It's like this, sheriff," Ray said. "You've lived in Barlow your whole life. You know that there are good folks here, but you also know it's not the greatest place in the world. If you're honest, you'll admit that Gayler County is dying a slow death. That's why most people get out and don't look back. How many deputies you lost to bigger precincts?"

Wilson didn't answer, so Ray just kept going.

"Now, George Young seems strange to you because he's different. He got out of the briar patch, put Arkansas in his rearview mirror, but he decided to come back. And not just to Arkansas, but to this little armpit of the state that we call home. To you, that seems suspicious. Why would this big shot author move to Barlow if not to upset the established order? You strike me as the kind of guy who believes in 'a place for everything and everything in its place.' Now along comes this George Young, and you can't make that piece fit into your puzzle. Percy's death just gave you a reason to speak up about your suspicions." Ray paused to take a drink and a breath. "I wasn't born in Edgewood, you know. I came here with my dad after my parents split up. I remember how people looked at us. Seemed like we'd never quit being the new faces in town."

Tate smiled like he was indulging an old man's nonsense talk. "Difference is, when you moved down here, a dead body didn't immediately pop up on your property."

Ray snorted at that one, but let it pass. If knowledge of his mother's chosen profession had spread around Edgewood, Ray had no doubt that he and his father would have been pariahs. Even a dead body on their front lawn wouldn't have lowered them more in the estimation of the locals. Elizabeth Chambers and her sisters were mediums, offering their services out of a house in Arnholdt, Washington. For the most part, their clientele consisted of giggling college kids looking to get a kick out of ten bucks' worth of palm reading or old ladies looking to commune with their dear departed loved ones. When Ray was an older child, on the verge of puberty, his father's skepticism shattered, and did so in such a radical way that he felt compelled to take his son halfway across the country and sever all contact with Elizabeth. But Ray hadn't spoken about that day—and hadn't thought about it much either—in years. He'd be damned if he owed the likes of Tate Wilson any explanations.

"I'm just suggesting that you might give George Young a little leeway before you summon the lynch mob," Ray said.

Wilson looked like he'd taken a bite of something sour. "I resent that comment, Ray. I resent the hell out of it. You know me better than that."

"I didn't mean anything by it."

"You know, this Young, he lives right around the corner from me. I took a walk by there last night, and he was just sitting there on his front porch. Near midnight, and this guy's just sitting there, staring at nothing like it was the most natural thing in the world."

"I don't know that sitting on the porch on a warm night is all that strange." Ray stopped short of asking what Wilson was doing walking around so close to midnight.

"You really don't think the guy's a little weird?"

"Doesn't matter. It's innocent until proven guilty, not the reverse. And it seems to me like you're coming down on the wrong side of the equation."

Wilson stood up, wiping his hands on his blue jeans. "I'll take that under consideration."

"Well, you have a nice rest of your Sunday. But you want my advice, I'd say watch pressing Young too hard. A harassment suit sure would look bad."

Tate walked away without a response.

There was a Cardinals game on, but Ray couldn't pay attention to it any more than he could to Brother Gibson's sermon. Something was eating at him, but he couldn't quite put his finger on what it was. If he'd been asked to explain the feeling, he'd have likened it to needing to sneeze but finding himself unable. He went to the kitchen and made himself a ham sandwich. He picked up another can of Coke, but thought better of more caffeine and filled a glass with water instead.

The Flannigan case—and yes, George Young's presence in Barlow—kept tickling at his brain, but he was unable to summon the power to mentally sneeze the whole thing out. Wilson had been right, just not in the way he wanted to be. There *was* something about George Young.

Two more innings and he gave up, turning off the TV and tossing the remote aside. He stared at the living room wall, as if the eggshell paint might offer some insight. He began ticking off the things he knew about Percy's death.

There'd been nothing natural about that crime scene. From the moment Ray had parked his car, he'd felt that old, almost forgotten sense—the one his mother had told him he'd inherited—start kicking up a storm in his gut. He'd nearly left his dinner right there on the asphalt. There was an aura over that little storage building, as obvious to Ray as a flashing neon sign. And standing there while the deputies yellow-taped the perimeter, Ray's past came roaring back at him like the world's biggest boomerang and smacked him upside the head.

It seemed his father was wrong, after all. Some things won't just wither and die, even if you did your best to forget about them. They came back, maybe even bigger than they were before.

Ray shook his head, trying to rattle things into place.

George Young's writing showed a depth of insight into the invisible world that the man himself denied having. Ray didn't think he was lying. He had no idea where Young—*Call me George*—thought his ideas for novels came from, but they were incredibly authentic. George hadn't published a book in years, but then he'd also spent most of that time deep in the bottle. Ray knew from experience that a stiff belt of booze could beat back that sense of the invisible world. He'd nearly killed himself locking out his own nightmares with a daily dose of whiskey big enough to fell an entire camp of lumberjacks.

The other thing Ray knew was that Tate Wilson was treading awfully close to being neck deep in waters that he wasn't prepared to swim in. The high-strung sheriff was right about George Young being connected somehow to Percy's death, but he was completely wrong about how George was involved.

You don't know that, Ray. There could be any number of explanations for what happened to that Flannigan kid. Just cause your stomach got upset when you were at a murder scene...when was the last time you'd seen anything like that? Of course, you got sick. Who wouldn't?

Ray shook that thought off. It hadn't been *that* kind of run of the mill sickness. That had come later—sure it did—when he actually saw the body. There were law officers so used to the sight of a dead human that they didn't so much as burp, but Ray wasn't one of them and doubted he ever would be. So sure, there'd been that regular old punch in the gut feeling. But the first sickness happened before he even knew that anything other than Percy's forgetfulness with passwords was to blame for the alarm. And it wasn't just being sick to his stomach, either. It was that old vertigo he'd felt whenever his mother was flipping cards or reading tea leaves at the kitchen table and he'd stumble into the room. Like the floor just dropped out from under him and gravity hadn't quite decided whether it was going to suck him down into the darkness below or just let him stand there dumbfounded like some cartoon character that just wandered off a cliff. And damn it, cliché or not, when Ray had walked through the gates of the U-Stor-It, the hair on the back of his neck stood at attention.

Well, if you're going to play poker, you might as well go all in. Quit fucking around and get to it, man.

Ray left his easy chair and went down the hallway that ran from the kitchen to his bedroom. There was a door to the attic on the ceiling. He tugged it open and let out the wooden step ladder that folded up on the underside. Dust fell on his face, a grey snowfall that got him sneezing. He wiped his face with his shirt and climbed up the ladder.

There were a few boxes in the attic, things he'd put up here after Emma left him. But the one he was looking for had been closed for even longer. It had in fact never been opened since he'd received it in the mail after his Aunt Jolene—the last of the Chambers sisters—died. Ray had been a young man then, working the line at the Bertram-Lowe bathroom fixtures factory. He'd had little time or energy to waste on sentiment, and even less to waste on superstition. Looking back on it, he supposed he was still a bit afraid. His father had drilled it into him over the years that the best way to avoid another incident was for Ray to put thoughts of such things out of his head. Even as an adult—his father long gone from this world—Ray studiously avoided thinking of his childhood in Arnholdt.

But he'd hung onto that box for some reason. Even after he married Emma and bought a house. She'd asked what was in it as he'd shoved the box into the attic. Ray told her that one day he'd explain, but he never did get around to it.

He went through the attic carefully. The last thing he needed was to plunge through the ceiling and break a leg—or worse, a hip—and be laid up for weeks on end. He was twice as careful on the way back, carrying the box carefully and taking small steps. When he'd finally negotiated the ladder back down to the hallway, he breathed a sigh of relief. He laughed, thinking it was funny how age could make such cowards of men.

He lugged the box into the kitchen and heaved it onto the table. The blade of his pocket knife snapped through the ancient packing tape, and he ripped back the top flaps to reveal a tangle of shredded newspaper. Years ago, someone had taken great care, packing the box as if it contained dozens of Faberge eggs, everything swathed in layers of protective newspaper. It was almost as if that person had known that someday Ray would need the contents. He wiped his hands on his jeans and got to it.

The first neatly wrapped packages were the standard items: photo albums, framed pictures, scrapbooks. The next few items were not so standard. There were decks of tarot cards and small leather bags full of silver charms. His mother's crystal ball—what she'd referred to as her "divining sphere"—was there as well, wrapped in layers of newspaper. And finally, at the bottom, the object of Ray's search: his mother's reference books.

That was what she called them, anyhow. No respectable library would have labeled them such. Most of them were slim volumes, printed by small and probably long-defunct presses. They had garish covers, the kind of thing you'd expect to see on old fantasy books, and their pages were yellow with age.

Vistas of the Soul by Baba Guru Johansen. The author photo on the back of this volume showed a bearded white man with an afro style hairdo. His eyes were half-closed, and he wore a smile of blessed contentment or drug-induced stupor, perhaps both.

Inner Dimensions: Awakening to the Spectre Realm by Robison Beardsley-Smythe. No author photo on this one, but the short bio on the dust flap described Beardsley-Smythe as a man with vague ties to British royalty.

The Complete Witch: Spells for Common and Exotic Use. There was no author listed on this one, just a listing for a PO Box in Massachusetts and the phrase (in bold typeface) "Donations for the Cause Always Welcome. Blessed Be."

The Seer's Ouija by Sonya Raven Nightwind. Ray suspected the woman on the cover—with an abundance of beaded necklaces making up for the sheerness of her blouse—was the author. She looked like Janis

Joplin, if Janis had been a vampire. There were plenty of dog-eared pages in this volume.

Sisterhood of the Oracle by Gertrude Wintergreen. The cover of this one—and some of the illustrations within—bordered on the pornographic. One of the chapters was called "Sex Magick and the Rituals of Intercourse." Ray shook his head. People thought that the swinging 60s invented free love, but the copyright on this one predated the Second World War.

The Angels of Mercy Cookbook. This one looked like some sort of diary. The few pages with anything on them contained recipes written in his mother's elegant handwriting. Probably useless, he decided.

There were a couple of big, leather-bound tomes called *Monmouth-Frasier Encyclopedia Demonica, Volume One* and *Monmouth-Frasier Encyclopedia Demonica, Volume Two*. A quick flip-through showed them to be filled with dense, impenetrable writing that Ray was sure would bore him into a coma.

Demons and Other Imps of the Perverse by Sir Gawain Roundhouse. This looked to be a vaguely scholastic work. There were footnotes, endnotes, and that sort of thing. It didn't look quite as dense as the Monmouth Frasier book, but it was clearly not light reading.

Attaining Bliss of Spirit by Alastair Grimsby. *Unseen Worlds* by Louise Gee. *The Ancient Portal* by Freidrich Orff. *The Golden Key of Dreams* by Eustace Fantoft. *Goblins and Sprites* by Constance Rutherford. And on and on until…

The Haunting of Harlowe Manor by George Young.

"Well, I'll be damned," Ray said. It was the same paperback edition that he had on his own bookshelf. There were also some dog-eared pages, and a quick flip-though revealed some notes scrawled in the margins.

He got out the can of Maxwell House and the filters. This was probably going to require a cup of coffee or three.

Chapter Twelve: Myrna

The clock on Myrna's bedside table said that it was a quarter past two, much too early to be awake. She lay staring at the ceiling, dreading the coming day.

It wasn't easy for a single woman of Myrna's age to keep her hours occupied in a town like Barlow. She had a part time job at the gift shop in the lobby of the hospital, where she sold balloons and stuffed animals and books of crossword puzzles to visitors. But her hours had dwindled until she was lucky to put in one shift a week. She also put in some hours at the Gayler Methodist's daycare program, cooking breakfasts and lunches for the little ones once or twice a week. She supposed she should be grateful Henry had left her enough money that she didn't have to worry about finding other employment. But there was still so much time to fill.

She had acquaintances aplenty, but no close friends. Her only family was Tate, and he was so busy with the sheriff's office. There was just no way to fill up the hours of the day without feeling lonely. Even if she went to bingo night at the VFW hall, there were still six other nights of dinners alone in front of the TV.

Myrna listened to the sounds of the old house. The ceiling fan whirred gently overhead. The refrigerator rattled then whooshed as the ice tray dumped a batch of cubes and refilled with water. The air conditioner stuttered as it cycled off. But there was something else. If she strained her ears, she could hear something like muffled voices from downstairs.

She slipped out of bed and crept into the hallway. The stairs were treacherous to negotiate in the dark, but she didn't dare flip on the lights. She crouched down, steadying herself with one hand on the banister.

"Who's there?" she asked, her voice little more than a whisper. She cleared her throat and called out again.

The murmuring downstairs stopped.

Myrna scooted down one stair, groping through the clutter with her feet and inching forward until her rear thumped down on the step below. She gathered her courage and went down one more. This time, her bottom came down on something slippery—a magazine or a catalog—and she was nearly on her back. She held the banister in a death grip, the knuckles of her left hand smarting with the effort.

She was wrong. The murmuring hadn't stopped; it had only grown fainter. Another two stairs, and she'd be able to peer around the corner. She cursed herself for not stopping by one of the boys' bedrooms for a baseball bat. But it's not as if she could face down an intruder, even with a baseball bat. She doubted she could do it with a bazooka mounted on her shoulder.

She pushed off with her heels and her right hand, held on with her left, and went down one more stair. She repeated the process, her rump already sore and probably bruised black and blue. As quietly as she could manage, she got to her feet and peeked around the corner into the living room.

Dale had returned once again. He was wearing the same clothes he'd worn before he'd been deployed, the last time she'd ever seen him alive: his favorite Harley Davidson t-shirt and a battered pair of jeans. Crowded into the living room around him were the hazy, insubstantial forms of the other spirits that lived in the house. They were so faded and indistinct that it was only with close inspection that Myrna could detect their vaguely human outlines.

The grey people.

Almost automatically, she rubbed her forehead, the spot where she imagined the tumor was growing. She could practically feel it in there, pressing against her brain, forcing these hallucinations. What would they tell her if she did go to the doctor? That she had only a few months to live? That she could look forward to hours of chemotherapy or brutal surgery? No thank you. Only, this scene taking place in the living room seemed so real. But it would, wouldn't it? Wasn't that the nature of hallucination?

While she debated the reality of what her eyes were reporting to her brain, the discussion between Dale and his ghostly companions went on. She cautiously descended another step. The landing was just two perilous steps away. Straining to hear what was being said, she inched forward, her bare feet sliding through the stuff piled on the stairs. She could almost hear…

Her big toe smashed into the sharp edge of something heavy and hard, and she cried out. It felt like she'd broken her toe. She sat down on the landing, holding her foot in her lap.

Dale turned toward her, his grey eyes wide with surprise. "Mom, what are you doing up?"

She sat there rubbing her foot and almost wanted to laugh. Here was her dead son, lecturing a room full of ghosts. And he was asking her what she was doing out of bed. As if this were the most natural scene in the world.

The grey people turned their featureless faces in her direction. They seemed to regard her for a moment before dispersing into thin wisps of vapor that dissolved into tiny motes and then into nothingness.

"Mom, are you okay? No one…nothing…tried to hurt you?" Dale glanced around the room, peering into the dark corners.

"Why would you ask that?" Myrna got up.

"Mom, has someone…" He looked around again. "I mean, have you bought anything that seemed strange lately?"

She moved to the couch and sat down. "No, just the usual yard sale stuff. You know how I am with those yard sales."

"And the flea market and the estate sales…"

"You're starting to sound like your brother."

Dale smiled a grey smile. "I wish I could see him. You should let him in the house someday. Of course, I'm not sure he could see me, much less carry on a conversation like this. Tate was never very open minded about…well, much of anything."

"You know I can't let him in here. He'd never let me keep all my things, and then where would you and all your friends be? But how about you tell me what's got you so scared. You look like…"

"Like I've seen a ghost?"

"Son, please."

Dale's face grew serious. "Okay, I think there's something, someone that's not right in the house with us. We've all felt it. Are you sure you haven't felt threatened?"

"I've had some of my nightmares, but you know I've always…" A sudden movement caught her eye.

It burst from the far left corner of the room, a thing made of darkness in an already darkened space. It was so dark that it looked less like a black thing than something so devoid of color that it was a dead spot in the fabric of the world. Myrna's panicked brain conjured up a snippet of Carl Sagan talking about black holes in outer space. Whatever the thing was—a black hole or a shadow with bad intentions—it swept across the room in an instant.

Dale threw his arms up protectively as it bore down on him. Black tendrils wrapped around his body, clamping his arms down tight.

"Mom, get out…" His voice was strangled by long black strands that reached into this mouth. More and more of them swarmed in until his lips stretched wide and his cheeks puffed out. The strands grew into thick ropes, slithering up from the main mass coiled about his body.

"Dale!" Myrna screamed, finally breaking free of her paralysis and reaching for her son. She jerked her hand back as it brushed the black substance engulfing him. The pain in her fingertips was so intense she couldn't tell if the shadowy stuff was extremely cold or hot. The sensation raced up her fingers to her shoulder and into her chest. It pinned her against the couch cushions, and she watched helplessly as mere inches away her son writhed.

The shadow was pouring into him now, and his neck bulged like a snake gorging on a large meal. His stomach swelled, stretching against the fabric of his t-shirt. It went on pouring down his throat and into his distended belly until it was all inside him, leaving only a few black wisps hanging from his lips. Dale slumped, his eyes wide open, his body twitching slightly.

Myrna whispered her son's name as she struggled against the force holding her fast to the couch.

Dale's head turned toward her. His eyes were black now, like tiny pits carved into his grey face. Blackness seeped out of them, spilling down his cheeks, his neck. It trickled upwards against the pull of gravity, blackening his forehead, his hair. Myrna watched in horror as her son began to change, completely engulfed by the shadowy substance. His body twisted itself into a different shape. His arms became longer, more slender, with hands that had unnaturally long fingers. His torso slimmed and flattened. His hair, normally short-cropped, now spilled over his shoulders.

But the worst change was the one that took over his face. Dale's soft features—the ones he'd inherited from Myrna—stretched and broke. His eyes pulled apart to make room for a long, blunted nose. His jaws stretched, pulling back his lips to reveal a set of sharp incisors. The face froze in an exaggerated smile. The figure beside Myrna was no longer recognizable as her son. It was an abomination that she recognized from her claustrophobic dream: the rat-faced woman who'd haunted that tight, dark space.

The nightmare creature rose and stood towering over Myrna. The horrible jaws parted as it shrieked, "Mine!"

Long black fingers, tipped in hooked claws, reached out for Myrna. They clamped down on her shoulders and shook her back and forth.

"Any time I want to, do you understand? Strong now, but growing stronger. All I have to do is reach out. Remember this," the creature hissed as it dug its claws into Myrna's flesh.

She screamed herself awake and laid there, tangled in the sheets, sweating and breathing heavily. The ceiling fan overhead whispered, but otherwise the house was quiet. She reached behind her shoulders and gingerly prodded the flesh there, expecting to encounter wounds left by Dale's hands. The skin back there was unbroken, if perhaps a little sore.

What do you expect? You were probably thrashing around like a madwoman. You pulled a muscle, that's all. It was a very vivid dream. But just a dream.

"One way to find out," she said, untangling her legs from the sweat-stained sheets.

She made a stop in the bathroom to splash some cold water on her face. The face that greeted her when she glanced in the mirror looked especially tired. Myrna wondered if there was any truth to that thing where the ladies on shows like *Sex and the City* took mud baths with cucumber slices on their eyes. Maybe she'd pick up some cucumbers next time she was at the grocery store. Only, should she get the bumpy ones or the smooth ones?

"Quit stalling," she told her reflection.

There was no point in keeping the lights off in the house. She knew well enough that trying to sleep after that encounter—*that dream*—would be a fruitless endeavor. She snapped on the light switch at the top of the stairway. There was a mess on the stairs as usual. Things landed there and never moved, despite her best intentions. Most likely, she was carrying something up or down the stairs in an effort at organization and had gotten distracted and just dropped whatever she was carrying. It was one more habit she needed to break.

Even after carefully surveying the mess below, Myrna was uncertain she could tell if anything had been moved. If she had indeed descended the stairs in the dark, she would have shifted things around. And her memory was most certainly not photographic. For all she knew, the little stacks—and the big piles as well—that were shoved to the side of each stair were completely undisturbed. Her toe was still sore, and she could see a heavy dictionary on the left side of the second to last step. That could certainly stub a toe. But its presence still didn't prove anything. One thing was certain: she must have been crazy to go down this staircase in the dark. She made a mental note to keep a flashlight by the bed. She knew she had one. She'd bought it at that yard sale over on Inman Street just a couple weeks ago. There was a whole toolbox with…

"Stalling again," she said. "What are you so afraid of if it was just a dream?"

She grabbed the bannister and picked her way down the stairs. With the light on, it wasn't so bad. She paused on the landing, steeling herself for what might lay ahead. She took a step into the living room. The gentle light coming through the windows didn't reveal any ghostly presence. She was reasonably certain that there were no dead bodies or black-oozing monsters waiting behind the couch. But the feeling was so strong…

The light switch was on the wall to her left, just a few feet away. She took two shuffling, sideways steps and flipped it on. The light fixture on the bottom of the ceiling fan came to life, lighting up the room and revealing its completely normal, non-supernatural contents in all their average, earthbound glory.

"Good heavens, what a mess," she said, looking over the disorder in the room. "I am going to clean this house up today. Find that stupid cell phone and get a handle on all this stuff."

She went to the kitchen and started to get out the breakfast things. Despite her proclamation in the living room, she knew she'd do little if any cleaning at all. The day stretched out before her, an endless parade of seconds, minutes, hours, all needing to be filled with something.

The Gayler County Public Library had a small store in the foyer that sold used books. Myrna forced herself to look the other way as she went through the front door. The last time she'd gone in there, she'd come out with a set of Beatrix Potter books and an entire box of tattered comic books, mostly those X-Men guys that Dale had loved so much.

If the first step on the road to recovery was recognizing that a problem existed, Myrna figured she was always on the starting line. She

Brad Carter | 107

had no illusions that her behavior was normal. She did not make—to herself, at least—any excuses or rationalizations. She was well aware of how strange her actions appeared. And because of this awareness, she set limits for herself. She did not own a computer with an internet connection. She knew that having twenty-four hour access to online auction and resale sites would be playing with fire. She'd sometimes wondered if her gift for recognizing and connecting with special items would even work in the online world. Would she be able to see the auras of these loved and treasured possessions through the screen? Would she be able to feel the same spark by tracing her fingertips across images on a monitor? The prospect both excited and horrified her.

She spent the morning in the library's computer lab, studiously avoiding eBay as she researched brain tumors and hallucinations. What she found only served to confirm her worst fears: that her amateur diagnosis was likely correct. Even the sleepwalking—if indeed she had walked down the stairs in her sleep—could be explained by a cancerous growth setting up shop in her brain. It was a grim hour of pointing and clicking and reading.

When her eyes were aching from staring at the screen, she logged off and took a stroll around the library. She needed to do the grocery shopping, but otherwise her day was free. There were only so many laps she could walk around the block, only so many hours of TV she could watch. So she roamed about the library aimlessly, sitting down to leaf through the current issue of *Redbook* for a few minutes, browsing through the latest erotic thriller paperbacks for a few more.

"Is that you, Mryna Wilson?" asked a chipper voice that Myrna instantly recognized as belonging to Luanne Samples.

Myrna reshelved *Operation: Man Hunt* by Gina Fielderman and let Luanne pull her into a quick hug. Luanne was one of those people who felt a hug was an appropriate greeting for just about anybody.

"Well, I just got through reading to the little ones back in the children's room," Luanne said as she released Myrna from her arms. "Thought I'd see if the new *Cosmo* was out, and there you were, looking at Gina Fielderman's last book. You know, I read it. Thought it was okay. The sex scenes weren't bad, although, between you and me, I think Gina's a bit of a size queen."

Myrna smiled politely. "You read to children?"

"Volunteer once a week. The kids really seem to like me, but sometimes their mothers give me some dirty looks. I'm not sure what that's all about."

Myrna had a pretty good idea what the dirty looks were all about. Luanne wore her beauty as nonchalantly as a pair of old comfortable shoes, and that made her the type of woman that most other women couldn't help but hate. Usually that type came with a good dose of bitchy superiority, but as far as Myrna could tell, Luanne was as grounded as anyone else. And although Luanne made no secret of her Hollywood dreams, her world seemed mostly to revolve around bringing fashion to Barlow via her job at the Primp 'n Perm, rehabilitating her no-good boyfriend Catfish, and acting as the conduit through which all the gossip of Gayler County flowed. It was this latter quality that made Myrna blurt out a question that had been nagging at her since her last visit to the flea market.

"Luanne, what can you tell me about George Young?"

Luanne giggled and dragged Myrna into one of the small study rooms to the left of the magazine rack. She pulled the two chairs back from the desk and dropped into one.

"Are you interested in him?" Luanne could hardly contain her glee. "I saw the way you looked at him when you bought those buttons. I know *the look*."

Myrna felt her face grow hot as she sat in the vacant chair. "Oh, come on, Luanne. I hardly know the man. I just thought…"

"Well, I know that he's a widower. He was a bigshot writer a long time ago, but I don't think he's written anything lately. He bought one of those houses on Bradshaw Street. You know the ones."

"Right around the corner from my son's house."

Luanne's eyebrows crinkled. "Things not good between you and Tate?"

Myrna thought about dishing out the cliché that her relationship with her oldest son was complicated. When Dale was around, he'd been a mediator, a dutiful go-between who smoothed out relations between Tate and Myrna. And now that he was gone, there was no one to ford the river between mother and son. Tate was just too much like his father, an orderly man with little tolerance for things that fell outside his neat and clean worldview.

"Things are never easy with Tate," Myrna said. "But I guess you know that."

"He's sweet," Luanne said. "A little high-strung though."

"I suppose that's one way to put it."

"I tell you what. I'll find out the story on this George Young guy. He seems nice enough. But I suppose you know about how Percy Flannigan got killed at that storage place in Edgewood. That was George Young's storage thingy that he died in."

"I don't think he had anything to do with that."

"I'm sure you'd know if he had. Tate would have told you all about it," Luanne said.

"Maybe not. He'd probably want to spare me the gory details." Not that he shared non-gory details, either. Tate wasn't one for discussing work with his mother.

"Oh, but let me tell you about what Crazy Annie did at the Methodist Church's Bingo Night," Luanne said, bouncing in her chair. "There's this old guy who's always asking women to help him to the bathroom…"

The conversation turned to the other town gossip, and Myrna half-listened and nodded politely as Luanne dished out all the latest tidbits.

Chapter Thirteen: Effie

Effie Landeros knew going in that the job would come with its share of bureaucratic headaches. A directorship of a branch library was, after all, the very definition of middle management. Just like her time in the service, there was a chain of command to be followed, and when it came time to fall in line, there was nothing to do but see that the right asses were kissed. One of her dad's baseball metaphors came to mind. *Sometimes, Effie,* he'd always say, *you just have to lean over the plate and take one for the team.*

Listening to Dr. Roberson, head honcho of the city's public library system, tell her why she wasn't free to fire one of her own employees, Effie got a clear mental image of hunkering over home plate as a fastball whizzed toward her.

"I'm sorry, but I just don't understand why this is such a big deal," she said. Even though she was seated behind the desk, she felt like she was the one being called out on the floor.

Roberson smiled his kindly country boy smile and brushed a speck of lint from his suit that was far outside the price range of a kindly country boy. "Effie, you knew it was part of the deal when you signed on. You get absolute autonomy when it comes to hiring. I'd never step on your toes when it comes to building a staff. But this is a government job, and if you want to terminate an employee, there's a protocol that has to be followed. I don't make those rules, but I do have to see that we all play by them."

"I have all the employee evaluations you need to see." She held up a manila envelope, but Roberson made no move to take it.

"And they don't make a very damning case against Chris Clanton."

"He's slower than all the other employees."

"And judging by those same evals, he also consistently outdoes those same employees in terms of accuracy, neatness, and thoroughness. Seems that he's punctual too." Roberson's smile widened, showing teeth. The fluorescent lights in the office gleamed off his pearly whites just as brightly as they did off his bald scalp. "Looks like his attendance has been exemplary."

"Not lately. He's been gone all week."

"He's called in, hasn't he?"

Effie nodded reluctantly. "Spoke to me at length about his intestinal problems."

Roberson laughed. "Probably ate at that taco stand down the street."

She didn't see anything worth laughing at. "Seriously, I have to let him go. The guy makes everyone uncomfortable. He's twitchy. He's condescending, insubordinate. To put it bluntly, I think the guy isn't right in the head."

"Want to elaborate on that?"

"Just a feeling I get."

"Answer's still no. Clanton keeps his job." He paused, gauging her reaction. "You haven't been here long enough to look at me that way, like I'm some micro-managing ogre that's overstepping his bounds."

She checked her expression, tried to keep it neutral. "Yes, sir."

"I really do like to get along with all the branch directors. I'm sorry I haven't gotten out here sooner to see how you were adjusting to the job, but things have been hectic." The way he said it didn't sound much like an apology. He paused for a moment . "You know, I served over there in the sandbox the first time, back when we went over to protect the sovereign state of Kuwait."

Effie nodded. "I'd heard that."

"It's one of the reasons you stood out from the rest of the applicants for this job, your time in Iraq. I'm partial to anyone who's been in the service, but I have a particular preference for those who have seen combat. I think combat teaches you something about yourself that nothing else can. When the bullets are flying, you learn all sorts of life lessons. And one of them is that things don't always go your way, and no matter what, you have to make the best out of the worst situations."

"But this is hardly a combat situation."

There was that *Aw, shucks* smile again. Effie wanted to barf.

"Exactly. This should be easy-peasy," Roberson said.

Effie sank a bit in her chair. She'd walked right into that one.

Roberson crossed his legs, sat back. "Now, that's all on the record and official. Everything after this point is off the record and not up for discussion in any shape or form. Understood?"

"Loud and clear."

"You can't fire Chris Clanton because of who he is. Or rather, who his father was." Roberson reached out and snagged a peppermint from the dish on Effie's desk. He took his time unwrapping it then popped it in his mouth. "If you were from around here, the name Clanton would probably mean something to you. His grandfather was a senator, and that was after the man made a fortune in the stock market. Chris' father was a well-respected attorney. 'Preeminent' is a word that got tossed around a lot in relation to Vernon Clanton. It looked like he was headed for a judgeship, maybe even a federal appointment, when he went off the rails a bit."

That got Effie interested. "Off the rails?"

"After his wife died, he quit his job, became a bit of a shut-in. Probably, his drinking got a bit out of hand. His name stayed on the law firm's stationary because it still carried considerable weight, but the man himself was more suited for the funny farm than a courtroom. My point is that he was raising his two sons—Chris and his brother—all alone in that big monstrosity of a house. Just the three of them there, probably driving each other crazy." Roberson crunched his peppermint.

"I can see why Chris is a bit twitchy, then. But I still don't see what that has to do with…"

Roberson didn't let her finish. "The Clanton family wasn't a big one, and Vernon had inherited a considerable amount of money from his father. He'd stacked up another considerable pile through his own work with the law firm and his own investments. The guy was loaded. Even after he became a hermit, he still dispersed charitable donations, set up trusts, and did all that philanthropic stuff that rich people do if they're decent human beings, or at least if they want the world to think they are."

Effie could see where this was going. "I'm guessing some of that money went to the library system."

"Combat also sharpens your instincts. You are absolutely correct." He took another peppermint. "Now, you're not the first one to say Chris Clanton is a pain in the ass to work with. Whether or not he came by it honestly, the guy is weird and he rubs people the wrong way. He's snotty, priggish, and he gets so bogged down in details that his pace is glacial. He's got a nervous energy about him that makes his coworkers uneasy. Members of the public avoid him when they come into the library for reasons they can't quite articulate. Effie, does it sound to you like I've had this conversation before?"

"Yes, sir, it does."

"Then I guess it wouldn't surprise you that there have been other complaints. Thing is, no one can really say what it is about Clanton that gets them so upset. And we can't exactly fire people just because their presence makes us uncomfortable. Lots of us wouldn't have jobs if that was the case."

"Agreed." She knew what Roberson was doing. He was reminding her that she was the only Hispanic director in the system. That alone was enough to ruffle some feathers, without even mentioning her sexuality. Roberson couldn't come right out and say it, but that's what he was doing. His smug expression told her so.

"Clanton has been with us for years. He's outlasted two of your predecessors, both of whom wanted him fired for the same reasons you've given me." He stood up, putting his spare peppermint in the pocket of his expensive pants. "Get used to having him around. If it makes you feel any better, I don't like the guy either. He's squirrely. But in this economy, we can't afford to lose that funding."

Effie stood up. "I understand."

Roberson put his hand on the doorknob. "I knew you would. You have a good day, now."

It seemed that, like the devil, discussing Chris Clanton would make the guy turn up. Effie was in the break room eating her lunch—a turkey sandwich from Subway and a handful of Cheetos—when he strolled in, looking like the cat that deep-sixed the canary.

"Feeling better?" she asked, leafing through the newspaper she'd brought to keep her company.

Clanton plopped down on the chair across from her. "I sure am. Everything seems to be back in order. I hope the place didn't fall apart without me."

"We survived." She tried to appear interested in her reading so that he'd leave her alone. She figured he might go away if he thought she had something on her mind.

He didn't take the hint, and went right on staring at her with that weird look of his.

"I noticed there was a big box of new paperbacks that had just come in. You mind if I process those? The other people here can't seem to ever get the stickers straight. It's like they don't care."

Effie put down her sandwich. Christ, the guy was so creepy she couldn't even eat around him. "I think that's a great idea. Why don't you go clock in and get started."

He sprang up from his seat, smiling. "And I can bring the cart by your office when I get done, so you can see if my work is up to standard. I try my best to use the ruler when I apply the stickers, but sometimes my fingers slip a bit."

She nodded. "That will be fine."

Good grief, was this guy for real?

Chapter Fourteen: The Prodigal

Ray made the drive to Memphis on Wednesday morning. It started pissing down rain once he got north of the county line, and he spent most of the trip cussing at the passing semis that splashed gritty water all over his windshield. By the time he actually made it to Madame Stephanie's Psychic Parlor, his nerves were completely shot. He thought about stopping off for a cup of coffee, but he was already running late, and this didn't seem like the time to make a bad impression.

Stephanie's place was just a house with an old-fashioned signpost outside identifying it as a psychic parlor. Ray's constable training had him questioning whether or not it was some sort of zoning violation as he rang the doorbell.

A sullen-looking young woman with arms covered in tattoos opened the door.

"Well, what?" she asked, fiddling with the ring in her left nostril.

"Is Stephanie around?" Ray wondered if he was going to be invited in or if he was just supposed to stand on the porch.

"Do you have an appointment?"

"Not exactly." The tattooed lady tried to shut the door, but Ray caught it with his foot. "Why don't you go tell her that her cousin Ray is here to see her?"

She sighed so heavily that her shoulders rose with the effort. She rolled her heavily mascaraed eyes. "Whatever. I guess you can come in. But make sure you wipe your feet on the mat. They make me clean the floors in here."

He followed her into a sitting room furnished with two wide imitation leather couches and a coffee table covered with outdated magazines. She exited through the room's single door, slamming it behind her. Ray looked around, wondering if he was allowed to sit or if it was also her job to clean the couches. He looked at the tasteful art prints hanging on the wall. They were tranquil landscapes, heavy on the soothing blues and greens. This could have been a dentist's waiting room.

But it wasn't. This place made Ray's skin crawl and his belly cramp up. Most people probably drove by this place and shook their heads, wondering how a place like this could stay open in the twenty-first century. But not Ray. He remembered what had happened to him in a place just like this.

He fought down the nausea, pushing the memory back into the mental closet it had slithered out of. If things were headed the way he thought they were, there'd be plenty of chances to revisit that horror.

"I never expected to see you again, much less have you standing in my waiting room, dripping rain all over the carpet."

Ray turned around as his cousin Stephanie entered the room. She'd become a big woman, so different from the little girl he'd known. Ray put her at just over six feet, her weight around a couple hundred pounds. Her grey hair hung loose about her shoulders. Her face looked like it smiled easy, but also like it didn't brook any nonsense.

"Hey, Stephanie," he said, feeling lame and out of place.

"You didn't show up for your own mother's funeral, so imagine my surprise when I get a call out of the blue, you wanting to meet to discuss family matters."

"Something's come up."

"Well, come on back and have a cup of coffee anyway." She pushed through the doorway, and Ray followed her into a hallway lined with framed portraits of Stephanie's semi-famous clients. Ray recognized a couple of pro ball players and some actors.

"Quite a collection of photos you got," Ray said.

"There's some politicians come to see me too, but they don't really want that getting out. Might put off their church-going constituency. So I don't get autographed shots from them," Stephanie said as she ushered him into a neat little kitchen. She gestured to the table in one corner. "Have a seat. I'll make some coffee. I've been trying to cut back, but if the prodigal's return isn't an occasion for a little bit of good living, I don't know what is."

Ray ran a hand through his wet hair. "I know I'm probably the last person you expected to see…"

"You got that right." She fired up the big stainless steel Bunn on the counter. "Your father made his feelings more than clear when he was still alive. And when you were an adult, you didn't respond to a single communication from your mother or mine. That's a pretty clear signal that you wanted nothing to do with your family."

"After what happened…"

Stephanie laughed, throwing her head back and braying at the ceiling. "You think your mother intended for anything bad to happen to you? You think she wasn't torn up about it? Grow up, Ray. Shit happens. You survived. Had you not run off with your dad, you could have…"

"Set up shop in some house, started giving out card readings to NBA players?"

Stephanie wasn't laughing anymore. "You came to me, Ray. I wouldn't have even seen you, but I promised your mother that I would look out for you if you ever came asking for help. It was like she knew there'd be a time when you'd finally have to acknowledge what you'd inherited from her side of the family. She said you'd come with your hat in hand, asking for help, and she made me promise I'd do what I could."

Ray sighed. He wondered if his shoulders heaved like Little Miss Creepy out there in the waiting room. "I'm starting to have…I don't know what you call them. Twitches or something. Feelings that I can't put my finger on exactly. I'm…oh, hell. I don't know what I'm talking about. This was probably just a waste of your time."

He stood up.

Stephanie put two steaming mugs down on the table. "Quit being so damn dramatic. Sit back down and tell me what's got your goat. You drove all this way. Might as well spill it."

He let himself back down into the chair. "I hardly know where to start."

"You could start with what it was that happened to you that got your daddy so scared he moved you halfway across the country."

That surprised him. "You mean you don't know?"

"Your mom wouldn't talk about it, and she made my mom and Aunt Jolene swear to never mention it again. You know how the Chambers women are with their secrets."

"Not really."

"We're fiercely protective of them, which is why you don't have to worry about whatever it is you're going to tell me ever leaving this room. All I know is that you had a scare, one that shook up your family so bad that your folks split."

Ray put his hands around the cup of coffee. "I haven't talked about it. Not since it happened."

118 | ONLY THINGS

"How about this?" Stephanie spooned sugar into her coffee. "Tell me what it is that got you to drive all this way to see a cousin that you haven't spoken to since she was just out of diapers. Then you can tell me why it's been forever since you've spoken to any of your family on your mother's side."

"You think the two are related?"

She smiled. "Won't know 'til you tell me. But our past is never really in the past, is it?"

"Faulkner would agree with you."

"So you've read some books since I saw you last."

"I've tried to better myself." Ray blew on his coffee. And he told her about Percy Flannigan's strange demise.

Ray was never certain why his parents had gotten married in the first place. Dervis McFettridge had been a hard man to know, and Elizabeth Chambers was just as inscrutable in her own way. But that was where the similarities ended. Dervis was small, dark, and hard, all wiry hair and bandy muscles. Elizabeth was tall, bright, and soft, blond hair cascading to her waist, big blue eyes always open wide to new possibilities. Her husband watched the world with cynical eyes, his brow wrinkled as if constantly staring into the sun. Those differences would have been enough to account for Ray's confusion, but there was more to it than just that. Elizabeth's profession was a constant point of contention between them. It was a conflict that was almost the embodiment of the town around them.

Arnholdt was part logging town and part artist colony. The two factions seemed to tolerate one another's presence but also regarded each other with suspicion and, occasionally, outright disdain. The Chambers-McFettridge marriage could have been like one of those medieval unions between royal families looking to cement a treaty, Ray supposed. But there was no joyous meeting of the minds between the workers and the artists, and a new kingdom of mutual respect was not forged. Arnholdt continued to be a town at a state of détente, and the Chambers-McFettridge union was, for all Ray knew, rocky from the very start.

"Mom used to ask her about it all the time, why she chose to marry the lumber shop guy," Stephanie said. She was sitting across the table from Ray at Rendezvous, a place she'd told Ray was mostly for tourists, but she liked anyway. After Ray had spilled his story—and after

Stephanie had cleared her schedule for the rest of the day—she'd offered to take him out for a late lunch so he could tell the other half of his promised tale over some ribs and beans.

"Hell, I asked both of them why they ended up with one another. I was young back when they were still married, but it wasn't hard to figure that they were a little mismatched," Ray sipped from his glass of sweet tea.

"Your mom said that she married Dervis just so she could give birth to you. She said she'd seen it in a vision and couldn't question it."

"About the same answer I got, when I asked her. I know the reason they didn't get divorced right off was Dad was a little bit scared of Mom. I think maybe when he married her, he just thought she was flighty. You know, some artist's kid who was into folk music and weird eastern mysticism. I guess Dad was amused by her interest in such stuff until he figured out that there was something to all of it. Maybe he thought she'd hex him if he filed for divorce."

Stephanie laughed. "I'm sorry, it's just the thought of your mother hexing anyone…"

"But that was the way Dad saw the world. He was suspicious of all women, not just Mom. Probably why he never remarried."

The waiter dropped their plates by the table, and Ray dug in. All this talking had worked up an appetite.

"Okay, this is the part where you tell me what it was that spooked old Dervis bad enough to overcome his fear of being hexed and take you all the way to Arkansas." Stephanie chomped a rib thoughtfully. "And come to it, why your mother never fought for custody."

Ray reckoned that if these were the ribs for tourists, he might consider relocating to Memphis. Stephanie had said part of her reason for settling here was the food, and he thought she was making a joke. Now he wasn't so sure.

"I think that, as scared as Dad was after what happened, Mom was even more scared," he said. "Way I figure it, she thought that it was best for me. After a while, that's what I came to believe. But lately, hell, I don't know."

"Well, now you just have to tell it. The suspense is killing me."

Ray paused to get a few more bites of food in him. He wiped his mouth with a napkin. "Dad didn't like me hanging around at your mom's house during business hours. Said that the witchcraft and evil doings would warp my young mind. It sounded funny to hear him say it, but he was dead serious. Most of the time, I obeyed him. But this happened during summer vacation. I was tired of hanging around the house all day by myself. So I went over to your mom's place. It was once I got over there that I started to get a little curious about what Mom did all day. I mean, I'd seen her flipping cards at the kitchen table, stuff like that. But I'd never actually seen her work."

Ray rode his bike to his Aunt Ellen's house. It was a few miles away, and Ray took a long, scenic route getting there, cruising through downtown Arnholdt to watch the hippie kids strum their guitars in the park and to snag a bottle of Coke from the drugstore. It was a warm day, and his shirt was sticking to his back when he crested Greenland Terrace, the steep hill that his aunt lived on. He let the bike coast, feeling the air blow through his sweaty hair. It was a good moment to be a boy. It was the last week of June, only a few short days until he could spend a glorious evening igniting firecrackers and Roman candles. With all of July and August stretched out before him, it felt like summer vacation could go on forever.

The Schwinn threw up a fine spray of road grit as it skidded into Aunt Ellen's driveway. Ray flipped the kickstand out and stowed the bike on the front porch. He poked the doorbell.

Aunt Ellen opened the door and spread her arms wide. "Well, Raymond! How are you today?"

Even though he was sweaty and dirty, his aunt smothered him with a hug. Aunt Ellen was great. She was always happy, and she smelled like cookies. Getting a hug from her made him feel light as air. She pushed him into the house, where a ceiling fan and two big oscillating fans were stirring up a breeze. His cousin Stephanie was seated on the floor, surrounded by what looked like every crayon in the world. There was an oversized book of artist's paper on her lap, and she was too interested in her scribbling to do much more than glance at Ray.

"Hey, cutie pie," Ray said as he passed the child. She giggled but didn't look up from her artwork.

"That little girl will be big as you before we know it," Aunt Ellen said.

"Awww, there's no way she'll catch up with me," Ray answered.

"Now, it's too hot to turn on the oven to make cookies. But there's Coke in the refrigerator and ice cream in the icebox. How about I make you a float?"

He responded by dashing into the kitchen. Most grownups were dead set against running in the house, but Aunt Ellen just laughed and ran after him.

She made him a float in a big Mason jar and stuck a spoon and straw in it. The drink was at least twice as big as the ones they made at the drive-in. His mom would have shaken her head at it. His father would probably have just flat-out told him that he couldn't drink it. The thought of his father made him pause mid-sip.

"Your daddy know you're here?" Aunt Ellen asked as if reading his mind.

Ray shook his head.

"You think he'd be happy if he found out you were?"

Ray shrugged and kept doing his best to slurp up the ice cream as fast as possible.

"And you came over here anyway?" Aunt Ellen asked.

Ray shrugged again.

"Why?" She plucked the straw from Ray's mouth. "And give me a real answer this time."

"I don't know," he said. "All my friends went to camp this year, but Dad said we couldn't afford it. I got tired of sitting at home all day."

"That right?"

"Well, yeah. I've read all my comics at least twice, and all those old paperback books you gave me. And besides…" Ray looked around, lowering his voice. "I wanted to see what it is you guys do over here. I've seen what Dad does at the shop, but I've never gotten to watch Mom work." He popped the straw back into his mouth.

"I don't see anything wrong with that. Your mother is one talented lady. But I bet that father of yours has filled your head full of all kinds of nonsense about what it is that she does over here, about what it is that all of us do. Your mother has said that when the time comes, you'll make up your own mind about it. Maybe that time is coming sooner than we thought. Now, how about an extra scoop of ice cream?"

Yeah, Aunt Ellen was pretty great.

They were slowing down with their food. Ray had just about scraped his plate clean.

"Did she take you right into the consultation room?" Stephanie asked.

"Not that day." Ray tossed his napkin onto the table. "But I kept going over there that whole week, pestering her. She made me wait until after the family get-together for the Fourth of July. That was the last happy time the whole family had together. After that, everything went to shit."

"Why do you think it took so long for my mom to take you upstairs?" Stephanie asked.

"Maybe she just wanted to see if I was persistent enough to really be serious about seeing it. Who knows? Your mother was a nice lady, but she could be a little mysterious."

"It's a Chambers woman quality."

"So there I am, eating a Dreamsicle and flipping through an old Batman comic one afternoon in the kitchen, and your mom comes in and asks if I'd like to go see what it is that my mother did all day. I just about bolted out of the chair. Well, I finished my Dreamsicle first. But then I bolted."

Aunt Ellen's house was old. Ray had heard his dad say the place had been built back around the turn of the century, and that's why it had high ceilings. It also had a big staircase, upon which the footsteps of an excited boy sounded like thunder. The stairs ended in a wide hallway, with three bedrooms to the left and two to the right, and a bathroom dead center. The rooms on the right were the ones where Aunt Ellen and Stephanie laid their heads at night. The ones on the left were used for psychic consultations.

Aunt Ellen snagged Ray's shoulder before he could burst into the room where his mother was working.

"Heavens, boy. You almost gave me a heart attack," she said as she reined him in. "Now what we're going to do is be real quiet and creep into that room. We'll sit in the back corner and watch what happens. You have any questions, you whisper them real soft in my ear, okay?"

Ray nodded vigorously, eager to see his mother at work.

"But you can't talk to your mom, okay? She'll need every bit of her concentration to do her job. Sort of like when your daddy is cutting up a stack of wood. Talk to him at the wrong time and he loses a thumb."

The thought made Ray wince a bit, but he nodded all the same.

Aunt Ellen smiled at him, ruffled his hair, and led him across the creaky floorboards into a darkened room. There were heavy curtains over the window, and the only illumination came from a tiny lamp that sat on the table in the middle of the room. Ray's mother sat on one side of the table, and a nervous looking woman with sharp features and grey hair swept up into a bun sat on the other. Both women had their eyes closed and their palms pressed flat on the table.

Ray took a seat next to Aunt Ellen on a small sofa pushed up against the wall. He watched his mother intently as minutes ticked by without either woman making a movement.

"What's going on?" Ray asked.

"This is Mrs. Lovelace." His aunt whispered in his ear. "Her son left town six months ago, and she hasn't seen him since. She wants to know what happened to him."

Then it dawned on Ray: he'd seen this woman before. Her face had been plastered all over the newspapers in the vending machine outside the drugstore. And he'd seen her on the nightly news that his father watched while drinking beer and muttering. The woman's son—the snapshot in the paper had been one of a gap-toothed kid with Buddy Holly glasses—had gone missing after the New Year's Eve fireworks display. When he thought back on it really hard, Ray could even recall the headline *Search Continues for Steven Lovelace*. Ray's father had scoffed at the whole thing, saying that the kid was probably shacked up with one of "those Beatnik whores that's always lounging around downtown." That was typical of Dervis McFettridge's poetic take on current events.

Ray frowned at his aunt. "Didn't she call the cops?"

"She did. And they haven't been able to find him. So she came to your mother for help."

This didn't strike Ray as strange at all. He knew she had a gift for seeing things that other people couldn't. His father often referred to her as a witch, but Ray knew that was just his dad being mean. There was no way Elizabeth Chambers—who made cookies, kissed skinned knees, and sang so sweetly—could be a witch. So Ray wasn't afraid or even taken aback as he watched his mother swaying gently in a trance. He was fascinated. He edged forward on his seat.

His mother's mouth was pressed into a tight little line. Only—Ray cocked his head to one side—he could have sworn that he heard her voice. It was faint, like a distant whisper, but it was her voice all the same. He strained, willing his ears to pick up the sound again. His heart sped up as he caught more quiet voices, his mother's, but now others as well. It reminded Ray of having the radio dial stuck between stations, being able to recognize the different sets of voices but not understand what any of them were saying.

"What is that?" he whispered.

His aunt looked at him with something like concern on her face. "What do you mean, honey?"

"Those voices." They were getting louder now and felt like they were coming at his ears from both sides, inside and out. It made his head hurt.

"Ray, honey, what do you hear?" Aunt Ellen asked.

The din grew and grew until Ray was sure his eardrums would burst. The voices seemed so numerous that he couldn't begin to separate them from one another. And there was more than just the feverish whispering he'd heard moments ago. Some of the voices screamed as if in terrible pain. Others sobbed with what could only be the deepest of grief. Still others chanted and gibbered in languages that Ray didn't understand. And the volume continued to swell. Ray clapped his hands over his ears, but the noise did not abate. He shook his head furiously. He filled his lungs and began to shriek, terrified to find that his own voice was drowned out, lost in the sea of mutterings, whispers, screams, sobs, and cackles.

Aunt Ellen hovered over him, her mouth working but no sound coming out. Ray's vision went swimmy at the edges, like he was looking through heat waves rising from a blacktop parking lot. It made him dizzy, and he turned his head and vomited his Dreamsicle onto the floor.

His mother was holding him now, rocking him on her lap like a baby. Like Aunt Ellen, her mouth was moving, but the only voices Ray could hear belonged to the invisible multitude filling his head with their chatter. He felt tears roll down his face. Fear gripped his guts, and he tried to vomit again, but there was nothing left to bring up, and he shuddered and convulsed. His mother and his aunt continued to make soothing gestures, smoothing his hair and wiping away his tears. Their faces were full of pure worry and fear.

The waves spread inward from his peripheral vision until everything he saw was distorted by the shimmering haze. His mother's face was pulled into hideous circus mirror contortions. Ray screamed and screamed until he tasted blood in the back of his throat. All the while, the voices, a million of them it seemed, hammered away inside his skull.

After what seemed like an eternity, he passed out.

When he awoke, he was in a terrible place.

"Jesus Christ, Ray." Stephanie let her spoon drop into her coffee cup. "I knew it was bad, but not like that. No wonder no one wanted to talk about it."

They'd left Rendezvous and gone to a small coffee shop that Stephanie had said was a good place for sitting and talking. She also said that if they went back to her house, Lucille (the girl with the tattoos and the bad attitude) would interrupt them every few minutes in an effort to eavesdrop.

They sat in a dark corner, both of them sipping oversized cups of coffee and picking at slices of sweet potato pie while jazz played softly over the shop's stereo system.

"I don't know how long it went on," Ray said. "Before I passed out, I mean. It felt like hours, but probably it was just a minute or two."

"Well, what then?" Stephanie made "hurry up" gestures with her hands.

Ray finished his bite of pie. "I went to sleep for two weeks."

"You *slept* for two weeks?"

"That's what Mom and Dad told me, that I went into a coma for two weeks and that everything I saw during that time was just some sort of fever dream. Course, I didn't have any fever. And then it was a pretty big coincidence about the dreams. It's not like I was too young to read the newspaper. And even if I was, you couldn't get away from a story like that."

Stephanie sighed. "Damn it, Ray, you really have a problem just coming out and saying things, you know that?"

"Get to the good stuff, huh?" Ray smiled for a moment then looked down at the table. "Only, this stuff isn't so good."

One second Ray was in his aunt's room, convulsing on the floor. The next, he was in the cramped and smelly interior of a vehicle roaring down the highway. It was one of those big vans with three rows of bench seats, and it rumbled along so noisily he thought it might shake apart into a million pieces.

126 | ONLY THINGS

The people in the van reminded Ray of the kids he saw hanging around the park, playing acoustic guitars and discussing poetry. The pair in the front seat, a guy with a little beard on his chin and a girl with a flower tucked behind one ear, wore faded blue jeans and outrageously patterned shirts. The young man on the bench seat behind them seemed familiar to Ray, but he couldn't quite place him. The guy's face wore an expression that said he was amused by everything around him, a little smile that twitched at the edges. His eyes were bright with a secret understanding, like he knew the punchline to the world's funniest joke and was taking his time sharing it. Ray saw intelligence in those eyes, but also something else. Something unsettling.

The windows were down in the front of the van, and wind whipped through the interior, stirring up the trash that had been strewn around. Gum wrappers and scraps of paper whirled through the air.

"Hello?" Ray asked.

None of the van's occupants acknowledged him. Ray looked down at his hands, his lap, and saw nothing. He stood up from his seat and peered into the rearview mirror. He saw a tight sliver of the view around him, saw the young man next to him and the back of the van, which was heaped with duffel bags and camping supplies. But he did not see himself.

"I'm invisible?" Ray asked, feeling like a character from one of his comic books. He repeated the question, shouting it this time. Still, no one so much as glanced his way. He was unseen and unheard. The realization unmoored him. Like a hot air balloon casting off its lines, he drifted up, moving across the top of the van. He examined the driver and the two passengers closely, but their voices were still lost to him. Ray realized that the din of voices he'd heard in his aunt's house was still with him, only now it was muted, distant, and soft, like ocean waves. It blended into the roar of the air rushing through the windows.

He drifted, relaxing into his invisibility. It was disorienting but not altogether unpleasant. He hovered above the young man in the backseat. Ray still couldn't place him. Then the kid reached into the breast pocket of his plaid shirt and brought out a pair of Buddy Holly glasses.

Steven Lovelace!

Ray looked at the two people in the front seat. They certainly fit the description for what his father referred to as "shiftless goddamn Beatniks." Maybe Dervis was right after all.

The van's occupants conversed, waving their hands and pointing their fingers for emphasis. To Ray, they sounded like people shouting underwater. They went on that way for some time: Ray floating around overhead and the people in the van arguing or at least discussing something vehemently. Ray looked out the windows of the van, searching the passing landscape for a landmark. They certainly weren't in Arnholdt. The scenery that whizzed by was nearly treeless, and the van's tires threw up a constant cloud of dust. The sun was setting, and it seemed to be resting out there in the distance on the flat brown line of the horizon.

"We were in Texas," Ray said. "Way out on the other side of nowhere, leaving some one-stoplight town and heading toward another. I found all this out later, after I woke up and after Steven Lovelace had been arrested."

Stephanie gave him a confused look. "That name, Steven Lovelace. You say it like it should mean something to me. It sort of rings a bell, but I'm not sure why. You know, like it's just on the tip of my brain."

"If Charles Manson's family hadn't stabbed poor Sharon Tate a couple months after my van ride with Steven Lovelace, you'd probably know the name instantly." Ray's cup was empty, and he considered the wisdom of having a refill. It was going to be a long drive back to Edgewood, after all. "That afternoon, Steven and his two hippie pals were discussing the wisdom of making another Statement. Capital 'S.' That's what they called it when they killed somebody."

Stephanie snapped her fingers. "*The Highway Kids*. Now I remember. There was that made-for-TV movie."

"It was a fictionalized account, but as far as the big picture stuff goes, the movie was pretty accurate," Ray said.

"I just remember that it had that guy from *Daddy's Place* in it. You know, the one who got arrested for jacking off in public?"

"I'll give you the *Sportscenter* wrap-up, then." Ray decided when the cute waitress came back, he would have another refill. He was getting damned near talked out and still wasn't to the end of his story. "My dad was wrong about what had happened. Steven Lovelace hadn't fallen in with some hippies that turned him bad; the hippies had fallen in with him. After Steven slipped out of dreary old Arnholdt, he hitched around for a while, trying out the typical hippie lifestyle. He never lost his taste for plaid shirts and Buddy Holly glasses, so he looked like a rube to most of the people he traveled with. Then he met Marty Lyman and Jeanne Brewster, a couple of college kids from Arizona who were looking to spend their summer vacations getting a taste of the turn on, tune in, drop out experience. They picked up Steven while he was hitching his way across Texas."

"Right where you joined the party."

Ray glanced around. The place was mostly empty and the few people working there looked too bored to bother eavesdropping, but Ray lowered his voice and leaned forward all the same. "That argument that I was watching? It was all about what had just happened a few miles down the road. They'd stopped for gas, and while Marty was filling up the VW, Steven and Jeanne had gone into the place, killed the cashier, and cleaned out the register. Apparently, Steven had a way with women and could talk them into things. Two female members of the jury at his trial were dismissed for improper behavior…"

Stephanie raised her eyebrows. "Improper behavior?"

"One of them flashed her breasts at him…"

"No way. During the trial, right there in the courtroom?"

Ray tried in vain to catch the eye of the bored waitress. "But we're getting way ahead of ourselves. And all that stuff is a matter of public record anyway."

"I can't believe I never heard of all this stuff," Stephanie said.

"Well, shit, less than a month after Steven was arrested, Sharon Tate turned up dead, and the world focused its attention elsewhere. There was no twenty-four hour news cycle to keep it fresh, and the Lovelace murders got buried deeper and deeper in the paper until they were just gone altogether."

"And here I thought it was just the young folks with short attention spans." She jerked a thumb over her shoulder to the counter, where the waitress was slumped, peering at her cell phone intently. "Arnholdt isn't exactly the Lost Kingdom of Upper Buttcrack. You'd think I would have heard more about it."

"Sometimes, people just want to forget. They figure if they move on, the bad stuff just fades away." Ray scooted his coffee cup around on the table. The waitress snapped out of her fog long enough to refill their cups and clear away the empty plates. He watched her leave then went back to his story.

The discussion in the van eventually lost its steam. Steven sat with his arm slung across the seat. He looked like he was on the verge of breaking into hysterical laughter. Jeanne lolled back in her seat with one bare foot hanging out the open window. Marty glanced her way as he drove the van. He looked at her like she was some alien creature that had taken up residence beside him.

The voices in Ray's head had subsided to a dull wash of white noise. He drifted around the interior of the van, blown about by the wind roaring through the open windows. The sun had finally disappeared below the line of the horizon, and the air streaming into the van cooled. Marty popped on the lights, switching on the high beams to cut through the darkness. Jeanne reeled her foot in from the window and put her shoes on. And Steven sat as motionless as a statue, the strange almost-smile unchanged. The miles of two-lane blacktop stretched on into the night. Finally, Steven leaned forward and said something to Marty. Ray could not hear his words, but it was clear that Steven had just given instructions to stop at the next rest area.

They all piled out of the van at one of those awful cinderblock public restrooms that served as a rest stop for tired truckers or tourists with full bladders. They walked through the parking lot, which was deserted except for an eighteen wheeler and a pickup truck. Ray drifted along with them, watching as Steven whispered something in Jeanne's ear. Marty looked on, his upper lip quivering.

Ray watched as Jeanne broke away from the group and approached the pickup truck. Steven grabbed Marty's arm and pulled him into the restroom.

"It's what they did," Ray said, sipping his fresh coffee. "They went hunting for normal people—those are Steven Lovelace's own words, by the way—and made a statement against the emptiness of modern straight society by killing them. Again, Steven's own words. They used Jeanne as bait. She'd get some trucker or traveling salesman going, and once they were really into the act, Steven and Marty would appear. Steven carried an old Bowie knife. Marty used a length of rope. At his trial, Steven maintained that Marty was a coward and that Jeanne was nothing more than a slut who got off on watching. The jury went easy on them, gave them life sentences but left the door open to parole. They shouldn't have. Whatever reservations Marty had about the gas station robbery were gone by the time they murdered the driver of that pickup truck. In the space of a few hours, he'd beat his conscience into submission."

"Dear God," Stephanie said, staring at her coffee.

"I'd drifted into that men's room with Marty and Steven, just because it felt like the normal thing to do. You know, the guys go to the men's room while the ladies go do whatever it is they do. Kid thinking. I say that because I think it's important for you to remember that I hadn't even seen my twelfth birthday when I watched that man in the truck die."

If there was some silent signal that passed between Steven and Marty, Ray didn't see it. One second, they were slumped against the bathroom wall, eyeing each other silently, and the next, they were walking out of the restroom, Steven lifting up his shirttail to withdraw his Bowie knife, Marty yanking a coiled length of rope from his back pocket. Steven pulled a dirty rag from his pocket and wadded it up in his fist. Ray swore that snapping arcs of electricity passed between them. By the time they were at the driver's side door of the truck, Ray could smell the ozone stink of the energy passing between them.

As an eleven year old, Ray had some inkling about the mechanics of what took place between men and women during their private moments. But he was not prepared for what he saw as he drifted past the driver's side window of the truck. Jeanne was shirtless, and Ray could see the tan line left by a two-piece bathing suit across her back. She was crouched over the driver's lap, her head bobbing up and down slowly.

The driver's head lolled back and to the side on the headrest, and his mouth hung open, a thin line of drool hanging at one corner. He moaned and grunted and wiggled around on his seat. Jeanne looked up from her work and saw Steven and Marty leering through the window. She smiled, licking her teeth. She buried her face in the driver's crotch again. He continued to moan and drool, grabbing a fistful of Jeanne's hair.

Abruptly, his eyelids flew open, revealing eyes that were bloodshot and panicked. He screamed. His shriek was cut short when Steven jerked the door open and stuffed the rag into his mouth.

What followed happened so fast that Ray could only perceive it in short bursts:

Jeanne's head rising from the man's lap and spitting something out of her blood-smeared mouth.

Marty slipping his rope around the man's neck, pulling it taut. The man's fingers scrabbling at the rough noose cutting off his air supply.

And Steven plunging his knife into the man's stomach again and again and again, blood streaming out onto the seat and floorboard.

The driver's feet drumming madly, his body thrashing. His eyes growing so wide with terror that Ray was sure they'd pop out of his head.

The murderous trio, covered in blood, laughing and clowning around with the dead body.

They'd gone back to Stephanie's house, to sit on the front porch and watch the rain while Ray finished his story. Lucille was off for the rest of the day, and they no longer had to fear her eavesdropping. They sat in silence for a while, listening to the storm drains gurgle. Ray swallowed, feeling a bit sick for having detailed his memory of his time with Steven Lovelace. He was sure that it would kill him to continue, but he pressed on nonetheless.

"I tried to run. To fly away or to just wake up. But it didn't work. Each time I got more than a short distance away, I snapped back, like I was connected to them by a rubber band. I could look away while they did their thing, but I couldn't close my eyes. I couldn't hear them speaking to one another, but the screams of their victims came through loud and clear."

"Good Lord, Ray…" Stephanie shook her head slowly. "I'm so sorry."

"They found the trucker asleep in his rig. They killed him for an encore. After they finished, they washed up in the restrooms and hit the road again. I was with them for two weeks, during which they killed seven more people and traumatized a few more just for kicks."

"And when you woke up?"

"The doctors watched me for a few days then sent me home. As far as they could tell, there was nothing wrong with me. They did a battery of tests and came up empty. There didn't seem to be any immediate danger, so they sent me home, told my parents to make sure I took it easy for a while."

"You didn't tell the doctors about what you'd seen, did you?"

"No. I had some idea that they'd lock me in the loony bin. But once I was home, I knew I couldn't keep it to myself. I cracked. Spilled the whole thing out while we sat at the dinner table."

"How'd that go over?" Stephanie asked.

Ray remembered the way the eerie silence had settled over the table, like storm clouds over his favorite meal—meatloaf and fried potatoes—made to welcome him home. He remembered the looks his parents exchanged, his mother's face pale, his father's jaw muscles twitching.

"My father told me it was a nightmare, but my mother believed there was more to it than that. I heard them arguing late into the night. Finally, Dad made an anonymous tip to the Texas state police, and Steven Lovelace was arrested a week later. Dad was livid. He called Mom every name in the book then served her with divorce papers. He went after full custody, and she didn't fight him on it. I think she was just as scared as Dad. Anyway, we didn't speak much about it, and after a while, I started to think I'd dreamed a lot of what I saw. I started to believe some of the horrible things Dad told me about Mom. And until recently, I just never thought about it much. Sounds terrible when I say it out loud, but there it is."

They sat for a minute without speaking, the only sounds the constant spatter of rain and the creaking of the wicker furniture beneath them.

"Well?" Ray asked.

"Well what?" Stephanie frowned at him. "I'm not sure what you're asking me, Ray."

His shoulders sagged. "What do you mean you're not sure? I'm the one that's been away from all this shit for the better part of forty years. You've been plugged right into it the whole time. Now I've told you everything—and I mean *everything*—because you should be able to offer some insight. Tell me something I can use. Tell me there's some dark secret evil bubbling up to the surface. Tell me that I'm just going crazy. Tell me *something*."

She gave him a funny look then got up and disappeared into the house. Ray pinched the bridge of his nose and squeezed his eyes shut. The mother of all headaches was setting up shop inside his skull. He cursed himself for a fool. The last time he'd seen his cousin, she was a toddler. Then out of the blue, he'd called her up, begging for help and refusing to explain over the phone what it was all about. If she could help him, why would she even want to?

Stephanie emerged from the house with a six pack of beer in her hand. She eased down into the wicker chair and tugged two cans free of the plastic ring.

Ray waved away the offer. "I'm sober these days."

Stephanie winced. "Sorry."

"Not like you could have known. We haven't exactly been close, have we?"

"Not exactly." She cracked one of the cans and took a long swallow. "But I figured out a long time ago that our family wasn't like others. This may surprise you, Ray, but we always kept up with you. Old Dervis may have thought you'd gone underground, but he should have known that your mother wouldn't let you off her radar. She kept up with all your milestones. Graduations, report cards, awards, all that stuff."

"She did? How'd she do that?"

She tapped her forehead with a finger. "How do you think? The same way you ended up keeping tabs on Steven Lovelace for a couple weeks."

Ray didn't quite know how to feel about that.

"So I heard about you plenty," Stephanie continued. "It sort of felt like you were the prodigal son who'd stroll back through the door at any minute. I guess you took your sweet time. But now you're here. Asking me for help. Ironic, isn't it?"

"I don't follow."

"Ray, honey, what I do is bullshit. I give advice and offer insight into people's problems. I'm really good at reading people, figuring out what it is they need to hear, and saying it to them. And would you believe I almost became a guidance counselor? Went to school and everything. But I guess old habits die hard, and after all, I did grow up around this kind of thing."

"What do you mean, it's bullshit?" Ray swiveled around in his chair to get a good look at her face.

"I don't have the gift. Your mother did. My mother did to some degree. Aunt Jolene had a bit. No doubt about it, though, your mom was the power hitter of the group. That's why she was usually the one up in that bedroom doing readings and séances while my mom and Jolene did the light lifting. I used to think it skipped a generation, but after talking to you, I guess I was wrong on that score. Some of your mother's talent obviously took hold in you."

"I wouldn't say…"

"Oh, is that right? Full-on, involuntary astral projection at age eleven doesn't sound like talent to you?" She ripped a decidedly unladylike belch and wiped her mouth with the back of her hand. "And what did you do with this talent? You put in some years at some factories, bought and later sold some alarm system company, and then became a part time cop. You know what someone like me would do to have that ability? What I'd give to have just a bit of that mojo? Talk about hiding your light under a bushel."

Ray shook his head. "But I didn't want it."

"That's why it's ironic."

"Pardon me if I don't laugh with you." Ray thought of all those years, learning to ignore his dreams, to never look too deeply into people's eyes. He'd spent his life consciously closing himself off from an ability that most people would have killed to possess. It was as if he was some virtuoso violinist who'd undergone voluntary finger amputation.

Stephanie kept going. "But you know, I did learn quite a bit from Mom and her sisters. I know the lingo, you could say. And I think I can at least get you pointed in the right direction. I'll help you as much as I can. I did make a promise, after all. I'll have my joyful assistant clear my schedule."

Chapter Fifteen: The Survivor

George arrived at the flea market early on Saturday to set up his wares. He wasn't even sure what was in the boxes he'd taken from the massive stacks in the garage. He'd grabbed the ones closest to the door, figuring he could work his way back to the house. Even after he'd wedged them into the car's trunk and backseat, the supply in the garage didn't seem diminished. An endless parade of weekends spent hawking the junk at the flea market had unfurled in his mind as he loaded the car, and he groaned inwardly. Ridding himself of Kathy's possessions was a millstone around his neck. He just wanted to keep his head above water long enough to get some writing done and see if the old spark was still there.

Luanne was one of the other early birds that morning, and she'd already filled her table with trashy romance paperbacks.

"Good morning," George called as he unloaded boxes from the dolly he'd borrowed from the comic book sellers across the room.

Luanne flashed him a smile. "How are you today, Mr. George? Looks like you got your issues straightened out with the storage unit. No more dead bodies in there, I hope."

He nearly dropped a box on his foot. "Not that I know of."

Just as Constable McFettridge had predicted, one of Sheriff Wilson's deputies had paid him a visit on Wednesday afternoon to let him know the contents of his storage unit were now available. The storage unit itself, however, was no longer available to him, as it was still considered a crime scene. And since all the other units were rented, George had been forced to relocate all the boxes to his house.

"I got some coffee in a thermos if you need some," Luanne said.

George smiled. "Do I really look that bad?"

"Just tired is all." She'd come from behind her table and started to help George unpack his boxes. "Arrange this stuff attractively. You can't just dump it on your table and expect people to buy it. What all you selling today?"

136 | ONLY THINGS

"Tell you the truth, I don't really know. I just grabbed the first boxes I could get my hands on." George looked at the commemorative Elvis Presley plate in his hands. His wife had loved the King, and she could be counted on to snap up any souvenir featuring his likeness. Something small fluttered inside him and then went still. Looking at Elvis' gleaming white smile didn't remind George of Graceland or take him back to Blue Hawaii; it was just another reminder that Kathy was gone and never coming back. Telling himself that maybe it was for the best was all well and good; actually believing it was something else altogether.

"You okay, Mr. George?" Luanne asked.

He cleared his throat. "Yeah, I'm fine. Just tired, like you said."

"Let me get you some of that coffee."

They sat behind Luanne's spread of lurid books and sipped coffee poured from her thermos. George's table—full of dolls, decorative plates, and other knickknacks—was now attractively arranged and awaiting perusal by the shoppers who'd soon be admitted into the building.

He must have reacted visibly to his first sip, because Luanne giggled and said, "I should have warned you that I make it strong. My boyfriend always says that some people like their coffee so strong that a spoon can stand up in it, but I like it so strong it just dissolves the spoon."

"I believe it," George said when he recovered.

She drank her coffee like it was water and not high-octane fuel. "Now, suppose you tell me what's got you so tired. I saw that Dr. Oz on TV the other day, and he recommended some kind of root that you chew on."

"It's not really that kind of insomnia."

"Is it what happened to Percy? Because I don't see how that can be your fault. I mean, if you'd done it, you'd be in jail by now."

George shook his head. "No, I don't think it's that. I mean, I'm plenty disturbed by that whole business, don't get me wrong. But that's not what's been keeping me up nights."

"Well, what do you think it is, then?"

There was something about her eyes—big, blue, and bright—that made her easy to talk to. Or maybe it was her expression, concerned and almost naïve. Still yet, maybe it was just that George was finally ready to unburden himself, and Luanne Samples just happened to be the one who'd stepped into his line of fire. Whatever the reason, he let it all out.

When he was finished, he felt light, as if he'd been carrying a heavy load on his shoulders and had suddenly shaken it off. He also felt like he might need to cry. Or possibly laugh.

This is the story that George related to Luanne, starting over a cup of coffee and finishing as the day's first customers streamed into the flea market:

In 1976, after *Speak Softly, Lover* became a modest hit at the box office, George Young wasn't exactly an in-demand name in the literary world, but he was making a good run at a career. Over the next decade, four more of his novels would be optioned for films—two of which were actually produced—and he visited the *New York Times* bestseller list with most of his books, even if the stays on that list were short-lived. But by the middle of the eighties, the ideas—and therefore the books—were coming slower. The market for horror was trending toward the fast-paced, gory stuff, far removed from the quiet ghost stories that George wrote.

First, his publisher quit putting out his titles in hardcover editions. It was pocket paperbacks only for George Young from then on. And when the next decade rolled around, when the Clintons were hugging as Fleetwood Mac blasted in the background, George found himself without a publisher.

He took a part time job teaching creative writing at a community college, hoping that he could recharge his creative batteries. Maybe a few years away from the grind of publishing a novel every sixteen months would rekindle the passion for the craft he'd felt as a young man. But the months slipped by, and he couldn't conjure up more than a few pages. His attempts at writing serious literary fiction were laughable, no better than the half-assed John Updike imitations that his most pompous students submitted to his workshops. He switched to an old typewriter, thinking that perhaps he could capture the spirit of Hemingway by clattering away on that ancient machine rather than clicking and tapping on his computer. It was a desperate gesture that proved fruitless.

The months became years.

He took to drinking. At first, he hoped it might spark something in him, get his muse back in order. Hemingway again. Then, when liquor failed to provide inspiration, it provided some solace. It became a crutch and then an excuse: how could he be expected to write in his condition?

Eventually, he gave up altogether. He'd written a dozen novels and cranked out short stories by the score, after all. Perhaps that was all he had in him. Some writers had less than that. He supposed he should be thankful, but somehow he couldn't make himself feel that way. No matter how much he tried to convince himself that his life had changed, probably irrevocably, the old frustrated drive remained. He felt he was meant to write, but for some reason, he could no longer do it.

They have a term for what George had become: a functional alcoholic. He didn't get blackout drunk and crash his car. He didn't go to class in vomit-streaked clothes. He didn't smash whiskey bottles when despair washed over him. If his colleagues suspected anything, they never voiced any concerns. There were no awkward talks with the head of the department, no staged interventions. He maintained a façade of normalcy, even when his hands shook in the morning, before he'd had his first two drinks of the day.

Then, early in the spring semester of 2001, he started dating one of his students from the previous semester. Part of his rational mind told him that he was treading on dangerous ground. Kathy Bowman wasn't too young to be in that sort of relationship—she was twenty-six—but she was, by most people's standards, too young to be in that sort of relationship *with him.*

"Some people just don't understand how love works," Luanne said, pouring more black sludge coffee into her cup.

George waved away her offer of more coffee. He figured he'd like to sleep sometime in the next month. "I suppose that's just how we're made. What seems so natural, so *right*, to us is often a mystery to everyone else. But the thing about Kathy and me is that if anyone had cared to really look, not just at the surface of things, they'd have known instantly why we were together."

Luanne laid a hand on her chest and sighed. "Star-crossed lovers."

"Sadly, no. What made Kathy and I perfect for each other was that she loved broken things, and I was very much broken when we met."

"Oh, that's so sad. But it sounds like poetry when you say it. No wonder you're a writer."

"There was more to it than just that. Nothing so simple as love is ever really simple."

Luanne clapped her hands. "More poetry!"

"You see, Kathy had money. She wasn't rich, at least not the way we've come to think of it by watching morons like Donald Trump flaunt their money. But the Bowman family had done well for themselves, and Kathy had inherited the entirety of her parents' estate. And the way she was behaving as head of that estate had some of the extended family quite worried." George nodded, remembering. "Going to community college to take creative writing classes from some washed-up horror writer was bad enough; dating the man was beyond the pale. They thought it was indicative of some sort of breakdown and even threatened to get the court involved. After all, Kathy had a troubled past. She had scars on each wrist from a suicide attempt back during her first pass at college. The lawyers made a good case for the relatives' bitching being sour grapes from people who were left out of the Bowmans' will. The sad irony is the family was right. Kathy was *not* well."

George wiped at the corner of one eye. After Kathy passed, he'd cried so long and hard during the lonely days that followed that he thought he'd exhausted his lifetime supply of tears. Apparently not.

"Well, don't stop now," Luanne said. "We still have a few minutes before the early birds start drifting in."

"Let's see, where was I?" George looked away, as if he might see the thread of the story suspended in the air like a strand of cobweb.

He'd known that Kathy had a problem the first time she invited him back to her place after one of their dates. The house was huge, and she lived there alone. The floors were hardwood and a kind of brown that resulted from years of regular polishing. They creaked in places, but not with a sound that was flimsy or brittle. No, these floors creaked with authority, like the voice of a wise old man might seem rough-worn. The ceilings were high, and from them hung lighting fixtures that were nearly works of art, some of them strong, others wispy-delicate. The furniture in the rooms was of the leather, wood, and velvet variety. Even the bathrooms, with their marble countertops and porcelain sinks, were beautiful.

It should have been a space that radiated class and refinement. It *should* have been. Mistaking the house for a haven of tranquil elegance was impossible, because Kathy's possessions—and there were so many of them—were strewn about in every available spot. The lovely antique furniture was draped with souvenir t-shirts and littered with stuffed animals of all colors and sizes. Velvet Elvis portraits had been hung crookedly on the walls among the fine art prints. The kitchen counters were crammed full of decorative plates, mugs, shot glasses, and silverware. Each step on the long central staircase had a heap of magazines or a box of shoes atop it.

The bathrooms were likewise a riot of clutter. If Kathy had told him that she'd bought out the entire bath and beauty sections of all the drugstores in the state, George would not have batted an eye. Had some terrorist ever pulled the trigger and blown the United States into the Stone Age, Kathy would have been prepared to outlast the fallout with plenty of bounce and shine in her hair, moisturized skin, deodorized underarms, no unsightly leg or armpit hair, a freshly waxed bikini line, and manicured nails. There was enough makeup in the master bath alone to keep several circuses and an Alice Cooper tour rolling in perpetuity. Enough bubble bath to turn Lake Michigan into a giant swingers' retreat. Stacks of towels. Boxes of facial tissue. Lotions, ointments, and ablutions by the gallon.

He'd made light of it, of course. By then, he was in love with Kathy. At least he'd come to depend on her for comfort and companionship. Although he knew this stockpiling was the symptom of some mental problem, he dismissed it. They'd gone to the bedroom and, after clearing the large four-poster of a metric ton of stuffed animals and clothes, made love atop expensive sheets.

"It was sweet of you to love her like that, even though she had some flaws," Luanne said. She'd put aside the coffee and was now chewing bubble gum that smelled sweeter than the cotton candy stand at the state fair. George got a sugar rush just inhaling the fumes from one of her burst bubbles.

"But it was dangerous. In recovery and rehab programs, they call that behavior enabling. That's what passed for love between us, enabling one another." George waved away Luanne's offer of a piece of gum. "Not that I went in for any of that stuff when I finally jumped on the wagon. But let me tell you, young lady, that's sure as hell what I was: an enabler. I never told Kathy the word 'no,' at least not for a long, long time. I never denied her this obsession with accumulating physical objects. Part of me figured that my love for her would eventually take the place of whatever fulfillment those things brought her. It never did. And when I began to suggest that maybe she should get rid of some of the things filling that house, she changed. In the end, I'm sure she hated me."

Luanne patted his shoulder. "Oh my God, that is so sad."

George pressed on. Now that he was rolling, he wanted to speak it through to the end. "And Kathy never told me no, either. When I wanted to quit teaching, even though I still hadn't published a lick, she smiled and told me to go ahead, that we had plenty of money. When my drinking increased, she helped me out by making sure there was a good supply of scotch in the house. When I had to puke in the morning, she made sure she was there with a chaser drink to steady me when I was done."

"She must have really loved you."

"No. That's not love. It's something like love, but not quite."

"Don't be so hard on yourself."

But George could see that Luanne was beginning to understand. "Despite the howls of protest from her family, we were married. I moved into the cluttered mansion, and we went on with our mutual self-destruction. A decade went by like that, in a blur of drinking and purchasing. Kathy collected my empty liquor bottles. Some of them, she stuck a candle in the neck and melted it down over the bottle. Some of them were sort of pretty. Most she just lined up on shelves. I used to walk past shelves full of liquor bottles, and I swear to you, I could feel my liver hating me."

"You said something changed, that you asked her to stop." Luanne prompted.

"Hollywood got a good taste for remaking old horror movies. I guess it's true that everything old is new again, which is nice, because it means there's still a chance for old farts like me. Since I didn't have an agent at the time, a producer contacted me directly. He was interested in remaking *Speak Softly, Lover* and wanted to know if I'd take a crack at writing the screenplay. Maybe he thought I was a charity case, or maybe he thought it would give the picture an air of authenticity or some sort of street cred with the critics. I was looking at a nice payday, but that wasn't what motivated me. It was more the prospect of getting to write again. It scared me a bit, because I wasn't sure if I could do it."

"You thought you'd have to clean up your act," Luanne said.

George nodded. "You got that one on the first guess."

He thought that Kathy would be overjoyed when he gave her the news. Most wives, George thought, would love to hear that their unemployed, drunk husbands were cleaning up and getting back to work. Not Kathy. She told him he was just setting himself up for disappointment. She made him a drink and then looked offended when he waved it away. He told her that they could do it together, both of them could let go of their addictions.

"If you ever throw one of my things away without my express permission," she'd said, sipping from the drink she'd made him, "I will kill you in your sleep."

George had laughed, thinking it was joke. After all, she'd said it so sweetly and with a smile. But when he pressed the issue, she retreated into the bathroom and slammed the door.

Nevertheless, he got down to work. If he was going to write, he'd need some private space, a room free of distractions. Nothing but a desk and a coffee pot. A chair that was comfortable, but not sleepily so. Maybe a tennis ball to toss against the wall to help him think. Problem was, there wasn't a single space left in the house that wasn't packed to the rafters with Kathy's things. He thought that just maybe, if he picked one of the small rooms downstairs, she might not even notice. There were three guest rooms on the first floor that Kathy never seemed to enter, much less keep an eye on.

He told himself she'd never notice. How could she possibly?

He should have known better.

"It wasn't even a real bedroom," George said. "Just a little space that was probably a servant's quarters back when the house was built."

"And filled with what?" Luanne asked.

George scratched his chin. "Well, let's see. There was just a bit of everything, as I remember it. Kathy didn't really separate her collectibles into different areas of the house or anything like that. It was all just one big jumble. Some of it was just trash: old magazines, junk mail, bumper stickers from politicians who were never elected, that sort of thing. I moved most of it to other piles, but I did throw some of it away. Bagged up the stray papers and broken things and put them out on the curb for the trash service to pick up."

"Oh no," Luanne said. "You didn't tell her, did you?"

"No. Like I said, she never used the room that I'd ever seen. I figured she wouldn't notice." George paused, thought that one over. "Or maybe not. Maybe I was hoping for a confrontation. I'd cut my drinking way back, but her buying and collecting hadn't slowed down at all. I was down to a couple drinks in the morning to get going, and then maybe two or three beers during the day, just to keep my hands steady. That's pathetic, I know, but nowhere near as pathetic as I'd been. I thought if I could do it, maybe she could just scale back a bit too."

"I have a feeling we're getting to the tragic part now."

"Don't take this the wrong way, Luanne, but there is no one like a woman for believing that old saw about revenge being best served cold."

For two weeks, Kathy ignored his writing. Each morning, she watched him bypass the living room couch and the TV, and disappear into the small room. She eyed him suspiciously when he emerged, but otherwise carried on with her usual routine. They chatted pleasantly enough at meals. They even made love at night when the mood struck, which wasn't quite as often as it had been in years past. During the day, he'd disappear into the room and tap the keys of his computer, and she'd make her pilgrimage to the area shopping centers, flea markets, and outlet malls. He'd hammer out a few hundred words—slowly, painfully—and she'd buy bags of clothes, beauty products, and whatever collectibles caught her eye. In many ways, life proceeded in the normal manner.

That changed the morning George went into his little room to discover his computer gone and the space once more heaped with Kathy's junk.

He stood there in the doorway, bewildered. Then, when it finally dawned on him what had happened, he stormed upstairs to the bedroom, where Kathy was modeling outfits from the previous day's shopping. She'd bought a dozen plaid skirts and was twirling in front of the mirror in one of them.

"Where is it?" he asked calmly, though the anger inside him was steadily coming to a boil.

"Where's what?" Kathy stood with her side to the mirror, looking over her shoulder at her reflection.

"You know what I'm talking about. Don't play innocent." His hands clenched into fists, the muscles in his forearms trembling like high-tension wires. "Where is my computer, all my work?"

She slipped out of the skirt and turned to face him. "I suppose that it's probably at the landfill by now. You know, with all of my stuff that you threw away without asking me."

He strode forward and grabbed Kathy by the shoulders, shaking her once, twice. "What the hell is wrong with you?"

Luanne gave George a troubled look, and he smiled reassuringly. "Don't worry, Luanne. I didn't hit her. I've done plenty of terrible things in my life, but that isn't one of them. I think I was close to it. Something held me back, though. Some part of me knew that if I got started that way, I might not be able to stop. What I did was shake her a couple more times, then turn and stomp out of the house. I went to the first bar I came across and drank until I blacked out. I woke up in a motel room the next day with the manager beating on the door and yelling that I had to either get out of the room or pay for another day. So I staggered out of there and went back home, stopping by the liquor store on the way for a case of beer and two fifths of scotch."

"Oh my God, this is awful. I almost don't want to know what happened next." Luanne spit her gum into a wad of Kleenex. She shoved a fresh piece into her mouth and commenced pummeling it with her jaws. "But I have to know. What happened?"

"Nothing. We never said another word about it. She went right on filling the house with worthless shit, and I went right on trying to pickle myself with booze. Something had changed between us, there's no doubt about that. We were never intimate again. Most of the time, we slept in separate bedrooms, if I didn't just pass out on the couch. I could have started writing again, but I didn't. I let the deadline on that screenplay pass and never heard from the producer again. What the hell, the movie never even got made, so I guess it was no great loss. No, Kathy and I went back to our old routine. Outwardly, it probably didn't look a whole lot different than before, but now the love had gone out of it."

Now it was Luanne's turn to dab at her eyes.

"We were both sick," George continued. "But Kathy was sicker than either of us knew. Along with her addiction to shopping and collecting, she had an intense fear of doctors. When she was a child, her parents had to sedate her just to get her into the doctor's office for a checkup. With both of them gone and with me barely able to take care of myself, there was no one there to force her to ever go near a doctor again."

"Oh, no…" Luanne clutched a fresh tissue.

"It was a brain tumor. Who knows how long it had been growing inside her head. If we had caught it early, would we have been able to do anything?" George paused, pursing his lips. "I guess there's no way to know. She had these…spells…that's what I called them, anyhow. Seizures. Not the kind where you shake all over and foam at the mouth and swallow your own tongue. These were just little stretches of time where she'd look blankly into the distance, maybe drool a little bit. She'd come out of it and say that she couldn't remember where she'd been."

One night, George was stalking around the bottom floor of the house, looking for a bottle that had more than a few drops of liquor left in it. He wasn't having any luck, and his desperation became greater with each empty vessel he uncovered. Kathy was upstairs, doing whatever it was she did, locked in the bedroom for hours at a time. She called out to George, and there was something in her voice that made him choose not to ignore her, as had become his custom. He flung aside an empty bottle of Cutty Sark. It fell softly on a pile of shirts that still had the price tags attached.

He stomped upstairs, muttering under his breath about how the next time Kathy went shopping she'd better return with a whole goddamn case of scotch or the marriage was over.

"What?" he asked, throwing open the bedroom door.

Kathy lay in bed, covered with stuffed animals and baby blankets. Her face peeked out from a forest of teddy bear limbs and Hello Kitty-patterned blankets. "George, I want you to make me a promise."

"Sure, whatever you want." He was eager to be out of the house, on his way to a bar or a liquor store so he could make the goddamn pounding in his goddamn head stop.

"I know you don't love me anymore, at least not like you used to," Kathy said. Her voice was small, almost childlike.

"That's not…" George started to protest but couldn't muster up any enthusiasm for it.

"Let's not pretend. But I know you loved me once, so I want you to promise me something."

George was stunned, and he didn't quite know what to do. It had been so long since they'd spoken about anything of consequence. He put his hands in his pockets then took them back out. He shifted his weight from foot to foot. Finally, because he felt that perhaps it was the right thing to do, he crossed the room, stepping high over the piles of clothes, and knelt by the bed. He almost reached out and took her hand, but pulled back at the last moment.

"Okay, tell me what it is. I'll promise you anything," George said. And he meant it, too. Despite everything, he still felt very deeply about his wife. Perhaps she was right when she accused him of no longer loving her, but there was still *something* there.

"When I die, I don't want you to send all my beautiful things to the landfill. You did that once and it nearly broke my heart. Promise me that all these things I've given a home will still have one when I'm gone."

He nearly laughed. He should have known that whatever she had to say would involve the material possessions with which she'd cocooned and entombed herself. He'd knelt down expecting some deep revelation that might set them back on the right path. But all Kathy could think of—all that she could worry about—was the vast collection of worthless shit that she'd used to ruin the house, their marriage, their lives.

"I promise. I'll make sure all your things have a home. But you're not going to die, Kathy. You're still so young."

"Remember that you promised me." There was an edge to her voice, something George had never heard before.

He rose from the floor. "I won't forget."

"Thank you."

"I'm going out for a while. Is there something you need me to bring back, like from the grocery store or something? Only, I might be gone for a while, so…"

She hugged her plush animals tightly and shook her head. "I have everything I need."

"I know you do," George said as he left the room.

The front doors were open now, and a few shoppers had already drifted in.

"Well, I guess I'd better wrap it up," George said. "Those were the last words I heard my wife speak. I was plenty miffed about what she'd said, making me promise to be the caretaker for her junk. I was plenty miffed about everything, I suppose. I went on one of my patented blackout benders. When I staggered home a few days later, the house was unusually silent. Kathy wasn't a loud person, but she also had a hard time being in the house without some sort of noise to keep her company. The TV or the stereo was always on, sometimes in more than one room.

But that morning, the big old house was as silent as a tomb. And that's because it was one."

"She passed while you were gone?" Luanne asked.

He nodded. "She had a massive seizure and just never came back."

"And you moved to Barlow because you couldn't stand to be in that house anymore?"

"After the funeral, I hit the bottle as hard as I could. And then I woke up one morning and started vomiting, which wasn't too unusual. But this time it didn't stop, and there was some blood in it too. I called 911 just in time to pass out."

"Bet you got one heck of a wake-up call, Mr. George."

"The doctor read me the riot act, that's for sure. Told me I wouldn't live much longer if I didn't stop drinking. So I went home and considered my options. On one hand, I could keep drinking and see how long I could make it. But on the other hand, maybe I could try cleaning up and see where that led me." He held up his hands, gestured around. "And it looks like this is where it led me. I won't lie to you; it hasn't been the easiest road. Plenty of times I've been tempted to get me a bottle, lock the door, and hide from the world. Who knows? Maybe that's the way it will work out yet."

"I'd sure hate for it to go that way."

"I boxed up all Kathy's things. Put the house up for sale, even though the whole housing market is in the tank. I took the first serious offer I got—from one of Kathy's cousins, as it turns out—and headed down here. I figured that both my parents are buried in Arkansas, so if I go back to drinking, at least I'll be close to the family resting spot." He laughed so that Luanne wouldn't get upset and further ruin her makeup. "Now, I'm just going through with that last promise I made Kathy. I'm finding good homes for all her things."

Luanne leaned over and gave him a hug. "Well, I'm glad you're here in Barlow."

He broke away from the hug and looked over his shoulder. "Now it looks like you have some customers headed your way. I'm going to slide back over to my own table and see if I can't get a little business done myself."

He sagged down into the aluminum folding chair behind his table. Telling that story—for the first time, he realized—had really taken it out of him.

Of course, he hadn't told the *whole* story. He'd left out the darkest parts about Kathy's mental state the last year of her life. She'd stopped sleeping through the night during that time, drifting off for an hour or two here and there but never adhering to a set schedule. George remembered hearing her roam about the house, talking to herself and her things. And there was worse. He'd catch her staring into the bathroom mirror for long stretches of time, probing her face with her fingers.

"What are you doing in there?" he'd asked once, pausing outside the bathroom door on his way to the kitchen for another glass of scotch. "Just staring at yourself?"

She'd answered without turning away. "You know exactly what I'm looking at. You've seen it. I know you have. It's why you never kiss me anymore. It's why the people at the stores and sales can't look me in the eye. I've become so ugly."

George regretted not telling her that she was just as beautiful as the day he'd met her, that if she could just get some sleep and a few good meals she'd be back to her normal self. He'd wished countless times that, instead of telling her that she was crazy, he'd taken her into his arms and told her that everything was going to be okay. But he'd done none of that. He'd shaken his head and told her to stop acting like a goddamn lunatic before refilling his drink. And every time after that, when he'd see her peering into the mirror, her eyes wide with horror and her mouth twisted with disgust, he'd done no more than laugh and again remind her that she was acting like a crazy person. Maybe things could have been different, if only he'd found it as easy to swallow his pride and anger as it was to swallow glass after glass of booze.

Of course he'd left this part out when he told Luanne the story of George and Kathy Wilson. There were some tragedies that were too awful to be anything other than private.

Chapter Sixteen: The Shopper

Myrna told herself that she'd skip the flea market and the garage sales this weekend and just stay home, but after breakfast, her resolve melted like ice cream left out on the counter overnight. The weather was perfect for getting out there. It was warm rather than hot, and there was a breeze. By the afternoon, it would be hot and muggy and suffocating. *That* would be the time for lingering inside with the air conditioner going full blast and the TV on.

There were sales aplenty—she'd glanced through the newspaper that morning while she ate her grapefruit and toast—and who knew what great, special things she might miss if she stayed in.

The Methodist church's Summer Rummage Spectacular was mostly a bust. There were nice looking things, sure, but none of them of them responded to her touch the way the truly special items did. She caressed many of the objects on display—always on the sly, she knew how people could misinterpret her behavior—but none gave off that pleasant electricity. She went away empty-handed. She wondered if she should call Tate and tell him that she'd just been at one of Barlow's biggest sales and hadn't bought a thing. Would he be proud of her restraint? No, more likely he'd start with the lectures and frustrated sighs.

The Crystal Falls Lutheran Church was having its bi-annual Trash 'n Treasure Sale, and although it was a bit of a drive, Myrna made her way there. She wasn't disappointed. Even before she'd entered the Fellowship Hall, she could feel a buzz radiating off the items for sale. She supposed that if she tried to explain it to Tate, he'd make some wise-acre comparison to a bug flying into one of those light-up zappers.

The Fellowship Hall was a large multi-purpose room that the good Lutherans of Crystal Falls used for church meetings, potluck suppers, and child care during Sunday services. That morning it was filled with four long rows of tables full of the congregation's cast-off goods. The room had that dusty, vaguely mildewed smell that was like a perfume to Myrna. There were things here, *special* things that were calling out to her.

This was her favorite part: strolling up and down the aisles and pausing for a moment when the tingle in her skin and the murmurs in her head were strongest. The anticipation of ferreting out treasured objects and rescuing them from an uncertain fate was her life's greatest pleasure.

"Those were Florence Jones' things," a woman said, pausing on the other side of the table.

Myrna snapped out of her reverie. She'd been hovering in front of a table full of tea sets of all colors, sizes, and descriptions. "They're very nice."

"Florence was a big fan of teapots and such," the woman said. She was a large lady with iron grey hair. Her cross-emblazoned t-shirt identified her as a "Proud Crystal Falls Lutheran Women's Missionary League Member."

"They really are something." Myrna lifted one delicate cup and saucer set. Her fingers tingled as she touched the porcelain.

"The poor old dear." The LWML lady shook her head. "She was in her nineties, and you know all her people had passed on. She had church and her tea sets, and that was about it."

"I can tell she loved them very much."

"But not as much as she loved her church. When she passed, her will said that her things should be sold to raise money for Crystal Falls Lutheran. She always put Jesus first."

Myrna put down the cup and picked up a teapot. This time the tingle rose almost to her elbow.

The helpful woman cleared her throat. "I have some of that bubble wrap. If you'd like to buy a set, I can pack it up nice for you."

Myrna looked over the saucers, cups, pots, spoons, and sugar dishes. They called to her. "Yes, I think I would like to buy them."

"And which set would you like, dear?"

"Oh, I can't decide on just one. I think I'll take all of them." Myrna's heart raced. Sweat tickled her palms.

The LWML woman sputtered. "There's more than what you see here. Those boxes under the table are full too."

"I'll take those also."

"Some of them are expensive. We don't want to overcharge, just what they're worth…"

Myrna waved this away like shooing a fly. "I have my checkbook. And besides, it's for a good cause, right?"

"Don't you want to even look in the boxes?"

"If the ones in the boxes are only half as nice as the ones on this table, I'll be getting a good deal." Myrna was eager to close the transaction. There weren't many people in the Fellowship Hall, but one of them could walk over and snatch up a cup or a saucer at any moment.

"Let me go get that bubble wrap," the woman said.

Myrna drove back to Barlow with several hundred dollars' worth of tea sets in the trunk of her car. She'd also picked out a box of toy cars because they reminded her of Dale. He'd loved his matchbox car collection so much as a child. She'd spent so much on the tea sets that the nice volunteer lady threw the cars in for free. How could she say no to that?

It was past noon, so she stopped for a sandwich and milkshake at the Frostee Tastee. It had been her boys' favorite place to eat, and she'd taken them there more than was healthy, especially on summer nights when a hamburger and a milkshake tasted so good.

After lunch, she intended to go home. She really was going to get some housework done, maybe start with the kitchen and work her way out to the living room. But the route took her past the Rosebud Flea Market, and the steering wheel practically turned on its own. She didn't fight it. As nice as the Trash 'n Treasure Sale had been, the flea market was a reliable spot.

And it has nothing to do with that nice man, that George Young who sold you those buttons?

Myrna feigned shock at her own thoughts and immediately felt ridiculous for doing so. True, she spent most weekends roaming the flea market, chatting with the people in their booths, picking up an item here and there. But then again, her heart did flutter a bit when she thought of George. There was something about him, something gentle and kind, but also sad, fragile. He was like one from her collection of Teddy Bears. Worn with age, sure, but also inviting. His smile…

Myrna! Where is this coming from? Just listen to yourself. You sound like a teenager.

She parked the car and took a deep breath before she got out. If George was in there this weekend, she didn't want him to see her looking all flushed and expectant. She walked to the front door, willing herself to look cool, calm, and collected despite the whirlwind within.

Stepping out of the rising heat and humidity into the cool, slightly dim interior of the building that housed the flea market was like entering a different climate. The thin layer of perspiration on her back felt icy. She glanced around. George was set up next to Luanne Samples, on the east side of the building. Myrna started on the west side and began working her way clockwise toward George's table. She didn't want to appear too eager. She actually had to force herself to take her time as she looked at the items for sale.

She bought a hummingbird feeder from a scruffy looking old man who sold lawn ornaments and gardening tools. He didn't say a word as he took her money. Although that normally would have unnerved Mryna, she hardly noticed. Now that she had something in her hand—something to explain her presence—she picked up her pace a bit, glancing over the wares on display but not stopping to inspect them.

Finally, as she rounded the bottom of the horseshoe arrangement of booths, she allowed herself a glance in George's direction.

He greeted her with a smile and a wave. "You made it just in time. I was about to call it a day and go get some lunch. Trying to sell this stuff has given me an appetite something fierce."

"You have some nice things on your table today," Myrna said.

In fact, they were *very* nice. The energy that clung to Florence Jones' tea sets was nothing compared to what was coming off the things on George's table. She didn't even have to touch them to feel the tingling in her fingertips. Just standing close was enough to make her skin prickle and her ears hum. These things didn't just call out, they demanded her attention.

"Tell you the truth." George adopted a dramatic whisper, leaning closer. "I've barely sold a thing. Luanne here has been raking in the cash hand over fist. I'll be lucky if I make enough money to buy my lunch."

"It's probably those pictures she has."

"I'm sure it is. And I've thought of using something similar to boost my own sales, but I'm just not sure Barlow is ready for pictures of me in the buff."

She laughed, and he did too. He had an easy way about him. None of the serious intensity she'd expect from a writer. But that spark that she'd felt the first time she'd been in his presence was back again. Her blood fairly sang through her veins as George explained to her all the different stuff he'd brought to sell.

"And here we have an entire set of Elvis Presley decorative plates." George waved his hand over the table. "A must for the home of any fan of the king."

She stepped forward and touched one of the plates. Electricity raced up her arm. "I think they're nice."

"Elvis fan?" He raised an eyebrow.

"I've been to Graceland."

"A rock 'n roll pilgrimage that everyone should make at least once, if only to stand in awe of the jungle room."

She laughed again. "You know, I think I'd like to buy those plates. And the dolls too."

He clapped his hands together. "And which plates would you like?"

"I'll take them all." She ran a finger over the rim of one of the plates, relishing the contact. "How much are they?"

He scratched his chin. "Well, what's a meal at that Pancake Hut down the street usually run?"

"They're not fancy. Six, seven dollars will get you plenty of food."

"Cheap eats are right up my alley. The doctor says I should get more leafy greens, which is why I get a hamburger with everything. All the vegetables they put on cancel out the cheese and red meat, right?" He started wrapping the plates in sheets of newspaper. "Since we're getting to the end of my business hours for the day, I'm going to make you a good deal on this stuff."

Myrna fished her checkbook out of her purse.

"If we were to go down to that diner," George said, putting the first set of plates into a box, "and you were to buy me lunch, I think we could call this transaction even. What do you say?" Her look of surprise must have thrown him, because his smile fell, and he apologized. "I'm sorry, I know that was abrupt. I didn't mean to be so forward."

She put her checkbook away. "I think lunch is a perfectly fair price." She extended her hand. "Shake on it?"

The jolt that ran up her arm as they shook hands was like the greatest sugar rush in the universe. She could have sworn that her feet left the ground.

Myrna smiled so hard on her drive home from the Pancake Hut that she thought her face might split right in two. Blueberry pie and warm, light conversation had restored Myrna to happiness following the morning's feelings of guilt and confusion. While he waited for the waitress to bring him the tab—George had just *insisted*—George asked Myrna if he could perhaps take her to dinner some night. Myrna had once again fought not too appear too eager as she accepted his offer. They made a date as they strolled through the parking lot.

She drove back home humming along to some bouncy polka music she found on the AM radio dial.

A writer.

Myrna could hardly believe it. No, not just a writer, like Mavis Kilgore—who lived over at the trailer court and put out those internet books with all the sex in them—but an actual *author*. Why, George had hardly batted an eye when he told her all about the movies they'd made out of his books. And for a man like that—educated, well-spoken—to be interested in her? It was almost too much to believe. But he *was* interested. Even as she'd sipped her coffee and told herself to batten down her expectations, she'd seen the look in George's eyes. He'd asked for her phone number, and she'd had to admit that her phone had gone missing.

"Oh, that's not a problem," he'd said. "It's a small town. I'm sure we'll run into each other again. Probably sooner than you think."

Her heart fluttered so hummingbird-quick in her chest that she almost passed by a yard sale on Crossland Street. Almost.

Chapter Seventeen: Chris

Sunday was the Lord's day, according to the nonsense that preachers spewed from their pulpits. Chris didn't agree at all with the concept of a day of rest. Time spent in quiet contemplation was time wasted. He awoke at dawn, showered, cleansed his colon with a hot enema, showered again, and went out to face the day.

Although he knew it was madness to do so, he drove across town, through a maze of narrow streets and decayed houses, to the scene of his first battle in the war against chaos. He parked his car a careful distance from the stop sign at the end of the road and strolled back towards the house. He put one hand in his pocket, whistling as he went.

It was strange to see Belinda's hovel in the morning sun. The last time he'd been here, rain had been pounding down, turning the weedy lawn to a muddy mess. Now, with the ground dry and the sun shining overhead, the little house appeared less grim. Oh, it was still a pathetic sight, with its pock-marked aluminum siding and curling shingles. But there was an aura of hope—a dim one, but an aura all the same—pushing through. It made him proud.

A bright yellow line of police crime scene tape still hung around the front of the house, and there was some sort of official paperwork stapled to the front door. Otherwise, one would never know that the place had been the scene of violent death. There was a battered pickup truck parked at the curb in front of the house. An open-topped metal trailer was hitched to the back, packed full of lawn and garden equipment.

A man dressed in khaki coveralls pushed a small mower through the tangle of weeds that passed for a front lawn. When he noticed Chris pausing to look at the house, the man let the mower's engine die.

"You looking for blood and guts, you best just be on your way. The police cleared all that out," he called, tugging a handkerchief from the pocket of his coveralls. He used it to mop his face and the back of his neck. He was one of those old men whose wrinkled skin was so worn and sunbaked that he'd probably look dirty no matter how much he bathed.

Chris walked closer, stopping at the edge of the yard, careful not to put his white sneakers into the row of freshly cut grass clippings. "No, I'm certainly not interested in that stuff."

"You interested in the house, then?" The man looked Chris over. "You look a little overdressed for the neighborhood, you don't mind me saying."

Chris nodded. He'd been concocting a story in his mind to explain his presence. He told the man that he was interested in buying houses to use as rental properties.

"Well, now, that makes sense. And you got a good eye, too. I know it don't look like much, but it'll be a steal. Current owner—that's my boss, Mr. Erickson—he's looking to unload it. Reckon that business with the last tenant getting murdered was too much." He offered his hand to Chris. "Name's Manning. I take care of Mr. Erickson's properties when something needs fixed or put right."

Chris didn't like shaking Manning's hand. It was dirty and calloused. But he went through the social ritual all the same.

"You want to take a look inside?" Manning stuffed the handkerchief back into his pocket.

"It's not a crime scene?" Chris asked.

"Mr. Erickson wants that tape left up to keep the crackheads from setting up shop in there. The police told him they were done with it, and then he told me to get to work cleaning the place up." He snorted and spat into the grass. "Lady that lived here, she was nice enough, not too hard on the eyes in her own way. She'd have visited a dentist and laid off the smokes, she could have been something. But she was one Class-A slob."

Chris' heartbeat kicked up a notch. "You don't say."

"Listen, you know how it is if you're in the rental business. You get tenants that ruin the carpet, put holes in the walls, let the cockroaches become roommates. And yeah, this one did all that shit, although not as bad as some. But the useless junk she had packed into that little house?" Manning whistled, shaking his head. "Two dumpsters worth of crap I hauled out of there. You wouldn't believe."

"Two whole dumpsters?" Chris knew there was a mess in the house, but it had been too dark the night of his visit for him to recognize the full extent of the problem.

"Crap piled damn near to the ceiling in some of them rooms. I wonder if the lady ever threw anything out. Ask me, she had a screw loose." Manning slapped away a mosquito. "Still feel like taking a peek?"

Chris nodded, trying not to appear too eager. He followed Manning up the cracked concrete path to the front door. The old man peeled away the yellow tape and opened the door, making "after you" motions to Chris.

Manning followed him in and threw back the curtains. Sunlight blasted in through the living room windows. All the furniture was gone, but the carpet was still stained and dirty.

"Going to replace that carpet. It's pretty well shot," Manning said. "Linoleum in the kitchen's all scratched to hell, so that'll come up too. Throw some paint up on these walls, give that aluminum siding a good once-over with a pressure washer, and this little house won't do too bad for you. Roof could use some work, if I'm being honest. Other than that, she ain't in too terrible shape. You could have it rented out in no time."

Chris nodded. "I can see how there might be possibilities."

"And the neighborhood really ain't too scary. There's a few rotten apples on every block. But you do a little background check, you could get you a decent tenant." Manning pulled out his handkerchief and swiped it over his forehead one more time. He took a step toward the door. "Well, you make yourself at home. I'll be outside whipping that yard into shape."

The door thumped shut as the old man let himself out, and Chris was alone in the house. His heart rate jumped again as he walked down the short hallway, toward the bedroom.

It was strange seeing the room so bare. Gone were the piles of stuffed animals, the mounds of clothes. And gone was that filthy bed, where Chris had allowed his body to be defiled. His teeth ground together at the memory. There were four divots in the carpet, marking the space formerly occupied by the bed. He stood at the center of the rectangular area marked off by these points and breathed in a lungful of the stifling, dusty air.

This was it, his Ground Zero. When the war against chaos was finally complete, and the dust had settled and been wiped clean, this would be the place for building a monument to man's eternal struggle. Closing his eyes, he imagined what such a monument might look like. Something simple yet striking. Clean lines and right angles. Gleaming gilt engraving of bold, all-capital print, proclaiming to the world that the only war that mattered had begun in this sorry hovel.

Chapter Eighteen: The Star-Crossed

The door leading from the living room to the garage was locked. George had kept it that way since he'd moved Kathy's things over from the storage unit. He didn't like to think about why he'd locked it or why he felt compelled to check it each night before he went to bed. Examining life's little obsessions when it came to writing a three dimensional character was one thing, but it was something else entirely when it came to his own life. Many people thought writers had to know themselves inside and out in order to write believable fiction. That always made George laugh. Writers were just as confused about life and the world around them as most people. So George kept that door locked. It was enough for him to know that the garage stirred in him some unexplainable dread. When he needed to get boxes out of there, he went to the front of the house and opened the garage door. He only did this during the day, when plenty of sunlight could flood into the dark space. A good dose of light dialed the dread down to a sense of vague uneasiness.

Thankfully, the boxes he was looking for were near the front of the garage. So far, it seemed that the police had been fairly diligent about getting the items into their correct boxes. He felt reasonably sure that he could trust the labels reading "Paperbacks" on the three large boxes. At least the contents didn't jingle or rattle when he picked them up.

He loaded them into the trunk of his car and closed the garage. Three more boxes out of there. It was slow progress, but progress nonetheless. He didn't consider that, at this rate, he'd still be selling off Kathy's junk well into next year. Like his silly fear of the garage, he didn't feel much like examining the long road ahead of him. The few AA meetings he'd gone to had hammered away at the idea of taking things one day at a time, and while George disagreed with much of what he'd heard at those meetings, he did agree with that part of the philosophy.

George parked the Chevy in front of the Primp 'n Perm (Barlow's Home for Chic, according to the sign out front). He couldn't help but smile. The building was actually painted hot pink. And open on a Sunday down here in God's country? These ladies were cutting-edge, indeed.

Luanne had given him her business card, telling him that although there were at present no male customers of the Primp 'n Perm, there was always a first for everything. George wasn't sure he was ready to put his hair into the hands of the three most fashionable ladies in Barlow, but he did want to pass along the boxes of paperbacks to Luanne. Selling them at the flea market would put him in direct competition with Luanne's enterprise. If she was indeed the pipeline for gossip in Barlow, George wanted to ensure that she only had good things to say about him. He may not have published a novel in years, but he still understood the importance of good PR.

A jingle bell atop the door announced his entrance into the building. Luanne was busy moderating a spirited debate among the two other employees and their customers about the age old question of whether or not Angelina Jolie was a better match for Brad Pitt than Jennifer Aniston. The overlapping voices fell silent as George entered.

"Hey, Mr. George. Feel like getting a haircut?" Luanne got up from her perch behind the front counter and joined him in the small foyer. "A little dye could turn all that grey into some highlights."

"No, I'm afraid I'll keep my grey for the time being. I feel like I've earned it." He smiled at the other ladies present and tipped an invisible hat. "Sorry to interrupt the caucus, and I promise I won't take too much of your time."

"No problem," Luanne said, her breath redolent of watermelon-flavored gum. "What can we do for you today?"

George told her that in the course of some house cleaning he'd come across three large boxes of books and thought she might like to have them. "I'd hate to take them to the flea market and sell them right next door to you. That's really your niche, and I'd feel bad butting in," he said.

"Oh, I'd love to have them. But Earl is always on me about bringing all those books into the house. Maybe I can take some for myself and take the rest to Mr. Talmadge over at the Book Nook?"

"They're yours to do with as you please as far as I'm concerned."

She slipped her arm through his and escorted him to the parking lot. "Let's go see what you got. This is like Christmas come early."

George had expected that she would transfer the boxes to her car, thank him, and that would be that. Instead, Luanne ripped open the packing tape on each box and began rifling through the contents. With blinding speed and precision, she sorted the books into three piles. These three piles went back into the boxes, the books now neatly arranged.

"These are the ones I've read and think I can sell at the flea market." She tapped the first box. "These here are the ones I haven't read yet. That last box is stuff for Mr. Talmadge. That way, I'm only bringing one box into the house. Earl can't really complain about that."

He helped her wrestle the boxes into her car, a bright yellow VW bug with a large pink flower painted on the hood. "You say there's a used book store in town?"

"Yeah, Mr. Talmadge's place down on Pleasant Street. Take Military Road all the way down to Luvene and take a right. Pleasant will be on your left."

"I might wind up giving him some business. I had quite a book collection at one time, but most of it got left behind up there in Wisconsin." He felt a quick sting of sadness, thinking back on the house he'd shared with Kathy. Browsing a used bookstore was the one time he found any common ground with her urge to purchase in quantity.

Luanne leaned back on her car. "So, did you ask Tate's mom out on a date? If not, you should. She's definitely interested in you, which is strange because I don't think I've ever heard of her going out with a man since her husband died. But I saw the way y'all looked at each other back at the flea market and then y'all went off together…"

George raised a hand to halt the torrent of words. "I did in fact ask Myrna Wilson out for dinner. But that's not news, is it? We already went out to eat together. You said so yourself."

"Oh, but dinner is a date. Going to the Pancake Hut, you can do that with anyone."

"Is that right?"

Luanne rolled her eyes. "Well, yeah."

George took a deep breath. He couldn't believe what he was about to say was really going to come from his mouth. "Luanne, don't feel like you need to spread this around to all your sources and contacts, okay? It's just two people with something in common going out for a nice meal."

"Stuff in common? Y'all hardly know each other."

She had him there. He and Myrna did hardly know each other. Their conversation had consisted of trivialities. They'd discussed the weather and the various vendors at the flea market. Myrna had brought him up to speed on local politics. She'd talked about how proud she was of her son, and even hinted that their relationship might be a little strained. He'd talked about hoping to get some writing done now that he was settled into his new house. But that was about it. Both of them seemed determined to avoid bringing up the spark that had almost visibly passed between them. It was as if they'd shared something sudden and intimate. Now they were too sheepish to look one another in the eye, much less talk about it. But what exactly was it that they'd shared?

"All the same, I'd appreciate it if you kept it under your hat," George said.

"I know what this is." Luanne bounced on her feet a couple times.

"Now, Luanne…"

"It's love at first sight!" She sighed dramatically, clutching her hands together beneath her breasts. "And you're afraid that Tate will give you no end of trouble if he finds out that you're stepping out with his mom. It's like Romeo and Juliet, except a lot older."

In truth, George hadn't even considered the sheriff's feelings. Now that Luanne had brought it up, he supposed that it might be a problem down the road. But just like his superstition about the door to the garage and the seemingly endless task of selling off Kathy's things, George thought it best to just take it one step at a time. After all, it was just one date, just dinner and maybe coffee and dessert afterwards. But if Luanne needed some extra motivation to not send the news of his social life rocketing through her grapevine, then so be it.

"That's exactly right," he said. "We're like a couple of star-crossed lovers, only older."

"That's so sweet!" Luanne looked as if she might cry. What she did, however, was sigh once more and bound back toward the salon.

"Hey Luanne, tell the ladies I've always been partial to Jennifer, myself," he called after her.

Chapter Nineteen: The Angler

Tate was pulling in the fish so easily that he actually quit worrying about whether or not his mother was buying cartloads of crap at the flea market. He even quit worrying about whether or not he'd catch a break in the Flannigan case. Instead, he just popped the top on a can of beer and watched Deputy Avery Cartwright continue his fruitless efforts. Tate had already hauled in two big catfish and a few bream that he'd thrown back. The few fish Avery had managed to hook were not much larger than the bait.

"I don't know how a fish so small could even swallow that cricket," Tate said.

Avery tossed back his latest catch and grabbed a beer from the cooler. "Man, maybe this fishing is just a white sport."

"Oh, I doubt your skin tone has anything to do with it. A poor craftsman blames his tools. Or his skin color."

Avery was the department's only black deputy and was also the closest thing Tate had to a real friend in the workplace. Although, when he was being honest with himself, Tate wasn't entirely sure that Avery didn't expect some career advancement in return for his friendship. It wasn't a very Christian way to think, but Tate knew most of his skill as a lawman came from considering the worst possible thing in every scenario. Expect the worst and you'll never be disappointed, he figured. But in Avery's six month tenure with the department, he hadn't been anything other than a good deputy and an equally good friend.

"How can I suck so bad at this?" Avery drank his beer and propped his rod against the side of the boat. "What do I want fish for anyway? I don't even like to eat fish. All those little bones can gag you, stick in your throat. And it stinks too, man. We should catch us some steaks instead."

"You want to catch cows?"

"Might be better than this."

"You catch a big fish, you could have it stuffed and mounted. Put it on your wall. Collect enough of them and you'll really have something."

"Collect dead fish?" Avery laughed. "Man, Latoya would have a fit if I tried to put that shit on the wall. She damn near exploded when I wanted to put up this neon Budweiser sign I got. Besides, I don't collect things. I hate clutter."

"You and me both. All that shit about how bachelors live in pig sties? I'm single and my place is pretty neat. I even dust every Sunday." He'd never actually admitted this. He knew that taking pride in his feather duster wasn't exactly manly, but the beer loosened his tongue.

"Well, I won't go so far as to say I actually dust. But those people that live in a house full of old newspapers and shit like that?" Avery shook his head. "I couldn't do it. I'd go crazy."

Tate was silent for a moment. No fish were attacking his hook, so he finished his beer, tossed the empty can back into the cooler, and grabbed another. He had the day off, so what the hell.

"My mother collects stuff," Tate said. It was the first time he'd unloaded this confession on anyone. He wasn't sure why he picked Avery for the honor. Tate had only known him these past six months, and they'd only been hanging out as friends for a couple of those. But who else would he tell? His social calendar was pretty empty. "You think a few stuffed fish is a collection of junk? Man, you have no idea. My mother, she collects *junk*. Stuff she'll never use, not in a million years."

"So what?" Avery said. "My momma collects copies of the Bible. She has a whole bookshelf full. A whole big bookshelf, nothing but Bibles. No way she'll ever read all them Bibles. They all say the same thing anyway. But it means something to her, makes her happy."

Tate gave Avery the full story, about how Myrna Wilson could have once been a candidate for the Housekeeper of the Century Award, so spotless was the Wilson house. Tate recounted how after his father and brother died, Myrna began hitting the flea markets and garage sales, gradually filling the house with loads of junk. Tate recounted the collections: magazines, books, children's shoes, teddy bears, bean bag animals, toy cars, ceramic angels, Barbie dolls, spatulas, scarves, wooden bowls, sunglasses, hats, license plates, glass jars, rubber ducks, commemorative plates, Christmas ornaments, lawn gnomes, clown figurines, and anything else that caught her eye. He told Avery about the garage so full of her collections that opening the door might cause an avalanche.

"Damn," Avery said.

"After Dale died, she kept his room exactly the way he left it. You know, I understand that. It's a pretty common thing, having trouble letting go. But that wasn't enough. She started out buying stuff that he would have liked. He was into Star Wars, so she'd buy action figures and stuff like that, put it in his room. He liked baseball, so she bought baseball cards."

"That's rough, losing a son like that."

"Yeah, but she's still got one son around. You'd think that would count for something."

Avery put up his hands. "Look man, I didn't mean nothing by that."

"Hell, that's okay. I didn't mean to pop off at you. This shit with the Flannigan case has me all stressed out." Tate checked his worm, cast his line out again, watching the ripples spread across the surface of Grouse Lake.

"You still liking George Young for being involved in that?"

Tate fiddled with his reel. "Probably not for the murder. He doesn't strike me as having the balls to do something like that himself. But you can bet your last dollar that he's involved. I just can't figure out how. And now this thing with my mom…"

"Never can have just one problem at a time, can you? Shit just piles up, huh?"

"I made her promise not to buy anything today, but I bet she's over there right now, at that damn flea market. She just can't stop herself." Tate pinched the bridge of his nose and squeezed his eyes shut. The worries that he'd banished by hauling in so many fish had come flooding back.

"You have any other kin around here? Maybe they can help," Avery suggested.

Tate reeled in his line, saw that the worm was gone from the hook. "No close family. Some distant cousins scattered around, but that's about it."

"Shit. What do you plan on doing?"

"Don't know. But I have to do something. She can't keep living like that." Tate baited his hook feeling guilty for unloading his worries on Avery. He prepared to cast his line and stopped. He tore the worm free from the hook and pitched it into the water. "Look man, I hate to cut this short, but I got to put in some hours today."

"No, it's cool," Avery replied. "I suck at this fishing shit anyway. Thanks for teaching me and all, but maybe I'm just not the fishing type."

"I'm sorry, normally this is a lot more fun."

"You got shit on your mind. Don't worry about it. Maybe we can try again next week. Besides, this way Latoya won't kick my ass when I tell her to clean and fry the fish I caught. And I won't have to lie to her about how good it tastes."

Tate fired up the boat's motor and took them to the shore.

Chapter Twenty: Myrna

Myrna had driven up to Little Rock to buy a new outfit. There was an Ann Taylor there, and those clothes just screamed "special occasion." And if her first date in years wasn't a special occasion, then nothing was. But after trying on a few dresses, she decided that her choices were much too formal and headed over to Old Navy instead. These clothes looked awful young, but she decided she didn't care. This upcoming date made her *feel* young, so she might as well dress to match it.

On the trip back to Barlow, she played rock music on the car radio.

Her heart sank when she saw the Dodge truck with the boat trailer parked in her driveway. Tate must have come back from his fishing trip early. Myrna stepped on the accelerator and sped the short distance to her house. The car hopped the curb as Myrna parked. Tate wasn't waiting on the front porch as he normally did.

"Oh no…Tate…" She released the buckle on her seatbelt and slid out of the car. The short walk to the front door felt like a march to her doom. Her hand trembled as she reached for the doorknob. She pushed the door open.

Tate had cleared enough space on the stairs to sit down. He was still dressed in his fishing clothes: a plaid shirt with the sleeves cut off, a pair of battered work boots, paint-stained jeans, and a sweat-ringed Razorback baseball cap pushed back on his head. His hands were balled into fists atop his knees. A mostly empty pint of whiskey sat on the stair between his feet.

"Son, how did you…" The question died in Myrna's throat when she saw her son's expression. The muscles of his jaw bulged from the sides of his narrow face, his mouth compressed to an angry slit.

"Jesus Christ and holy shit, Mom! This place is a disgrace!" Tate picked up a fistful of old *Reader's Digest* magazines and flung them in the air. "People don't live like this! They… just….*don't*."

"How did you get in here?" Myrna watched the magazines flutter to the floor around her.

Tate's eyes bulged in their sockets. "How did I get in here? I grew up in here. It's not right for you to keep me out like this. So I broke in. What are you going to do, call the law? I *am* the law."

He grabbed a nearby teddy bear and wrenched the head off its shoulders. He tossed the plush carcass over his shoulder.

Myrna recoiled at the fury contorting his face. She took an involuntary step back. "Stop destroying my things. Please, son."

He stood up, rising to his full six feet and three inches. His prominent Adam's apple bobbed up and down as he spoke. "How do you live like this? You can't even walk around in here with all this shit piled everywhere."

"Don't say that," Myrna snapped.

"Don't say what? That it's shit? But that's exactly what it is. What else would you call it, Mom?"

"My special collections! You don't know their value, because you can't see it. You can't feel it. But I can!"

Tate smashed his fist on the banister. "Collections of shit!"

He turned and stomped up the stairs, kicking things out of his way as he went. His incoherent shouts of rage seemed to shake the house. Myrna fled crying to the front porch.

Chapter Twenty-One: Avery

Avery was getting down to business with Latoya on the couch, expertly using the one-hand technique to unhook her bra while he kept one eye on the baseball game playing on the TV across the room. The broadcast went to commercial, so Avery turned his attention back to the task at hand. Latoya was pliant beneath him, and he whispered a few dirty words in her ear, which made her gasp and giggle. The game was back on, and Avery looked up as Latoya attacked his neck. She worked her way up to his ear and whispered something. Avery muttered a reply. Abruptly Latoya pulled away. She turned and looked at the TV then pushed him away.

"Were you watching the TV?" she asked, pulling her shirt closed.

"What?" Avery did his best to look indignant.

Latoya snatched her bra off the couch. "Don't you act all innocent with me. I saw you looking at it."

"Maybe I just checked the score, but it's not like I was watching it." He reached for her. "Look, I recorded it on Thursday and I've been trying to watch it for three days…"

"Wait a minute." Latoya slapped his hand away. "You were trying to look at a *recorded* game while we were about to do it?"

"Look, girl…"

She put up a hand to silence him. "Don't you 'girl' me, Avery. From now on, you want to get it on, you call up ESPN."

He watched her stomp out of the room then zipped up his pants and turned the TV back on. Latoya would calm down and decide that she wanted some attention after all in a couple hours. At three months pregnant, she was just more emotional than normal.

Then came the banging on the front door.

Avery sighed and tossed the remote aside. He slouched across the room to the front door.

Bart Stilwell, one of the other deputies was standing on the doorstep. Avery sighed again. He'd only been on the job in Barlow for six months, but it had been enough time to figure out that he didn't much care for

Brad Carter | 169

Stilwell or his buddy Lee Watkins. Neither of them had said anything directly to him (or course not; he could have kicked both of those pot-bellied rednecks into next week), but he knew their feelings about a black man living with a white woman. Avery had heard a comment during his first week when he was using the station house crapper. Watkins and Stilwell must have thought he was out of ear shot. Avery remembered the exchange:

Stilwell: *At least she's got a black name. What kind of white parents name their daughter Latoya. I mean, Latoya? What the fuck is that?*

Watkins: *The same kind raise their daughter to live out of wedlock.*

Stilwell: *Living in sin.*

Watkins: *They do that. Easier for them to walk away.*

Stilwell: *You ever hear the one about the definition of mass confusion? Father's Day in Memphis.*

Watkins: *Yeah, that's a good one.*

Avery had waited in the bathroom, taking deep breaths and counting backwards from ten until he heard them leave. He'd reminded himself that he and Latoya had a kid on the way and starting fatherhood as unemployed would be twice as bad as just letting it go. He was still trying to decide whether or not to bring it up with Tate.

Avery didn't invite Stilwell inside. "It's my day off, but please tell me what I can do for you."

Stilwell looked down at his feet for a moment then back at Avery. "Sorry to bother you, but I got this call about a disturbance over in the Maple Oaks subdivision. On Biscayne Avenue."

"I'm waiting for the part where you tell me what it's got to do with me."

"That's Myrna Wilson's address. The boss' mother."

"Yeah, he said they'd been having some problems."

"It ain't good over there. The boss has sort of popped his cork. One of the neighbors called in a complaint, said the sheriff and his mother were in some sort of shouting match. I figure we better get out there." Stilwell hitched his pants up under his beer gut. "I know y'all are buddies, and this might be delicate work."

Avery knew the question was bugging Stilwell: why was the sheriff such good friends with this black kid and not me?

"Sure, I'll come along." Avery leaned back inside to grab his keys. "Hell, I was just fishing with the man earlier today. He seemed a little distracted, but he didn't seem like he was about to go crazy. Had a few beers, but not enough to get drunk. He must have gotten down to some serious drinking."

Stilwell looked surprised. "Really? You went fishing with the boss? Out on his boat?"

"Yeah. Over on Grouse Lake. Didn't see the Sasquatch in the woods, but then again, we weren't really looking that hard. Don't all the deputies go fishing with him?"

He shouldered past Stilwell, not waiting for a reply.

Chapter Twenty-Two: Tate

"It's no wonder you can't find your phone," Tate said. "You could look for years and not find it in this mess."

He bulldozed his way up the staircase. Had he been sober, he'd no doubt have fallen. But drunkenness made him bold. He gripped the handrail so hard his knuckles popped, and tramped his feet down on whatever was in his path. Magazines and paperback books tore beneath his shoes. The sound of ripping pages didn't slow him. If anything, it spurred him on. He pumped his fists before him like a prize fighter as he crested the staircase. He stood in the cluttered hallway, wondering where he should start.

To his left was his mother's room. To his right were the three other bedrooms, one for each of the Wilson brothers and one that had been their father's home office. Dead ahead was a bathroom packed with unfolded towels, unopened cartons of beauty products. God knew what else was heaped on every available surface, including the floor. Even the sink was full of stuff.

"That's enough of this shit." He reeled from the alcohol he'd poured down his throat.

He went right, to his old bedroom. He had to put his shoulder to the door to open it. An avalanche of his mother's precious collectibles rumbled as he staggered into the room. His luck with keeping his balance finally ran out, and he went down hard on his rear, his head landing on a conveniently placed mountain of small beanbag animals. Rage rather than relief washed over him, and he lashed out at the beanbag toys as he struggled to his feet. He grabbed the edge of his old dresser for support and upset a mountain of comic books that slid to the floor.

The room in which he'd spent countless hours daydreaming as a boy was gone, buried under layers of yard sale and flea market curios. He thought of the PBS program he'd seen years ago about the destruction of Pompeii, how an entire city was buried under hot ash. His room was similarly destroyed. Maybe it still existed somewhere deep beneath all this worthless crap, but it would take serious excavation to unearth it.

He stomped back into the hallway. Dale's old room was next door, close enough that they tapped messages through their shared wall when they'd discovered Morse code via their Cub Scout troop. Tate took a deep breath and put his shoulder to the door of his brother's room. What he saw inside made his jaw drop open. Whiskey and resentment boiled through his veins.

Whereas his own room had been a riot of disorder, little more than a dumping ground for his mother's hoard, Dale's room was an orderly display of collectibles. It was cluttered, yes. It was packed full of enough things for five rooms its size. But there was an order that had been imposed upon it. The bed had been kept clear and was neatly made. The comic books and magazines had been neatly put away in boxes. The action figures and model airplanes were displayed in tight clusters on shelves. Baseball cards were mounted in neat frames on the walls. It reminded Tate of an absurdly overstocked collectibles store, one which had barely enough space to admit one customer.

His own room had been reduced to an above-ground landfill. Dale's had been made into a shrine for all the things the youngest Wilson brother had loved in life. Tate was still alive and in the same town, and his mother couldn't be bothered to take more than a passing interest. But Dale, dead and gone, was still her favorite. Dale, the sensitive one, the smart one, the athletic one. If there was ever any question about the favorite Wilson brother, it was now put to rest.

Tate lurched out of the room, feeling like he might puke right then and there.

"Tate! Please stop!" his mother called from downstairs.

He ignored her and ducked into the bathroom. He snapped on the light and shouldered the door closed. Walking into that space was like kicking through a snowdrift. He slogged ahead heavily, plastic bottles of lotion, shampoo, and whatever else piling up around his feet. His hands shook as he scooped out the contents of the sink, tossing the toiletries and knickknacks to the floor with their fellows.

Amazingly, the sink worked. The faucet sputtered, the pipes coughed, but the water ran clear when it finally came. A couple splashes against his face didn't do much for his nausea. The whiskey was kicking around in his belly, and he figured it would simply have to run its course.

There were magazines piled atop the closed lid of the toilet, and Tate knocked them aside. He pulled up the lid and crouched over the bowl, waiting for what he knew was coming. His stomach heaved, but nothing came up.

"Come on, come on, come on," he chanted, his eyes squeezed shut.

His mother was still calling to him, but her voice sounded distant and muffled. Tate slid to the floor, hugging the cold porcelain toilet for support. The room seemed to be revolving around him. He crossed his arms over the toilet and laid his head on them. The worst of the nausea had passed, but he wasn't sure that there wasn't more in the mail. Best to just wait it out. His mother would be pacing with worry by now. He didn't care. She'd brought this on herself.

The thought was petty and bitter, but it seemed to settle him somewhat. The world was still spinning, only now it was relaxing. Less like a roller coaster. More like being rocked gently to sleep. He *was* sleepy, now that he thought about it. His anger had taken a lot out of him. He closed his eyes, let the room spin him into relaxation.

Tate awoke with a sledgehammer headache and no idea how long he'd been out. It could have been seconds, or it could have been hours. He was afraid to open his eyes, knowing that even the soft light of the bathroom would be like a needle jammed into his brain. He groaned, leaning back against the wall and massaging his temples. The whiskey had really done a number on him. He steeled himself with a deep breath, opened his eyes hesitantly, and saw…nothing.

The room was pitch black. He looked to his left, where a sliver of light should have been leaking under the door. Nothing there but darkness. Maybe there was too much stuff piled in front of the door to admit any light. He *had* been pretty agitated when he kicked his way in here. But why was the light turned off? Maybe his mother had come in and seen him asleep against the toilet then turned off the light so he'd have some peace.

Tate shook his head. That didn't sound right.

His skull felt like it had been packed full of broken glass. He was paying the price, all right. Memories of the mornings after high school parties swam back to him through the agony.

He got to his feet, unsteady in the total darkness, stiff from sleeping in that cramped position. Pins and needles raced up and down his legs.

He leaned forward, hands outstretched to grab the counter and use it as a guide to the door. His hands encountered something other than the smooth surface of the counter. His fingers brushed against something papery to the touch.

What the hell?

He tugged his phone out of his pocket and turned on the display to use as a flashlight. And even that small light revealed enough for Tate to know that he was no longer in his mother's bathroom. The tub, sink, and toilet had been replaced by a maze of cardboard boxes stacked to the ceiling.

The disorientation was worse than the aftereffects of the whiskey. He decided that he was dreaming, still asleep on his mom's toilet while his brain turned cartwheels. It was probably his subconscious mind punishing him for losing control the way he had. Tate didn't go in for a bunch of psycho-babble theories of human behavior, but this was too obvious.

You've been feeling lost, what with the Flannigan case about to get kicked over to the state police without any leads and now this bullshit with your mom, so your brain has you stuck in this maze. Probably would take some head shrinker to figure out what the dark room meant. No doubt the doctor would come up with some sex metaphor. They were always doing that…

A faint scratching noise pulled Tate back to the situation at hand. He moved forward with small steps, sweeping his phone light around as he went, searching for the source of the sound. Claustrophobia was never something he'd seriously contemplated, but the sense of confinement—dream or not—that enveloped him made breathing difficult. His heart rate jacked up, and he could hear his pulse pounding away in the silence of the maze. He came to a T-shaped intersection and stopped.

Left or right? Too dark to flip a coin.

He decided to go left. He'd gone three steps down the narrow cardboard corridor when something slammed into his back with enough force to send him sprawling. It felt like he'd been kicked in the back with the largest available steel-toed boot. The air whooshed out of his lungs. The phone spun out of his hand, clattering across the floor.

Tate wished he'd been in uniform. He would have pulled his Maglite in one hand, his Glock in the other, and gotten very quickly to the bottom of just what the hell was going on here. But even his dreams were sources of frustration lately, and he was still wearing his fishing clothes. It occurred to him how unfair this whole thing was. This was *his* dream.

Shouldn't he get to decide what he wore? Only this was one hell of a vivid dream. Everything about it was so real. The hot, stale air was real enough to make him sweat. And the pain in this back, where he'd been kicked, was sure as hell real.

He rolled onto his back, peering into the darkness as he groped for his phone.

"All right, whoever you are," he said in his best peace officer baritone. "Step forward slowly and identify yourself. You've already got assaulting an officer on your tab. No sense adding to the bill. We can do this the easy way or the hard way."

Although he'd put as much authority into his voice as he could scrape together, he didn't feel very confident. For one thing, he was in complete darkness. And for another, he was unarmed. Whoever had planted that boot on his lower back could have been the size of a rhino and just as unpredictable. He told himself again that this was just a dream, that sooner or later he'd wake up. But the longer he sat there on the floor, the less dreamlike the situation became. The floor beneath him felt solid. The boxes around him felt real enough as he clutched them for support and got up from the floor.

Something emerged from the sea of darkness in front of him. It was like fog, low-hanging and creeping around the corner of the intersection where he'd been knocked down. Fog or mist or whatever it was, it gave off a faint glow. There was a main mass of the stuff, like a cloud, and it trailed little wispy strands as it moved. It carried with it the wet smell of mildew and stale attic air. It seemed to move with a purpose, gliding around the boxes toward Tate. He stepped back as it drifted nearer. Whatever the stuff was, he wanted no part of it.

Over the sound of his own double kick drum pulse and his ragged breathing, Tate heard a voice. It was raspy, choked, and distant, but he heard it all the same.

"Who's there?" Tate called.

"Even in this dead shell, I have returned." The voice was closer now. "And now I will reclaim what is mine. Behold!"

The thin wisps trailing from the dark cloud shot forward, wrapping around his ankles, dragging him back down to the floor. For something that appeared so insubstantial, the stuff had real strength. It coiled around his legs, holding him fast. Other strands shot up his pants' legs. It felt the way that it smelled: cold and clammy. Still more pieces separated from the cloudy mass and snaked around his wrists and across his belly.

Every bit of the authority had fled from Tate's voice as he screamed. His cries were cut short as another grey tentacle reached into his mouth. A salty, wetness spread across his tongue. He closed his eyes, tears streaming from their corners. He gagged. His stomach did its best to heave up its contents.

The raspy voice returned. "Look at me."

Tate shook his head furiously. He squeezed his eyes even tighter.

"Look at me," the voice commanded.

He felt wet pressure against his eyelids and knew that tendrils of solidified mist had attached themselves to his face. They pulled at his eyelids. He knew from the steady pressure that if he didn't obey, the lids might be torn from his eyes. He relaxed, allowing them to be pulled open.

There was enough of the glowing mist around him now that darkness had been replaced by a dim half-light. The mist parted, revealing a dark figure that stood at its center.

Tate could see that the figure was that of a woman. She was clad in a black, formless garment that was somehow even darker than the total darkness around her. She drifted closer, and he saw that the garment was less like something made of fabric than an oil-slick liquid that flowed over her body in a slow eddy. Tate shook his head. That didn't make sense. But then nothing about this dream—*and it was a dream, it had to be*—made any sense.

The muscles in his legs burned from the effort of trying to tear free. The woman in liquid black came closer and closer. As she neared, Tate saw that her face had been so distorted that it hardly resembled a human at all. Her face with its protruding jaw and flattened nose—had a rodent quality.

Tate tried to close his eyes as the rat-woman thing crouched over him and straddled his hips. Her knees pressed into his ribcage with such force that he was sure his bones would snap. Her fingers, unnaturally long and thin, threaded through his hair, her sharp nails digging at his scalp. The pain brought tears to his eyes.

She leaned down so close that her snout brushed the tip of his nose. "You must be made to see. I cannot be stopped."

With one finger, she scooped the substance clogging his mouth. Tate gagged as he felt it tear against his teeth. She tossed it aside, where it hit one of the boxes and dissolved into mist. Her black eyes shined in the dim light as she pressed her face closer and closer until her leathery lips pressed down on Tate's mouth. Her tongue, cold and slimy and vibrating, probed around his teeth and then slid down his throat.

He gagged and choked, straining his limbs against the bonds that held him. The tongue continued to travel into him. He could feel his stomach swell with it. And then, mercifully, he blacked out.

He awoke into another nightmare. He stood at the center of a sea of curios and keepsakes and collectibles of every stripe, an ocean of broken toys and outdated magazines that stretched to the horizon in every direction. It rose and fell with a symphony of clacking plastic and crinkling pages. The smell of old paper and mildew permeated the air. He sank, sucked down by the riptide of junk, tossed about like one of the ragdolls that swam through this ocean like schools of button-eyed fish. He paddled his arms and kicked his legs, but the things were piled so thick and deep about him that it was like swimming through quicksand. Each panicked movement drew him deeper. He sank to his waist then to his chest. Finally, only his head remained above the surface.

He screamed that he just wanted to wake up. He thrashed as he cried out. The frenzied motion sucked him under, into the depths of that awful sea, into the choking darkness, down and down as his face was battered by blunt plastic and torn by the sharp edges of paper.

178 | ONLY THINGS

Chapter Twenty-Three: Avery

Seemed like the boss had gone batshit crazy.

Avery got the rest of the story from dispatch as he drove to Myrna Wilson's house. It sure sounded like a hell of situations. And who was coming to the rescue? The newest member of the department, low man on the totem pole, and probably scapegoat Avery Cartwright. No doubt those idiots on duty today thought this was a situation that could go from bad to career-ending real fucking quick, and therefore, it was something better handled by someone who was too dumb to cover his own ass. Maybe he should have just told them that he was off the clock. But the truth was that the boss was his friend, and he owed it to him to get him out of this shit.

Tate's mama lived in one of those older neighborhoods where the houses were built to look like miniature plantations, with big front porches supported by white columns and long driveways snaking through oversized lawns. There was a weeping willow tree right there in the middle of all that green grass. One of those metal old-time Negro porters wouldn't have looked out of place. The house across the street had one.

Avery parked his truck and slid out. He hadn't bothered getting into his uniform. As far as he was concerned, he wasn't here in the line of duty. Sheriff Wilson was his boss, but Tate was just his buddy. And his buddy had gotten himself into a bit of a jam. Avery had just thrown on a pair of basketball shorts and an old Razorbacks t shirt, keeping it real casual. That made it easy to dispense with writing up reports should anything happen, because, hey, you just never knew with these family things.

"Afternoon, ma'am," he said, approaching the porch. The woman sitting on the steps looked distraught to say the least. He put on his best sympathetic smile. "I'm Avery, one of Tate's friends. He's told me an awful lot about you, and I wish I was getting to meet you under better circumstances."

She smiled up at him weakly. "He's mentioned you, too. The few times we've talked lately, that is. I'm glad to meet you. Tate doesn't have a lot of friends. Never has, really."

"Mind if I sit?"

"Go ahead."

He eased down on the stair beside her. "Want to tell me what's going on in there?"

She told him how she'd come home after running a few errands and found her son sitting inside the house. He'd been fairly drunk at the time and had started making all kinds of wild pronouncements before storming upstairs and locking himself in the bathroom. He'd damaged some property as well. Nothing big, just a few knickknacks, that sort of thing.

"I don't know what's gotten into him," she said.

"Would you mind if I go in there and see if I can't talk him down?" Avery asked

Her eyes were red from crying as she looked at him uncertainly. "I…I don't know. I'm not really comfortable having people in my house. I'm afraid I'm not much of a housekeeper."

"Neither was my mama. You should have seen how the dishes used to pile up. And dust bunnies? Not in our house. We had dust elephants." It was bullshit, of course. Lucille Cartwright kept plastic on the couch, blue disinfectant in the toilet bowl, and the whole house smelled like Pine Sol. But Tate's mama didn't need to hear that right now. "You know, the longer he stays in that bathroom, the harder it'll be getting him out of there. Before long, some of the other deputies—the ones on the clock and in uniform, you understand—they'll get here, and then the whole incident will get official. I know you and your son are having some disagreements, but you don't want this to escalate no further than it already has, right?"

She nodded, staring out at the lawn like that grass held all the answers. "Go on inside then. Just please, try to understand…"

"My mama didn't throw out a newspaper for going on fifteen years, I bet." More bullshit. His mama couldn't even stand a newspaper left on the breakfast table after the dishes were put up. They went into the magazine rack by his dad's recliner and stayed there until the next morning, when they got thrown out and replaced with that day's issue.

"Okay, go ahead. Just please…" She left that one hanging, showing him eyes full of tears and reluctance. "The bathroom's at the top of the stairs."

"Don't you worry none." Avery got up off the steps and pushed open the front door.

Two steps in and he'd already figured out that the boss hadn't exaggerated one bit about his mama's tendency to hold onto things. If anything, he'd undersold it. There was shit piled up everywhere, stacks of it on every available surface, seemed like. No wonder the boss was so pissed. It wasn't just messy in the house. It was dangerous. Never mind the fact that all the books and magazines and newspapers were a fire hazard, it was damn hard to just walk through the place.

"Sweet Jesus, would you look at this," Avery whispered.

Just walking up the stairs was a chore. He couldn't imagine being older and doing this every day. Tate's mama looked good for her age, even after she'd been crying, but even if she had Tate when she was young, she was at least fifty. Avery was only a month past his thirtieth birthday, and the ascent up the stairs was scary shit. He paused at the top to thank the Lord he hadn't broken his damn neck. After he'd talked Tate down—if he *could* talk him down—this little venture had damn well better put him in the good graces of the Gayler County Sheriff's Department for the remainder of the Wilson tenure. Not that Avery was the type to keep score, but still.

He knocked on the door. "Hey there, boss. Avery out here, just wondering if you were planning on staying in there all day. You eat some bad tacos or something?" He tried a laugh on for size and found it an awkward fit. "Seriously, man, you might think about coming out. Your mama's awful upset. I know y'all have your differences, but this ain't worth it."

Silence from the other side of the door. Shit. Of course this couldn't just be easy. Family problems never were.

He knocked again. "You okay in there?"

Still nothing but silence.

"Okay, look. Your mama called dispatch, so it's out there, you know. Maybe someone might be inclined to make this thing official."

Now he was starting to lose his patience. Tate was his friend and all, but there was only so far that Avery could be pushed. This was disgraceful behavior for a grown man, locking himself in the bathroom like some teenage girl. Once the boss had sobered up, he'd probably be ashamed. Avery put his shoulder to the door and forced it open.

The boss was slumped over the toilet, looking like a man having deep regrets about some serious drinking. It didn't take a veteran detective to connect the dots on this one. Something had snapped in the guy after he'd had a few. It was still disgraceful behavior, but understandable. As bad as the downstairs had been, the second floor was worse. It looked like the place had its own weather system and tornadoes rampaged through it daily.

He made his way through the trash covering the floor and squatted down by Tate.

"Hey, man. Time to wake up." Avery shook him gently.

Tate's eyes fluttered open. He groaned. "We have to stop it. She's going to kill us with all this stuff. We'll drown in it. Stuff everywhere, choking us."

Looked like the boss was going to need a few more hours of sleeping it off before he could get right.

"Sure thing, man. We'll get it cleaned up. Just not today." Avery grabbed him under his armpits and hoisted him up. He held onto him for a moment until he was sure Tate wouldn't fall.

"You don't understand." Tate shook his head. "She wants everything."

"I'm sure she does. Let's just get out of here, and you can tell me all about it." Avery used his patient voice, the one he reserved for sad drunks that he had to haul into the tank.

Now Tate's face grew tight. He let out an exasperated sigh. "She's *living* here. And she's somewhere else also. She was dead, but now she's in our world."

"Don't you worry, we'll get it taken care of. But right now, it's time to get you home and into bed. Been a hell of a long day."

Tate squared his shoulders. His eyes narrowed to slits. "Don't you patronize me."

"Look, man. I'm on your side here."

"Then you'll be happy to help me clean this up before it's too late."

There was a small window in the back wall, set about two feet above the toilet. Avery figured it was there so you could look out at the backyard while you were doing your business. Like in case you forgot to bring the sports section, you could watch the birds or the squirrels or whatever else was out there. Tate turned around and pulled this window open. There was a screen there, but he didn't even bother trying to open it. He just knocked it right out of the frame. Then he bent down and grabbed a stack of old magazines. They were the ones Avery usually saw women thumbing through while they waited in the checkout line at the grocery store: the ones with low-fat recipes, tips for the bedroom, and plenty of ads for makeup and sanitary napkins. Tate chucked them right out the window. He scooped up a handful of sample-size bottles of shampoo and conditioner then tossed them as well.

Avery put up his hands. "Easy now. You're making a mess of that backyard."

"We get rid of all this stuff, and then she won't be able to stay here." Tate sent another handful of stuff flying out the window.

Avery grabbed Tate by the shoulders, forcing him to drop his armload of empty Kleenex boxes. "I think you've put enough of your mama's stuff out on that lawn. You may not think much of it, but it is her stuff. And this is her house."

It wasn't that Tate's fist was like a battering ram. But the shock of the blow having been delivered at all knocked Avery off his feet. He threw out his arms to break his fall and grabbed the shower curtain, tugging it free as he went down on his ass. Anger like an electrical shock coursed through him, but he tamped it down, telling himself that there was something wrong here, something more than a guy chugging down a few too many drinks. There was an unhinged look about the boss as he worked at a frenzied pace, slinging things out the window by the armload. And all the nonsense he was talking? It was like he'd blown a fuse or something.

"Sorry about that," Tate said over his shoulder. "But I can't put this off any longer."

Avery got up, working his jaw where the punch had caught him. "And I don't think I can put this off either. Sorry, man."

"Huh?"

Tate paused for moment as he stood with another handful of stuff. That gave Avery the opening he needed. He dropped his shoulder and swung his fist into Tate's stomach. The fight went out of him right along with his breath. He sank down to his knees, one hand clutching his stomach and the other holding onto the toilet for support. He hung his head over the bowl and vomited.

Avery recoiled at the sight of his boss puking. The stuff running out of his mouth just didn't look right. Instead of a mostly recycled version of the sausage biscuits they'd eaten this morning at Grouse Lake, the stuff pouring out of Tate was like nothing Avery had ever seen. It was a thick grey substance that poured out of Tate's mouth in thick ropy clots.

And it just kept coming. Avery thought it might go on forever, the strange grey goo flooding out of Tate until his body shriveled into a dry husk.

Finally, it stopped. Avery winced as he watched Tate slump sideways then fall to the floor. Avery stood there watching, half expecting the boss to start vomiting again. He glanced over at the toilet. It was full nearly to the brim.

Should he flush it? Avery reached out tentatively. He paused with his fingers on the lever. No telling what that stuff might do to the plumbing. But he couldn't just leave it there for Tate's mama to find either. He sure didn't feel like explaining that one. There was a plunger on the other side of the toilet, and he snatched it up, holding it at the ready as he flushed. The grey goo gurgled and swirled around the bowl, going down the pipes with no trouble. But as it circled around the bowl, patterns rippled through its surface. It was moving so fast that Avery couldn't be sure, but he could have sworn that the ripples and bubbles converged for the tiniest fraction of a second into something recognizable: the horribly disfigured face of a woman. Then just as fast as it had appeared, it was gone.

He blinked his eyes, sure that he'd been hallucinating.

A little cold water splashed on his face brought Tate back to the bright side of consciousness. He looked up at Avery and made a face.

"What…what the hell happened to you?" Tate slurred. "Look like you got into a fight."

"Yeah, I got sucker punched." Avery offered his hand to help him to his feet.

"Really? Give me a minute to get my shit together and we'll go arrest the asshole." He peered at his face in the mirror and winced. "Who was it anyway?"

"Someone above the law."

He cut his eyes in Avery's direction. "Oh man, no way. I mean, I was sure drunk…I think I'm still drunk…but there's just no way…"

Avery slapped him on the back. "Believe it. But don't feel too bad. That pain in your gut ain't just those sausage biscuits fighting it out with the whiskey. I gave you a pretty good shot in the belly. Wasn't much fight in you after that."

Tate leaned down near the faucet so he could splash more water on his face. He came up looking just as haggard, only this time he was wet from his scalp to his chest.

"Think I've told you before that I'm not much of a drinker, that I avoid spirits pretty much altogether." He looked around in vain for a clean towel. "This here is why I have that light beer only policy. I remember coming in here so I could have a talk with Mom about the state of the place. One good look around and I decided I needed a drink or two, so I went out for a pint of Wild Turkey. Next thing I know, I'm stomping around up here, cussing at the top of my lungs. Then I got to feeling like I might puke, so I fought my way into this bathroom and locked the door."

"That's it? That's all you remember?"

Tate tugged the bottom of his shirt up to his face and wiped away most of the water. "Well, I had some pretty wild dreams while I was out."

"You were talking some pretty crazy shit when you woke up."

"There was this woman…." Tate shook his head. "There was something wrong with her face, like she wasn't human. I think she lived in this house…or maybe she was trying to get in…I don't know. Like I said, I was pretty damn drunk."

Avery looked at him. "That's it?"

"What? The damage I did here ain't enough for you?"

Avery shrugged it off. "You better get downstairs and make your apologies to your mama. Wouldn't surprise me none if some of the other guys are out there too, so try your best to look normal. Last thing we want is people getting the idea that you're doing a perp walk or something."

Tate nodded, and they each took a deep breath, bracing themselves for the treacherous descent of the stairs.

They passed Tate's mama on the way out of the house. She was still sitting on the front porch, tears leaking out of her eyes. Tate mumbled something in the way of an apology, but let himself be led to his truck.

"You okay to drive?" Avery asked.

"Yeah, I think so." Tate fished his keys out of his pocket. "I just feel really tired."

"How about I follow you home just to make sure?"

"Okay. But I'll be fine."

Avery watched the sheriff climb into his truck then waved to Mrs. Wilson. She raised a shaky hand and waved back.

Brad Carter | 185

Chapter Twenty-Four: Ray

Ray was three days into the sick leave he'd taken from his constable post and feeling like very little progress had been made. Whatever psychic abilities he possessed hadn't come to the fore, even with Stephanie's relentless prodding. She said that it would happen, that he just had to be patient. She said that it would be like a light switch being flipped. One second, he'd be regular old earthbound Ray McFettridge, and the next, he'd be in tune with the spirit world or some such. Ray thought himself a patient man. But this process was testing that notion.

The sun wasn't up yet, but he was already on his second cup of coffee. He felt lucky to have snagged a little sleep. Lately, that was as good as it got.

Part of it was having a houseguest. He didn't realize how accustomed he'd become to being alone until Stephanie had packed up a couple of suitcases and followed him from Memphis to Edgewood. Now there was another physical presence in the house. The guest bedroom wasn't just some place to vacuum once a month, and the other bathroom wasn't just a convenient place to take a leak without walking all the way down the hall to his bedroom.

The other part was harder to define. It was just some vague gut feeling that they were running out of time with this project. Something was drawing near, and he'd either be ready or he'd end up dropping the ball in a big way.

"You're up early," Stephanie said as she bustled into the kitchen.

Barely five in the morning and the woman was already dressed and had her makeup on.

"Couldn't sleep. Besides, this is a working vacation, right?" He got up from the kitchen table and started rummaging around in the refrigerator for breakfast makings. There were eggs and cheese, onions, and peppers to go with them. "I got to tell you, though, if we don't have some sort of breakthrough today, I might decide to call this whole thing off."

She poured herself a cup of coffee. "Still having those nightmares?"

"Nightmare. Not plural. It's the same one every night." He fired up the stove and set a skillet on the burner. "Claustrophobic to say the least, and then that woman…"

"We're going to have a crack at something new today."

He finished chopping the vegetables and threw them into the skillet. "Good. I don't think I can take any more chanting and meditation and staring at crystals."

"Okay, smartass. Remember you're the one who asked for my help. I can go back to Memphis whenever you want."

Her voice had an edge to it that made Ray lift his hands in apology. "You're right. I'm sorry. Just hope we'll get somewhere is all."

So far, all they'd managed to do was give him a headache after hours of peering into a pair of crystals. Stephanie was hard at work on that pile of books Ray had pulled out of the attic, reciting relevant passages to him and explaining some of the terminology. But they weren't a bit closer to figuring out a damn thing. Percy Flannigan's murder was still under investigation—now by the state police and the honest-to-God FBI. And Ray's own theory—that George Young was somehow involved without his own knowledge—was beginning to look more and more absurd.

"Here's a thought." Stephanie joined him at the counter and started cracking eggs into a bowl. "Maybe you should just talk to this George Young guy. Tell him straight up that you think he's involved. You know, do your bad cop routine and get the guy to crack."

He handed her a whisk and she went to work beating the hell out of the eggs. "I don't want to spook him. We read about poltergeists in that one book, remember? If it's something like that following him around, we're likely to set it off."

"You think it's a poltergeist?"

"Hell, no. But you keep telling me to keep an open mind." He took the bowl of eggs and poured them into the skillet. "I'm afraid if we go in without at least some hint of a sound theory, we're going to sour the whole thing. When I talk to him, I want my ducks all in a row."

"Fair enough."

Stephanie had told him his psychic ability was ingrained, that he couldn't have gotten rid of it if he tried. Thing was, through skepticism and booze and downright stubbornness, he'd been applying layers of duct tape over its mouth for years. It was going to take a whole lot of cutting to get through those layers, and the last few days had been spent trying to find the right knife for the job. When it finally happened, she'd assured him, it might not be pleasant, but it would be powerful.

She'd asked him dozens of times if he was sure he wanted to do this, if he was sure he wanted to embrace the power that had put him into the mind of Steven Lovelace for two weeks. Ray had thought long and hard about that one. In the end, he came to one simple conclusion: he'd wasted much of his life. He'd been an average student with little ambition. He'd lucked into the alarm business more than anything. And what had he done? Drank until his wife left him. Selling off the company and getting elected to a constable post that was so low paying and such a pain in the ass that he ran unopposed in the last two elections. In short, he'd wasted his talent. It might have been a little late to start making up for that waste, but he'd be damned if he wasn't going to try.

He toasted up a couple pieces of sourdough bread and smeared them with some strawberry jam he'd bought at the church bake sale. Alongside the eggs, it looked like a decent breakfast. They carried their plates to the table and chowed down.

"So, what's on the agenda for today?" he asked.

"I thought we could try the Ouija board." Stephanie put up a hand before he could protest. "I know it's corny as hell, but I figure it's worth a shot. You know what I've been telling you, how all this stuff with the crystals and everything is just a way to focus your mind? Well, same thing with the board. You have one hanging around, don't you?"

"Why the hell would I have one hanging around?"

"You don't have to sound so offended. We can get one at the toy store, I imagine."

"We're going to focus my mind to enter the ethereal realm with something we can pick up in the toy aisle of Walmart?" Ray wiped the last of the toast crumbs from his mouth. "Forgive me for remaining skeptical."

"You still think this is funny on some level. It's not. Those dreams you've been having aren't just run of the mill nightmares, you know. That's your instinct waking up, trying to tell you something."

Ray sighed. "Thing is, I feel like a character in one of George Young's novels. Of course, those old writers and professors that he wrote about always had such an easy time adjusting when things got strange. Even though I know all this shit is real and I've actually experienced it firsthand, it still seems whacky."

"Where'd you pick that term up? The ethereal realm?" Stephanie asked.

"It was in one of George Young's books, *The Haunting of Harlow Manor*. Pretty scary stuff. I read it back when I was taking classes at the junior college. Think I studied his novels harder than my textbooks. Mom read his stuff too. Funny little coincidence."

"Maybe it's not coincidence that he's here." She gave him a pointed look.

"He's a hardcore skeptic. Said supernatural stuff made good stories, but that didn't make it real."

"Inspiration comes from somewhere," Stephanie said. "Even if he thinks he just wrote that stuff at random, his books sound awful damn accurate. You see any other fiction books in your mother's things? She usually read romance paperbacks. Never went in for that Stephen King stuff. There had to be something in Young's books that struck her as useful."

Ray slumped down in his chair and pinched the bridge of his nose between his thumb and forefinger.

"What?" Stephanie asked.

"Do you ever stop and look around, really think about the things you're doing and the things you're saying, and then wonder how the hell your life got to that point?"

She paused. "No, not really. Why?"

They had to drive all the way to Little Rock to find a Ouija board. The Walmart in Edgewood didn't carry them, and the Toys 'R Us in Benton only stocked them around Halloween. There was a novelty shop in southwest Little Rock called Crazy Eddie's that had two different models, and Ray deferred that decision to Stephanie, figuring that she had more experience in such matters. She chose the one made by Parker Brothers.

"So the people that make Monopoly also make the tool that's going to help flip my psychic switch?" Ray asked as they climbed into his car.

Stephanie reached behind him to put the board in the backseat. "I told you that it's not so much the board as the person using it. Besides, this one has a cool box. The picture on the back, those people look like they're having a blast with it."

Ray gave her a look.

"What?" she asked, poking him in the ribs with an elbow. "Part of your problem is that you're trying too hard. You need to remember that you're a natural at this. It's not something you need to stress out over. Just open up and let it come in."

"I thought you told me to quit being a smartass. Now you say I'm trying too hard."

"Loosening up and not being an asshole are not mutually exclusive."

"It's just that you make it sound so easy." Ray winced as his voice crept dangerously close to whining.

"Well, it should be. You're *making* it hard," Stephanie said.

They stopped for lunch at Fred's Fish House, and engaged in a battle to determine who could consume the most catfish. They decided to keep score, and that the loser would pick up the tab for the meal. In the end, Stephanie came out ahead, and Ray blamed his loss on the numerous hushpuppies he consumed along with the fish.

"That's your own damn fault," Stephanie said, watching him dig out his wallet. "They put those out to distract you from the fish."

"I'll keep that in mind for the rematch."

"Rematch hell! I don't even want to look at another piece of fish for at least a couple months. And certainly not now that I've given away my secret strategy."

Ray settled the bill, laughing the whole while. It was nice to smile and carry on. Just being away from Edgewood for a few hours had done him a world of good. Stepping outside that house where he'd been slaving away like some old time apprentice was like being underwater for a long time and finally coming up for air.

As they left the restaurant and walked across the parking lot, some of that good cheer went out of him. They had to go back, after all. And he had to get cracking again, trying for that elusive breakthrough. If it didn't happen soon…well, what then?

"You've got that look again," Stephanie said.

Ray drove out of the parking lot and back onto the road towards Gayler County. "What look?"

"Like you're having doubts. I may not have the same psychic abilities as you or your mother, but I read people for a living. So don't act like you're not an open book to me."

"I just wish I knew what the hell I was doing."

She laughed. "Hon, that's just life, ain't it?"

Conversation dwindled as they neared Edgewood until all talk gave way to a duel of barely stifled yawns. The lunch sitting in Ray's belly was making him tired, and he didn't have to possess Stephanie's fine-tuned intuition to know that she was suffering the same effects. Even with the air conditioner going full blast, he was still feeling just as heavy as if he'd been out in the summer heat.

"Listen, I know we talked about hitting it pretty hard today," he said, "but I need at least a few hours off. I'm so tired right now that it'll be a wonder if I don't fall asleep at the wheel."

She yawned again. "I hear you loud and clear."

One problem: tired as he was, Ray couldn't sleep. He half suspected that he was just too afraid he'd have the nightmare again, but it was hard to admit that to himself. He slipped out of bed and stepped back into his jeans and old tennis shoes. His t-shirt was wrinkled from lying in bed, but he didn't suppose changing it was going to win him any fashion contests.

Stephanie was sawing logs in the guest bedroom. Even with the door closed, he could hear it. The woman could snore like nobody's business.

There was a cold can of Coca Cola in the refrigerator. Ray popped it open and took a long slug, wincing as it burned on the way down. Now *this* would be a good occasion for a glass of whiskey. Even something cheap that he could mix into his Coke would do just fine. A little drink to take the edge off.

And that's how it always starts. One little drink will become five or six stiff ones, and next thing you know, you'll be stewing in your own juices, too pissed off to think straight and too drunk to care.

He took another drink of soda and sat down at the kitchen table. The Parker Brothers Ouija board was in the middle of the table, still in its plastic shrink wrap. It looked absurd, like the child's toy that it was. Ray guessed it was no more absurd that the crystals and the tarot cards and all the rest. Stephanie wanted him to keep an open mind, and he really was trying. But what if he didn't have any gas left in the old psychic tank? What if he was like a volcano that had erupted once long ago and fallen dormant for the rest of time? Stephanie said that his ability couldn't fade, but how did she know for sure? The smiling faces of the séance participants on the Ouija board box seemed to mock him. He snatched his car keys off the counter and left the house with no particular destination in mind.

He drove around aimlessly for a while, burning up gasoline and listening to the radio, before he wound up at Barlow's literary epicenter.

The Book Nook was one of those used book stores that defy the laws of physics, seeming to have a great deal more room inside than the dimensions of the building should allow. The squat cinderblock structure didn't look like much, but the interior was honeycombed with enough sagging shelves to occupy a building twice its size. The sign out front indicated that Larry Talmadge, the aging hippie who owned the place and was its sole employee, had been in business since 1979. How such a place had remained in business for over thirty years in Barlow, a place in which books other than the Bible were regarded with deep suspicion by most residents, was one of the mysteries of the universe. Tate Wilson had once suggested that it was probably a money laundering front for Talmadge's marijuana operation.

Ray pushed through the front door and was instantly assaulted by the patchouli scent of the incense that Talmadge burned constantly. Sitar music jangled through the overhead speakers. Talmadge was seated behind the counter, his sandaled feet thrown up beside the cash register, his eyes hidden behind a pair of wire-rimmed black shades. Standing beside the counter was George Young. The two broke off their conversation as Ray walked in.

Ray covered his shock by smiling. "Well, if it isn't our local author. Written anything good lately?"

George returned the smile. "And if it isn't the cop with the good taste in books. Yes, I guess you could say I'm taking baby steps toward getting something down on paper."

"Good to hear. I see you've discovered the cultural center of Gayler County."

Talmadge rummaged around on the desk. "I got to write that one down, man. Put it on the sign out front. Cultural center, I like that."

"I take it that you're a regular?" George asked.

Ray explained that he came in once or twice a month to buy a load of paperbacks. Once he'd read them, he donated them to the Gayler County Library. Probably some of them made their way back to the Book Nook shelves.

"It's sort of like the water cycle. If I don't remember whether I've read it or not, I might buy it again. My bad memory might be the backbone of this little economy that he has going here," Ray said, pointing to Talmadge.

"Guess I could think of worse economies to prop up," George said.

There were some trashy romance novels on a rack near the counter, and Ray scooped them up for Stephanie. When they took breaks from their psychic pursuits, he noticed that she usually stuck her nose in something with Fabio on the cover. Maybe she'd read these, but at a buck apiece, it was hard to worry about that. And getting a few right here at the counter meant not having to brave the Romance section in the back corner.

"Broadening your horizons?" Talmadge asked.

"I'm a bit old for that, don't you think? No, these are for a friend."

"No shame in it if they're for you, man."

Ray started to feel a faint itch way up in his nose, like the world's biggest sneeze might be building. The tingling felt like it was jammed way up in his sinuses, almost to his brain. And rather than traveling down into his nose, it seemed to be climbing deeper into his head. He wiped at his nose furiously for a few seconds then forced himself to stop.

"Excuse me." He snorted sharply. "Must be the incense."

Talmadge looked offended. He pulled the smoldering stick from its little holder and extinguished it with two spit-slicked fingers. "Hey, you guys going to be here for a few minutes? I could use a little bathroom break. Watch the store for me, huh?"

"What do we do if someone wants to buy a book?" George asked.

Talmadge laughed as he disappeared into the labyrinth of shelves. "Yeah, okay," he called over his shoulder.

Ray shifted his weight from foot to foot. The itching in his skull was maddening. He remembered some old episode of *Night Gallery* about an earwig that burrowed into a guy's brain, driving him crazy. He held the bodice ripper paperbacks in his hand with a death grip.

"Looks like that incense really got to you," George said.

"Yeah, maybe I'm allergic." Ray gestured at the stack of books on the counter. "You pick out some good ones?"

George nodded. "I didn't pack a lot of my books. You know, I took my wife's stuff because I'd made her a promise. Long story there. Anyhow, her stuff took up most of the space in the U-Haul, so a lot of my own stuff went by the wayside. But now, I have all this space for bookshelves, so I'm restocking."

Ray rubbed his forehead. The poison ivy itch had set up shop in there. He began to wonder if the big sneeze ever manifested itself, would it send his brains spraying out of his nostrils like ropy grey snot? Would he be dehydrated after the blast? The hairs in his nasal passages seemed to be on fire, blazing a trail straight up to his frontal lobe. It was, in a word, maddening. He squeezed the paperbacks in his hand like they were one of those stress-relief balls.

"Are you sure you're okay?" George put a hand on Ray's shoulder.

"Oh yeah, Talmadge's incense gets me every time." This was a lie, pure and simple. Ray was in the Book Nook every couple weeks, digging through the paperbacks, and although he found patchouli to be stinky, he'd never had any sort of allergic reaction before.

The itch was so bad that it was making his ears ring. He fished his wallet out of his back pocket and took out some bills. He took a deep breath and managed a few words about how Talmadge could keep the change and how he'd be seeing George around.

"You go home and take some Benadryl," George said.

"Fresh air," Ray wheezed as he banged through the door. "Some fresh air is all I need."

The typically soupy atmosphere of an Arkansas summer greeted him. He sucked in great gulps of air, blowing them out through his nose. It was a lot of effort for nothing. The itch remained firmly planted beneath the bones of his face. Little motes of black swam across his vision, like he'd been rubbing his eyes. He gripped the books in his hand and put one foot in front of the other, crossing the small gravel parking lot with the sort of fierce determination he'd seen in documentaries about the men who explored the Antarctic.

Once he was in his truck, things improved somewhat. The itching subsided to discomfort rather than agony. He fired up the engine and put the air conditioner on full blast. The rush of cool air was bracing. He wrestled his cell phone out of his pocket and dialed Stephanie. It rang through to her voice mail.

"Listen, Stephanie, it's either happening right now or I'm about to have a heart attack," he said when prompted by the beep. "Might want to fire up that Ouija board."

He tossed the phone onto the passenger seat with the paperbacks and got the hell out of there.

Although AR-421 was a straight shot from Barlow back to Edgewood, Ray kept to the back roads, those two-lane blacktop county roads with numbers rather than names. He figured if some spell or fit was coming on, the last thing he wanted to do was jerk the steering wheel and send the truck into the wrong lane, where he'd no doubt get himself or someone else maimed or killed. Instead, he whizzed past the soybean farms on the outskirts of town. He had the radio cranked up, hoping that some loud rock music would give him some sort of focus. Bachman Turner Overdrive started taking care of business on KRCK, and Ray did his best to keep it between the lines. His eyes began to water as BTO stepped aside to make room for The Who and their magic bus.

Ray almost laughed. Isn't that what he was preparing to do, climb aboard a magic bus and take a ride?

He stepped down on the accelerator. If he could keep his speed up, he'd be home in fifteen minutes. But those fifteen minutes might as well have been fifteen hours. His body seemed determined to do its best to prevent him getting there. Tears continued to drip down his face, and the little spots still danced at the outside edges of his vision, reducing his sight to a narrow tunnel. He ripped off his sunglasses and wiped at his face with a tissue, but the more he scrubbed, the worse his eyes became. A steady stream of commercials poured out of the radio, loud voices hawking used cars and light beer and fast food. The DJ came back on and mentioned that caller number seven would get a pair of tickets to a tractor pull and monster truck show in Jacksonville. He introduced a pair of back to back ZZ Top songs. Billy Gibbons sang about a sharp dressed man and then how he needed to be taken downtown for some tush. Tammy from Bryant snagged herself a pair of tickets to the monster truck rally. And Ray's head kept itching and leaking and spinning.

He pulled into his driveway with a fishtail of gravel announcing his arrival. His right foot aimed for the brake but missed, stamping down hard on the accelerator. The big oak tree in the front yard halted his progress and smashed out the left headlight for good measure. He got the door open by shoving it with his shoulder and slumped out onto the grass. Overhead the clouds moved listlessly across the bright blue sky, and Ray watched them as he lay there. One of them looked almost like an elephant, and wasn't that funny? Distantly, he heard the front door of the house open and slam shut. And maybe that was Stephanie's voice calling to him.

Chapter Twenty-Five: Chris

Chris jumped out of bed and ran for the shower. It was Wednesday, one day closer to the weekend, when he was free to go hunting again.

After he bathed himself thoroughly, he popped two tablets of something called Stay Sharp. He'd bought them from a truck stop out on Highway 10. They were marketed for long haul truckers who needed to drive all night, but Chris had figured they'd suit his purposes just fine. Two tablets in combination with a pot of coffee would perk him up sufficiently.

He'd stopped sleeping normally last week. The way he saw it, sleep was a waste of time, minutes and hours and days that could be spent fighting the good fight. Now he limited his nightly rest to four hours. And that wasn't exactly wasted time either. His dreams were not so much nightly excursions into the musings of his subconscious as they were planning sessions for his ongoing battle against the Chaos. Each night, when he closed his eyes, he conferred with his other self, that version of Christopher Wayne Clanton who lived in a separate universe, where Order had triumphed and the world was born anew in a glorious utopia of clean surfaces, right angles, and thorough hygiene. This Chris wore a flowing mane of golden hair, and his body was a perfectly toned suit of muscular armor. But he shared Chris' features, and he spoke with Chris' voice. Chris called him the Golden Knight of Perfection, for surely one who had remade his entire world in his own image could be nothing short of perfect.

The Golden Knight, with his smooth, hairless skin and his clean scent, had become something of a role model. This satisfied Chris greatly. In a way, he was now his own ideal, his own lord and master. He'd been liberated from the mundane world of mess and clutter, free now to shape his world according to what he knew was best. Each day was exhilarating.

He arrived at the library while the stars were still in the sky. He was, of course, the first person to arrive for the day, and he'd be alone in the building for hours. This was all according to the Golden Knight's plan.

The war against Chaos must start at home, he had said. *You must impose glorious, strident organization on every aspect of your own life. If you turn a blind eye to mess and filth, you are no better than the unwitting agents of Chaos that you have rightfully dispatched.*

Chris had taken the lesson to heart, scrubbing his already clean apartment with bleach and antibacterial soap. He'd even washed the ceiling. But he knew that it was not enough to sanitize his living space. His workspace was also his responsibility, and for too long, the library had been a filthy place. The janitorial staff only made vague gestures at cleaning. If they managed to empty all the trash cans and keep the bathrooms supplied with toilet paper, they'd exceeded expectations.

Mess reigned supreme. Sure, the books were neatly aligned on the shelf and in good order (at least in the sections Chris shelved), but the workspaces were cluttered and disorganized. People that worked in the library shouldn't be so slovenly. And the worst offender was their leader, the director of the branch, Effie Landeros. Her desk was a riot of loose paper clips, uncapped pens, stacks of periodicals, and computer print outs. The calendar on the wall behind the desk still displayed last month. The books on her shelves were arranged with little thought. It was disgraceful, disgusting, and sad.

Chris' father used to say that a fish rotted from the head down. If a person was going to lead, that person should do so by example. If that example showed that it was okay to have a messy office, how long before the library's other employees began to let things slide? Where would it end? In complete disregard for the Dewey Decimal System? In a smelly staff who didn't care one jot for the rules of basic human cleanliness?

Not on Chris Clanton's watch.

He crouched before the door to Effie's office. It wouldn't take him long to pick the lock.

The work day went much like any other. Working at the library was as close as one could get to living the same day over and over again. With few exceptions for special events and projects, a Friday in June wasn't substantially different from a Tuesday in December. The same people came in with the same questions and problems. It was an endless parade of routine, a quality that Chris appreciated. After all, what was routine if not a manifestation of order? Knowing most of what the day held before he even started it was as comforting as a warm blanket on a cold night.

He was nearly finished shelving a cart of books when Effie tapped him on the shoulder.

"When you finish shelving those books, I need to see you in my office," she said.

"Your nice, clean office, you mean?" Chris gave her his most winning smile.

"Yes, that's right. I'll need to see you in my nice, clean office."

"Of course."

Chris watched her walk back through the stacks. She was a short, powerfully built woman. He'd heard that she'd served in the army before she became director, and he didn't have a hard time believing it. She looked like she could hold her own. Plus, she was a no-nonsense type. No flashy clothes or ridiculous shoes or overly made-up face for her. On one hand, she cut a figure of military precision. On the other, she clearly had little regard for order in her personal space. The contradiction bothered him. Contradictions were the enemy of order. They were things that couldn't be neatly categorized and put into little boxes. Chris liked categorization. He liked little boxes.

He tried to keep his attention where it belonged—on getting the books properly aligned—but his mind kept returning to Effie. She hadn't seemed angry when she'd asked to speak with him. She'd even told him to finish his cart of books before coming to her office. If she wanted to berate or chastise him, wouldn't she have insisted on his dropping everything and coming at once?

Maybe she's come around. Maybe, after all these long months of her tenure as director, she's come to see your value.

Chris paused with his hand halfway to the shelf, a volume of cat mystery stories in his grip. Now there was a thought.

Maybe she's figured out that there's a war being waged between Chaos and Order. Maybe she's decided it's time for her to choose a side.

This thought excited him. So far, he'd planned on fighting this war by himself. Even his own brother was allied against him. The idea of having someone to stand by his side while he did battle was enough to make his hands shake. Of course, those tremors could also have been the Stay Sharp and the coffee. He'd had more than enough of each.

He shelved the book then clenched his jaw hard enough to make his neck hurt. In his daydreaming, he'd put the book in the wrong place. He *never* did that. For the remainder of the hour (or however long it took him to do the job *correctly*), he'd have to put his daydreams about Effie out of his head. He allowed his jaw to unclench and took a deep breath. Shelving the books took every bit of his concentration, but he saw it through by making a deal with himself. He could pause between each book to consider the pros and cons of sharing his crusade with Effie.

A book went onto the shelf…

His dream of standing alone against the Chaos would never come true if he had another person by his side. But then again, this was such a hard battle to fight by himself.

Another book in its proper place…

It was a well-known fact that bonds formed in the heat of war were especially close ones. Effie might want to seal their bond with a physical act that led to the emission of so many disgusting fluids. Perhaps he would have to endure another messy coupling of body parts in the name of the good fight.

Another book shelved in good order…

On one hand, Effie had served in the military and undoubtedly had tactical expertise far exceeding the scraps that Chris had cobbled together. But then again, this was a war that had room for only one commander. No matter what combat training and experience Effie possessed, she hadn't fought in *this* kind of war.

He shelved a few more books, finishing the cart off. The ruler he kept in his back pocket was an ideal straight edge for making sure the books were well aligned and looking good in their rows. This was a quick process; it took him no more than five minutes to check all the shelves he'd worked on. He stood back and admired his job well done. If only the whole library could be so thoroughly organized. The thought of the other sections, those shelves currently entrusted to less dedicated employees, made him shudder. Here, in this place that should have been an oasis of tranquil order and peaceful organization, chaos was creeping in. Entropy had unfolded its tentacles over much of the world, and the library was not out of its reach. It was always there, lurking in even the unlikeliest places.

Chris' hands clenched into fists at his sides, and he had to force them to relax one finger at a time. There was no sense getting so worked up. The war he was fighting had just begun, after all, and it would undoubtedly rage for a long time to come before the final confrontation. Enthusiasm was a necessity, but left unchecked, it could burn him out. Only, there was so much to be done.

He wheeled his cart back into the circulation office and stowed it with the other empties behind the sorting shelves. Two of the other clerks—Darryl and Martha—were chatting in hissing whispers at the front desk. They turned and looked at him, their smirking faces full of false friendliness as they watched him squirt a thin spray of WD-40 onto the wheels of the cart. He kept a can of the stuff back in the sorting area, and he was certain he was the only employee conscientious enough to use it.

"You feeling okay, man?" Darryl asked. He was a college student who could barely be bothered to comb his hair before coming to work. And his pants had probably never seen the business end of an iron. He was perched on a swivel chair behind the checkout desk, engaged in the project of stringing together a box of paper clips.

"I'm fine." Chris put the can back on the shelf and made sure the carts were lined up evenly.

"You look a little ragged, if you don't mind me saying." The paper clip chain trailed all the way down to the floor, where it rested between Darryl's battered sneakers.

"I do mind you saying that, actually."

Martha giggled. She was sitting at the desk where periodicals were processed, attaching property stickers to magazines. Chris ignored her. Although he disliked her intensely, Martha was always neatly attired and appeared to have rigorous standards of hygiene. She smelled of expensive soap and moisturizers. And Chris knew from peeking into her car that she had the vehicle detailed and washed often. She may have been bitchy and snide, and her work may have left much to be desired, but at least Martha hadn't let her appearance devolve.

Darryl gathered up the chain, clipped the ends together, and slipped it over his head like a necklace. "Sounded like Effie gave you the 'see-me-in-my-office talk' earlier. She did that to me when I wore my flip-flops to work the other day. You want my advice, wear a flak jacket, man."

"I'm not worried," Chris said. Of course he wasn't. *He* wasn't the type to push the boundaries of the dress code.

"She probably wants to give you a commendation for making sure the carts were oiled up and lubricated," Martha said over her shoulder. Chris couldn't see her face, but he knew she was laughing.

"I don't think there's anything funny about doing my job properly." He swallowed the hot bile that had risen in the back of his throat and turned away from them and walked down the hall to Effie's office.

A moment of truth—one of many that Chris was sure he'd face in this war—was at hand.

He squared his shoulders, took a deep breath, and knocked on the door. Effie's clipped, unaccented voice told him to come in.

"You wanted to talk to me about something?" he said, walking into the office.

"Have a seat, Chris." She was sitting behind her desk, and Chris was immediately disappointed to see that some of her clutter had already returned. A sheaf of papers was spread out on one corner, an empty coffee cup squatted on another. There was a sheet of wax paper in front of her, supporting a breakfast burrito that oozed cheese and salsa out of one end. Some of it had dribbled off the edge of the wax paper and onto the desk. Chris looked at it and winced. How could she just leave it there? A paper napkin lay not six inches away. Had she not noticed?

He sat down in one of the uncomfortable chairs. His heart was hammering away so hard that it was difficult to sit still. He wondered if he could get up and do jumping jacks while she talked.

Effie snatched up the napkin and wiped the corner of her mouth. She did nothing to stem the slow lava flow of melted cheese that crept onto her desk.

"So I came into my office this morning and couldn't find my stapler," she said, giving him a pointed look.

"In your front drawer." His reply was quick, automatic.

"And you know that because you were in her without permission, am I correct?" She raised a hand before he could answer. "Don't bother. I know you were in here. I've seen the security camera footage of you picking the lock on the door."

"But I just wanted to clean…"

"In an area that's off limits to you."

"I work here…"

"Not in this office." She whipped off her glasses, folded them up, and tossed them onto her desk. They narrowly missed the oozing burrito. "What you did, Chris, is a firing offense."

"You don't understand." He wanted to tell her about entropy and the Dragon Who is Called Chaos and the war, but he could do no more than stammer nonsense syllables. Surely, if she could just be made to see, to *understand* that what he'd done was an act of valor in defense of all humanity.

"I think I understand just fine," she said. She snatched up the remains of her burrito, crumpling the wax paper. More drips escaped and spattered onto the desk. She tossed the crumpled wad over Chris' head at a trash can behind him. The shot was a near miss. It bounced off the rim of the trash can and rolled back across the carpet, coming to a stop between Chris' feet. He looked down at it, horrified.

"I bet that just kills you, doesn't it?" she said.

Chris swallowed, his dry throat clicking. "Why would you do that?"

"You have a problem, Chris. You need help."

His eyes flicked from the trash on the floor to Effie's smug face. So much for being a fellow defender of order. This woman was nothing more than an agent of chaos.

"You're bringing about the destruction of the world," he said as evenly as his anger and dismay would allow. "You're bringing it all down and you don't even know it."

The smug smile gave way to something like a look of sympathetic concern. "I'm sure it seems that way right now. But it's just a piece of trash. It's just a little mess."

"That's how it starts. With little messes. Then little messes become big ones. And where does it all end? I'll tell you where: the heat death of the universe." His palms were sweaty. A spot between his shoulder blades itched fiercely. He squirmed in his chair.

"As a longtime employee of the library, you're eligible for some mental health leave. Eight whole weeks of it, in fact. I think it's time you took some time off so that you can get some help." She stood, holding a piece of paper out to Chris. "Here's a list of preferred providers from our insurance plan. I hear great things about Dr. Ashawatti."

"I am *not* sick."

"Chris, I'm not the only one who's noticed that you're not well. Now take this list of providers and get yourself some help."

Her face was a mask of false concern. But Chris saw what was lurking beneath that feigned benevolence. Under the surface was the grinning, mocking face of chaos itself, of entropy manifest. It was right here in this room, possessing this woman and daring him to do something about it.

"We all just want you to get the help you need," Effie said.

With a low, bestial snarl, Chris sprang from his chair with his arms outstretched. He snatched the paper from her hands. He wanted so badly to tear it to shreds and throw them in her face. But he couldn't. Instead, he folded it neatly and slipped it into his pocket.

"You are wrong about me," he said lamely as he stalked out of the office.

Chapter Twenty-Six: Myrna

After Tate's episode, Myrna had been unsure about keeping her date with George. At first, she'd been so shell-shocked by the whole thing that she could hardly consider leaving the house again, much less going out on a date. But she shook off her sadness as best she could and ventured out to the grocery store. When no one gave her funny looks or whispered behind her back, she came to the realization that word had not gotten out about the incident at her house. She breathed a sigh of relief, thanking the Lord above that it was Avery Cartwright who'd come to the house and not one of the older deputies, who were as gossipy as a church ladies' knitting circle. Wanda, who also worked in the kitchen at the daycare, squealed with delight when Myrna let it slip that she had a date. Backing out after such a reaction was unthinkable. When the big night rolled around, she was ready, or at least as ready as she was likely to get.

She waited on the front porch for George to pick her up. She wore her clothes from Old Navy: capri pants and a light blue blouse. Wanda had told her that she should show a little leg, but Myrna wasn't as adventurous as her coworker, who wore glittery eye shadow and tops with plunging necklines that revealed much of her two hundred-plus pound frame. No, capris and a regular blouse were just fine. Luanne had given her a touch-up trim at the Primp 'n Perm and had also offered some advice that involved spritzing a little perfume in what Luanne had referred to as the "hot zone," gesturing to her waist and below. Myrna had sprayed a little Chanel on, but hadn't ventured that far south. It wasn't going to be that sort of date, she told herself. And besides, it was all well and good for people like Wanda and Luanne to flaunt what they had, but Myrna, even when she was much younger, had never been that type.

George parked his car, a conservative navy blue Impala, in the driveway and crossed the lawn to meet her. He wore a pair of khaki pants and a short-sleeved plaid shirt that wasn't tucked in. His shoes were

Converse All-Stars. The outfit gave him the look of a prematurely grey college student. He had a bouquet of flowers—modest carnations rather than extravagant roses—that he presented to her with a flourish.

"Just a little something I picked up for you," he said, handing them over.

Myrna had a brief moment of panic. She'd have to go inside to put them in water, and he'd expect to be invited in. He'd see the mess, and he'd run screaming back to his car. That would be the end of this date and all future dates. Her heart sank down into the pit of her stomach.

"You know what?" George smiled. "Let's take them with us. We can get some water at the restaurant. Might be nice to have some flowers on the table at dinner."

Her heart jumped right back up into its proper spot, but it didn't slow its pace one bit. "I think I'd like that."

"Of course, I'm not certain this is a flowers-on-the-table type place we're going to." His smile took on a mischievous glint. "I hope you don't mind, but I'm not much for fine dining. And, I guess I should have asked beforehand, but you do like rock music, don't you?"

There were three signs outside Grouchies. One proclaimed in blue neon that the beer served inside was the coldest in Barlow. Another, located directly below the first, screamed in red neon that the chicken wings were the hottest in Barlow. The third was a small marquee above the door. It said that a band called Booze Hammer was appearing all week, playing two sets a night.

"They have a separate room in the back for the music," George said as he pulled into the gravel parking lot. "But it's not exactly soundproofed. If you'd rather go somewhere else, I won't be offended."

"Oh no, I love this place," Myrna said. This was not entirely true. She'd never actually set foot inside Grouchies, because it was not the sort of place Tate would think to take her, and him taking her to the occasional meal was her only opportunity for dining out. It occurred to her suddenly that most people would interpret this as a sign of her loneliness.

"I came here for dinner the first night I was in town," George explained. "I was dead tired from moving in, and nothing sounded better than a big plate of American junk food. So I guess what I'm saying is, I hope you're hungry." He opened the car door, hesitating before leaning out. "Last chance to go somewhere else."

Brad Carter | 205

"Oh come on!" she said. "Let's go eat."

He trotted around the car and opened her door for her. Myrna wasn't used to that, but she decided she liked it just fine.

The neon signs advertising various brands of beer provided as much illumination as the mismatched light fixtures hanging over the tables. A generous soul would have called it "mood lighting." The band hadn't started playing yet—it was just past six o'clock—but the jukebox in the corner was pumping out rock music loud enough to drown out much of the usual restaurant noise. They obeyed the "Seat Yourself" sign and chose a booth along the back wall. They were just barely in their seats when a pale skinned girl with blue-black hair shuffled over to take their drink orders.

Myrna ordered some complex cocktail with four kinds of fruit juice and three types of liquor. George went with the iced tea.

"And a large glass of water to put the lady's flowers in, if you don't mind." He pointed to the carnations that Myrna had laid on the table. "They're fresh cut and thirsty."

The waitress, whose nametag indicated that she was called Dru, said that it was so sweet that they brought their own flowers, only she said it with a complete lack of inflection. She was clearly not impressed.

George waited until the waitress departed then explained why he was probably the only man in the establishment not drinking a beer.

"Oh, should I flag down our waitress and change my order?" Myrna asked.

George laughed. "No, don't do that! It won't bother me if you drink your daiquiri chiller or whatever it was called. Even when I was down in the depths, I couldn't stand to drink that fruity stuff. Tiny toothpick umbrellas terrify me."

"Oh," she said.

George leaned down to catch her eyes. "That was a joke. What I mean is that I'm okay. You don't have to worry about me. Now, my friend Luanne says that if we're going to have a proper first date, you should tell me all about yourself. She seemed pretty taken aback that we don't know one another's life stories after eating together at the pancake joint."

"Well, there's really not much to tell on my end. For a long time, I was just a full-time Mom to my boys. Then, once they were off at school all day, I got a job working at the Methodist daycare. I still do that a

206 | ONLY THINGS

couple days a week, putting together lunches for the little ones." She suddenly felt awkward, trying to spin her life story into something that might be the least bit interesting to this man who was a bestselling author, who'd met movie stars, and run in literary circles. Then he reached across the table and patted her hand. There was no flash of electricity this time, but there was a sensation that reminded her that it was not a normal touch. Gentle, tingling warmth radiated from the tips of her fingers to her heart, and all at once, she didn't feel so awkward anymore.

She smiled at him, inching her fingers forward until they interlaced with his. And she told her story, all of it, from her childhood on her parent's farm to her early marriage to Henry Wilson to the deaths of her husband and youngest child. She paused to thank Dru for bringing their drinks and then continued with her tale, getting George up to present. Of course, she left out the parts about the grey people and Dale inhabiting her house. And she skipped over that terrible episode with the black shape that forced itself inside poor Dale. There was something inside her that urged her to tell George everything. It took every ounce of willpower she possessed not to blurt out that her house was either haunted or she was descending into a type of madness, most likely brought on by the growth of a brain tumor.

Dru returned to take their orders, receiving them with all the enthusiasm of someone attending a funeral.

"I guess it's my turn," George said.

Myrna had to remind herself to eat as George spun out the tale of his life. He did it conversationally, laying out the details of his tragic marriage in between bites of his Derrick's Special Burger and sips of sweet tea. The first part of the story was the sort of thing that Myrna imagined would form the basis for one of those paperback books that Luanne Samples loved so much: the famous writer falls on hard times but begins to work his way back by teaching, only to discover that the love of his life is one of his students. But one of Luanne's books would no doubt play out with the hapless writer finding his inspiration in his new love and writing the Great American Novel while siring a series of beautiful, intelligent children with his younger wife. The second part of George's story was more the sort of thing that would happen in some foreign film, the kind that's shot in black and white and has subtitles.

"I know it's not a happy story for the most part," George said, wiping his mouth with his napkin. "But you know, since I've moved here,

I've had a hopeful feeling. I haven't started writing yet, but I'm getting ideas."

"I…I don't really know what to say." Myrna settled for forking up another mouthful of her strawberry chicken salad. If her mouth was full, she wouldn't be expected to talk.

"Say that you're not afraid to be out on a date with me. Say that you won't think it strange when I give you Kathy's old snow globe collection later."

Myrna tried to hide her surprise at that last part. "I'm not afraid to be out on a date with you. And I'll accept your gift. I'm not sure why you'd want to give it to me, though."

"The snow globes were something I was going to keep for myself. So much of her collections were just thrown around the house, but she kept the snow globes neatly organized on a set of shelves in her childhood bedroom. She wasn't much of a housekeeper, but she kept that room dusted and clean. They were her first collection, something she'd started when she was just a little girl. Her parents traveled a lot. They left her with a babysitter. But they always brought her a snow globe from wherever it was they'd visited." George got a thoughtful, faraway look on his face. It seemed for a moment that he was finished speaking, but then he cleared his throat and continued. "So I thought that I'd keep them, that maybe I should adhere to the spirit as well as the letter of the promise I'd made. But I think she'd have wanted someone who cares for sentimental things to have them."

Myrna smiled. "You sound like you know me awful well for someone on a first date."

"I've been around the block, you know. I think I've earned the right by age and mileage to just shoot straight and use the direct approach."

"I don't mind that at all."

He tossed his napkin on the table and pushed his plate away. "Now, I'll say something else, since I've already started down this road. In the old days, I'd have ordered a glass of scotch to give myself the courage to do it, but I've left those days behind. Now I just have to work up the courage on my own."

Myrna pushed her own plate away. "Now I'm intrigued. What is it?"

"I don't believe much in the supernatural. I know I made my living for a while writing about that sort of thing, but I've always been a skeptic to the core. Rational, straight forward. But lately, something has me questioning all that. Lately, I've been thinking that maybe there is something like fate or destiny...and oh hell, I realize this is going to sound like a line..."

Without thinking, Myrna grabbed his hand. "Quit beating around the bush. Just say it."

"When I met you, when we shook hands, I felt something. I don't know how to explain it." He looked down at their hands. "I even feel it now." He paused, giving her a look. "Well, I can tell by the way you're not pulling your hand away and running for the door that I haven't creeped you out too badly."

"I felt it too. I thought I was..."

She stopped herself short. She'd almost blurted out that she was relieved that the electric tingling wasn't another symptom of her probable brain tumor, like her sleepwalking and visits from her dead son. George may have come into this date ready to throw all his cards on the table, but she wasn't that courageous. Besides, she didn't know if he was talking about the same type of jolt she'd felt when they'd first made contact. Maybe he just meant that he had a good feeling about her, that he felt like they could be compatible. There was nothing in what he said to suggest he'd gotten the same physical shock that she'd...

You don't really believe that, do you? He said fate. He said destiny. He began by saying he didn't believe in the supernatural. You know he felt it. You know.

She realized that their conversation had hit a lull. But it wasn't so bad, sitting there and holding hands. "Well, we like each other. It's good that we've gotten that out of the way. Now we can breathe easier."

"I'm sorry. I'm so out of practice at this sort of thing," he said.

"Don't worry. I'm even more out of practice than you."

"So, is this how normal people do the first date these days?" He gestured around. The night time crowd was starting to drift in. The jukebox music had given way to the sound of Booze Hammer tuning up in the back room. The smell of hot grease, charred meat, and hot wing sauce wafted out of the kitchen.

"Who cares about normal?" she asked. And she meant it. She could almost forget how Tate had leveled his accusing stare at her and then stomped up to the bathroom. She could almost forget how haunted and tired he looked as his friend Avery led him away.

"Let me ask you a serious question," George said. "How do you feel about Booze Hammer?"

Chapter Twenty-Seven: Chris

Three tablets of Stay Sharp and a large coffee had Chris so wide awake that he could hardly blink. Sweat as thick as cooking oil bubbled up from his pores and ran all over his skin. After leaving the library, he'd driven aimlessly through the night, stopping in parking lots to rest every few hours. He was afraid to go back to his apartment and face the disappointment of the Golden Knight, who would surely be waiting for him on the other side of the wall of sleep. The car's air conditioning turned his sweat into a cold sludge that coated him. He needed to be out of the car. He couldn't breathe. The seatbelt strangled him.

He whipped the car into the parking lot of the donut shop and sat for a few minutes, trying to catch his breath. Although it was early morning, the summer heat was ferocious, and it quickly turned the car into an oven. He unclipped his seatbelt and nearly spilled himself onto the hot asphalt. Waves of heat shimmered up from the black surface as he crossed the parking lot.

The booth nearest the entrance was vacant, but the table was flecked with bits of donut glaze and droplets of cream-clouded coffee. Chris recoiled in disgust and collapsed into the neighboring booth, which was spotless. This was familiar territory, and it felt safe. Despite the nasty state of the neighboring booth, this place was kept neat and clean.

But the caffeine and pills wouldn't let him relax. His fingers drummed a relentless tattoo on the table. His feet shuffled back and forth. Every inch of his skin itched or tingled. He was the only customer in the shop, and he was suddenly aware that the man behind the counter was staring at him.

"Hello there, sir," the man, whose nametag identified him as Amjad, said. "I must stand on our policy that our booths are reserved for paying customers. The park down the road has plenty of benches by the shade trees."

Chris frowned. What sort of insolence was this? He was a regular customer of this establishment. He should be valued, not treated like some dirty ragamuffin blown in off the street.

"In that case, how about a dozen donuts and a large coffee?" Chris strode proudly to the counter. He produced a crisp twenty-dollar bill from his billfold and tossed it down in front of the man. "Does that qualify me for one of your fucking booths? Or would you like to remind me about the park down the street again?"

He rang up the sale and returned Chris' change. "There's no need for that language. It's just that we sometimes get vagrants…"

"Me, a vagrant?" Chris threw back his head and laughed once sharply.

"I apologize again. Let me throw in a couple of apple fritters and we can just call it even, okay?" Amjad opened the box back up and put in two large sugary discs. He handed over the cup of coffee.

"You know, one day you'll tell people that you remember the day the savior of the human race came into your humble donut shop. You'll probably leave out the part where you treated him so shamefully, though. I bet you'll gloss right over that." Chris ripped the lid from the cup and gulped down two boiling hot mouthfuls without hesitation.

"Okay, look, I've been nice. Maybe I was a little quick to make assumptions, but I apologized and made it up to you with the free fritters. There's a limit to how much abuse and foul language I'll take out of any customer. You can get out or I can call the police." Amjad shoved the box across the counter.

Chris poured the rest of the coffee down his throat. It seared a line of fire from his tongue to his stomach. He slammed the empty cup down on the counter and grabbed his box of donuts. "I'm growing tired of everyone being so damned thankless. You keep such a clean place in here, you'd think a little understanding might pass between us. But no, you're just like the rest of them."

Amjad stepped back from the counter. "I won't ask you again."

Chris snarled as he left the building.

He awoke in tangled, sweat-soaked sheets without a memory of coming home to his apartment, much less getting undressed and into bed. The air conditioner had turned the sheets into a wet, sticky mess that clung to Chris' skin and had to be peeled away like soggy bandages. His stomach roiled at the sensation. The morning's donuts and coffee spewed out of his mouth without warning, splashing into a hot puddle on the bed.

"Well, that was not so nicely done. You should have more control of yourself."

Chris turned towards the source of the robust, honey-coated baritone. He was standing there in the corner of the bedroom as if he'd stepped out of a dream: the Golden Knight himself. Clad in a blinding white tunic and clasping his hands before him, he looked like a messiah. A messiah with Chris' face. The fact that they could have been twins made Chris feel even more ashamed and inadequate. Here he was, covered in sweat and lying in vomit while his doppelganger was scrubbed to glorious cleanliness and smiling with an expression of pure serenity.

"Easy for you to say. You've beaten entropy out of your world," Chris said. "It's just an unpleasant memory for you."

"It's more than that, I'm afraid," the Golden Knight said. "Entropy is a force that sweeps across all worlds. If it destroys your world, it will move on to the next one. If it destroys that one, sooner or later it will turn back and attack my world again."

Chris scrubbed his mouth with the back of his hand. His nostrils burned with the acrid smell of vomit. "So it can never be destroyed completely?"

"Who knows? Perhaps if it is beaten back from enough worlds, it will one day lie down and die for all time. That is not for us to know. But I tell you this truly: if you do not pull yourself together and start to act the part of a crusader for order, you will most certainly fail when the time comes to strike."

"I'll be ready!" Chris threw his arms in the air. Flecks of vomit flew from his fingertips. "I've already begun the fight. I erased a filthy slut. And I took out a couple of dirty hippies. You should have seen their houses. Disgusting. There was filth everywhere, and so much…"

The Golden Knight tossed his head and sniffed. "Pathetic. You removed a few pawns from the board, and you act as if you're mounting an assault on the king. Perhaps this world is truly lost if it depends on you to be its savior. Perhaps I should just move on to the next one and make preparations there."

Chris tried to jump from the bed but was too tangled in the sheets to pull it off properly. He tumbled to the floor. His head smacked into the carpet with a muffled thump, and his vision swam for a moment.

Grabbing the side of the bed with all his might, he hauled himself to his feet and stood naked in front of the Golden Knight.

"You can't abandon me now that I've finally found my purpose. I need you. I can't do this alone. I thought that Effie was an ally, but she's one of *them*. Please…" Chris winced as a note of pleading crept into his voice. It made him more ashamed, but he repeated the word over and over in the same tone until the Golden Knight's ramrod straight posture softened.

"First, we'll get this room cleaned up. And we'll scrub your person until it has a shine befitting a true crusader." The Golden Knight put his hand on Chris' shoulder. "Then we'll make plans. It's time for hostilities to escalate."

They'd gone down to the apartment complex's laundry room and put the bed sheets into one of the washing machines. Then they'd gone back to Chris' apartment and sprayed the carpet in his bedroom with a foaming cleanser. After Chris had run the vacuum cleaner over the floor as thoroughly as he could manage, he was already beginning to feel better. The Golden Knight nodded his approval.

"Very good. Now let's get you cleaned up, soldier. We're going to scrub you until you shine," the Golden Knight said, plucking at Chris' t-shirt. "Come on, now. I'll help."

Chris removed his shirt and tossed it into the hamper. He stuck his thumbs in the waistband of his gym shorts and hesitated, looking at the Golden Knight, who stood opposite him.

"If it helps to ease your discomfort, I'll disrobe first." The Golden Knight stepped away, and in one quick movement, removed his tunic. He stood with his hands on his hips, his shoulders thrown back to afford a better view of his smooth, hairless body.

Chris swallowed again. His heart thundered away in his chest as he stripped off his shorts. It was a strange sensation, standing there naked with the Golden Knight. It was like looking into a mirror. Aside from the Golden Knight's flowing mane of golden hair and his thoroughly shaved chest and pubic region, he looked to be a carbon copy of Chris.

He smiled softly, taking Chris' hand and leading him into the bathroom. He turned on the shower, running the water hot enough that the room was almost instantly filled with steam. He pulled the shower curtain open and gestured for Chris to enter.

"I'm sorry, I don't…" Chris glanced down at his stiffening manhood.

The Golden Knight followed him into the hot spray. "There is no need to be ashamed. This will bring us closer, just as if we were standing shoulder to shoulder, engaged in the heat of battle."

Chris gasped as those smooth, confident hands worked the soap all over his body. He groaned as they washed his most sensitive areas. His mind reeled, filled with images of a world without mess and disorder.

Chapter Twenty-Eight: The Man Behind the Curtain

Ray awoke in a familiar place. It was the upstairs bedroom in his Aunt Ellen's house back in Arnholdt. He opened his eyes and groaned, more in the anticipation of pain than any real discomfort. As he sat up, he found that he was a bit sore, but it was probably just from sleeping all curled up on Aunt Ellen's old red velvet couch. He ran his hands over his ribs, his neck, his face: all the spots he'd expect to be howling with pain from the car wreck. Everything seemed to be more or less intact and in good working order. He chalked it up to the logic of dreams. Back in the waking world, he was probably laid up in a hospital bed with tubes sticking in him. If he was lucky, maybe he was already back home and soaking up the painkillers the doctor gave him.

He walked across the creaking floorboard to the heavy black curtains that covered the room's lone window. He wanted to see if the backyard still looked the same in his dream.

"You're not dreaming. And the car wreck wasn't that bad."

Ray started at the sound of the voice. He turned and saw his mother seated at the table where she'd once done her readings and consultations.

She stood and spread her arms. "Hello, son."

He hesitated, but only for the briefest moment, before throwing himself into her arms. She wasn't the frail, older lady she would have been when she died. She was still the vibrant woman that Ray had known before his father moved him across the country. Her smell—a mixture of the cheap perfume Dervis bought for her at regular intervals during their marriage and the Clorets gum she chewed after she smoked a cigarette—split open the dam holding back his emotions. He wept on her shoulder, thanking his subconscious mind for granting him this reunion, however insubstantial it might have been.

"I told you that this isn't a dream," she said, pulling away so she could study his face.

"How do you know what I'm thinking?"

"When a man encounters his dead mother in a room of a house that burned down years ago, it's not hard to guess what he might be thinking. Especially after he's been in a doozy of a car smash-up." She held him at arm's length, looking him over. "Well, here we are."

A million things raced through Ray's mind at that moment. All the things he wanted to say about how he'd wanted to come home for years, about how he hadn't wanted to let his father poison his memories of her, about how he hadn't come to hate and fear her, not *really*...all those things. He wanted to tell her that he'd decided—too late, as it turned out—to bring Emma to Arnholdt to meet her. He wanted to tell her that he now understood. But he said none of that. Instead, he lamely asked, "So if this house burned down years ago, where are we?"

"Ray, son, we're behind the veil."

He blinked in surprise.

Behind the veil.

He'd become familiar with the phrase in his last few days of intense study with Stephanie. So many of the books they'd pored over—whether written by wild eyed and debauched poets, shaggy hippies, or kaftan-clad mystics—featured it prominently. None of the texts had yielded any answers about how they could get Ray acquainted once again with the spirit world, but many of the books referred to a place—physical or metaphysical—that existed beyond the ken of normal humans. Sometimes this place represented some sort of afterlife. Sometimes it was a parallel plane of existence. One of the books had even posited that it was a new level of consciousness that could only be reached through prolonged and vigorous sex in the strangest positions (diagrams were included). Nearly all of the books referred to this destination as behind (or sometimes *beyond*) the veil.

Ray had figured that you had to be dead to actually step behind the veil. Most of the books agreed with him on this point, explaining that in rare cases, people could sneak a peek behind it in dreams or during near death experiences. Only the nuttiest of the books—and something had to be pretty goddamn far-out for it to stand apart from the pack as nutty—mentioned the possibility of a living person setting up shop and actually interacting with someone permanently on the other side. Stephanie had told Ray that his childhood excursion into Steven Lovelace had been something akin to astral projection, meaning that his spiritual mass had left his body and traveled behind the veil as a sort of shortcut to Lovelace's trail of death in Texas.

"You know in that old show *Lost in Space* how the family got sucked into a black hole and shot to some remote corner of the universe?" she'd asked during one of their study sessions.

"Yeah. I was always more of a *Buck Rogers* guy myself, but I remember," Ray had replied, washing down some aspirin with a slug from his can of Coke.

"Well, something, some kind of a force like a psychic black hole reached out and found you. And like that black hole dragging the Robinson family to the ass end of outer space, this force snatched your spirit right out of your body, carried it behind the veil, and spit it back out on this side. Only when it spit you back out, you were miles away from your body."

"And then I woke up..."

"Something brought you back. Maybe it was the same something that sucked your spirit out of your body in the first place. Maybe not."

Ray had slumped in his chair. "So we're nowhere. Are we wasting our time with all this?"

"This isn't an exact science. Hell, I'm not even sure you could call it a science at all. You need to remember that on a lot of this stuff, I'm as in the dark as you. I know the vocabulary, but the mechanics of it are vague. It's like explaining to someone how to ride a bike. You can talk all you want, but until the person actually does it, your words are just moral support more than anything."

"So why hang around then? Not that I don't appreciate a sympathetic presence."

Stephanie had smiled and given him a playful punch on the shoulder. "I'm sticking around because I want to be here when you have your breakthrough. I don't have your talents, but I do have a knack for intuition. And I can feel that big things are coming. I want to be in the presence of real, behind-the-veil psychic contact, even if just one more time before I die. I want to know that the family's talent lives on, even if it's not in me."

That wasn't what Ray had expected to hear. It was an awful lot to live up to.

His mother sat down at the table, and Ray took the seat opposite her.

"Stephanie was such a sweet girl growing up," she said. "It was so sad to see her trying so hard to develop a talent for the family business and coming up short."

Ray nodded. "She's been a big help."

She beamed, her smile as wide and warm as Ray remembered from his childhood. "It's nice sitting here, just looking at you. I wish we could sit here forever and catch up."

"I sense a 'but' coming," Ray said.

"Son, I don't really know that there's an easy way for me to explain all this. And I'm not sure how much time we have. So what's coming might sound like a lecture." She paused to consider for a moment. "Actually, I guess it will probably sound more like a plot dreamed up by a horror writer like that George Young. You're going to have to suspend your disbelief, I'm afraid."

"My disbelief took a hike when Percy Flannigan got himself killed by something invisible. And now that I've got some rat-faced woman attacking me in my dreams, it's like I'm living in a George Young novel."

"Rat-faced woman?" She crinkled her brow.

"Yeah, the one in my dreams. You don't know about that?"

"I'm behind the veil, son. That doesn't grant me any special privileges for peeking into your dreams. There are laws of physics over here the same as there are on the other side. Different laws, but laws all the same. I'm sort of out on a limb as it is, just talking to you like this. All I know is that there's something big coming down the pike on your side of the curtain. And it involves something from my side, something that found a way through the veil and back into your world. I wanted to make sure you were ready, because there have been rumors over here that you were involved. And I knew Dervis didn't leave you prepared for that."

Ray took a breath and let it out slowly. "I need to ask you something. It's a question that's been itching around in my brain for a while now."

"You want to know why I let Dervis take you away, why I never tried to contact you for all those years."

"There goes that Chambers intuition."

She looked down at the table. "More like mother's intuition, I'm afraid. This has been a long time coming, hasn't it?"

"Most people don't get a chance to tie up loose ends with someone after that someone is dead. I know you said our time here is short, but I figure as long as I'm here I might as well ask."

"When you took your trip with Steven Lovelace, it wasn't just your father who was scared. I was sick with worry. You were gone, and there was nothing I could do to bring you back. At the time, we didn't even know what Steven had gotten up to. I think if I'd have known that, I might have gone out of my skull. It was my fault that you'd gone wandering."

Ray shook his head. "You passed some of the talent on to me, that's all. You can't help what's in your genes. It wasn't your fault any more than a parent with a colorblind kid is at fault."

There were tears in his mother's eyes, big fat ones that hung tangled in her lashes then plopped down her cheeks. "But I should have prepared you. We all knew how strong your talent might be. We could all feel it, the potential you had. But the thing was, you were a boy. It shouldn't have been so strong with you. It never is with men. Stephanie should have been the one to carry on, but for some reason, she never had the spark. It was like the wires got crossed somewhere along the line. We should have been teaching you from the time you could crawl, but we just didn't know…"

"Dad never would have allowed that."

"We just didn't *know*," she repeated. "Then you were gone so long, I started to think you weren't coming back. And when you did finally open your eyes, the story you told us…"

"I remember the way Dad looked at you. I remember that he grabbed you by your arm and hauled you out of the room. There was arguing, but I couldn't hear what was being said."

"Your father said that what I was doing was dangerous, and that he wasn't going to sit still for it any longer. He said that you belonged far away from me and my sisters, some place where our influence couldn't hurt you."

"And you agreed?"

"I was a mother first and a seer second. Anyone in my situation would have done the same." She sniffed. "That didn't make it any easier, knowing that it was the right thing. Or at least thinking it was the right thing."

"But all those years between then and now…" Ray cleared his throat. "I know that the phone lines run both ways, but you never called."

"I called and wrote plenty, but Dervis made sure that you never knew it. I imagine the letters went straight into the trash. I thought about driving down to Arkansas, but I didn't know how safe it would be."

"You think just being in the same room would have caused another…incident?"

She sniffed again, her eyes continuing to leak. "Maybe that was it. But some of it was self-preservation. Believe it or not, there are still groups of people out there who take a very dim view of the way the Chambers sisters earned their money. That type has never been shy about expressing their distaste for people like us, and they can be violent. I'm guessing it wouldn't surprise you much to know that some of those people are very well connected."

Ray thought of the upstanding citizens that made up the church he attended. They were judgmental and often petty, but could they be moved to violence? He thought that, given the right motivation, they would jump at the chance to start burning witches in the town square.

He sat there, watching his mother cry and considered how different his life could have been. It was sad and useless.

"Well, here we are," he said. "It may not be the type of family reunion you had in mind for all those years, but we're together now. How about we get to it? How about you tell me just what the hell is going on with my town?"

"Here's what I know: everything boils down to two opposing forces: chaos and order. That's what makes the universe work. Existence is really just a careful balance between the two. With me so far?"

"I have a feeling that my poor head will need an aspirin or two before this is over, but yeah, I think I can follow."

"For some reason, that balance is upset over on your side. It's like a seesaw tipping back and forth." She bit her lip, looking at him intently. "Ray, something got through. Something that never should have gotten into your world managed to slip through the veil. And, for reasons that can't possibly be known, it's settled in Arkansas."

"But what can I possibly do about it?"

Her eyes were sad as she said, "I don't know. For the sake of everyone around you, I hope that you'll know when the time comes."

"Thanks for the vote of confidence, but if everyone is depending on me, I'm afraid the outlook might be grim. I'm sort of groping along in the dark. I can't even believe that I'm here right now."

"But you *are* here. And that means you've awakened to your talent." She looked around as if making sure they were still alone. "The only thing I can tell you is this, son: when you're poking around on this side of the grave, you leave yourself open to all sorts of things. Be careful that you don't let anything unwanted get inside your head."

His stomach sank as he looked back into her worried eyes.

Chapter Twenty-Nine: Stephanie

Ray was finally out of bed. He stumbled into the kitchen, still looking like a guy who'd been hypnotized by a stage magician.

"Are you hungry?" Stephanie asked.

Ray grunted. "Need to eat. Need to keep my strength up."

She took his arm and guided him to a chair at the kitchen table. "Here, you just sit and I'll make a pitcher of tea and some sandwiches."

Another grunt of assent.

She busied herself getting the ham and cheese and mustard out of the fridge. "You were asleep back there for a while. I was starting to think maybe I should call the ambulance and just have them take you in."

"No ambulance," Ray said. He did his slow-blinking thing and looked right at her. "I'm fine. I'll be back soon."

"You'll be back?" Stephanie paused. "Ray, where are you?"

"I'll be back soon. But I need to eat."

She nodded. "Sure, it'll be ready in just a minute."

When Ray clipped the side of his truck on the tree out front, Stephanie had flown from the house without even stepping into her flip-flops. Once she'd given up trying to talk Ray into going to the doctor, she'd spent the next few hours picking splinters out of her feet. Ray had used the time to stare off into space. The truck didn't look so bad, but Ray had a bruise on his forehead where he'd whacked it on the steering wheel. To Stephanie, the bruise and Ray's behavior just screamed "concussion." But he'd been adamant that he was fine and that if she wanted him to go to the hospital, she'd have to drag him there. His voice was thick and monotone as he pleaded his case, and his eyes blinked a lot less often than they should have, and when they did, his eyelids took their sweet time opening back up.

Now he was scarfing down his third ham and cheese, taking big bites, chewing them methodically, and every once in a while, draining a whole glass of sweet tea in one go. He didn't speak, just stared straight ahead like he was looking at something beyond the plain kitchen wall. Stephanie had hardly touched her own sandwich. It was fascinating, watching her cousin operate on autopilot.

He'd really done it.

Stephanie shook her head in amazement. He'd actually flipped his psychic switch and gotten out there on the ethereal plane somewhere. She wondered where he was, who he was observing. This was what they'd been working for. Poring over those musty books, chanting all those nonsense-sounding prayers, staring at crystals for hours on end…it had been exhausting. And then, just out of the blue, while he was driving around, Ray has some breakthrough? It was strange.

She watched Ray put down another sandwich. Who could have known that traveling the ethereal plane could work up such an appetite? After Ray had gone off on his journey as a little boy of eleven, he must have woken up ready to eat a horse. Did they put a feeding tube in him while he was laid up in the hospital? She supposed they would have. If so, he must have been hooked up to a fifty-five gallon drum of whatever they pump into the comatose.

He polished off his glass of tea and moved his dishes aside, his eyes still fixed straight ahead. The Ouija board was still in the middle of the table, and the plastic wrapper crinkled and rustled as Ray took the board out. He tossed the wadded-up plastic aside. Without ever taking his eyes off whatever invisible thing he was staring at, he took the board and planchette out of the box. With a sweep of his forearm, he knocked the empty box to the floor.

Apparently, people traversing the ethereal plane were not much concerned with housekeeping.

Stephanie pushed her own dishes aside, her appetite forgotten as she watched her cousin place his fingers on the planchette. At first, he did nothing but sit there slack-jawed, his fingers resting atop the little eyepiece pointer. His eyes did their slow-blinking thing. She thought that maybe he'd slipped away, gone into some coma like he did when he was a kid. But then he started talking, whispering really. His words were coming so rapidly that they were slurred together and unintelligible. Maybe he wasn't even speaking English at all. It was hard to tell.

Abruptly, he shut up. There was a brief pause, and then his fingers flew across the board, pushing the little plastic eyepiece over letters and numbers so fast that they nearly blurred. Had smoke started rising from the surface of the board, Stephanie wouldn't have been shocked. Then, as suddenly as it had started, the furious movement stopped, and Ray went back to his incoherent muttering. He carried on that way for a few minutes before going back to blazing a trail across the Ouija board.

He sat there, alternately mumbling and working the planchette for all it was worth, for hours. As fascinated as she was, Stephanie managed to get back to her sandwich. The bread had gone dry and scratchy sitting out that long, but she ate it anyway.

Chapter Thirty: The Author

George had always laughed at the pompous asses who spoke about writing in mystical terms. All that bullshit about communing with your muse or tapping into some vein of archetypal stories from the collective unconscious was just a way for people to avoid writing. He was of the opinion that writers were unique in that so many of them loved the idea of writing but actively avoided, even hated, the actual process. After all, it was easier—and much more fun—to sit at the bar or in the coffee shop and tell people how deeply talented and/or tortured you were than it was to park your ass behind the desk and bang out word after word. Writing was work. And it could be thankless and low-paying. For some people, that was just too taxing to contemplate. For others, for people like George, the act itself was satisfying enough. Maybe once upon a time he'd enjoyed the accolades almost as much as the writing, but that time was long since passed.

The morning's outburst of writing was nearly enough to make him reconsider his position on the muses. Since rolling out of bed at dawn, he'd only left his desk to go to the toilet or refill his coffee cup. At times it felt as if the words were writing themselves and his fingers were struggling to keep up.

None of it was Pulitzer material. He had the barest bones of a story forming in his head, and the few pages he'd pounded out that morning were only first draft material. But the words were good, and they were flowing out of him the way they had back in those glory days when he could turn out two novels a year.

He pushed back from his desk and looked at the computer screen. It was like coming up from the depths of the ocean and gulping down a lungful of air. His eyes scanned the sentences. It was a solid opening, something to build on.

His joints popped as he stood and stretched. All the coffee he'd poured down his throat was finally catching up to him, and his feet had the urge to do some walking. First, he went to the kitchen and got a glass of ice water. He made a sandwich while he was at it, spreading a layer of pimento cheese between two slices of white bread. He ate while prowling around the house, his mind alternately turning over the morning's writing and his date with Myrna.

His ears were still ringing from the walloping they'd received from Booze Hammer's set. And his restless feet were still a bit sore from all the dancing they'd done. He wondered if she'd had as much fun as he had. Certainly, she'd smiled and laughed enough. And at the end of the night, when he'd stacked the three boxes of snow globes on her porch, she'd let him sneak a quick kiss. They'd agreed to have another night on the town on Saturday. But, standing there chewing the last mouthful of pimento cheese on Wonder Bread, George felt that the days between now and Saturday were a vast gulf of time.

He admonished himself for acting like a love-struck teenager. But was that really so bad? It was certainly a hell of a step up from being so pickled with scotch that he couldn't even string together a coherent thought, much less knock out a few thousand words in one go.

The thought stopped him in his caffeine-addled tracks. Whether or not Myrna was his new muse, there was no denying that he wanted to see her again, and the sooner the better. It wasn't just a simple desire, either; it was damn near a compulsion. He *needed* to see her. He recognized the feeling for what it was. A yearning that strong couldn't just slip by an old drunk. But as strong as the need was, it didn't have that ragged, desperate edge that he'd felt when it had been too long between drinks during his dark times. No, this was a pleasant aching, clean and sharp as gulping cold spring water.

But one thing was clear: there was no way he could wait until Saturday.

•

The last box of snow globes was in the back corner of the garage. George had no idea why he remembered this. He couldn't have said what was in the other boxes stacked shoulder-high in that cramped space. But for some reason, he remembered that one of the boxes of snow globes had been separated from its fellows and placed in the far corner of the garage.

It was ridiculous, standing there in front of a simple, everyday door, fighting down a creeping sense of dread.

Ridiculous, hell. How about stupid? How about downright silly? It's not dread that you feel my friend; it's guilt. Kathy's dead, you're alive, and that makes you feel guilty. Double guilty now that you're smitten with some woman you've just met.

George waved his hand in front of his face as if swatting the thought away like a pesky insect. But the feeling persisted, and damned if his forearms weren't pimpled with gooseflesh.

It was broad daylight, lemon yellow bars of sunlight crisscrossing the floor as they streamed in through the blinds. If there was ever a time for reacquainting oneself with childish fears, it was in the pitch black of night. Every child knew that light was the bane of all monsters, just as surely as pulling the covers over one's head was adequate defense against whatever lurked in the shadowy corners of the bedroom. Bright summer mornings weren't good settings for horror scenes.

So why are you just standing there? You want to go see your lady friend, you need an excuse to show up at her doorstep on a Thursday unannounced. Those snow globes are your excuse.

The ice in his water glass had melted and fat drops of condensation slid down the side onto his hand. He gulped down the rest of the water and set the glass on the coffee table. Cursing himself for a fool, he took three hurried steps forward and unlocked the door.

No crazed, hockey-mask clad killer rushed in to hack him up with a power tool. No screaming banshee glided in, eager to suck his soul down to hell. A snootful of hot, musty air was all that greeted him as he groped around the corner for the light switch. The single light bulb did little to dispel the gloom, but it also didn't reveal anything out of the ordinary. All the boxes seemed to be present and arranged just the way he'd left them after his possessions had been released from the Sheriff's Department.

He stepped down into the garage.

The tight little rows he'd left between the stacks would have brought a claustrophobic to his knees in agony. He had to go sideways through the narrow spaces, feeling one box slide across his back while another brushed his belly. He made a mental note to lay off the pimento cheese and ice cream. Maybe this tightness was why he dreaded coming into the garage? He tossed that possibility away immediately. No, his dread wasn't going to be so easily explained. He'd save the rationalizations for someone else, should the topic ever arise in conversation.

Oh, you write scary books? So, tell me, what is it that scares you? Ghosts? Goblins? Serial killers?

No, none of that. But wouldn't you know it, I'm scared of my garage! Damnedest thing, but I can't even walk out there without having a panic attack. I think it goes back to the trauma I experienced in the womb. You see, my mother had a difficult labor…

He stopped. There'd been a sound, something like scratching over in the corner. Were there rats in here? The house was new. How could it have rats already? He edged forward, cocking his head to one side as he listened for the sound. Maybe he'd imagined it…no, there it was again, a sharp, insistent scratching.

He slid through the cardboard maze until he found the box he was looking for. All the while, the scratching persisted. It moved around, seeming to come from a point almost right in front of him one moment and then starting up again to one side a moment later. George's imagination—primed and ready from the morning's writing session—conjured up a dozen different horrible possibilities for the source of the scratching. All manner of hideous creatures and deformed monsters swam into his mind. It would have been a treasure trove of ideas for his newly begun novel if not for the strange, undefined fear. He was sweating, his shirt soaking through in the hot, stale air.

He knelt beside a box to read his scrawled label.

Snow Globes—Fragile!

The boxes piled atop it were relatively light, and it wasn't much of a chore to move them. It was likely that they were filled with larger plush toys, the bow tie-wearing teddy bears and goofy eyed elephants that Kathy favored, but George didn't take the time to read the labels. He just wanted out of there. Down close to the floor, the scratching seemed louder. He half expected to move a box and find himself face to face with some buck-toothed, whiskered monstrosity. But the only horror he came across was a spider web loaded with desiccated insects.

The return journey was even more arduous than the first. He was forced at some points to hold the box over his head to slide through the narrow passageways. Worse was the creeping unease that clung to him as tightly as his sweat-soaked shirt. It was the sort of prickly sensation that comes with being watched or followed, the phantom twinge that comes from walking an unfamiliar street after dark or sitting alone in a crowded restaurant. Or, as Ben McCauley, the intrepid ghost hunter from George's novels, would have theorized, it was the feeling of being watched by eyes that were not of this world.

Good old Ben McCauley. What would he do in this situation? Well, he probably wouldn't need to fetch snow globes as an excuse to see a woman. McCauley was too cool for that.

At last he came to the end of the line, setting foot on that one concrete step that led to the door. His free hand was slick with perspiration. His fingers slipped across the smooth surface of the doorknob.

"Goddamn it," he growled, shifting the box higher on his hip.

He scrubbed his hand on his jeans then tried again. The doorknob turned reluctantly.

He paused with his foot on the threshold, gulping down the cool air of the living room. The sweat on his chest was instantly cold and slimy. He leaned forward to set his burden down on the carpet, but something clamped around his left ankle and sent him sprawling. He threw his arms out to break his fall, dumping the box onto the floor as he fell.

The top flaps of the box, the packing tape sliced from the police search, popped open, and one of the snow globes flew loose from its nest of crumpled newspaper. The large glass sphere atop its heavy wooden base traveled end over end in a quick downward arc.

George looked up in time to see the globe shatter on the corner of the coffee table, spraying him with water, fake snow, glitter, and thin shards of glass. He scrabbled up onto his left knee, kicking his right leg out against whatever held him. His foot encountered no resistance, no matter what direction he kicked. Terrified that his lashes were full of bits of glass just waiting to slash his corneas to shreds, he risked a quick glance through squinted eyes over his shoulder.

And there, framed by the darkness of the garage, stood Kathy.

She was clad in a long-sleeved black dress. Her dark hair hung about her face, wisps of it stirred by some phantom breeze. Her mouth was contorted into a sneer that pulled her face out of alignment. It looked as if her nose had been broken. George squeezed his eyes shut and counted to ten while he waited for the hallucination to disappear. He planted his hands on the carpet, pushing himself up to a seated position. Taking a slow, deep breath, he opened his eyes.

She was still there, staring back at him through the strands of hair that hung loose across her face. The garage had gone dark behind her, and the blackness of the atmosphere looked thick and oily. It was as if it was a tapestry woven from millions of wriggling black threads.

"Still mine," she said, her voice low and hoarse. "Forever and ever and ever mine."

George rose shakily. "Kathy, you have to understand…"

"All mine, you lying bastard!" she screamed.

Something unseen slammed into George's stomach with sledgehammer force, dumping him back onto the carpet. His neck whiplashed, and the back of his head thudded onto the floor. Stars burst across his vision. Lightning bolts of pain struck his skull.

He looked up into Kathy's face, and for a moment, her features were no longer a contorted mask of pain and anger.

"George, I'm sorry but I can't stop it," she gasped.

The door to the garage slammed shut. A raspy voice cried out suddenly, as if in pain, and then was silent. George fought against the warm tide of unconsciousness. It was a fight he lost.

George awoke with a steady throb of dull pain in his head. It was as if the Ghost of Hangovers Past had paid him a visit while he was out. He pushed himself up to a seated position and rubbed the back of his head gingerly. There was a good-sized knot on the back of his skull, but he was pretty sure nothing was broken. His neck hurt like a son of a bitch, but he could turn his head without too much trouble.

He sat there for a moment, searching for some rational explanation for what had just happened.

Like an old man, you lost your balance carrying that box. You fell flat on your face and cracked your skull then panicked because you hallucinated a vision of your dead wife. Amazing that your brains aren't spilled out all over the carpet with that snow globe water.

He stood up warily, his eyes fixed on the door. He stepped forward and opened it cautiously, peeking out into the dark garage. Nothing there but the stifling air and dusty smell of cardboard.

Feeling ridiculous, he called out, "Kathy?"

Silence greeted him. Silence and a fresh batch of goosebumps that raced over his forearms. A phantom breeze of hot air puffed out through the door. He jumped back and slammed it shut. He spun on his heels, sure that he'd find himself face to face with Kathy. She'd grab hold of him with her cold, dead hands. She'd pull him close and speak a cloud of graveyard breath into his face, demanding to know why, after he'd promised to care for her things, he was practically giving them away at the flea market.

Of course, the only thing he saw was his sparsely furnished living room.

"You're as bad as that superstitious constable," he said, forcing a laugh. The sound seemed overly loud in the quiet room.

Back in the 70s and 80s, what George thought of as the "glory days," the little critical acclaim his novels received often centered on the way in which the books depicted ordinary people facing the supernatural. For all his ghost-hunting acumen and courage under pressure, Ben McCauley, the protagonist of George's four most successful books, was still just a beleaguered bartender doing the best to provide for his family. He never sought out a career as a ghost hunting detective. The fact that McCauley divorces his wife and becomes estranged from his oldest son during the course of the four books endeared him to readers. George liked to think that he'd jerked a few tears from their eyes with McCauley's death scene in the final chapter of *Whispers at Midnight*. His publisher at the time had told George he was killing the goose that laid the golden eggs, and George had scoffed. He'd come around to the publisher's view in the years since.

So when he was finally able to calm down, George took a seat on the couch and asked himself what Ben McCauley would have done in this situation.

Good grief. You wrote paperbacks with bad covers and raised metallic lettering for the titles. They're hardly guidebooks for the paranormal. Besides, some fleeting vision brought on by a guilty conscience hardly qualifies as a supernatural occurrence.

George pushed the voice of doubt aside for the moment. He didn't see much use for turning a skeptical eye on what he'd seen and felt. If it was all in his head, he'd have nothing to worry about.

Of course! Because those sorts of vivid hallucinations are nothing to worry about. Perfectly natural.

But if there was more to it than that…well, what then? In the real world, how did one go about ridding one's house of a ghost? Was there an office where he could file a complaint? Really, he had to laugh.

Then the thought that he'd be facing this thing alone sobered him. He'd moved to Barlow almost on a whim, the last desperate measure of a writer who would do anything to kickstart his long-dead career. He had no family here. And the sum total of his friendly acquaintances could be counted on one hand: Constable Ray McFettridge, Luanne Samples, and Myrna Wilson.

George considered that it was times like this when he would have formerly sought answers in a few stiff drinks. Even before his drinking had taken on monstrous proportions, he'd been known to empty a few glasses of scotch to clarify life's more difficult situations. Now, that option was unavailable. It was pure, unassisted brain power from here on out. He'd broken enough promises in his time, but his promise to himself to keep a clear head for the rest of the ride was one he intended to keep.

He paced the living room floor, scratching his chin and contemplating the door to the garage. At last he came to a decision. His inner psychiatrist told him that the whole thing was just some psychosomatic manifestation of his guilt over Kathy's death. But he still didn't feel comfortable standing in front of that door. His hand trembled as he reached for the lock. The deadbolt thudded into position. He dragged one of the chairs in from the kitchen and wedged it under the knob for good measure.

He tried not to think too much about the implications of this last action.

Chapter Thirty-One: Avery

The sheriff's department owned one unmarked car, a loaded Chrysler they'd acquired as part of a drug interdiction a few months before Avery joined up. He'd seen it sitting in the lot and wondered if it ever got any use. Now, he was behind the wheel, parked in the cul-de-sac a few houses down from George Young's place. The stereo was good, although he'd blow his cover if he gave into the temptation to crank it up. The air conditioning was nice and chilly too, which was a good thing since he didn't feel like sticking to the leather interior in this heat. Everything in the car was top-shelf. But even that couldn't make up for the crushing boredom of the assignment. This George Young was one boring motherfucker. He hadn't been out of the house all morning.

His phone buzzed in his pocket and he scooted around on the cushy seat to get to it.

Shit. LaToya again.

He thought about letting it go to voicemail, but then felt guilty because the girl was pregnant. Besides, talking to her about what sort of junk food he needed to bring home to answer her cravings was better than sitting here staring at a house.

"Hey, girl, what's up?" he said, putting the phone to his ear.

Here's how Avery came to be saddled with this boring as shit detail:

Once the boss sobered up, he'd called over to apologize, and rattled on for what seemed like a full hour about conduct unbecoming an officer of the law and other such bullshit. Avery had accepted his apology, telling him to forget it, that it was no big deal. He wasn't going to file any damn complaint. For one thing, he wasn't one to go rocking the boat. And besides, now the boss owed him big time. His time on the job had taught Avery to never pass up a chance to get someone higher up the food chain into his debt. Discretion about something like last week's incident was the sort of thing that could open doors for him.

He just hadn't expected it to happen so quickly.

"Listen, there's another reason for my call," Tate had said. "There's a seminar up in Little Rock on new innovations in law enforcement. I'm thinking that I might head up there, check it out."

"Yeah?" Avery wondered where this was heading.

"After what happened…I need a little time off. I'm going to stay up there, knock around Little Rock, maybe go see a ball game at Dickey Stephens. And I'll be posting this next part in a memo so everyone knows what's up, but I wanted to let you know first. I'm leaving you in charge of the department while I'm gone. I know everyone has seniority on you, but I don't care. I trust you to do it right, it's my call, and that's all there is to it."

Avery had tried to keep the excitement out of his voice when he said that he'd give it his best effort all around.

"One more thing," Tate said. "Keep an eye on George Young. I still don't trust the guy. Keep it low profile just in case the state police are sitting on him too. They tell me that he's been cleared as a suspect, but you never know."

"I'll make it a priority, boss," Avery said.

It was not the type of stakeout that Avery had seen in cop movies. He wasn't spying on some criminal mastermind. He wasn't even keeping tabs on some paroled felon who was likely to lapse on the conditions of his release. There was no suspenseful game of cat-and-mouse going on. Hell, it looked like George Young only left the house to eat at fast food joints or walk laps around the block. After two days of watching the guy's house, Avery had been ready to pack it in. But then, something happened that caught his attention.

LaToya started in with one of her pregnancy cravings, and she just had to have fried pickles and fried cheese sticks. So even though all Avery wanted to do was drink a couple of beers and watch *Sportscenter*, he'd thrown on some shoes and taken her to Grouchies. It was the type of place that fried just about everything, and they had a couple of big screen TVs on the wall, so it was a good compromise. He'd been listening to LaToya go on about how she just couldn't decide which baby bed to buy when in walked George Young himself, and with Tate's mama hanging on his arm. That sure as hell got his attention. It was impossible to eavesdrop on them once they got seated at the other side of the room.

234 | ONLY THINGS

Hell, with the noise in that place, Avery had a hard time just hearing his woman go on about side rails and organic mattresses and all that shit.

But come morning, it was back to the same old routine.

So far, Young hadn't even left the house to scoop the paper off the driveway, and Avery was getting a little restless. To make matters worse, he needed to piss. Like, really urgently. The need had just sprung itself on him, and his eyes were drawn to the two empty Gatorade bottles on the floorboard. He shifted around in the seat. Maybe he could sneak over to the Walmart and take a leak there. Maybe get some snacks while he was at it. It wasn't like Young was going anywhere…

Shit. Speak of the goddamn devil.

Young was out of the house now.

You got to give it to him, the man has timing.

Avery groaned. He shifted around some more, trying to cross his legs and finding the steering wheel in the way. He snapped off the stereo, as if that could somehow settle his bladder down. The Gatorade bottles were becoming an attractive option. It wasn't like there was anyone to see him. Just about all these big ass houses were empty. This made him reconsider the wisdom of parking the car down the street the way he had. It wasn't exactly inconspicuous. That was the sort of thing Tate would have thought of, no doubt. The boss was a little high strung, goofy even, but when it came to the job, he was thorough. You don't get elected to the office of sheriff at thirty-three, not even in Gayler County, by being a fuck-up.

But it didn't seem to matter to Young that the Chrysler was parked out here in front of a vacant house. The man was standing there in the middle of his driveway, just staring at the garage door. He had something in his hand—a flashlight, it looked like—and he was thumping it against his thigh. Just standing there watching the garage door like it was something fascinating.

What the hell?

Minutes of bladder-straining agony ticked by. Avery watched Young step forward hesitantly and put his hand on the garage door. He stepped back, tapped his leg with his flashlight a few times, and then stepped forward to put his ear against the door.

Seriously, what the hell?

Young stayed there with his ear pressed against the garage for a while then straightened up. He walked back to his car and leaned in. The garage door started to rise. Young stood on the threshold, holding his flashlight in front of him. But it looked to Avery like he had the business end pointed the wrong way, like the old guy was planning on using it like a weapon instead of for its intended purpose. It was a big Maglite, just like police-issue, so why not? Maybe the old guy had a possum or squirrel in his garage and was tired of putting up with all the noise at night. Avery couldn't imagine beating a possum to death with a flashlight, though. It just seemed a little overboard. Didn't they make traps for that kind of thing?

The pressure on his bladder pulled him out of his thoughts on pest control. He'd heard the expression about back teeth floating before but never really understood it until now. Goddamn Gatorade. Once he opened a bottle, he couldn't let it be until it was empty. And LaToya, this was her fault too. She was the one packed him off this morning with two cold bottles, one Lemon-Lime and one Sour Melon. She had to have known he'd drink them both, one after the other.

"Aw, fuck it," he growled.

He grabbed one of the bottles and uncapped it. He stuck it into the console's cup holder and started unzipping his pants. Even though he knew that the houses around him were unoccupied except for Young's place and a couple of others on the other end of the block, he still looked around nervously. He pulled himself out of his pants, grabbed the empty bottle, and slipped inside. Relief washed over him instantly, and he was going like a fire hose. Only problem was, now Young had come out of the garage and gotten in his car.

"Motherfucker, not now, not now, not now," Avery chanted, trying to manage the bottle and keep an eye on the target of his surveillance.

Young's car backed out of the driveway and went down the street. It made a right at the Stop sign and kept going. It wasn't the only thing that kept going. Avery had nearly filled the first bottle. Gritting his teeth, he forced himself to stop. The bottle was warm and full. He screwed the cap back on and put it in the cup holder. He barely had time to get the second bottle in position before the flow started again.

"Mother*fucker*," he repeated, his voice half anger and half sweet relief.

This time the flow eased off and eventually stopped. He capped this bottle and set it next to its partner. There was a moment of terror as he zipped back up and nearly snagged a sensitive area in the zipper's metal teeth, but with a little wrestling around, he got everything put back in its normal resting position without too much trouble. Problem was, now Young was long gone.

The way Avery figured it, if Young wanted to have a reasonable expectation of privacy, he should lock the back door of his house. Barlow was pretty damn backward, at least compared to what Avery was used to up in Little Rock, but it sure as hell wasn't any fucking Mayberry. Besides, it wasn't like he was going to steal anything. He just wanted to have a quick look around, see if anything jumped out at him. He'd be in and out in a couple minutes. Even if Young just went out for a Big Mac and fries, Avery would be out of there with time to spare.

The back door was one of those sliding glass jobs that burglars love so much, and it opened right into the kitchen. Young was one hell of a housekeeper. The place was damn near spotless, so much so that Avery thought about taking a picture so he could show LaToya that it was possible to have a kitchen sink that wasn't constantly filled with dishes. There sure as hell wasn't anything incriminating in here.

He moved out of the kitchen and into the living room. There wasn't much furniture, just a chair, a small two-seater couch, a coffee table, a modest TV, and a bookcase. But here was something: there was some broken glass on the floor and a big wet spot in the middle of the carpet. A big cardboard box sat just this side of the wet spot.

And what the fuck is this shit?

The guy had a chair jammed up under the doorknob of the door that must have led out to the garage. Was he afraid of something getting in? Maybe that possum he was listening for earlier? Avery laughed, but he didn't feel very funny all the sudden.

Something was wrong about the whole thing. First, there was Young's weird behavior outside. Then there was this mess in the living room. And finally, that chair wedged up under the doorknob. Too fucking weird.

He tiptoed around the wet spot and looked into the open flaps of the box. It was full of those snow globe things, and not the little plastic ones that his mama used to put in their stockings at Christmastime. These were the type that grandma put on her shelf of stuff that no one was allowed to touch. Big, heavy, glass things. Well, there was one mystery solved. But what the hell was up with that door? This old guy, maybe he wasn't as boring as Avery thought.

Avery approached the door. He reached down for his gun but decided against pulling it. He settled for unsnapping his holster. Then he felt silly just doing that, so he fastened it again. There was a mess in here, that was for sure, and the chair under the doorknob was strange, but there wasn't much evidence of foul play. There didn't look to be any evidence of anything other than someone getting clumsy with a box.

Still, there was a strange feeling in this house. It was like how the air got all charged up right before a thunderstorm blew in. And the place was quiet too. Sure, it was an empty house, and empty houses should be quiet, but this was different. It was eerie. Strange word to just pop into his head, but that's what it felt like: eerie. His hand hesitated as he reached for the chair. He pulled back, deciding that he'd better get out of the house before Young got back.

Of course he knew there was some weird shit going on in Barlow. You'd have to be fooling yourself if you thought things were normal lately. First there was the Flannigan case, a man torn up in a storage unit with no evidence that anyone other than him was in there in the first place. Then there was the whole thing over at Myrna Wilson's house. He hadn't discussed it with Tate afterwards, other than to tell him not to worry about apologizing all over himself. He wouldn't have known how to bring that up, especially not with the boss.

Hell, he hadn't even been able to bring it up with LaToya, and he told her everything. She'd asked if everything was okay with the sheriff, and he'd just nodded and told her that yeah, it was just a little family dispute that had gotten out of hand, no big deal. That night, lying in bed and listening to her soft breathing, he'd asked himself why he'd been so afraid to tell her about what had happened. And he'd also wondered just what the hell *had* happened. Maybe he'd just been seeing things. LaToya was all the time telling him how he misremembered the way things happened. He'd always thought she was just using that to slip out of an argument, but maybe there was something to it. Maybe that whole scene in the bathroom hadn't been anything out of the ordinary at all.

But he didn't believe any of that. He'd taken exams that tested his observational skills as part of his training. He'd scored high. It was just that it was easier to think that something was off with his own observations than to imagine that something might be off with the world as he understood it. Far easier to just put it out of his mind, pretend it

238 | ONLY THINGS

hadn't happened at all. Sure, he'd seen the boss puke up his guts, but it was just regular old liquor sick and not some swirling grey vapor.

Only thing was, forgetting about it wasn't so easy. Something was wrong here, and not just in the way that so much shit that he saw on the job was wrong. He just couldn't quite put his finger on what it was. He didn't like to speculate much about that kind of shit. That story he told the boss about his mama collecting Bibles was true. What Avery left out was that she did it because she believed that those Bibles had the power to ward off demons. She figured that having all those old books around was the best kind of home protection. Avery figured that having all those old books around meant that Mama was a bit crazy. He didn't want any part of superstition. Open the door to that just a little bit, and who knew what sort of crazy shit would start to seem perfectly natural.

He told himself that he wouldn't let it get that far. He'd keep an eye on Young, figure out what the guy was up to. If he was up to some shit, the old guy would get the bracelets and a patrol car limo ride. If he was clean, he'd go on acting weird in his garage. Avery settled back into the front seat of the Chrysler, where two bottles of piss sat in the cup holder.

Chapter Thirty-Two: George

On most days, Walmart was, in George's view, as close as one could come to an earthly manifestation of hell. Populated by those who'd clearly abandoned all hope long ago, the Barlow store was as bleak as anything his imagination could conjure up. But it was a good place to clear his head. Wandering the long aisles of discounted merchandise and food products, he could let his brain ride on autopilot. It was his sincere wish that his subconscious mind would be able to use this respite to put together a rational solution to recent circumstances that defied rational thought.

He pushed his empty cart through the sporting goods section. There was an impressive array of fishing gear and lures. Maybe he'd take up fishing. After all, he'd have to find something to fill the hours when he wasn't turning out page after page of outstanding prose. He smiled at that. It was easier to think back on the morning's writing session than it was to think about what had happened afterwards. So he meditated on the good, clean energy of banging out words and feeling satisfied with the way they looked on the page. He was so intent on keeping this positive thought in his head that he became reckless with his cart as he turned a corner. Only a last second swerve prevented a collision between his cart and one pushed by Myrna Wilson.

"Well, fancy meeting you here," he said.

She gestured at her cart. "I came in for shampoo and cream cheese. Now it looks like I'm buying half the store."

He abandoned his cart altogether and walked alongside Myrna. "Tell you the truth, I was looking for some excuse to come by and visit. I promise that I'm not some creep. It's just that I woke up this morning and started writing. I went at it hard and heavy for some hours."

"That's great. Maybe you're turning a corner with your writing."

"For some reason, I felt like I needed to thank you for that. Does that sound funny?" He felt nervous admitting this stuff, but he just couldn't help himself. He already regretted giving her that sanitized version of Kathy's last days. The omission felt like a lie.

Myrna stopped her cart and gave him a look that he didn't quite understand.

"Okay, I don't know that look," George said. "So I'm going out on a limb here when I ask what's wrong."

She smiled, but it was a nervous, quick-fading smile. "George, we're moving awful fast. There are things you don't know about me. Things that might change the way you feel. Standing here with you, even right here by the bottles of Quaker State, I want to tell you everything. But I'm afraid of how you'll see me once you know all this stuff."

"There's nothing you can say that will make me…wait, you're not one of those nice, lady-next-door types that actually has a basement full of jars of shrunken heads and malformed fetuses, are you?"

The smile returned to her face, this time full of mischief. "I don't have a basement. I keep my jars in the bedroom."

"Well, now that we have that sorted out…"

"Be serious for a minute," she said. "And let me be serious too. You make me laugh, and I like that in a man, but right now, I need you to stop."

He held his hands up, doing his best to look innocent. "I mean it, there's nothing you can say that's going to scare me off. I could even get used to the shrunken heads."

And it was true. He couldn't think of a single thing she could tell him that would make him turn around and walk away. It didn't make a lick of sense, but that's how it was. Whether it was the inexplicable energy that seemed to bounce between them or the understanding look in her eyes or even just the way it had felt holding her when they danced to the pounding noise of Booze Hammer, he was bound to her now. Could he articulate that? Could he tell her over dinner that he felt a need just to be near her that was so intense it was nearly unsettling?

She looked at him with those deep brown eyes, and it seemed that she was staring straight into his mind, reading his thoughts as easily as if they were a flashing neon sign. She nodded, as if coming to some long awaited decision.

"We need to go somewhere quiet to talk." She stepped around her cartful of merchandise and took his hand. "Then I'll have to show you something. And if you don't want to run away screaming after that, I want you to hold me close and tell me everything will be okay."

"Myrna, is something…"

"Not here. Come on, before I lose my nerve."

"But your stuff." He pointed to the cart.

"There's nothing in there I really need right now."

Grouse Lake Park had been a huge swath of land encircling a shallow, muddy lake on the west end of Barlow. Then the county had sold the northern half of the circle as private real estate a couple years ago to offset the financial straits strangling Barlow. The parks service installed a few picnic tables and some boardwalks to mitigate the development on the north shore, and now Grouse Lake Park, or at least the half that wasn't occupied by houses and boat docks, was a respectable little spot for an afternoon stroll. George had learned all of that from a pamphlet his real estate agent had left at his house.

If not for the swarms of mosquitoes and fat, droning flies, the park could have been a delightful picnic spot. As it was, George thought that there should be a kiosk offering malaria treatments at the park's gates. But even the vampire mosquitoes, loud and brazen and thick as thieves, couldn't put him off his curiosity as he watched Myrna get out of her car and cross the little black top parking lot.

They'd driven to the park in separate cars. Myrna had insisted, just in case what she had to say made him want to flee. That way he would be spared an awkward car ride back to the Walmart parking lot. He'd tried again to convince her that whatever it was couldn't be so bad. But she'd stood firm. So he'd walked her to her car without saying anything. She'd given him a kiss, one that wasn't deep but lingered all the same, then told him she'd meet him at the east entrance to the park.

He took her hand, and they walked onto the concrete pathway that snaked through the woods and down to the shore of the lake.

"They should be selling quinine-laced ice cream out here," he said, swatting a mosquito with his free hand. "Do you want to head down to one of the pavilions by the water? Normally, I'd say those places are hot zones for these bloodsucking bastards, but I don't see that it could be much worse."

"No, I think I'd prefer to keep walking. For some reason, I think it will be easier to confess that way."

"Confess?" He stopped, pulling her around to face him. "Listen, whatever it is…"

"Can we just walk?" She turned away, looking at the trail. "I'm afraid that I'll lose my nerve if I don't get this out soon." She dropped his hand and started walking. "Promise me that once I get started, you'll just let me finish."

"I promise to wait for the question and answer session following the lecture." He trotted a few steps to catch up.

"I almost spilled some of this the other night. I asked you if you actually believed in any of the things you wrote about. You laughed it off, and that made me hold back." She kicked a pebble, and it went skittering across the pavement.

George had to bite his lip to keep quiet. She seemed not only reluctant to tell her tale, but also *afraid*.

"For a while, I thought it might be a brain tumor. Now I know that's not true. I haven't been to the doctor or anything, but I know. Don't ask me how. I just *know*."

George kept to his promise about maintaining his silence.

She told him about losing her son, how she imagined it was the way amputees never quite got used to the absence of a limb. "That's sort of how it was for me. I'd wake up at night and expect to hear him down the hall in his room, playing his video games or maybe talking on the phone with some girl. He had a few after him, you know."

There were tears in her eyes when George sneaked a look at her. The air was full of the wet dog smell of the shallow part of the lake, where it was little more than stagnant pools choked with vegetation, and they slowed their pace as if the thick air offered some resistance.

"And then, just as I was starting to finally accept it, that my baby boy was gone and never coming back, that's just what he did. He came back, George. My house is haunted by the ghost of my son. Do you want to run now?" She paused. "It's okay. You can answer."

"No," he said.

"Do you believe me? And don't say yes if what you mean is that you believe that I *think* the ghost of my dead son comes back to visit me a few times a month. That's patronizing, and I don't know if I could take that from you."

"I believe you. I really do." He felt a strange sort of relief. Hearing her confession—if indeed it could be called that—would make his that much easier. It also meant that, even if his encounter with Kathy had been the first signs of madness overtaking him, it was at least a shared madness.

"At first, it was nice. Maybe a bit scary, but nice all the same," she continued. "And there were others too, but they weren't like Dale. They were grey, silent, almost like shadows. I guess you could call them ghosts. Dale told me that I was their caretaker and that they meant me no harm. I've never felt threatened by them, but they can give you one heck of a start when you get out of bed at night for a glass of water and see some of them lurking around."

She paused for so long this time that he thought she might be done. They had emerged from the canopy of trees into the blinding afternoon sun as they followed the path that wound around the public portion of the lake.

Then she took up her story again. She told him about the dreams—horrible, claustrophobic nightmares that plagued her—and the sleepwalking episode that ended with her son's ghost consumed by some shadowy substance. George stopped walking when she got to that part. His heart nearly leapt into his throat as she described it. He stopped walking.

"Myrna, I've…"

She threw up a hand. "Now, it's time to show you something. After you've seen it, if you still want to be close to me, you can say whatever you need to say."

Her eyes were so full of pleading that he swallowed his words. He nodded.

"Let's walk back to the cars," she said. "I'd like you to follow me to my house."

George made his second lonely drive across town, following Myrna's car as they drove from Grouse Lake Park to her house. His brain worked overtime, firing questions, possibilities, and scenarios so fast that he could hardly latch onto one before it was knocked aside and replaced by another.

It wasn't hard for his imagination to throw up some likely theories. This was the sort of thing he'd made a living writing about for the better part of two decades. It was an uncomfortable possibility, but it had to be voiced all the same: Kathy was haunting his garage. She was out there among all her things. Perhaps she was there to see that he followed

244 | ONLY THINGS

through on his promise to find good homes for her stuff. But why would she lash out at him the way she had that morning?

He gritted his teeth. Was Kathy's ghost jealous? Only, she'd softened there at the end, said something about not being able to stop herself. What could she have been talking about? Her compulsion to acquire things? Her anger at his selling them? George shook his head.

He pulled the car into the driveway outside Myrna's house. She was already there, having gotten ahead of him at the Church Street intersection. She sat on the front porch with her legs dangling off the edge. She had two glasses of iced tea with her, and she offered one to George as he sat down beside her.

"I should tell you again that I had a really great time on our date," she said. "I'd sort of resigned myself to never having a night out like that ever again. And part of the reason for that is that my life is pretty messy. And I don't mean that as a figure of speech. Last night at dinner, when you were telling me about your wife, about Kathy…my heart fell right down into my stomach. You sounded sad that she was gone, but you also sounded relieved."

He opened his mouth to protest but thought better of it. He'd promised to let her get this all out in the open without interruption. Presumably, she'd gotten through the hard part already, telling him that her dead son haunted her house along with a silent army of half-formed grey figures. He let her continue.

"It's okay, I understand that. Henry wasn't the gentlest or kindest man. He took good care of us financially, but he wasn't much of a companion. I wouldn't say I was relieved when he passed, but I wasn't as sad as I thought I should be. I've never said that out loud, but it seems like today is my day for confessions." She drank down the rest of her tea. "No, the reason my heart sank is the way you talked about her collections. You sounded, well, not disgusted exactly, but maybe disappointed. I put it out of my mind. I swore that you'd never have to see what I'm about to show you. I told myself that I'd have time to fix it, but even as we were dancing around like teenagers, some part of me knew that I'd never fix it. I've told myself that a thousand times, and still nothing gets done."

She stood up and motioned for him to do the same. "You should probably kiss me now. After I open the door to the house, you might not want to again."

George took her in his arms. He put his lips on hers, kissing her deeply this time. The electricity that seemed to pass between them every time they touched was there, but this time it was less urgent. The arcs of white hot zapping lightning were gone, replaced by a deep thrumming. When their mouths parted, he held her face next to his, cheek to cheek.

"Whatever it is…" he said. But he'd have to be dense indeed not to know what was waiting for him beyond that door. And though he meant what he said, that he would still stand by Myrna no matter what, he could feel dread like a heavy weight pressing down on him.

The house was a cluttered mess.

No, that wasn't right. A cluttered mess was something that described a living room after a raucous party. A cluttered mess was what happened when you were tired and let the dishes and laundry pile up for a few days. This was something else entirely.

"It started to happen after Henry died, but Dale kept me reined in. Once he shipped out, I got worse. Then, when I got the news about what had happened, things got out of hand," she said.

George swallowed and found his voice. "You were depressed. It's not uncommon."

"No, that's not it. I mean, sure, I was down. But I never thought that this…" She swept her hand around. "…this *stuff* would fill the hole that Dale left. I'm not crazy. At least, I don't think I am. It was just that these things started calling to me."

"I think that's how it usually works."

"No." She crossed her arms and stamped her foot once. "I don't mean they called to me the way that a nice dress in the window calls to a mall shopper. I mean that they literally called out to me."

"I don't understand."

She softened a bit, uncrossed her arms. "I didn't either, not for a long time. All I knew was that some things at the flea market started to have this glow about them, this aura. And when I'd lay my hands on these things, I'd feel this electric tingle…"

"An electric tingle?" He raised his eyebrows. He reached out and took her hand in his. "Anything like that?"

"Not as deep and not as pleasant, but yes, like that." She squeezed his hand and let it drop. "Dale explained it to me. These were things that were very important to people during their lives. These are things that were *loved*, things that were *valued*. Somehow, something of their owner remained after death. Those are the grey people."

George stood there, looking around at the mess that had taken over the house. The ghost of a dead son, grey people lurking around the trinkets they loved in life…it was a lot to take in. But then again, so was the ghost of a writer's dead wife floating around in the garage. It seemed to George that suddenly his whole world was a lot to take in.

"You can say something," Myrna said. "Or if you want to leave, please just do it. I don't want to get my hopes up now, only to find out later that this was over from the moment you stepped in and saw…" She looked around, shaking her head slowly. "…and saw all this mess. Or that it was even before that, when I started rattling on about ghosts and such."

He'd been taking a step forward, almost purely on instinct, to take her in his arms and comfort her. He was a lot of things, but George wasn't the type who could stand idly by while a woman's bottom lip began that tell-tale quiver. It was hardwired into him, the impulse to hug and comfort. But he took her advice, and examined his feelings. It didn't take long.

He hated what Kathy became. He could admit that now. A large part of it was her insistence on the importance of things. She took him for granted. She took all people for granted. She just couldn't see that all her precious collections, they were only things. But Myrna was different. He knew it deep down in his being.

He wanted to tell her that. He settled for telling her that everything was okay, that everything would work out just fine. Because he loved her. He expected it to sound awkward coming out. It always had the first time he'd said it to a woman in the past. Now, although his pulse quickened at the words just as it had those other times, it felt right. She melted into his arms. And quietly, her face pressed into his chest, she asked him if he would stay with her.

"It's a hard climb up these stairs to the bedroom," she said. "But I can show you the way."

The bedroom was not as cluttered and packed as the rest of the house, which is to say that there were several wide paths through the junk, leading to the bed. They moved slowly, holding one another and kissing as they went. Myrna paused to a clear away the dozen stuffed animals that were scattered across the bed. George pulled her back into his arms and pressed his mouth against hers. When at last they broke apart, they stood looking into one another's eyes, breathing hard.

"It's been a long time for me," she said, sitting down on the edge of the bed. "I hope I remember how to do this."

"We'll figure it out," George said.

Afterwards, they dozed, tangled up in the sheets.

When they awoke, the afternoon was dying slowly, the warm rays of the sun spilling through the blinds, fading from bright yellow to deeper orange. George kissed her before she could open her eyes, and she sighed, snuggling closer. These kisses softer, less urgent, and they went about it lazily, breaking apart to smile at one another.

"I'd make you dinner, but I don't have much in the house other than breakfast cereal," Myrna said. "As you may recall, I was swept off my feet at the store and forced to abandon my groceries."

"That was an awfully short-sighted gentleman. Probably some slick gigolo who is not to be trusted." George tickled her ribs, and she squealed with laughter.

"Stop it!" She swatted him away playfully. "I'm serious about being hungry. And I'm also serious about not having much more than Grape Nuts. There might be a TV dinner hiding in the back of the freezer, but even that might be wishful thinking."

"You think it might be Salisbury steak? I practically lived on those during my bachelor days."

"Gross," she said.

"Woman, my palette is world renowned."

"Your silliness is world renowned."

They both laughed then settled into silence. The house made its usual settling noises, but there were no ghosts rattling chains or mysterious moans from the attic. He considered for a moment commenting on how normal it seemed for a haunted house, but he knew she wouldn't take it lightly, and he didn't want to spoil the moment.

"It comes and goes, you know. All the weirdness, I mean," she said, as if reading his mind. "It's early yet. Tonight, that black shape could tear through the house, screaming like a cat in heat. Or maybe my son Dale might pay me a visit. I might get up for the bathroom and see the grey people milling about. Then again, it may just be like a night in a normal house. You'll see."

248 | ONLY THINGS

"Myrna, did you just ask me to spend the night?"

"Maybe. Tell you the truth, I'm not so sure I want to be on my own. Now that I've actually told someone about everything, it feels strange to be here. I'm not sure I could be alone." She gave him a quick peck on the cheek then sprang out of bed. "But you better buy me dinner first."

She picked her way across the clutter-strewn floor with practiced ease and disappeared into the bathroom.

Once again, they feasted on deep fried delights at Grouchies before listening to Booze Hammer's set of raucous rock music. When they returned to Myrna's house, their feet were sore from dancing and their mouths stretched and tired from smiling and laughing. They made another careful ascent of the staircase then collapsed into bed, too tired to do anything but find a comfortable position in which to hold each other as they fell asleep.

George woke suddenly, unsure for a moment what had caused him to wake. Then the noise started up again, a symphony of shattering glass, tearing paper, and cracking wood. He sat up, groping around blindly. Myrna was gone. He stumbled across the room, stubbing his toes on stacks of unseen objects, barking his shins on the corners of the furniture. A large cardboard box tripped him up. He threw his arms out, grabbing the wall for support. He found the bathroom and managed to flip on the light switch. Blinded for a moment, he turned away. As he blinked his eyes to get adjusted to the light, he saw that the box that almost sent him sprawling was one of his own. It was one of the boxes of snow globes he'd given Myrna after their date. There was a similar box still sitting in the trunk of his car, forgotten after the day's events.

The noise downstairs rose in volume. Now he could hear Myrna's voice. She was shouting, screaming really, at whatever was causing the cacophony.

George ducked out of the bathroom. He stepped through the bedroom door and saw Myrna standing halfway down the staircase, gripping the bannister with both hands as she screamed, "Leave me alone! You won't spoil this for me! Go away!"

George picked his way down the stairs and stood at her side. He looked first at her frantic, panicked face then at the chaos engulfing the living room. A black tornado swirled through the space, tearing through Myrna's vast collection of objects. Paperback books flew into the air,

Brad Carter | 249

their pages fluttering like startled birds before being torn out and shredded into yellowed confetti. The cyclone—a whirling centrifuge of black fog—smashed the furniture to matchsticks and ripped away the curtains. The tornado trailed long streams of oily black shadows that seemed at once to be liquid and vapor. The stench of mildew and dry rot assaulted George's nostrils.

"Myrna!" He threw his arms around her, dragging her back up the stairs and into her bedroom. He pushed her gently inside, kicked aside some clothes and magazines, and closed the door behind him. They stood there for a moment just looking at each other.

"Don't look at me like that," she said. "You told me that you believed me."

"I did believe you. It's just…"

"But you *said* that you believed."

There was no time for argument. Black tendrils had begun to seep into the room through the space between the door and the carpet. The sounds of destruction tapered off as more of the black substance flooded in. It swirled over the carpet and around their feet. A steady droning, like an insect chorus trying to mimic human speech, filled the room.

Myrna clapped her hands over her ears. George pulled her into his arms, and she buried her face in his t-shirt. The droning voice rose in volume until George could feel it in his teeth, his eyes. Cold, clammy streamers of liquid shadow made contact with his bare feet and he recoiled, pulling Myrna back with him.

The black substance changed, solidifying into something vaguely human-shaped. George could see hair and features. They were generic, blank almost, but feminine. Lines and detail spread across the face, twisting the nose, eyes, and mouth into a recognizable form. As he realized the form that the substance was taking, he added his own screams to the deafening din. The person who stood before him, molded out of material that was at once as insubstantial as fog and as palpable as thick and reeking tar, was his departed wife Kathy. She seemed to sense the recognition in his eyes, and her horrible dripping face broke into a smile. The insect voice snapped abruptly to silence.

Shadow Kathy drifted closer, until she was standing toe-to-toe with George. She raised her rippling arms, and for a terrible moment, George was sure that she meant to draw them into a group hug. His skin crawled at the thought of being embraced by the stinking black arms, caressed by the mildew-scented hands.

"Mine," she whispered, her voice like a knife edge drawn across a whetstone. "It's all mine."

Myrna pulled her face away from George's shirt. She stared defiantly at the shadow Kathy. "Go away. You're not wanted here. You go away!"

The mocking smile on Kathy's face fell away. Her features twisted, becoming something primitive, bestial. George recalled for a horrible instant all those times he'd seen Kathy staring at her reflection in the mirror, prodding her face and mumbling. Goose bumps broke out over his arms.

"You will listen to me. Growing stronger every day, even in this dead shell." Kathy's raspy voice climbed in volume and pitch. Her hands, the fingers stretched to grotesque length, grabbed fistfuls of Myrna's nightshirt and ripped her from George's arms. Kathy screeched wordlessly and flung her across the room. Myrna slammed into the wall, her shoulder leaving a hole in the drywall. Kathy's rippling face froze for a moment in a satisfied smile. "Mine. It's mine, all of it."

George lunged, making an awkward grab for the shadowy figure. His hands closed around her throat, but it was like grasping an oil slick. She laughed as his hands scraped through her flesh, little dribbles of black tar clinging to his closed fists.

"You," she said, her face twisting as if it were clay manipulated by an unseen sculptor. "Faithless, lying drunkard."

Clammy fingers wrapped around his neck, at first so gently that their grip was almost a caress. Suddenly, they applied pressure that steadily increased until George's airway choked off. Panic seized him as he realized that he was being lifted off the floor, held aloft by the thing that had once been his wife. His vision blurred, going dark around the edges.

The sudden impact of his rear end dropping to the floor pulled him back from the edge of unconsciousness. As his vision cleared, he saw that Kathy had retreated to the far corner of the room, crowded into the space between the bed and the window. One after another, the glass snow globes she'd once treasured whizzed through the air like grenades. They smashed against the wall or against the bed frame. George turned to watch Myrna. She rummaged in the box for another globe, tore the newspaper wrapping away, and hurled the bauble at the cowering figure.

"Go away!" she screamed, reaching into the box for more ammunition. This time she found a miniature plastic globe, the once clear covering scratched and yellowed. She wound up like a fastballer and whipped it across the room. When she had finally exhausted her supply, she picked up the box and slung it like a shot put.

Kathy rose from her crouch, her body now less tar and more fog. Her features dissolved, and her form became indistinct. In moments, the strange mockery of human form became a swirling black cloud. It whirled about, gathering enough force that some of the clothes strewn across the floor whipped through the air. George's hair blew back from his scalp. He threw his arm across his face and staggered blindly back to Myrna. Bits of debris—shards of glass, loose change, and broken figurine pieces—pelted his back. Stuffed animals whirled through the air, thumping against him.

He opened his eyes just enough to get his bearings as he crouched down next to Myrna. He picked her up, surprised by his own strength, and staggered to the walk-in closet adjacent to the bathroom. The closet, which would have been spacious had it not been crammed waist-high with clothes, seemed to be outside the storm's reach. He kicked aside enough of the clothes to gain entrance and then deposited Myrna onto one of the soft piles. The clothes he'd moved out of the closet whipped through the air as the wind seized them. He turned and slammed the door shut then settled down next to Myrna. On the other side of the door, the storm continued.

Chapter Thirty-Three: Ray

Ray's mother bid him farewell. They embraced, both of them pressing their tear-streaked faces into the other's shoulder. And then, she started to fade. First, the color leached out of her, like a photograph bleached by the sun. And then she began to grow less and less substantial, becoming weightless and delicate in Ray's arms. Gradually, she disappeared. He prowled around the room, drying his eyes and wondering just what the hell he was supposed to do.

It happened to the walls first. Tiny holes appeared in the wood paneling, as if they were made of wool and a horde of moths were nibbling away at them. The tiny holes merged, becoming bigger and bigger holes until the walls dropped away entirely. The ceiling wavered and was gone. Ray was surrounded on all sides by a black expanse deeper than a starless midnight. The floor beneath his feet trembled as it became less solid. And then it was gone. He fell for what seemed like hours. It wasn't the hair-blown-back plunge of a roller coaster, but the gentle descent of an autumn leaf leaving the highest bough and drifting on the cool breeze. Ray relaxed as he was drawn back to the world of the living.

His head smacked down on the kitchen table, and he slid out of his chair and onto the floor. He came painfully awake, trying to sit up and hitting his head on the underside of the table.

"Ray!" Stephanie shouted, dragging him from under the table and helping him to his feet.

Pins and needles shot from his toes to his kneecaps to his ass. It seemed everything below his waist was still asleep.

"I'm okay," he said, his throat dry and ticklish. "I'm just…let me sit down."

Stephanie hoisted him up, getting under his arm and ushering him forward. She marched him into the living room and released him onto the couch. She flopped down next to him. "Where were you? Tell me all about it. I mean, I knew you were somewhere else, but it was like you were on autopilot, walking around with these zombie eyes. And man, did you eat while you were gone. Come on, tell me what happened!"

Ray raised a hand to halt the onslaught of questions. "Get me two, three aspirin and a Coke, I'll tell you whatever you want to know."

"I have some Advil in the bathroom." She jumped off the couch and thundered down the hall.

Ray sat up and rubbed his legs, getting some of the circulation going there. He was sore all over and had a supersize headache beating on the inside of his skull like it was a bass drum. He straightened up and rolled his head around on his shoulders. His neck popped like dry kindling.

Stephanie trotted back into the room and presented him with three tablets of Advil and a frosty can of Coke. Ray cracked open the soda and washed the medicine down with three long, burning gulps. He tipped his head back and belched.

"I was behind the veil," he said. He liked watching Stephanie's mouth fall open and her eyes get big. "Mom was there, and she had quite a story to tell."

"Is it George Young?" She was practically bouncing around.

"She wasn't that specific. But she said that there was something big on the horizon, that Gayler County was about to be ground zero for some serious supernatural shit. Two opposing forces meeting, something like that." He took another slug of Coke and felt it hit his empty stomach. "You said I ate a lot while I was over there? I feel pretty damn hungry right now."

"We can eat after you tell me what this big supernatural event is."

"Some Chinese food sounds awful good. There's a buffet over in Barlow…"

"How can you be so damn calm right now?" She grabbed him by the shoulder, gave him a little shake. "Damn it, you were just on the other side of existence. Mystics and seekers have gone to ridiculous lengths to get just the tiniest peek behind the veil, and you've just been over there because you got a little bump on the head. And all you can think about is egg rolls!"

"I'm not sure what you want me to say. I'm thinking about egg rolls because my stomach is growling like a grizzly bear just woke up from hibernation. And I can be calm because I don't see what jumping up and down like my hair is on fire is going to accomplish." Ray stood up and stretched his legs. "Mom said that I had a talent for intuition and that I'd soon know how to proceed. Now that I think about it, she didn't really tell me much of anything that sounded useful. But at the moment, all my intuition is telling me is that it's way past dinner time. And by damn, if I'm going to start flexing my psychic muscles of intuition or what the hell ever they're called, then I'm sure as shit not doing it on an empty stomach. Now you can sit there and wring your hands, but I'm going over to that buffet for some General Tso's Chicken."

"You'd better let me drive," Stephanie said. "You remember what happened the last time you were behind the wheel."

Stephanie drove over to the Happy Okay Buffet in sullen silence. She claimed that she wasn't hungry and probably would just get a drink, but once inside, she grabbed a plate and filled it up with noodles and bright orange chunks of fried chicken in spicy sauce.

"So, she couldn't tell you specifics?" Stephanie asked between mouthfuls.

Ray shook his head. Now that he had some food in his belly, he felt better about talking. "No, all she said was that there had been something that escaped from her side of the curtain and was stirring up shit in our world, and it had to be stopped before it spread. If it really was my mother that I talked to, that is."

She twirled up some noodles on her fork. "Who else would it have been?"

"Could have just been my own subconscious mind talking back to me. Could have even been something evil trying to lead me astray. The one time I did anything like this, anything involving the talent I inherited, it wasn't exactly roses and rainbows, you know."

"Well, what do you think? Was it her?"

He paused a moment to consider. "I think it was her. I like to believe that she's on the other side, cheering me on. But to tell you the truth, I'm shitting myself. I'm standing between Gayler County and the forces of the supernatural? That doesn't sound good, does it?"

She dropped her fork onto her plate. "Could have fooled me. You're hardly dragging around like there's an albatross around your neck. So, what's our next move?"

"My gut is still telling me that George Young is the linchpin of whatever is going on. Now, I've sounded this guy out once before, and he's a hardcore skeptic. I can't just go in guns blazing and say, 'Hey partner, I know you don't believe in anything supernatural, but the

Brad Carter | 255

reason you're such a good writer about such things is that you're a magnet for it, and right now you have some seriously bad ju-ju hanging onto you.' He'll think I've flipped my lid. All I can think of is that I set up surveillance over at Young's house. If he really is in the eye of the storm, there has to be something going on around him that I can point to and say, 'Look at that. What other explanation can you give me?' Then, who knows?" George shrugged. "That's all I got. Just keep my eyes open and hope shit doesn't get too bad before I can do something about it."

Stephanie laughed. "Oh man, a stake-out. I was hoping when I came down here I'd get to see you do some real police stuff."

"I'm just a town constable. That's hardly real police."

"But you're better than that. You're like a supernatural detective now."

It was Ray's turn to laugh. "Like Ben McCauley?"

Stephanie narrowed her eyes. "Who?"

Chapter Thirty-Four: Effie

There wasn't much on TV—just the usual sexy doctor shows and reruns of *Law and Order*—but Effie resolved to spend the night with the remote control in one hand and a glass of wine in the other. She tossed the remains of her Stouffer's single serving lasagna in the trashcan, poured a second glass of pinot noir, and trudged back into the living room. Her late dinner was already sitting like a brick in the bottom of her stomach. Eating that shit was bound to put the weight on her, now that she was in a job where she mostly sat on her ass all day. She added joining a gym to her list of things to do.

She flopped down in her recliner and slung her feet—shod in fuzzy bunny slippers—up on the footrest. The tension that didn't come out with her heavy sigh would soon be pummeled into submission by a couple hours of mindless TV and wine, she decided.

The job was a lot more stressful than she thought it would be. She'd popped off about how the directorship of a branch library was nothing compared to combat missions, and for the most part, it was true. But there were times when combat had its advantages. After all, you couldn't shoot people at the library. You couldn't even yell at them. And according to Dr. Roberson, you weren't even allowed to bust someone down a rank. It was bullshit, plain and simple.

Sooner or later, she'd have to start getting out of the house. As much as she dreaded the dating scene, Effie figured she'd have to at least dip her toe in the water. She hadn't had a girlfriend since high school. For all those long years in the service, she'd kept a lid on that part of her life, mostly out of necessity. Even though she was in Arkansas—not the most progressive place—she'd be damned if she was going to keep it in check. Let the rednecks gape and gawk. She needed someone to rub her shoulders, someone to warm up the bed.

"Later for that," she said to the empty room.

She thumbed the remote, jumping from channel to channel in an effort to get away from the blaring commercials. Her eyes drifted away from the screen to the clutter in the room. There were still some boxes that she hadn't unpacked. And here and there among them were the stacks of things she'd accumulated since moving in: little household items she thought she might need, books she would eventually get around to reading, and other assorted junk. She smiled at the mess. It was her rebellion after years of spic-and-span army life, when her tiny house on base had been as neat as an operating theater. As a young woman, she'd been impulsive and unorganized. The army had beaten that out of her, but civilian life was allowing it to creep back in.

Let the organization stay at the library, she figured. A little chaos is good for the home. And it beat the hell out of housework.

There was a made for TV movie on the Lifetime channel about a single mother with a gambling problem. There were actors she recognized, but not well enough to know by name.

"Look, it's that guy that was in that thing!" she shouted back at the TV.

She laughed. The wine was doing a number on her. She'd never been one for drinking to excess, but something about the last week had persuaded her that it might be a good idea to tie one on. Dealing with Dr. Roberson's golden egg-laying goose, Chris Clanton, was grating on her nerves. All week he'd been even twitchier and weirder than usual. Twice, she'd caught him using a ruler to make sure the books on his shelves were arranged perfectly. And he'd been talking to himself too. All damn day, while he was sorting or shelving or mending, he kept up a steady stream of whispered monologue, too quiet to require a reprimand, but too damn strange to just ignore. This shit with her office, breaking in and cleaning it top to bottom, it was way over the line. But she was stuck with him. Word had come down from on high. Dr. Roberson would be meeting with her when he got back in town from the ALA conference, according to the terse voice mail he'd left. Effie had no doubt the subject of the meeting would be Clanton's looming reinstatement. Oh well, it was worth a shot, sending Clanton on a little forced vacation. Maybe the time off would do him some good. Maybe he'd come back a changed man.

"And maybe when I look in the mirror in the morning, I'll see Angelina fucking Jolie staring back at me," she said.

Her wineglass was empty. This time when she filled it, she brought the bottle back with her. There was no sense pussy-footing around it. She was going to get drunk and forget about work for one night. Hell, she was already well on her way. She had Friday off this week, a day she'd taken with the intention of finally getting her things unpacked and put away. So what if she spent that day hung over and lying around in bed? It wasn't like it would be the end of the world if the house stayed messy for another week. The last thing she needed was to start obsessing over a little mess. She wasn't Chris Clanton, after all.

Fucking Clanton.

She wondered if there was enough wine in that bottle to scrub his image out of her brain. Hell, was there enough booze in the *world* for that?

This glass of wine didn't seem to last as long as the one before. Good thing she'd brought the bottle. That way she wouldn't have to wait for commercial breaks to run to the kitchen for a refill. Not that she was too concerned about missing any of the movie. It had moved into some hot and heavy bedroom action between the hot gambling mama and the guy that was in that thing. But this was just regular old cable, so there wasn't much skin on display, and besides, the actors really didn't seem that into it. She was considering reaching over to grab the remote—wondering if it was even worth the effort—when the doorbell rang.

"Shit!" She nearly spilled wine all over her shirt as she climbed out of the chair. It was a ridiculously overpriced recliner and easily the best piece of furniture she'd ever owned, but it was apparently not set up for the less than sober.

The short walk to the front door gave her a few seconds to regain her composure. She felt like she made a good effort in that direction, although the wine was working its magic on her. That was why she forgot to use the peep hole, why she just unchained the door and poked her head out without a second thought.

She paused a couple beats, just long enough to put a name to the stupidly grinning face looking back at her.

"Clanton, what the hell…" she drew her robe up around her. She considered slamming the door in his face, maybe even calling the cops, but she stopped herself. He creeped her out—no denying that—but she'd shot people who were shooting back at her, and she'd watched men and women torn apart by bullets and shrapnel. No way was this Clanton asshole putting a scare into her. Probably, he was just drunk and looking to mess with her. No doubt he knew that he had friends up high on the library food chain and got his kicks lording it over his supervisors. Maybe he'd done this to those other supervisors that Roberson had told her about.

Drawing back? Acting scared? Not a goddamn option.

"Hello, Effie." Clanton's idiot grin spread even wider. "You're up awful late tonight. You know, your neighbors' lights are all out. Just you burning the midnight oil." He turned his head and stage-whispered to some imaginary friend. "You were right. This is how great things are accomplished, by bold moves. I feel good. I feel very, very good right now."

"I don't think there's any way that even you can think this is appropriate behavior," she said in her best soldier voice. "You've overstepped your bounds coming here. Even you have to know that."

"Really?" The stupid smile fell away, replaced by something like feigned embarrassment. He leaned over and spoke again to his invisible companion. "You see how she is, why she's impossible to work with? And the rumor going around is that she's a dyke. Can you imagine?"

"And I don't care who your friends are at the main library or on the board of fucking directors, if you don't get off my property double quick, you won't have a job to come back to. This little vacation of yours will become permanent." Effie squared her shoulders.

"What's that?" he asked, leaning over to his imaginary buddy. "Oh, yes, by all means. I'm tired of her voice too. For someone who was supposedly a badass soldier, she's a bit shrill."

"Who the hell are you talking to?"

Had she been sober, she would never have missed it. She'd have seen his arm creep to his back pocket. Hell, she wouldn't have needed to see his forearm tense up as his hand came back around, this time gripping a length of metal. Had she been at her sharpest, she'd have seen it in his eyes, and she would have had him down on the floor screaming for her to please not break his arm as she twisted his hand up between his shoulder blades. But with most of a bottle of wine in her, the best she could manage was some half-ass tussle.

His strength surprised her. For a guy that looked so scrawny, he wrenched his arm out of her grasp with shocking ease.

"Here we go!" he shouted with undisguised glee in his voice as he dealt her a backhand blow with what looked to be a pipe of some kind.

It caught her on the side of her head. Her world spun for a moment then she charged forward swinging, landing a couple of quick jabs to his ribs and finishing with an uppercut that he mostly dodged. For good measure, she tried to recover with a left hook, but it wasn't her good arm and she was way off balance anyway. He stepped aside like a matador dodging a slow bull and smashed the metal bar across the base of her skull.

Clanton carried on talking to his imaginary friend while she flailed about, trying not to fall. Just as she was coming up, he whipped the bar into her ribs. He hooked the fingers of his free hand into her hair and wrenched her head back. A line of blood spilled out of his lower lip, where one of her punches had landed.

"Just look at the state of this place, Effie. It's a disgrace. But that's okay. We'll get it cleaned right up." He slammed her again and again in the ribs.

She tried to pull free, but he had seemingly all of her hair twisted up in his fist, and his grip had the strength of a crazed animal. The harder she struggled, the more he slammed his weapon into her ribs. It felt like her abdomen was full of broken glass. She screamed, and he responded by smashing her in the face. Jagged fragments of teeth shot down her throat, and she gagged, bringing up a mouthful of blood.

Then she was face down on the floor. She tried to say something, anything, but all that came up was more blood. The breath went out of her as Clanton sat down on her back. He placed the metal bar beneath her chin, pulling it back against her throat. She pinwheeled her arms, reaching back to find some purchase which would allow her to dislodge him. But he held on against her struggles with the sort of unfeeling strength that belonged only to the truly mad.

Well, shit. This is how it ends?

Effie's world grew dark.

Chapter Thirty-Five: Julian

Despite what his stuck-up, stick-in-the-ass brother thought, Julian was well aware of the mess in the house. He knew it was cluttered and filthy. And that's just the way he liked it. The way he saw it, this was man's natural state, in the dirt, the dust, the grime. It was his way of keeping the world at bay. The things around him formed a protective shield, through which none of the world's nerve-wracking rules and regulations could penetrate. And that's not all. There were health benefits to leading a disordered, natural life. Julian could not remember the last time he'd fallen ill. He chalked it up to his prolonged exposure to the microbes in his surroundings. And to his good protective layer of dirt. A bath once a week during the summer seemed excessive, but it was his one concession to modern standards.

There was another reason for the state of the house, one that Julian would never admit out loud but believed as deeply as he believed that the sky was blue. Keeping the maximum amount of disorder in this place kept the ghost of his father alive. Late at night, when the house was dark and Julian lay in his bed beneath a thick cocoon of stained sheets and dusty blankets, he could still hear Vernon Clanton's thundering voice. If Julian were to give in and follow his older brother's edicts about order and cleanliness, he knew that he'd only banish his father's memory to the void of death. Chris would never understand something like that. He was simply too practical-minded.

Julian shifted around on his squeaky mattress. Sleep was elusive, and he came to the conclusion that a stiff nightcap was just the thing. He threw aside the blankets and was halfway down the stairs when the pounding on the front door started.

"Hold your damn horses. I'm coming," he muttered, pulling his bathrobe around him. "Little late to be calling on people, anyhow. Should mind your damn manners and come back at a decent hour."

He kicked aside a stack of old magazines and junk mail to punctuate this burst of false anger. The truth was that he was happy for the diversion, whatever it was, a mis-delivered pizza, a complaining neighbor, or a motorist with a flat tire and no spare. He never really thought that it might be his brother. Wasn't Chris an early-to-bed, early-to-rise type? Didn't he need to get the proper amount of sleep so he could get up at the crack of dawn and starch his collars and pluck his nose hairs before going off to his stupid and completely unnecessary job? But when Julian opened the front door, there stood Chris.

"Just what in the blue hell is this shit? Don't you know what time it is?" Julian emphasized the point by looking down at his wrist, where his watch would have been had he not misplaced it last month. "And maybe you forgot about that restraining order. I thought you were the type to read all the fine print, but since you're here, let me spell it out for you. It means Chris Clanton is not fucking welcome on this property. The words on that little mat beneath your feet no longer apply to you."

His brother grinned like a fool. He turned his head to one side and spoke to some invisible friend he'd brought with him. "You see how he is? My own brother, living in abject disorder."

"Not this crazy shit again." Julian leveled a hard stare right at his brother. "Or maybe you want to come in and have another food bath?"

"There just is no hope for some people," Chris said.

Julian couldn't tell whether he was talking to his imaginary friend or him. Either way, Chris brushed past him and stepped into the house. He carried something at his side, thumping it against his leg. It looked like a metal pipe. Julian looked closer and saw that it had little musical notes engraved down its length.

What the hell, a wind chime?

Julian spun around and grabbed Chris' shoulder. "Hey, asshole. Do I need to call the cops?"

It happened so fast that Julian didn't even have time to throw up his hands protectively in front of his face. Not that it would have mattered. Chris swung the length of metal with such force that it smashed out all Julian's teeth on the right side and broke his jaw. A second blow, delivered quickly on the heels of the first, caught him on the ear. Pain sheared through his skull. Little pinpricks of light lit up tracers across his vision. Through the ringing in his head, Julian heard Chris launch into some crazed monologue, his voice giddy, delirious.

"We could have stood together as brothers, united against the Chaos. But you see how far gone he is. And you also see how deep is my dedication to the cause." Chris punctuated his lines with a third strike,

Brad Carter | 263

this one to the back of Julian's neck. "My own brother! You of all people should have been able to see the truth!"

Julian staggered, his hands clutched to his bleeding face. The room spun around him. He didn't see the next blow coming, but it landed across the bridge of his nose. Blackness wiped away his vision. He thudded heavily to the floor. His head whiplashed on his neck as Chris kicked him again and again. And then he was using the wind chime, hammering away at Julian's skull.

Soon enough, he felt nothing, and that was a mercy.

Chapter Thirty-Six: Amjad

The best part of the donut business was being off by noon every day. The worst part of the donut business was being at the shop so damn early in the morning. At the beginning of his tenure as manager, Amjad had been there promptly at 3 AM, but he'd become so adept at the opening procedure—mixing, frying, glazing—that he could now slide in a half-hour later and still get the show on the road in advance of opening time. No way would his father have approved of such a late start. But his father was enjoying retirement in Tempe, and Amjad was stuck in Arkansas, running the family's donut empire, carrying on the proud tradition of making sure the good people of Little Rock were properly caffeinated and filled with sugar and grease. It wasn't what Amjad thought of as a noble calling, but it was what he had. Lately, he'd thought of getting back into UALR, finishing up his degree. But he was short enough on sleep as it was, and more student loan debt was the last thing he needed. No, he was better off sticking to what he knew.

"And Alexander wept when he saw the breadth of his kingdom," Amjad sighed as he pushed his bike in through the Employees Only door at the rear of the shop. He kicked the door shut behind him.

Actually, it wasn't so bad. For the most part, the customers were nice enough, and business was always steady. But he'd be damned if he ever strong armed his kids into taking over the family business. Of course, to treat his offspring magnanimously, he'd first have to produce them, and that meant getting out and finding a mate. Not so easy to do when his ass was in bed before nine most nights.

Heavy is the head that wears the donut crown.

He was arranging the first few batches of regular glazed in the display case when he noticed the guy pacing around in front of the door. Amjad recognized him as one of his regulars, one that normally popped in for three glazed and a large coffee, but who had also been acting pretty twitchy lately. On his last visit, Amjad had to tell the guy to take a hike. Was it Monday or maybe yesterday? The days ran together sometimes in one long blur of hot coffee and hotter grease. Whenever it was, that guy—Mr. Three Glazed, Large Black Coffee himself—was doing his best to wear a rut in the sidewalk. For a guy all by himself, he seemed to be having one hell of a conversation, swinging his arms in wild gestures, like he was giving someone a recap of a thrilling sporting event or maybe having some sort of seizure.

Amjad ignored him for a while, concentrating instead on getting the coffee going and scooping donuts out of the fryer. He hit this hot batch with some strawberry glaze and white sprinkles then slid them into the display case. He punched out a few rings of dough, slipped them into the fryer, and looked out front again. The guy was still there. If anything, he looked even crazier now. He was usually smartly dressed and neat as a pin, but now he looked wild, as if he'd been doing hard work in the hot sun. His shirt was unbuttoned and hanging askew. His hair was disarrayed. And even at this distance, Amjad could tell the guy's eyes weren't right. They were so wide they looked like they might jump right out of his face.

Amjad checked his watch and sighed. Opening time was coming, and if this weirdo wanted to stomp around and talk to himself, he'd need to find a different location. Nothing can scare off business like a crazy person loitering near the entrance. If Amjad called the cops, they could probably clear him out with a minimum of fuss. Or not. It could turn into a big scene with Tasers and guns drawn. That kind of scene could be even worse for business. Then again, maybe the guy just really wanted a donut and coffee. Even the insane need a morning pick-me-up, so why the hell not? Get the guy fixed up with his donuts and coffee, and maybe he'd take his nutjob act elsewhere. Worth a shot, anyway.

This was the kind of thinking that made his father such a beloved presence. He was always taking the day old donuts to the homeless shelter or the drug addiction treatment homes. No way would his father have called the cops on this guy.

Amjad boxed up a trio of fresh donuts, poured a large coffee, and made a mental note to start taking the leftover donuts down to the Samaritan Center again. Just because his dad wasn't here to look over his shoulder, Amjad could still do the right thing. Even if it meant going out of his way after a long shift.

He walked from behind the counter and set the donuts and coffee on the table nearest the door. He dug his keys out of his pocket.

"Three glazed and a large black coffee, am I right?" he asked as he unlocked the front door. He opened the door and leaned out, offering the on-the-house breakfast and what he hoped was a neutral smile.

The crazy man stopped mid-gesture to stare at Amjad. There was something red-brown and crusty in the man's hair. Flecks of the same stuff dotted his shirt here and there. Amjad thought it might be blood. Suddenly, this act of charity didn't seem so smart anymore. There was something in the man's eyes that was a step beyond normal crazy and into the territory that you could call madness without doing a Vincent Price voice or pulling some silly face. The little fires dancing in his dilated pupils were too intense to call this simple insanity. No, this was *Madness*, capital "M," and there was nothing funny about it.

"You know why I like coming here?" the crazy man asked. "It's not for the food or the coffee. It's because your place is so neat and clean. That's important."

"We have an A-plus rating from the health department." Amjad was caught halfway through the door. He tried to ease back inside, but the crazy man took a quick step forward. He stood close enough that Amjad could feel his hot breath.

"That's the least of it. You have the approval of a power beyond your reckoning. When you asked me to leave, I realized it was only because you didn't understand." He looked to his side, cocking his head and nodding as if listening to someone speaking. Finally, he turned back. "You've been chosen, you know. Chosen to fight alongside me in a war that has just now begun. Two battles were fought tonight and decisively won. But you must answer me now. Will you join me in the war against the Dragon Who is Called Chaos?"

Amjad's mouth hung open. How the hell was he supposed to respond to that?

"I see that you're confused," the crazy man continued. "It's my appearance. How can a man so disheveled hope to be a leader in this fight? This is the blood of my enemies, and proud as I am of it, I plan to wash it away as soon as possible."

Amjad's eyes flicked down to the guy's shirt. Holy shit, he'd just opened up the door without even noticing that the psycho looked like he'd just walked through a slaughterhouse. Was it really blood? Amjad decided he didn't want to find out. He shoved the crazy man in the chest, knocking him back a couple steps.

"Sir, I'm going to have to ask you to please leave. I'd really hate to call the police. Amjad slammed the door and locked it. He scooped up the coffee and donuts from the table and walked back to the counter without looking behind him.

Please, please, please, let him be gone when I turn around.

He repeated this like a mantra as he puttered around behind the counter. More than anything, he dreaded a confrontation. His imagination threw up a dozen ways that this little scene could escalate. None of them were particularly pleasant.

Whatever gods listened to the prayers of donut shop proprietors smiled upon him. When he turned around, the crazy man had left.

Thank you, donut gods.

A long sigh of relief was only halfway past his lips when he heard the back door creak open. He was bad about not getting it closed all the way on the mornings he rode his bike. Sometimes he just didn't have enough pop to his back-kick to get the latch to click. Just last week, one of the dumpster cats hat nosed his way into the shop and raised hell for the fifteen minutes it had taken Amjad to chase it back out. He threw his hands up in the air and grunted a few choice words. Those fucking cats were going to get their tickets punched one way to the animal shelter. He was a peaceful man, but he could only be pushed so far. The cup of coffee he'd poured for his new least favorite customer was still sitting on the counter, and he picked it up, removing the lid carefully. He could hear the cat padding down the hallway, and it must have been one of those fat little shits, overfed from the dumpsters of all the area restaurants. It sounded fat, deliberate.

We'll see how fucking deliberate you are after a nice coffee shower.

His muscles tensed. He'd have one good shot at this, and suddenly, for some unknown reason, scalding the feline intruder meant so much to him. The confrontation with the crazy man had left him a bit shaken, and he was ready to take it out on something. Then he heard the breathing. And the quiet laughter.

Oh shit. No…

He spun around just in time to register the fact that the crazy man had drawn back his fist and was clutching in it a length of dull grey metal. Panic jumped up rabbit-quick into Amjad's throat. The cup of coffee slid out of his hand. Hot liquid splashed onto his pants. He didn't have time to steel himself for the blow. The metal bar smashed into his forehead.

Lightning bolts of agony struck his brain. His feet went out from under him, and he collapsed to the floor.

The crazy man stood over him.

"You disappoint me." He poked Amjad in the chest with his weapon. "I thought you'd understand. But you're just like all the others."

The crazy man planted his foot on Amjad's chest and raised the metal bar over his head with both hands, like a lumberjack hefting an axe. His eyes blazed with feral intensity.

Amjad had one final chance to whimper.

Chapter Thirty-Seven: Ray

Ray had told Stephanie that she didn't have to come, that most of what he would probably be doing was just old fashioned police stake-out work.

"Mostly what we're going to do is sit in the upstairs room of a vacant house, watching George Young's place for anything out of the ordinary," he'd said as he took his binoculars off the top shelf of his closet. They hadn't been used in years, not since he'd tried in vain to take up bird-watching during his first painful year of sobriety. "If any psychic phenomena or whatever you call it starts to manifest, I swear I'll call you. I'll probably need you to explain it to me."

But she'd stood firm, saying, "No way I'm sitting on the sidelines now, buster. I'm coming along for the ride, and you'll just have to deal with it."

"Suit yourself," he'd said, dusting off the case that held the binoculars. "But just so you know, there's no utilities in those houses, which means we'll be sweating like pigs and using a bucket when nature calls."

She'd seemed to consider that for a moment before reiterating her stance.

"Suit yourself," he'd repeated.

The air in the house hadn't been too bad when they'd let themselves in. They'd opened a few windows, but not the one facing Young's house. They needed the reflection on that one to hide the presence of the binoculars staring out. A few hours later, the heat was already past comfortable. Ray knew that in no time it would be stifling.

"See, this is why I could never be a real cop," Ray said.

"A real cop would have had the air conditioning turned on before starting a stakeout," Stephanie answered from the room across the hall. She was seated by an open window, fanning herself with one hand and paging through an enormous book with the other. A cooler containing the day's provisions—cans of soda, plastic bottles of water, and some sandwiches—sat beside her.

Ray got up from his crouch and paced around the room, careful to stay away from the window. So far, the morning had been just as boring as he warned Stephanie it would be. There were no phantoms hovering over Young's house, no demons flying out of the chimney, and absolutely no sign of Young himself. The car wasn't in the driveway, and there were no lights on in the house. Of course, there was nothing to say that the car wasn't in the garage and the man was still asleep. He was a writer, after all. Maybe he burned the midnight oil working on his latest book and then slept late.

Ray walked into Stephanie's reading room and caught a bit of the gentle breeze wafting in through the open window. "It's going to be hot enough to burn the Jesus out of you come lunch time."

Stephanie laughed. "You've been spending too much time at that Baptist church. You're starting to talk like one of them."

"Well, hayseed talk or not, it's the truth. Going to be one hot sonofabitch." He fished a bottle of water out of the cooler and pressed it to his forehead. "All right, what's that you're reading? Sure as hell ain't one of those paperback romances you love so much."

"Speaking of which, you were talking about what happened before your little excursion to the other side, and you said you'd stopped to pick up some used paperbacks for me, right?"

"Yes, and wasn't I just a bit embarrassed to be seen buying that smut. They're still in the truck, you want to go down and grab them. Just keep that garage door shut."

"I'm not hurting for reading material, but it did get me thinking. I'd be willing to bet the family business that those paperbacks made their way to the store via George Young."

Ray opened the bottle and took a long drink. "Why the hell would he have had some paperback romance books? I've been in the guy's house, seen his bookshelf in the living room. He didn't really strike me as part of the Fabio fan club."

She held up the book she was reading so he could see the cover. It was a plain, black cover with the words *Monmouth-Frasier Encyclopedia Demonica, Volume One* stamped on it in gold type. He remembered pulling the book out of the box from the attic. Stephanie let the book thump down on her lap. "While you were sleeping, I was hitting the books. This is one of your mother's old favorites, and compared to what the fine folks at Harlequin are putting out, it's pretty goddamn dry. But I think I'm getting to the heart of the matter. There's all kinds of shit about physical objects absorbing psychic energies that can be powerful or even dangerous if handled by folks with perception beyond what's normal. That's you, by the way."

"He still doesn't seem like the romance type to me." Ray screwed the cap back on the bottle and tossed it back in with the ice.

"So now I want to see what old Connor Monmouth and Alastair Frasier have to say about the forces of chaos and order, that stuff your mom was telling you about."

Ray rubbed his head. "Yeah, some of that stuff is still a bit cloudy. Something about two primal forces responsible for the birth of the universe…it was a lot of information in just a little time."

"You sure were burning up that Ouija board."

"Yeah, it's too bad you couldn't take dictation."

He walked back to the front window and looked out at Young's house. There was something about the stillness of the place that made him sure it was unoccupied. It just had that empty look.

There was something sad about this street, he decided. A bunch of new houses standing empty. He put the binoculars to his face and scanned the rest of the street. There wasn't much going on except for the fancy-ass black Chrysler backing into the driveway of the house at the end of the street. It looked an awful lot like the car that Tate Wilson was bragging on after it was seized as part of some drug dragnet. And yeah, that looked an awful lot like one of his deputies trying to look inconspicuous behind the wheel of that monster.

"Well, would you believe that we're not the only ones on a stakeout today?" he called over his shoulder. He put his binoculars on his eyes and watched.

Ray knew what a hard-on Wilson had for George Young. Now that he'd lost the Flannigan investigation, Wilson was probably more pissed-off than ever. That such a by-the-book guy like Wilson would allocate the resources necessary to set up surveillance on Young spoke volumes about how angry the sheriff really was. Ray wondered how much this would complicate his plans. He also wondered just what the hell his plan was.

The deputy was out of his car, looking up and down the street. He seemed to come to a decision, nodding his head and hitching up his pants. Then he ran across the road and scrabbled over the fence into Young's backyard.

Now just what the hell do you suppose he's up to?

After a maddeningly slow half-hour, Ray gave up watching the house and went back to where Stephanie was still poring over her demonology book. There wasn't anything to watch anyway. The deputy was still inside, and Young was still a no-show. He was half-tempted to call it a day, but he wanted to know what the hell that deputy was doing breaking and entering like that. Surely his boss would not have approved.

"He still in there?" Stephanie asked without looking up from her book.

"Yeah." Ray snagged a Coke and one of the sandwiches from the cooler. He wasn't hungry, but he needed something to do. "How's the research going?"

She looked up at him. "Like I said, this ain't exactly a page-turner, but I've found some interesting stuff. This thing isn't really indexed by subject, so basically I've just been poking around, hoping something would jump out. Back when we were looking for something to flip your switch back to the 'on' position, I thought these suckers would be too big to be much help." She hefted the book and groaned to illustrate her point. "But now that we know a bit more about what we're looking for, I figured I might give these old guys a try. Besides, last night I couldn't really sleep, so I went looking for something to read. I was too excited for my first real stakeout."

Ray wrapped half of the sandwich back up and dropped it in the cooler. "I hope it's lived up to all your expectations. Look at it this way, we're losing weight like we're in a sauna. Can you believe some assholes actually pay for this?"

"So here's what I've found so far," she said. "And before I start, let me just say that despite everything, we might still take this with, well, maybe not a grain of salt, but at least a healthy dose of skepticism. The Monmouth Frasier is a favorite of mystics and seers the world over, but any Western Civ professor worth his tweed jacket would drum you out of his classroom for citing it."

"And what would a Western Civ professor have to say about me burning a hole in that toy store Ouija board while I was communing with my dead mother?" Ray laughed.

Stephanie waited for him to finish, giving him the kind of look that a patient parent gives a stubborn child. "I'm just saying that it wouldn't surprise me if you couldn't find another reference to this stuff anywhere else. Monmouth and Frasier were occultists first, historians second, and it's hard to know where the lore stops and the facts begin. There are lots of folks out there—and I'm talking about people who are hardcore occult researchers—who believe most of the shit in these two volumes is just a bunch of bunk made up by a couple of rich, perverted British fops."

"I'm not going to drive up to the UALR library and try to find secondary sources to refute your claims or anything like that. At least the guys that wrote those books don't have names like Baba Guru Lowenstein Moonraker or some such nonsense."

"Are you finished?"

Ray got himself under control. "For the time being, yeah."

"According to the esteemed authors, the source of this legend or myth or whatever you want to call it is a set of cuneiform tablets that were entrusted to this English nobleman who also happened to be a charter member of the Mystical Order of the Silver Goblin. And that group still has the original tablets under lock and key at their secret temple. If they really do exist, I bet these tablets could make a career for some museum curator."

"So we're talking old, right?"

She reached behind her and grabbed a bottle of water from the cooler. "We're talking older than old. Ancient. Old, as in the birth of civilization." She gave that little bit of information time to sink in. "This is a creation myth that comes from some forgotten Mesopotamian cult. Sort of like their version of the book of Genesis, I guess you could say. This little congregation believed that before the universe came into being, whatever darkness was out there was home to one being, a god called *Xax-Ghuzuul*. Here things get a bit fuzzy, as they tend to do with nothing to go on but a pair of cuneiform tablets that may or may not exist, but apparently this god was a sort of yin-yang, male-female package that had an internal dispute or something like a split personality."

Ray smiled. "Let me take a shot in the dark here. They became two separate entities: *Xax* and *Ghuzuul*."

"You'd sweep the obscure cults category in *Jeopardy*," Stephanie said, at least pretending to be impressed.

Ray took a bow.

"So this split released a burst of energy, sort of like the Big Bang," she continued. "And that energy increased as *Xax* and *Ghuzuul* fought for control of the new universe. They basically fought to a stalemate. Neither was strong enough to beat the other, but it didn't stop them from fighting continuously for eons. The stars, the planets, life as we know it, all of that was just a byproduct of this lover's spat."

"I'm guessing by the significant look you're giving me that this is the part where you tell me how all this relates to what we're doing."

"It was when you told me what your mother said about good and evil really just being a simplified way of looking at the only two forces in the universe: order and chaos." Stephanie wiped a hand across her sweaty forehead. "That rang a bell, but it wasn't something I could call to mind instantly, so I had to go back to the Monmouth-Frasier, which I read cover to cover as an impressionable youth. *Xax* represented the order side of the equation. *Ghuzuul* was the bringer of chaos."

"I don't know…" Ray shook his head.

"But wait, cousin, that ain't all." She tapped the book. "Remember when I told you that I bet those paperbacks you got me came from your buddy George?"

"Yeah, so what?"

"Here's what: there were two very different groups within the *Xax-Ghuzuul* cult. They both basically worshipped the same two-faced god, but they differed on how to go about it."

"Even back then, the Baptists and the Methodists couldn't get it together, huh?" He snorted, thinking of how many times he'd sat in the pews at church, listening to the people around him bitch about how the other churches in Edgewood were crammed full of godless heathens.

"Something like that. But it makes sense, if you think about it. A god with two faces, there's bound to be some folks who favor one face over the other." She held up one hand, made a fist. "The worshippers of *Xax*, the orderly face of the god, were ascetics. They didn't believe in the accumulation of material wealth. They believed that by purging the world of disorder, they could delay the inevitable end of the world." She held up her other hand, made a second fist. "And the other congregation favored *Ghuzuul*. They took it to the other extreme. Believing that their god wanted them to revel in every type of filth and excess, they accumulated material goods as a form of worship. They were like packrats. And, here's what I've been working up to: both groups believed that their god—and those who were holy enough to attain that god's enlightenment—could imprint their psychic energy on physical objects."

"These characters, Monmouth and Frasier, they got all that from some clay tablets?" Ray let out an appreciative whistle.

"Ray, I think your mom was dropping clues about what was going on. She told you that there were limits to how much she could tell you, right? I think she wanted us to find this chapter, but she was afraid to come right out and say it."

Ray sat down on the floor to get closer to the faint breeze coming in through the window. "Jesus Christ," he said.

Stephanie laughed. "Hardly. According to the book, one reason that the cult of *Xax-Ghuzuul* burnt itself out so quickly is that it was a fatalist religion. As long as the two gods fought, there would be strife in the world. But if they ever reconciled, the universe would cease to exist. And for another thing, the religion was probably based around ceremonies that involved demonic possession. That could be just a theory, or maybe it's based on something in the tablets. Like I said, this book isn't exactly accepted scholarly research."

"No, it's not that," he said. "It just finally dawned on me. Those books probably came from George's wife. He said that she'd passed away, and now he was selling off all the stuff she'd accumulated. And you should have seen how much shit was packed into that storage unit. Mostly, it looked like trinkets and old clothes, but I wouldn't be surprised if some of those boxes were full of old paperbacks."

Stephanie clapped her hands together. "I think you just found your murderer."

"The dead wife of a washed-up horror writer?"

She nodded. "Spurred on by some pair of ancient and long-forgotten gods that have been camped out behind the veil for thousands of years, just waiting for a chance to slip back into this world."

"Shit. Anything in that book about how to put a stop to all this and get things back to normal?"

"Actually, it says that they can be dispelled back into the ether—their words, not mine—by a person adept at the ethereal arts." She slipped a bookmark into the pages and snapped the book shut. "I guess that would be you, big guy."

"So I'm the best hope we have at getting rid of whatever it was that bit Percy Flannigan's neck damn near in half? Sure you don't want to just head back to Memphis, hunker down, and wait this out?"

"And abandon you in your hour of need? Ray, we're family, remember?"

Chapter Thirty-Eight: Avery

The air inside Young's house seemed heavy even compared to the soupy summer humidity outside. Avery didn't like it one bit. Something was wrong with this place. He didn't feel much like hanging around in the living room, where pieces of the broken snow globe still littered the floor and that chair was still wedged up under the doorknob. He told himself he needed to make a more thorough search of the house.

There was a set of stairs on the opposite side of the living room, and Avery took them two at a time to the second floor of the house. The rooms up here were smaller than the open plan of the first floor. Still, it was a hell of a lot bigger than Avery's place. Two of the bedrooms were completely empty. Not one stick of furniture, and there were still marks in the carpet from the vacuum cleaner. The bathroom had some soap on the counter and towels hanging on the rack, but none of it looked to have seen any use.

All this space and the guy didn't have anything to fill it up? Avery shook his head. People could be damn strange.

The master bedroom and bathroom had been used, it looked like. There was a toothbrush and a razor on the bathroom counter. The bed had been slept in, and there were some dirty clothes in a plastic basket in the corner. Some clothes hung in the closet, but not many.

George Young was a mystery. If there was nothing in the house to give Avery some insight into the man, there had to be something in that garage.

He told himself that he was being stupid, that there was nothing to worry about. Whatever was out in that garage, it couldn't be that bad. Standing there in front of the door, he ran through the possibilities. Maybe the old guy had a meth lab set up out there. But there was no cat piss smell of cooking crank, and Avery just didn't figure George Young for the type. Maybe it was some sort of sex freak set up, with whips and chains and leather suits. Again, Young didn't seem the type.

Brad Carter | 277

"Aw, fuck it." Avery pulled the chair from under the knob. "Can't be no cop if you're scared of some old man's garage."

He opened the door and groped around on the wall for a light switch. The only light was from a single bulb at the center of the ceiling, but it was good enough for him to get that the room was packed full of cardboard boxes. It looked like Young was preparing for the world's largest rummage sale. Avery figured it was all the shit Young had in his storage unit. He must have moved it here after the Flannigan murder went down. But it didn't explain why the guy was carrying on like there was some rare disease or awful monster contained in the garage.

Avery moved out among the stacks of boxes, wishing that he had a flashlight to cut through the shadows. It seemed way too dark and somehow much bigger than it appeared from the outside. Was it some sort of optical illusion? Something to do with the low lighting and all the boxes stacked up nearly to the ceiling?

"You should not be here." The voice was sharp-edged and raspy, and it came from somewhere in the back of the garage.

"Who's there?" Avery drew his pistol and held it at his side.

"It's mine." The voice was closer now. "Everything you see. Mine."

The musty smell of the garage was suddenly stronger, so thick that it made Avery cough. His eyes watered, and as he looked down to wipe them, he saw that shadows had gathered about his ankles. They moved and twisted as if they were living creatures.

"Mine!" The voice was right behind him, screaming into his ear with a blast of hot, moist breath.

Avery spun around, but the shadows coiling around his ankles materialized into solid ropes that pulled him to the concrete floor. The impact was jarring, and Avery's gun danced out of his fingers. It spun away from him as it hit floor.

The thing hovering above him looked vaguely like a woman that had been shaped from the shadows. Streams of mist dripped down from her outstretched hands. Her fingers were cold as they caressed his face. Avery recoiled in disgust as he looked up at her. Her features, those of an attractive woman, began to twist until her face was no longer recognizable as human. She swiped one of her fingers across his forehead, the hooked nail opening a cut that poured blood into his eyes.

"It's mine…" The voice that came from the woman's throat reminded Avery of the sound that movies used for a sword being drawn out of a sheath.

He closed his eyes against the hot flow of blood, bracing himself for whatever horror came next. But then, she was gone.

Avery heard the door to the house open and then slam shut. The next sound was glass breaking. And then there was silence. He allowed himself a minute to catch his breath before he clambered uneasily to his feet. He picked his gun up from the floor, and held it at the ready as he stepped back into the house. Once inside, he kicked the door closed behind him. George Young stood there watching him.

A voice from the kitchen called out. "The window in here is broken right out. You think it might have been her that did it?"

Avery turned toward the kitchen and saw Myrna Wilson staring out a window rimmed with tiny shards of glass.

Chapter Thirty-Nine: Ray

So much time had passed since there had been any movement at all at the house across the street that it took Ray a moment to react when he saw George's car pull into the driveway.

"Hey, shit, we've got something going down across the street," he called over his shoulder.

Stephanie had dozed off, and she snorted herself awake at the sound of his voice. The sleepy grunt she uttered sounded like it ended with a question mark, so Ray repeated the breaking news.

"It looks like our guy finally got home. And I think we can assume that he had a good time last night, because his girlfriend is with him. It's Sheriff Wilson's mother, if you can believe that. And shit, the deputy is still in the house."

Stephanie came into the room, her hands pressed to the small of her back as she stretched. "Finally. I was worried that I was going to have to give up my romantic notions of police work as something exciting."

"Did you hear me say that the deputy hasn't come out yet?"

She yawned. "We're about to see some fireworks, aren't we?"

Ray bit his lower lip, watching George take Myrna Wilson's hand and lead her up to the front door of the house. "What the hell is that deputy still doing in that house? He's been in there going on two hours now."

"Is this good or bad for our little investigation?" Stephanie asked.

Butterflies danced around in Ray's stomach. "I don't know. I guess it was bound to happen sooner or later. Tate Wilson was never going to let this guy be."

"But you already warned him that the sheriff was keeping an eye on him."

"Like I said, I don't know. But..." He paused, looking out at the house.

"But what?" Stephanie asked.

"But I'm starting to get that feeling in my gut, like something's happening."

280 | ONLY THINGS

"That old Chambers intuition." She patted his shoulder. "Use the force, Luke."

"I wish you'd be serious," he snapped. The butterflies had multiplied, and it felt like the sandwich he'd eaten earlier might be gearing up for an encore appearance on the carpet.

"Fine. You're really not one to talk, you know that?"

His cell phone buzzed in his pocket, tickling his thigh. He was groggy the way one can only be after spending too long in a hot room, but at least the butterflies in his belly were starting to settle down. The number on the screen wasn't familiar, but Ray answered it anyway.

"Ray McFettridge." He gave it his best peace officer voice.

"Constable? This is George Young."

"What can I do for you, Mr. Young?"

"It's George, remember?"

"George, yeah. What can I help you with?"

"When you gave me your card, you said to call you if I needed anything. I didn't expect to cash that in, but here we are." There was a note of desperation in George's voice that clashed with his casual phrasing. Ray could tell the guy was upset and trying to keep it under control. "Do you think you could swing by my place as soon as possible? I have a sort of legal situation here. Maybe you can help me out."

"Sure. I just happen to be in the area, so I'll be there before you know it."

"Seems like a lot of cops happen to be in the area," George said.

Ray had tried to argue Stephanie into staying back at the stakeout house, but she wouldn't have it. The last time Ray had gotten near George Young, he'd gone on a little trip to the land of the dead, and she'd be damned if he was going off alone to risk that again.

"Think about it, Ray," she'd said. "You knock on the door, he answers it, and you drop down like a sack of potatoes on his doorstep because your body's on autopilot, and you're really off communing with the spirit world. How's that going to look? Just waiting to get a phone call from him was enough to get you all queasy. You never know what might happen."

He conceded the point, and they went across the street together. He supposed they probably should have slipped out the back and walked around the block, but there was really no point. Besides, this stakeout, only a day old, had already gone on too long for Ray's tastes. He felt like he was going to sweat himself into the grave.

Brad Carter | 281

George opened the door before Ray could knock. "Thanks for coming so fast," he said. "Although I guess it wasn't much of a problem since you were in the vacant house over there."

Ray didn't see any point in denying it, so he just shrugged. "This is my cousin Stephanie. She's working for me these days as a sort of consultant, I guess you could say."

George shook her hand. "Charmed. Wish we were meeting under better circumstances."

"What can we do for you?" Ray asked.

George stepped aside and motioned them inside. "It's not so much what you can do for me, but what you can do for him."

He pointed to the living room couch, where the deputy was laid out. Myrna Wilson knelt beside him, pressing a cloth to his bleeding forehead.

"We looked at his ID," George said. "Imagine my surprise when I see that he's a deputy with the Gayler County Sheriff's Department. I figured that maybe you could give me some advice on how to handle this situation. Imagine my further surprise when I see you walk out of that vacant house over there."

"Yeah, I can see how it might look."

"It looks fucking weird. Pardon my French, but what the hell is going on around here? First, all this stuff last night…" He exchanged a meaningful look with Myrna then went back to Ray. "And now, there's some zoned out cop bleeding on my living room floor and another cop watching my house from across the street. Why do I get the feeling that you know a lot more about what's going on here than I do?"

Ray looked at Myrna then back to George. "What about last night?"

George shook his head. "You first, constable."

"The deputy stable?" Ray asked.

"A little cut up and a lot freaked out. I offered to get him to the hospital, and he flat out refused." George sighed. He looked tired. "Tell you the truth, I think he probably wants to hear what you have to say as well."

Ray licked his lips. "You still got some soda pop in the house? This is a story with a lot of telling, and I'm going to need something to keep my throat lubed up."

"Fridge is in the kitchen. Help yourself."

When Ray returned from the kitchen with his can of soda, the deputy, who George introduced as Avery Cartwright, was sitting up on the couch. He looked a little less freaked out than when Ray had entered the house, but the kid still had a nasty gash on his forehead.

"Look at it this way," Ray said, "you're going to have one hell of a cool scar to show off to all your buddies."

Avery didn't smile. "Yeah, and I'll just explain to everyone how I got it. They'll throw me in the mental hospital, and I'll get to wear a cool bathrobe and a cool pair of slippers for the rest of my days."

Ray took a long drink of Coke, belched silently into his fist, and looked at the sober faces around him. "Well, I can see y'all want some answers, and I'll try to give them to you as best I can. I'll warn you before I start that a lot of it might inspire disbelief. I got no excuse for that. For what it's worth, I swear that every word of it is true, but I guess I can't make you believe it."

George raised a hand. "I think that right about now, everyone in this room is willing to believe just about anything. So how about you cut the preamble and get right to it?"

Ray took one more drink and got started.

He gave it to them straight, starting with his childhood in Arnholdt as the son of a bona fide seer and medium. And for the third time in his life, he told aloud the story of his sojourn in the presence of Steven Lovelace. By the time he'd gotten to the part about his relocation to Arkansas, he was already feeling talked out. It wasn't particularly pleasant, laying out all his secrets to a trio of strangers, but since they were evidently a part of it, he owed them all the gory details.

To their credit, everyone in the audience listened without crying out that the whole thing was a bunch of bullshit. That was nice.

Ray did skim over the bits about his time as a functional alcoholic who drove his wife away with long periods of sullen indifference. He just didn't see the need in telling that in great detail, but he could tell by the look in George's eyes that the man sympathized.

Then he got to the part that everyone really wanted to hear, starting with his nighttime trip to the scene of the Percy Flannigan murder.

"My hackles went up, I guess you could say. I didn't recognize the feeling at first," Ray said, rolling the soda can between his hands so the aluminum crinkled. "Then it came back to me in a rush the next night. It was the same thing I'd felt in my aunt's upstairs room. Same sweaty, seasick feeling. Same dizziness. So when I got home, I went digging through my attic for a box of my mother's old things, her books and whatnot. About that time is when I thought of my long lost cousin Stephanie."

"Really, it was *you* that was long lost," Stephanie said.

She perched on the arm of the recliner in which Ray sat. The others were packed shoulder to shoulder on the couch. No one looked the least bit comfortable. Ray wondered if that had anything to do with the seating arrangement or if it was all down to the business at hand.

He continued, "The family's all but gone. My mom is dead, and so are my aunts. Me and Stephanie are all that's left, really. I guess I was just desperate for someone who might listen sympathetically. So, I got on the computer and looked her up. Imagine my relief when I found out that I wasn't going to have to take my ass all the way to Arnholdt."

He drank the last of his soda. It was warm and half flat, and it made his throat sticky. He coughed a few times to clear it then got on with his story. The long days of research into his mother's books, the trip to purchase the Ouija board, and finally, his encounter with George at the bookstore.

"So it wasn't the incense that had you acting strange," George said. "You're not allergic to patchouli, are you? You're allergic to me."

"Not to you." Stephanie pointed at George. "Or else he'd be laid out on the floor convulsing right now. He's got a psychic allergy to the spirit that's attached itself to you. Big difference."

"You mean the spirit of my dead wife. You mean Kathy." George smiled weakly as he took in the shocked expressions of those around him. "That's what we're talking about, right? Kathy's spirit somehow attached itself to her old possessions, and now she's making her presence known. Remember, I write this kind of thing for a living, or at least I used to. It hasn't been hard putting the pieces together over the past twenty-four hours."

Ray nodded. This was going a lot smoother than he'd thought it would. Maybe his first intuition about George—that his writing betrayed a certain depth of knowledge of occult matters beyond most authors—was correct. It was a relief to have him finally come around.

"We've seen her, so don't go thinking that I've developed some new psychic talent," George said, as if reading Ray's mind. "Well, we've seen the thing that she's become, at any rate. Last night, at Myrna's house. She was twisted and deformed, but it was Kathy, no doubt about it."

"Maybe," Ray said, "it's time for me to let you have the floor. It sounds like there's something you need to get out in the open."

George sighed. "I can tell you about last night. Not that I'm very eager to revisit the memory."

Chapter Forty: George

The hardest part about telling his story was sitting next to Myrna and confessing again that until he saw the inky banshee tear her living room apart, he didn't really believe in the supernatural. At least not in the same way he believed in something like gravity. He'd worked himself into accepting that something beyond the understanding of man's science might exist, but he hadn't really swallowed it down yet. It wasn't until Kathy's shadowy form was standing so close that George could smell her that George banished all doubt from his mind.

"I was prepared to stand by Myrna because there is something between us that goes beyond normal attraction, but my mind couldn't accept what she told me. It was too much like something out of one of my old books," he said.

Myrna grabbed his hand. She squeezed it gently. "If you feel our connection so deeply, you would have believed me. And besides, you'd actually *seen* her already. She was standing out there in your garage, so you weren't just taking my word for it."

He nodded, still looking at nothing in particular. "You're absolutely right."

"Don't be too hard on him," Ray said. "Some of us have lived with this stuff for so long that it's easy to forget how far out it really is. I'd almost talked myself out of believing in it, even after everything that I've seen. Our brains just aren't wired to accept this stuff, I've decided. Something we lost when we evolved into a civilized, scientific species. It's easy to reject the evidence our own eyes give us if it doesn't fit our worldview."

George shook his head. "I appreciate that, but Myrna's right. Even after I saw what I saw, I just couldn't talk myself into believing it. But let me tell you, after watching some black fog shape itself into my dead wife then start smashing apart everything in the room, I'm ready to believe anything," George said. "Catching a quick glimpse of her standing in that garage was nothing compared to last night."

He circled back to the beginning of his story, explaining the creeping dread he'd begun to feel once he moved the items from his storage unit to his garage.

"I even considered nailing the door shut, but I stopped myself. Having an irrational fear of the crowded garage is one thing, but nailing a board across the door is something a crazy man would do. I tried to rationalize the fear, telling myself it was some latent guilt about Kathy's death that made me uneasy. I told myself that I was just overreacting. You know, after so long living in absolute disorder, I was not okay with the idea of being so close to it. I thought it was just some psychological quirk." He looked over at Avery, who was staring impassively forward. "I guess the deputy here found out otherwise."

Ray jerked a thumb over his shoulder at the shattered window in the kitchen. "Well, she's gone now. Doesn't mean she won't come back, but I'm not feeling a thing in here right now."

George chewed on that for a moment.

"You said that your switch was flipped back on after I ran into you at the bookstore." He pointed at Ray. "That was after you handled some of those romance paperbacks, right? I can't be sure those were the ones, but I gave Luanne Samples three big boxes of books that belonged to Kathy. Trashy paperback romances. She mentioned that she might take some over to the Book Nook."

Stephanie nodded. "What we're probably dealing with is a ghost that attached itself to a boat load of physical objects. You know how people talk about spirits imprinting themselves on a house as an explanation for a haunting? Well, same thing here, only it isn't a house. It's all that useless junk Kathy loved so much."

"Just like the grey people," Myrna said. She gave a brief explanation of the silent figures haunting her house. "They stick around because I'm the caretaker for the things they loved."

Stephanie nodded again. "Sure, why not? Our problem now is that her stuff is spread out. There's stuff at the bookstore, at Myrna's house, and wherever else it ended up after someone bought it at the flea market."

George groaned. "There's no possible way I could remember who bought stuff from me. I mean, I didn't exactly do booming business, but I did sell some odds and ends. No one bought big batches of it. Well, no one except Myrna."

"The amount may not matter," Stephanie said. "I think that maybe getting rid of the bulk of it might be enough to weaken her. Then Ray can send her back to where she came from. But we should start at Myrna's place. That house is like one big psychic battery with all those grey people hanging around. Kathy's spirit could be using it to boost her power, sucking up those half-formed spirits like a baseball player shooting steroids."

"Just where are you getting all these theories?" George asked. "You said yourself how you're not able to plug into any of this supernatural stuff, so how are you just letting all this arcane knowledge slip like you're talking about the weather?"

"A music critic doesn't necessarily know how to play an instrument. A sports writer didn't necessarily have to be an athlete. I've spent a lifetime studying this stuff. You know the saying about how those who can't do, teach? Maybe those who can't do, learn all they can about the thing that was denied them." She cocked her head to the side and smiled a funny little smile. "I have a stack of the kind of reference books that you won't find in most libraries."

George opened his mouth to say something, but Avery stopped him short.

"Look, this is all real interesting," the deputy said. "All this supernatural shit, it's fascinating. Y'all are some strange folks, and your lives must be exciting. But I want to know what we're going to do about this ghost. I tell you, that thing was ready to kill me as dead as Percy Flannigan. If y'all hadn't got home…" He looked at George and Myrna. "I don't know what would have happened. Maybe you'd have been scraping me up off that garage floor. But now that damn thing is somewhere out there. I don't think it's just going to stop. So whatever y'all plan on doing, best get your asses in gear and do it."

There was an uneasy silence as everyone stared at one another.

Ray cleared his throat. He nodded in George's direction. "First things first, we have to get rid of all this stuff that belonged to your wife."

"That will get rid of…" Myrna trailed off, her eyes flicking over to the door to the garage.

Stephanie shook her head. "There's no way of knowing that. It may have no effect at all. But I'm hoping that it will weaken her. Toss that stuff into the landfill, and it will be like taking a couple pints of blood out of somebody. At least, I think it will. This is just an educated guess."

"Still," Ray said, "it's worth a shot."

"So, what, we clean out the garage and her house? And we just wait around, hoping that is enough to get rid of this thing?" Avery asked.

"Got any better ideas?" Ray asked, looking around the room. "I'm all ears."

No one volunteered anything.

"Well, you wanted to hear my side of things, so here it is." The deputy stood up. "I'm getting the hell away from you people. That…ghost…thing…whatever you want to call it nearly killed my ass. I don't want no part of this shit. Truth is, I can't wait for the sheriff to get back so I can wash my hands of the whole thing." He walked over to the front door and paused with his hand on the knob. "I hate to be the one to ask this, but what if you're wrong? What if all these theories you cooked up amount to jack shit?"

Everyone looked at each other silently.

"Yeah, that's what I thought." Avery stomped out of the house, slamming the door behind him.

"What now?" George asked, looking at the constable and his cousin.

"First things first: we get rid of stuff. Anything that's in Myrna's house could be tainted at this point," Stephanie said. "Fire would work best, but the landfill will have to do. Ray here will get to work on finding a way to get your wife's spirit back to the other side."

After the discussion group broke up and everyone went their separate ways, George took Myrna upstairs and showed her into his bedroom. She protested that she wasn't tired, but her red-rimmed, puffy eyes told a different story. She was out within a few minutes of her head hitting the pillow. George lay beside her for a while, listening to her soft breathing. When it became clear that he wasn't going to join her in sleep, he slid out of bed and tiptoed downstairs.

He called up Roll Away Disposal, a place that rented dumpsters and hauled away junk, and was told that they could have a dumpster available in the morning. He didn't much like the prospect of staying in the house with all of Kathy's things. Maybe when Myrna woke, they could go check into a hotel.

He forced himself to take a quick walk in the garage, and found that it didn't inspire the same crushing dread. It felt like a cramped and musty room, nothing more. But who could tell how that might change after dark? Or did that even make a difference? In George's books, Ben

McCauley had always done his battles with ghosts after dark, usually around midnight. But Kathy had attacked the deputy in broad daylight.

He went into the kitchen and fixed a pot of coffee. While the machine hissed and burbled, he sat down at the table and stared at the broken window above the sink. Maybe when this was all over, he'd change a few things around and work it into a book. If he lived to see it through, that was. Maybe in the novel version, Kathy's ghost would tear him to pieces in a fit of jealous rage. Now, that would be a hell of an ending.

The coffee was strong, and he drank it black, just the way Ben McCauley did when he was working a case. George realized how ridiculous it was, thinking of this whole thing as a book he might write, but he told himself it was the reflex action of his long-dormant skills coming back to life. If Ray McFettridge could have his psychic switch flipped after rubbing up against the supernatural, why couldn't George have his author switch flipped by the same?

He ran through the characters of the story.

There was Ray McFettridge, who, George had to admit, wasn't much of a hero. Ray seemed to have more going on than his redneck appearance suggested. And he accepted all the strange goings-on with Zen calm. He sat there talking about his out of body experience like a guy describing a particularly good blue plate special he'd eaten at the local diner. *The meatloaf had the perfect amount of ketchup glaze on top, and oh yeah, I floated around invisibly inside a serial killer's van.*

Then there was his cousin Stephanie. A seer from Memphis who advised musicians and pro athletes, but was ironically deaf, dumb, and blind to the spirit world despite being born into a family stuffed to the gills with psychic talent. George would have written her as sympathetic, but he sensed that the real Stephanie had a considerable amount of jealous resentment for her cousin. He'd seen the way her eyebrows twitched when Ray talked about his long years of drinking to suppress his talent.

And poor Myrna. George sighed, thinking of all she'd been through. She was likely to go through a lot more once her son got back in town.

Now where exactly did George himself fit in? Ray had given him a deadpan look and told him he was the linchpin of whatever was happening in Gayler County. He'd said that George was the eye of the coming storm, whatever that meant. George had wanted to ask if the eye of the storm was so calm, why did some shadowy ghost version of Kathy try to strangle him last night? That didn't seem very damn calm. George tried to see himself as Ben McCauley in *Speak Softly, Lover*, a rational man who was drawn into a web of supernatural intrigue, only to emerge as a reluctant hero. George nearly laughed out loud at that one. It was part of the dust flap synopsis from the first printing of that book.

The coffee was doing its job a little too well. George felt restless. He put his cup in the sink and walked through the living room and back into the garage. If there was anything sinister lurking out here, he couldn't feel it. Even the light from the single bulb seemed brighter. He walked sideways through the boxes, for some reason reluctant to brush up against them.

He cleared his throat and spoke. "Kathy, are you here? If you are, please just know that I'm sorry. For everything. But this isn't you. Even if you are angry, you were never the type to hurt people. You have to let go."

Silence answered him.

Chapter Forty-One: Ray

"Goddamn it, I can't just sit here waiting for something to happen," Ray said, pushing the Ouija board across the table. He stood up and stomped over to the refrigerator. There was some store-bought iced tea in there, and he drank two big mouthfuls right from the jug.

"Well, with that attitude, you're certainly not going to get anywhere fast," Stephanie said. "You have to visualize, let yourself be taken in."

"Quit talking about this shit like it's easy."

"Oh, I definitely don't talk about it that way." Her tone of voice was short, peevish. "Believe me, I understand how hard this shit is. You don't want to know how many hours I sat with my fingers on the planchette, just hoping against hope that I'd feel some little twitch. So no, I don't think it's easy. But the universe, in its infinite wisdom, granted you the talent for it."

She glared at him, and he tried to look back blankly, but after a moment, he dropped his eyes. It was as if she blamed him for being born with abilities that she never had. Like he'd sucked up all the talent from the gene pool and left her high and dry. But the truth was he didn't even want this talent. If he'd been able to transfer it to Stephanie somehow, he would have done so.

"Maybe he's not there anyway," Ray said. "You know, some souls probably pass on. They go to the light and become little angels with harps or something."

Stephanie shook her head. "You don't believe that at all. You think he's there. You had some flash of insight, and that's why you got this idea in your head. You think he'll help us for the same reason he felt compelled to catalogue all that stuff in his books."

Ray drank some more tea then returned the jug to the refrigerator. What Stephanie said wasn't exactly correct, but it was close enough. The idea for contacting Sir Connor Monmouth via Ouija hadn't come to him in some brain-jarring burst of psychic insight. It had just come to him the same way a difficult crossword puzzle clue revealed itself. He might actually feel better about the whole thing if lightning bolts of supernatural inspiration had struck. Deciding to contact a century-dead occult philosopher shouldn't come to you the same way as thinking of an eight-letter word for bloodsucker.

He sat back down at the table and took a deep breath.

"Just think of it like a telephone," Stephanie said. "Your mom never used a Ouija board that I remember, but she used to say that her deck of cards and her crystal ball were her telephones to the dead folks."

Ray put his fingertips on the planchette and closed his eyes. He imagined pulling his cellphone out of his pocket and punching in a number. He visualized bringing the phone to his ear. It rang and rang and rang. Minutes passed. Frustration began to set in. He was on the verge of shoving back from the table and cursing his failure, and then…

"Hello?"

The voice that answered was soft but clear.

"I say, is anyone there? Hello?"

When Ray opened his eyes, he was standing in a cozy room with a roaring fireplace. The rug beneath his feet was Persian, and the air around him smelled of pipe tobacco and bergamot tea. Near the fireplace, in a leather wingback chair, sat a neat man in a smoking jacket. A large book was spread across his lap, and a pipe dangled from his lips. He studied Ray for a moment. Then he slipped a ribbon in the book to mark his place, closed the volume with a soft thump, and set it on the small table at his side.

"I get so few visitors that my manners seem to have gotten a bit rusty." He plucked the pipe from between his teeth. He gestured with it to another chair, this one on the other side of the fireplace. "Please have a seat, sir."

Ray looked around. The furnishings in the room looked like museum pieces. A grandfather clock stood in one corner, its gold pendulum swinging silently. Tall bookshelves lined the walls, packed full of leather-bound volumes with gilt writing on their spines. Above the mantelpiece were mounted sets of horns and antlers from animals that Ray couldn't identify. He wiped his hands on his jeans and sat down.

"My name is Connor Monmouth." The gentleman raised his hand and tipped a casual salute.

"Ray McFettridge." Ray raised his hand but didn't know what gesture was appropriate for greeting a long dead English gentleman, so he let it drop back into his lap.

"An American!" He clapped his delicate hands. "So, tell me, Mr. McFettridge, to what do I owe the pleasure of this visit? It must be frightfully important for you to risk a trip behind the veil. And let me say that I'm impressed. You must be frightfully talented to have managed it. Really, my interest is piqued."

Ray shifted about in his chair. The seat itself was perfectly comfortable, but the situation made Ray uneasy. There was something cold and alien about Monmouth's smile.

"I've been reading your book, the one you wrote with Alastair Frasier…" Ray began.

"Ah, good old Alastair!" Monmouth's smile stretched so wide that it nearly split his face in half. "How I miss that chap. We were such close friends despite our disagreements later in life."

Ray didn't know how to follow that, so he just kept going. "In the chapter 'A Cruel and Malicious Entity Manifests at the Hollingsworth Estate,' you make reference to something called *The Spell of Summoning for the Purpose of Banishment.*"

"That Frasier, he was very keen on his proper titles for every incantation we came across. They sometimes reminded me of the menu descriptions at a French restaurant, in which the chef felt it was necessary to take a paragraph to describe pastries filled with cheese."

Ray shifted around some more. "But that spell isn't in the book. It's mentioned, but the words or the incantation or whatever, they aren't there."

Monmouth rose from his chair. He tugged the hem of his smoking jacket to smooth it then walked across the room to a cart loaded with decanters and glasses. He poured two glasses of brown liquid and returned, handing one to Ray.

Ray took the glass, giving it a suspicious look.

"Oh, now." Monmouth said, pursing his lips. "It's only scotch. A fellow writes a few books on the occult and suddenly everyone thinks any drink he passes out is some witches' brew." He took a sip from his own glass to prove a point.

"It's not that. I don't drink. I had a problem with it, so I gave it up." Ray placed the glass on the table at his left.

"Ah, a reformed man." Monmouth drank more of his own scotch. "Well, more's the pity. Now, let's see, you were interested in one of the spells used during that Hollingsworth business. Poor Lord Hollingsworth, he was struck down by grief."

Ray nodded. He'd read the chapter as soon as he left George's house, opening the second volume of Monmouth and Frasier's book right to what looked like a relevant passage. It concerned two British aristocrats who lost their only child to a mysterious fever. Grief-stricken, they put aside their religious convictions, and with the help of a medium of some repute, they conjured up the spirit of their daughter. But the sweet ten-year old girl they remembered had changed. When the girl's spirit grew bored with smashing the furnishings in the house, it ravaged the livestock of the nearby villages. Finally, they went back to the medium, who told them that nothing could be done.

"Of course, what she told them wasn't strictly true," Monmouth said. "There was such an incantation. But she was frightened of the risks that it entailed. Relocating a spirit back to its roost behind the veil is no simple act, you know. Doing so involves opening doors that most people believe should remain closed."

"Sometimes you don't have a choice."

Monmouth spread his hands. "Just so. And that is exactly how my esteemed colleague Lord Frasier persuaded this medium, one Madame Livinia Zita, to perform the ritual."

"And?" Ray asked.

Monmouth shrugged. "And what? The medium performed the rite, and the ghost went back where such things belong."

"That's it?"

He laughed, a sharp sound like rocks thrown at sheet metal. "Why, what else did you think would happen?"

"Then you were there? You witnessed the ritual?" Ray asked.

"Why, of course I did, old man. I witnessed a great many rituals in my time."

Ray's mind played the scene out for him like an old time horror movie. He saw Madame Livinia Zita as an angular, sharp-eyed gypsy woman, complete with silver bangles on her wrists and oversized hoops in her ears. He imagined Lord and Lady Hollingsworth, their eyes raw from crying, pleading with the medium to deliver them from the terror that the ghost of their daughter had brought into their lives. Their shoulders must have sagged with the double load of grief, of having lost their daughter once, only to be forced to do so again. Such a story *couldn't* have a happy ending.

"Yes, you see how dire the situation was," Monmouth said. "Madame Zita, of course, felt the sting of guilt most acutely. It was her recklessness that brought the child's spirit back into the world. Had she not felt that sting, she would not have attempted the incantation that Sir Alastair whispered in her ear."

"Why not? She was a powerful medium, right?"

"The smallest act of magic carries a risk."

"But you can tell me the spell?" Ray didn't give a damn how desperate he sounded. He leaned forward in his chair, his hands gripping the armrests. "You can teach it to me?"

Monmouth drained his glass of scotch and placed it delicately on the table at his side. He took up his pipe, filled it from a leather pouch of tobacco, and began tamping it. "I can indeed. But you should know that this spell, this incantation, it comes with a price."

"I'll pay it," Ray said.

"Splendid." Monmouth's smile showed a mouthful of gleaming white teeth. "Only are absolutely sure that you won't join me for a drink? I feel reasonably certain that once you hear what I have to say, you'll wish you had one."

"Just tell me. Whatever it is, I can handle it."

"Very well." Monmouth leaned forward, his bony hands gripping his knees. "I want you to bring it back to me, this thing you've found. When you work this spell, you will be able to direct the spirit to any place beyond the veil that pleases you. Direct it to me."

"Why? What could you possibly want with this thing?"

Monmouth rose from his chair, beckoning Ray to follow him across the room to one of the crowded bookshelves. The occultist's long white fingers danced across the spines of the volumes in front of him, pausing on a bright red leather tome. He grasped the book and pulled it a few inches from the shelf then let it slide back into place. There was a faint metallic groaning, and the shelf spun slowly away, revealing a dim room. It was the type of hidden room gag you'd see in a bad spy movie.

Ray snorted. "You have a secret room, even in this little world you've created for yourself?"

"Did you know that it was one of the few things I wanted in life that I was never able to have?" Monmouth stepped inside. "I lived in London, in sad little buildings like boxes. And besides, what I have in here deserves a little secrecy."

"Secrecy? From who?"

Monmouth half-turned, raising his eyebrows. "One never knows. In the old days, it was Scotland Yard that paid me visits. There are agencies on this side of the veil as well. I find it best to avoid their notice."

Ray followed him into the room. It took his eyes a moment to adjust to the dimness, but he saw that three of the walls were lined with glass cases. Stepping closer, he saw that the cases were full of butterflies and moths pinned to a corkboard. Their wings fluttered and their legs twitched in a futile attempt to free themselves from the board.

Monmouth put his hand on Ray's shoulder. "I'd like to draw your attention to one particular specimen."

Ray allowed himself to be led forward, although the atmosphere of the room was so strange and sinister that he felt queasy just breathing in the air.

"Here." Monmouth tapped the glass in front of him. "I believe you're familiar with this one."

All Ray saw was a sickly black moth, its ragged wings beating erratically. "I don't know anything about bugs."

"Oh, I think it is quite more than that, sir. Lean closer and look. Really *look*. I think you'll find that you know this specimen very well."

Swallowing down his nausea, Ray peered at the struggling insect. He squinted, studying each detail. Then the moth stopped squirming. With excruciating slowness, it turned its head around. Ray could hear the cracking of its shell as it faced him. He gasped. Staring back at him was not a pincer-faced, giant-eyed insect head, but the panic-stricken face of Steven Lovelace. The moth's wings began to beat again, thumping against the corkboard with a soft, irregular rhythm. Its murderer's face twisted, its jaw distending as it screamed a tinny shriek that made Ray clap his hands over his ears. He staggered back from the case, looking around frantically at the other specimens. They were all turning their heads now, straining in a symphony of creaking, cracking exoskeletons to get a look at Ray. Their faces stood out in sharp detail to his horrified eyes. He recognized among them famous murderers and psychopaths. A Midwestern cannibal, famous for fashioning furniture from his victims' skin. A mother who drowned her children because she thought they were demons. An acne-faced teenager who opened fire on a daycare center.

And there were others, famous monsters from history: Nazi doctors, slave traders, and cult leaders. And still others, which were not even human. Howling demons, clawed and fanged monstrosities, misty ghosts. All of them crushed into insect form. Somehow, Ray recognized them all. He saw their faces and knew their deeds, which spun across his vision in a blood-soaked highlight reel. Their screams drilled into his eardrums.

Monmouth slung his arm around Ray's shoulders and led him from the room. As the bookshelf swooshed shut behind them, Ray fell to the floor, breathing heavily as the nausea abated.

"I do so love my little menagerie," Monmouth said as he stood over Ray. "It provides me with a welcome distraction from the tedium of eternity. And your friend on the other side of the veil sounds like a welcome addition to my collections. That is the price. You must carry the entity back to me."

"How?" Ray's legs felt weak as he stood.

"That's quite up to you, chap." Monmouth's eyes lit up as he smiled.

Chapter Forty-Two: Chris

"Here," **the Golden Knight said**, pointing to a long driveway leading off the two-lane blacktop. He reached over from the passenger seat and placed his hand on Chris' arm. "Turn off here."

Chris looked at the perfect version of himself questioningly. "We don't know what's up there."

The Golden Knight smiled, his straight, white teeth gleaming even in the car's gloomy interior. "Oh, ye of little faith, have I steered you wrong yet?"

Chris shook his head as he turned onto the narrow gravel path. He couldn't find fault with any of the Golden Knight's tactical advice. At first, he'd been resistant, not wanting to abandon the clean familiarity of his apartment for the open road. But the Golden Knight had made him see sense. Three bodies in one night—Effie, Julian, and Amjad—all of them with connections to Chris. The police were by and large incompetent, but they would put the pieces together soon. If the war against Chaos was to be waged, then Chris would have to leave his home. He'd given himself a bracing enema, taken a scalding shower, and packed a bag of supplies, making sure to include his trusty windchime. He'd come to think of the weapon as his sword, and the idea of going into battle without it was unthinkable. The Golden Knight had told him to drive south and to stick to the back roads.

"Where are we, anyway?" Chris asked, flicking on the high beams to cut through the darkness.

"A place called Gayler County," the Golden Knight said. "A few miles outside of Edgewood. Do you know the area?"

"Not really. There's some sort of big craft fair down here every year. There was a billboard for it a few miles back. But I make a point of avoiding that sort of thing."

"As well you should. But there is something here that calls to me. An instinct long forgotten, perhaps." The Golden Knight leaned forward in his seat. "I believe we've arrived. Turn off the headlights, if you would."

They'd come to the end of the driveway, emerging from the tree-lined path into a weedy patch of land occupied by a single trailer house and rusting piles of broken down machinery. The oxidized shells of cars crouched in the half-light cast by a bug zapper which hung from the corner of the trailer.

"Surely this isn't the place for us," Chris said.

The Golden Knight responded by cuffing him across the jaw with a casual backhand. "We are behind enemy lines from this point on. You expect spotless luxury? Are you really a warrior, or are you just the foppish son of a rich man playing at soldiers?"

Tears stung Chris' eyes. "I *am* a soldier."

He turned off the car's engine and followed the Golden Knight as he walked toward the trailer.

The man who answered the door wore a stained denim shirt, khaki trousers, and a camouflage baseball cap. A patch above the breast pocket of the shirt identified him as Marvin. He scratched at his stubbly chin as he looked Chris over.

"You lost or something?" he asked.

"Oh, I'm not the one who's lost," Chris said. With his wind chime in hand, he felt confident once again. He could see past Marvin's considerable bulk to the trailer's interior. Even though the only light was the pale flashing of a television screen, he could see that the place was not fit for habitation by a right-minded person. Boxes were piled to the ceiling in every corner. The walls between were full of shelves laden with knickknacks.

Marvin snorted. "Look, I ain't got time for this. You go on and get out of here or I'll be forced to take measures, understand?"

But it was Chris who took measures. He swung his sword into the side of the fat man's head. The impact was enough to rupture Marvin's eyeball, and a stream of viscous fluid shot onto his cheek. Chris planted both hands on his chest and shoved. Marvin collapsed to the floor. His meaty hands pressed to his face, he began to howl. Chris stepped through the doorway, gripping his sword tightly. This was becoming an easy process. Maybe he'd take his time with this one.

"Marvin, we're going to need to talk about the state of this place," he said, giving the man a kick in the ribs. "Just look at all this clutter."

Marvin made an odd, high-pitched sound somewhere between a scream and a blubbering sob. Righteous fury filled Chris as he looked down at the pathetic wretch at his feet. He raised the wind chime above his head and smiled.

Later, after they'd dragged Marvin's body into the woods, Chris and the Golden Knight explored the trailer, taking stock of the depth of the late inhabitant's depravity. On first glance, Chris had assumed that the interior would be much like Jube and Moonflower's hovel. Once the lights were on, it was immediately clear that Marvin's madness was quite unlike that of the hippies. There was hardly a speck of dirt or dust in the trailer. Of clutter and junk, there was plenty. But it was junk that had been well cared for and meticulously maintained. The orderly stacks of boxes contained thousands of Barbie dolls, most of them still in their original packaging. Neat lines of ceramic unicorns filled one set of shelves, arrayed like fragile cavalry. Another set of shelves supported dozens of tiny tea sets, the kind of thing a little girl might set on a table between her and her dolls. The bedroom was a shrine to Shirley Temple. The walls were plastered with movie posters, the closet bursting with reproductions of the costumes the child star had worn.

"The man wasn't just an agent of Chaos," Chris spat. "He was some sort of pederast."

The Golden Knight nodded. "It was a good thing you did here. Perhaps you are the savior this world has been waiting for, after all."

Chris' chest swelled with pride. At last, his efforts were acknowledged. It was as if his whole life had been building to this moment. He'd been slogging uphill, up a mountain, and now that he'd finally reached the top, he didn't quite know how to react. He sank to his knees, covered his face with his hands, and wept tears of joy. A warm hand squeezed his shoulder.

"I'm proud of you," the Golden Knight said.

Chris looked up into his smiling face, and he saw for an instant the image of Vernon Clanton. That stern visage filled him with a sense of awe. It was as if his departed father was reaching out to him from beyond the grave and offering at long last his approval.

"I knew that if I kept to the path long enough, you'd understand," Chris said, clutching at the Golden Knight's leg as he stared up into a face that was at once his own and that of his father.

They cleared the majority of the clutter out of the room, shoving it into the spare bedroom. It was far from ideal, but at least it was out of sight. Tomorrow, they could burn it. But the day had been a long one, and Chris found himself physically and emotionally exhausted. When the Golden Knight pulled the covers back, Chris slid into the bed with a deep sigh. It seemed completely natural when the Golden Knight slipped in behind him. They were, after all, closer than brothers. Closer even than lovers. And for that reason, it seemed just as natural when Chris felt the Golden Knight's hands slide over his body.

Chris sighed again as the honeyed voice whispered in his ear. "You have proven yourself worthy of command in this most righteous of crusades. It is time that you take on the full mantle of responsibility."

"You're leaving?" Chris asked as the firm hands slipped inside the waistband of his shorts and tugged them down. "I'm not ready to fight alone."

"I will always be with you, although you may not always see me. We'll soon grow so close that we will never truly be apart."

"But how?"

A gentle yet insistent pressure between Chris' buttocks answered him.

"Breathe deeply," the Golden Knight whispered. "As with all things worth doing, this will be painful at first."

At the first thrust, Chris cried out. At the second, he turned his head to bite the pillow.

Chris awoke in the small hours of the night to the distant drone of summer insects and an empty bed. The sheets were crusty with the salt trails of dried sweat and semen. He fumbled with the switch on the small bedside lamp then winced as the light stung his eyes. The muscles in his thighs and buttocks felt tense as he swung his legs out of bed. He walked the few steps to the bathroom gingerly. The light spilling in from the bedroom was soft, but it was enough for him to examine his reflection in the mirror above the sink.

The changes were small but apparent, even in the half-light of the bathroom. His eyes had taken on the bright, intelligent shine that he'd seen when he met the Golden Knight's gaze. And his skin was so smooth that it seemed without pores. He rolled his shoulders back, squaring up to his full height. Yes, his body was stronger, suppler. The blood in his veins was white hot, his pulse steady and assured. He smiled at the mirror, and his teeth fairly gleamed.

"I am become the Golden Knight," he said to his reflection. "I am the destroyer of chaos, the bane of entropy."

He closed his eyes for a moment, imagining his hair grown out to a flowing blonde mane. He saw himself gripping a sword of flaming steel, riding a steed of purest white.

The shower didn't run as hot as the one at Chris' old apartment, but he didn't mind. He stepped into the steaming spray, and let the water sluice the dried fluids from his skin.

Chapter Forty-Three: George

George and Myrna spent the night at the Motel 6 by the Interstate. They checked out early, stopped at the Pancake Hut for breakfast, and then went back to Myrna's house, where they waited on the porch for the Roll Away Disposal truck to arrive. A man named Doug Horton—the name painted on the side of his truck in swooping red script—showed up at eight. His battered truck was towing a large trailer, a big metal box on wheels. He pulled the truck into the driveway, leaned out of the driver's side window, and asked where they wanted the dumpster dropped.

"As close to the house as you can get it," George called over the rumbling diesel engine.

"Sure about that? These dumpsters can be hell on the grass."

"The yard will be fine." George pointed to a spot in front of the porch. "Just bring it up this way."

Horton shrugged. "You got it."

The man was right: the truck's tires and those on the bottom of the dumpster did tear the grass up. But George was more comfortable with a torn-up yard than a torn-up back, and the more he could shorten the distance he'd have to carry things, the better. Myrna didn't seem to mind, either. She'd been silent most of the morning, only picking at her breakfast. Her face was pale, her eyes red.

Horton unhitched the dumpster a few feet in front of the porch. He wiped his hands on his jeans then fished a business card out of his pocket.

"This here's got my cell number on it." He passed the card over to George. "Give me a holler when you need me to pick her up and take her over to the landfill."

"Actually, we'll probably need you again tomorrow."

Horton raised one bushy eyebrow. "Got another place needs cleaning out? Well, my moving fee still applies. If that ain't a problem, I'll haul it wherever you want."

"Fair enough."

Horton climbed back in his truck and rumbled off down the road, leaving behind two tire track scars across the lawn.

George turned back to Myrna. She was still seated on the edge of the porch, looking down at her dangling feet.

"You want to get started now or wait for Ray and Stephanie?" he asked.

Myrna took so long to respond that he thought she might not have heard him. When she finally did speak, her voice was so soft that he had to step closer just to hear her.

"I don't want to do this," she said.

George sat down beside her and put an arm around her shoulders. "Look, I know this isn't going to be easy. Believe me, I know. But hanging onto this stuff isn't making you happy."

"But the grey people are only alive because I keep their things. They'll die if I get rid of my stuff."

"Myrna, those grey people, they're already dead. Whether they know it or not, they need to move on. Their time in this world is over, and whatever is waiting for us beyond the veil, that's where they need to be. You need to let them go. It's the right thing."

She leaned into him, pressing her face against his chest. "I know."

They didn't wait for Ray and Stephanie. After Myrna had gathered her strength, she said that she was afraid her resolve might crumble if they waited. So they'd picked themselves up off the porch and headed into the house. The living room looked like a war zone. Kathy's ghost had smashed up all the shelves and torn apart the furniture. But there were still some boxes that hadn't been emptied among the debris.

"Where do we even start?" Myrna asked, standing just inside the front door.

George caught a shadow of defeat creeping across her face, and he made a move before she could sink any further. He grabbed the first thing he saw, a box of model airplanes. The broken bits of plastic made a faint tinkling as he picked up the box.

"We start right here and work our way up," he said. "You eat an elephant the same way you eat a peanut butter sandwich: one bite at a time."

Clutching the box in his arms, he swept out through the front door. He heaved the model airplanes—box and all—into the dumpster, where they landed with a crunch. He turned back just in time to catch Myrna's wince at the sound of the impact. But then she nodded and took up a bag of children's clothes and strode onto the porch.

"One bite at a time," she said as she tossed the bag into the dumpster.

By the time Ray and his cousin arrived, George's back was already starting to ache. Most of the living room's stacks and piles had been moved to the dumpster, leaving behind tufts of dust and broken bits of plastic, glass, and ceramic. The enormity of the task in front of them hit George full force when he peered down into the dumpster and saw how much had come from just one room. He'd thought renting the largest dumpster that Roll Away Disposal offered might be overkill. But after just an hour's work, he'd begun to think that it might not be enough.

"Morning, constable." George waved to Ray and Stephanie as they approached the house. "Hope you don't mind, but we started without you."

Ray looked like he hadn't slept a wink. The corners of his mouth made a feeble effort at smiling as he shook George's hand. "Sorry it took us a while to get over here. I was indisposed, if you know what I mean." He looked over his shoulder at the dumpster. "Guess you already know that thing's going to tear up the yard."

"I thought that, under the circumstances, the landscaping was a low priority."

"I guess you're right." Ray nodded. "Reckon we better get started."

George stood aside, gesturing for him to enter the house. "After you."

The constable grunted and went in. "Jesus Christ, y'all weren't lying about the damage that thing did in here. Looks like a goddamn tornado came through."

George caught Stephanie by her elbow before she could follow. "This is going to work, right?" he asked. "Getting rid of all this stuff, I mean. And are you sure about starting here instead of my place?"

She shrugged. "How the hell should I know? But it's bound to be a step in the right direction." She lowered her voice and leaned in to whisper. "But I'm worried about Ray. He was doing some…research last night, and when he got done, he wasn't looking so hot."

George watched the constable stoop to pick up a crushed cardboard box. "We'll just keep an eye on him, okay?"

"Sure," Stephanie said, walking into the house.

By noon, the entire downstairs was clear. They'd worked fast and indiscriminately. There was no dithering or dickering from Myrna. Most of what she'd collected was in pieces anyway. Aside from a few blankets and pillows that had belonged to her for years, everything went. The downstairs closet, packed to the ceiling when they began, now contained a few jackets and coats. The kitchen and dining room had likewise been purged. All the unopened boxes of dishes and silverware went into the dumpster. The old cookbooks joined them.

"Seems a shame to get rid of some of this stuff," Ray said, looking over a set of decorative wooden bowls as he walked from the kitchen to the front door. "It's not like it's all, I don't know, *infected*."

Stephanie shot the idea down. "You don't really want to take that chance, do you? Besides, these grey people of hers, they need to move on. You ever see someone keep a pet alive way past the point where it has any quality of life? Same thing. It's hard to let go, but it's what needs to happen."

George watched Myrna wince at this exchange. But she remained silent as she emptied the china cabinet of all but the place settings she'd had since her wedding.

"I don't think my husband's ghost is hanging around for these cups and saucers," she said, smiling weakly at George. "He always hated the fancy china. Called it frippery. That was his word for it. His word for a lot of things, actually."

George called a halt to the proceedings. "Let's take a lunch break. I'll spring for pizza."

Myrna nodded. "I could use a break."

They ate lunch on the porch, lifting slices of pepperoni pizza out of the grease-stained box and sipping from sweating cans of soda. Their clothes were dusty, sweated through in spots. They ate ravenously, polishing off two pizzas. George was amazed at his own appetite. But looking out at the dumpster, he could see the amount of work they'd done. All four of the downstairs rooms were almost completely empty. The living room and the TV room were even clean. Stephanie had run the vacuum cleaner over the carpet in both rooms and wiped down all the surfaces with a rag sprayed with furniture cleaner. It was real progress they were making, and it would have made George feel something like pride had he not looked at Myrna.

The woman looked like she'd been swimming against a terrible tide with no shore in sight. Although he and Ray had done the majority of the heavy lifting—the boxes of books and old wooden toys, the smashed up furniture—it was Myrna that looked as if she'd been put through the paces. Her shoulders slumped as if bearing up against an invisible weight.

He touched her arm. "I'd say we're closing in on the halfway point. If our bodies don't just give up, we might finish it today. Once we get those stairs cleared, we can work it bucket brigade style. It'll be okay."

"Will it really? Do you know that for sure?"

Her sharp tone had George drawing back his hand for a moment, but he scooted closer to her and put an arm around her shoulders. "I know for sure that I love you and that this is the right thing."

Her shoulders trembled under his arm. "Dale's old room. It's upstairs. All his things…"

George looked at Ray and Stephanie like a man up to his neck in water casting about for a life preserver. The two cousins seemed suddenly interested in pushing pizza crusts around on their paper plates.

"Look, we'll cross that bridge when we get there," he said lamely. "We have a lot of work to do between now and then."

Myrna nodded but continued to stare into her lap. "I know it's for the best. I just can't bear to think…"

They sat for a few minutes in uncomfortable silence before heading back inside. There was work to be done, and not all of it would be easy.

Chapter Forty-Four: Myrna

The others were down the hall, getting her bedroom cleaned out. That almost made Myrna laugh. Just a couple weeks ago, she'd have practically had a fit just at the thought of people poking around in her house, let alone her bedroom. Now she didn't care one flip. Yes, it *almost* made her laugh. All those things that she thought were so precious, they'd been torn and smashed and shattered. Now the broken pieces were going into a dumpster, destined to rot in the county landfill.

She stood in front of the closed door to Dale's bedroom, her hand on the knob. She hadn't quite worked up the strength yet to actually walk into the room. No matter how many times she told herself that this was for the best, she couldn't make herself go through with it. Tossing away her collections, and banishing the grey people to whatever place awaited them, that was bad enough. But this, well, it was something else altogether. It felt like a betrayal. And how could she explain that to the others? Ray, Stephanie, George: they were all childless. How could they understand what throwing away Dale's things would mean for her?

She took a deep breath. The doorknob seemed to turn on its own. Stepping into the room with her eyes closed, she half expected her son to be standing there. Maybe he'd be lying on his bed, reading a comic book. Maybe he'd be flipping a baseball into the air, letting it fall into his mitt. His presence was so immediate, so *real*, that she thought she might be able to hug him close to her, to stand on tiptoe and kiss his stubbly cheek. But the room was empty when she opened her eyes. Empty except for the vast collection of neatly organized items.

Dale wasn't there.

Of course, he hadn't been there—not *really*—for some time. The washed out grey version who paid her sporadic visits wasn't the same as her baby boy. She knew that. She'd known it from his first visit. But cleaning out this room, well, she knew it would be like taking out all his baby pictures and burning them.

"I was so cavalier about clearing out the house after Kathy died."

Myrna turned at the sound of George's voice. He was standing in the doorway, his hair sweat-slicked back from his forehead. Myrna sat down on Dale's old bed and patted the space beside her. George crossed the room through the narrow alley between boxes of comic books and baseball cards, and sat down.

"Afterwards, I felt guilty," he continued. "I knew that most of what I was packing away was just junk that she'd bought out of some compulsion. It didn't *mean* anything. That's how I rationalized it when I set that table up at the flea market. But all the same, I knew how hurt she'd have been had she lived to see it. As much as I hated her sickness, I never hated her."

"I'm not ready," she said. "Maybe some of the things I bought for him after he'd gone. Maybe I can let that stuff go. But all the things he'd treasured while he was still with me, I just can't do it. I'd rather cut off my arm."

"Letting go isn't easy. I think it's supposed to be painful."

She stood up, crossing her arms over her chest. "I'm sorry, but you can't understand. Dale was my child. You can take everything out of this house—the furniture, all my clothes—but this room isn't to be touched."

"Myrna, you know…"

"No!" she snapped. "End of discussion. Nothing leaves this room."

George stood, rubbing at the small of his back. He gave her a look—something like a weak smile tinged with pity—and left the room. He hesitated on the threshold, but said nothing before shutting the door gently behind him.

Myrna thought that she might cry, but no tears came. The sadness that fell on her was something too profound for simple tears.

Looking around, she realized that although she'd maintained this room more than any other in the house, she'd actually spent very little time in it. Her visits were limited to furious bursts of dusting and organization of the collections within. She'd run a feather duster over the room once every couple weeks or whenever she added more items to the shelves or boxes. But that was it, really. She never had occasion to come in here and just sit, not the way she was doing now. And she knew why.

Sitting on Dale's bed, surrounded by all his treasures, she was buried beneath an avalanche of memories. His childhood played out a bittersweet highlight reel across her memory, a montage of first days at school, skinned knees, Little League games, Cub Scout meetings, bicycle rides, and birthday parties. These things had happened and would never happen again. When they'd taken place, they'd gone by in a whirl, the days, months, and years whizzing by until her baby boy was a man. And now that he was gone, the days, months, and years stretched out before her like an endless, empty road.

She fled the room, closing the door behind her. They could clean the rest of the house, but this room would remain untouched. She didn't care if all the demons in hell rose up to torment her, Dale's room would not be stripped of those memories.

Chapter Forty-Five: Doug

Those people had paid him to haul the dumpster to the landfill, but Doug didn't reckon it made a bit of difference where he took the stuff. They wanted it gone, and it would be gone. Whether it was gone to the landfill or to Weird Marvin's place, who gave a shit? Soon as Doug had seen what was in that dumpster, he knew that Weird Marvin would want to take a look. Weird Marvin was a sucker for that cutsie-kiddie stuff, and these people had thrown away a lot of that shit. Just the quick once-over Doug had given the dumpster while he got it hitched to the back of the truck had told him all he needed to know. There were kiddie toys and books and little knickknacks that Weird Marvin would give good money for. Sure, a lot of it was broken to pieces, but just as much looked like it could be salvaged. He'd let Weird Marvin sort it out. That was their arrangement: Doug got to use Weird Marvin's property for storing some of the machines he'd one day get around to fixing, and for a modest finder's fee, Doug would deliver any kiddie stuff he came across during his job.

For Doug, it was a classic win-win. He wasn't sure what Weird Marvin got out of it, other than a yard full of junk and a house full of dolls and toys. But Doug didn't concern himself too much with that. There was a reason that the guy was Weird Marvin instead of plain old Marvin. It had crossed his mind that maybe Weird Marvin might be one of those kiddie diddlers, carrying on the way he did about Shirley Temple and Cabbage Patch dolls and Barbie dream cars. But he preferred not to dwell on such thoughts. Instead, he thought of ways to spend Weird Marvin's money.

He knew he should go by the salvage yard and drop the dough for the parts to get one of the cars in Weird Marvin's backyard up and running. But Doug reckoned he'd probably treat himself to a steak dinner and an evening of lap dances at Rhoda's Cabaret over in Crystal Falls. And that was just what he had planned for the money from tonight's haul. According to the old boy who'd paid the tab—George something or other, it was printed there on the invoice—there was another load of stuff he needed hauled away in the morning from a different address. If that job was anything like this one, Doug would wind up getting paid four times out of the deal: twice for the dumpster rental and twice for bringing the shit over to Weird Marvin. It was shaping up to be a good week. Mayhap there'd be shrimp cocktail with that steak and a second lap dance in the deal.

Doug took the turn onto Weird Marvin's long driveway at a slow creep. Last time he'd been up this way, he'd gotten careless and nearly slid into the ditch and dumped the whole works. The big diesel engine growled. The contents of the dumpster shifted with each bump. There'd be some breakage. But that was Weird Marvin's problem.

When he crested the hill, the truck's headlights illuminating the junked cars and other assorted machinery, Doug leaned on the horn. When he'd given it a few good blasts, he killed the engine and jumped out of the truck.

"Hey, old Marvin, get your weird ass out here!" He sauntered over to the trailer's front door.

This was another part of their arrangement. Doug always came unannounced. He didn't want Weird Marvin's phone number, and he damn sure didn't want Weird Marvin calling him at his work number. The less contact they had, the better. The money was good, and the work easy enough, but that didn't mean he had to like the guy.

He mounted the stairs leading up to the trailer's door and hollered again. "Hey, I ain't got all night. You want to come look at this stuff I got or not?"

There was a noise of someone scuffling around inside. Doug jumped down from the stairs, muttering to himself about how Weird Marvin was probably in there braiding the hair on his My Little Pony collection or posing his Barbie dolls in obscene positions. That thought made Doug laugh as he looked out over the graveyard of junked cars. Weird Marvin sure was good to let him store all these clunkers up here, but damned if he wasn't a character, what with his dolls and toys and such. Doug was still chuckling to himself when he heard the trailer's screen door creak open behind him.

"Took you long enough," Doug said, turning around. "You choking the chicken over a pile of Barbies or…"

The words died in his throat. The man standing at the top of the stairs sure as hell wasn't Weird Marvin. This old boy was considerably younger and thinner. He was naked except for some white briefs and a pair of running shoes. And he held in his hand what looked to be a metal pipe. Clearly, the old boy was off his rocker. Weird Marvin was one thing. This old boy was a different kind of crazy altogether, and Doug didn't need more than a glance to know it.

"Who the hell are you?" Doug asked, taking a step backwards.

The old boy hopped down from the trailer. "I'm a friend of the owner. He owes me a great deal, for I freed him from the grip of chaos."

Doug swallowed. He kept a gun in the glove compartment of the truck, but it felt like it was ten miles away rather than ten feet. He took another step back, wondering if he could run a few strides back to the truck, open the door, dive in, and get his piece before that crazy guy could grab hold of him.

"You a friend of Marvin?" he asked.

"That's right."

Doug kept moving. He was close to the truck now. Another few steps and he could reach out and touch the door handle. He watched the old boy move into the beams of the headlights.

"Then you probably know about our arrangement. I got a whole load of stuff back there in the trailer. This woman cleaned out her house. She had all kinds of stuff," Doug said.

"I know all about your kind."

It happened so damn quick. Even if he'd had his gun, there was no way he could have aimed and fired in time. One second the crazy guy in his tighty whities was standing there with his eyes shining in the truck's headlights like some wild animal, and the next he was waving that metal pipe of his like a Major Leaguer. Doug threw up his arms in front of his face and got himself a couple of broken bones for his trouble. He screamed as the pipe clocked him in the ribs once, twice, three times.

"I am become the Golden Knight of Perfection!" The crazy man bellowed as he swung his weapon.

Doug stumbled, his broken ribs stabbing at him with each breath. Pain exploded at the base of his skull, where the metal pipe smashed down. Everything started spinning, like he was on some carnival ride doing endless loop-the-loops. He hit the ground with teeth-rattling impact. The pipe smashed into his back in a sledgehammer rhythm as the crazy man hollered his nonsense.

Doug's hands scrabbled for purchase on the weedy ground. He tried to hold on as everything went dark.

He awoke to a world of hurt. Each breath was a dull knife stuck between his ribs. The back of his head throbbed in time with his heartbeat. His eyelids were gummy. When he opened them, it felt like ripping away the Velcro strips on his shoes. And once he did get them open, he didn't feel at all reassured by what he saw.

He was in Weird Marvin's trailer, tied up to a straight-backed chair. He could tell the first part by glancing around at the shelves full of children's toys. The old fashioned console TV, the antique coffee table, the floral patterned curtains, Doug recognized all of it. The second part of his predicament became apparent when he tried to move his arms and legs. They were held fast in place. Whatever was holding them there bit into his flesh as he tried to move.

The crazy man sat on Weird Marvin's plastic-covered sofa. Still wearing nothing but his shoes and his drawers. Still grinning like a fool and talking an endless stream of bullshit.

"I'm so glad you're awake," the crazy man said. He got up from the sofa, his skin coming away from the plastic with a tearing sound. He put his hands on his hips and threw one foot on top of the coffee table like it was some big game animal he'd just gunned down. "We have so much to talk about."

"Fuck do you want with me?" Doug's voice sounded strange to his own ears. His mouth felt mushy.

"Straight to the point, eh?" The crazy man disappeared into the kitchen and came back with a chair. He placed it in front of Doug and sat down. Their knees nearly touched. "What I want to know is where you picked up that horrific collection of junk that you were bringing to your pederast friend?"

"Marvin weren't no molester. He was just weird, that's all." Doug had no idea why he was wasting his breath defending Weird Marvin. He didn't even like the guy. Of course, he supposed that the poor old weirdo was probably dead now. The crazy man didn't look like he'd just dropped in for a glass of iced tea and conversation.

"The man was a disgusting pervert. The world is a better place for his death."

Doug's shoulders sagged. There you had it. This nutcase had killed Weird Marvin. And now that he'd told Doug, that probably meant he'd kill him too. Doug began to cry. Each sob made him feel like he was going to split right open, but he just couldn't stop himself. It just wasn't fair, dying like this. An hour ago, his biggest fear was that the blonde with the C-section scar that worked at Rhoda's might have given him a dose of the clap after their encounter in the VIP room. And now, he was wondering if he was right enough with Jesus to die. Damn it, he didn't plan on this, not at all.

The crazy man shook his head, tsk-tsking like a disappointed parent. "A grown man shouldn't cry. You're making a spectacle of yourself." He reached out and slapped Doug across the face. "Now tell me where you picked up that disgusting load of trash, and all this will be wrapped up, neat as you please."

Doug blubbered out the address.

The crazy man stood. "There, was that so hard? You know, driving down the road, I could practically smell the entropy coming off this place. But still, I wondered why it called out to me so. Then you came to me, and when I tasted the aura of the things you towed onto this property, I knew at last why I was brought here."

Doug grunted. Part of him was scared shitless, but the other part just wished the crazy asshole would get it the hell over with.

"My oldest enemy, after all these years…" The crazy man dissolved into a fit of laughter. When he finally recovered, he patted Doug on the shoulder. "That rat faced bastard will be so surprised to see me. I can hardly wait."

He left the room, humming as he went. Doug took a deep, shaky breath and waited. He didn't have to wait long. When the crazy man came back into the living room, he was carrying his length of metal pipe. He stood in front of Doug like a batter crowding home plate. Doug closed his eyes, bracing for impact.

Chapter Forty-Six: Tate

The idea of hotel bedding had never sat well with Tate. Sure, he supposed they washed it plenty, but that didn't change the fact that untold numbers of people had slept on it. Slept on it and done God knows what else. During the day's seminar on forensic equipment, some of the nerds from the State Crime Lab had shown off the latest advances in fluid detection. Tate shuddered to think what that equipment might reveal in his hotel room. But that didn't stop him from tugging his shirttail out of his pants, tossing his wallet and phone onto the nightstand, and flopping down on the bed. He was dog-tired.

Not that bouncing around the convention was all that taxing. Other than the panel discussions on hand-to-hand tactics and new SWAT weapons, the whole thing had been a bust. Bunch of lawyer mumbo jumbo, civil rights discussions, that sort of thing. The FBI profiling class had seemed promising, but it was standing room only an hour before Tate even got near the Grand Ballroom. Disappointing, that was for sure, but it was still better than being back home.

Hiding out forever wasn't an option, and even these few days of running away from his problems made Tate feel like a coward. But he'd really lost it at his mother's house. God only knew what he'd have done if Avery hadn't shown up.

Tate swung his legs out of the bed. He crossed the room and got a can of ginger ale out of the mini-fridge. His stomach was doing flip-flops just at the thought of home. He took a long slug of soda and belched. The belch brought on a yawn. Damn, but he was tired! Sleep hadn't been easy to come by since he fell in his mother's bathroom and had that horrible dream. And that's all it was. Just a dream. No matter how real it felt, it was just some stupid, meaningless dream brought on by a bellyful of whiskey and too much work.

His phone buzzed, rattling and jumping on the nightstand. The screen said "Stilwell" and showed a picture of Deputy Bart Stilwell's gap-toothed grin.

Tate groaned. He couldn't get away for a few days without something going to shit at the office. He thought Avery could handle things, but apparently not. Of course, Stilwell wasn't the type to take orders from someone so much younger, not to mention so much darker. And that was a problem that Tate knew he'd have to sort out eventually.

He tapped the screen and put the phone to his ear. "Sheriff Wilson."

"Howdy, boss. How's it going up there in the big city?" Stilwell's voice was full of false cheer.

"It's great." Tate hoped that the deputy would just get to the point so he could fire up HBO and drink his ginger ale in peace. "This seminar has been really interesting. What's up on the home front?"

"Wish I had good news, but I got to tell you that it ain't all roses down here."

The deputy paused so long that Tate thought the call might have been dropped. But then he realized that he could hear Stilwell's heavy mouth-breathing. "Is that so?"

"Homeboy ain't doing such a hot job holding down the fort."

"You mean Deputy Cartwright? The deputy that I left in charge?"

"Sure, that's right. *Deputy* Cartwright has taken sick leave for the last two days."

"Maybe he ate something that didn't agree with him. Maybe he got one of them summer colds. You know, folks do take ill from time to time."

Stilwell laughed. "Mayhap he does just have a case of the sniffles. But I'd think he'd have at least kept you up to date about what's going on with your mama. Guess he hasn't bothered to give you a holler to tell you she's been stepping out with that George Young character. It ain't much of a secret that you still like him for being involved in the Flannigan thing. I didn't figure you'd be too happy, him gallivanting around with your mama."

Tate's mild indigestion blossomed into a full blown bellyache. He left town for a few days, and everything went to hell. He wracked his brain for a reason that Avery might have held out on him, and although he couldn't come up with anything plausible, he was sure the deputy had an excuse. Maybe he was sicker than Stilwell made it sound.

"That all you got, deputy?" Tate slumped down on the bed. "My mother is a grown woman. She gets to decide who she dates."

"But I thought you'd…"

Brad Carter | 317

"If you did any thinking this week, I'd be shocked. How about you let Deputy Cartwright do the job I left him to do? If there's some crime wave down there and he doesn't call me, then you be sure to give me a holler."

He ended the call and tossed the phone back onto the nightstand. His stomach continued to churn as he lay there staring up at the ceiling. He supposed he should start packing. If he checked out of the hotel at sunup, he could be back in Barlow by breakfast time. Then, he could start picking up the pieces. He made a mental list of what needed to be done, ticking off each point with a heavy sigh. Figure out this business with his mother and George Young. Find out what the hell was wrong with Avery. See if the state police were making any progress with the Flannigan case. And maybe check with Dr. Philips about getting some pills to make the damn dreams stop.

He clutched his belly and rolled over onto his side. Nothing was ever easy.

Breakfast was more ginger ale and a sleeve of saltine crackers purchased from a convenience store on the way out of Little Rock. No matter how much he felt that he needed coffee, Tate knew that there was enough disruption going on in his gut without dumping a cupful of hot black acid onto it.

By the time he rolled into Barlow, his hands were shaky. He felt emptied out. The dreams had come back to him again last night. Visions of drowning in a sea of junk disrupted his sleep so much that he couldn't be sure he'd gotten more than a few total hours of shut-eye. It was sure as hell catching up to him.

The Crown Vic wasn't in the driveway at his mother's house, but Tate got out and rang the doorbell a few times anyway. The two most likely explanations for her absence both made him want to scream: either she was out shopping for more crap to stuff into the house, or—*please, God, no*—she was somewhere with George Young.

Tate climbed back into his truck. He considered driving over to Young's house, maybe throwing a scare into the guy. Sure, Tate figured, his mom would be madder than hell, but he could live with that if he could get Young to back off. He shook his head. The whole thing could just backfire and make them dig their heels in on a relationship that clearly was going nowhere. Better to just let it run its course.

That left Avery.

Tate had been a guest at Avery's apartment once before. He'd sat on the couch and eaten nachos and watched a baseball game with the deputy. It had been a nice time. Avery's girlfriend, LaToya, had endured their crude man-talk with good natured shakes of the head as she sat with them and leafed through a magazine. Tate had been comfortable there. But that was a different time, different circumstances. Now, he felt awkward as he sat on the couch. He had to force himself to sit still and quit fidgeting. LaToya sat there beside him, her hands folded on her pregnant belly. She wore a concerned frown as she stared at Avery, who sat kicked back in his recliner.

"I don't get it." Tate shook his head. "You went into Young's house, and the old guy fired at you?"

"No, it wasn't him." Avery didn't look at him as he spoke. He just kept looking at some point in the middle distance. "Listen, nobody fired at me. Whatever was in that garage, it wasn't some person."

"You're not making sense."

Avery finally turned to look at Tate. "I don't care if you think it sounds crazy. I know what I saw."

"A ghost attacked you in Young's garage? You even listening to the stuff you're talking?" He didn't like the look in the deputy's eyes. They were red-rimmed and puffy, like he hadn't been sleeping. They were a lot like his own eyes.

Avery snapped the footrest down and leaned forward. "Boss, I don't care how it sounds. And I bet you know I'm not just talking shit. I think you saw it too. That day up there in your mama's bathroom. I'm guessing you did more than just fall and bump your head. And I'm guessing the reason you look like shit right now is that you ain't been sleeping so good ever since. Tell me I'm wrong."

Tate's mouth had gone dry. "You're wrong."

"That's the way you want to play it, fine. But there's something fucked up going on in this town. Can't believe I got out of Little Rock for this." He looked over at LaToya. "Girl, you mind giving us a few minutes? Maybe you could run up to that restaurant, get you some of those fried pickles you been craving."

LaToya's forehead creased. "Honey, I don't think…"

Avery raised a hand. "Please. Just give us a little while to talk."

Brad Carter | 319

She got up from the couch and went to Avery's side. She bent and kissed his cheek. "Okay, but just a few minutes. Then I want you to promise me you'll try to get some sleep."

She gave Tate a pointed look then grabbed her purse off the coffee table and headed for the door.

After she left, Avery just sat there for a few minutes. Tate wondered if he should talk first, but he didn't know how to begin. Finally, Avery spoke up.

"LaToya, she's afraid. I knew I shouldn't have told her about what happened in that garage, but I just couldn't keep it to myself. Thing is, she knows that my mama is little off. Probably thinks some of the family crazy is starting to come out in me. And her being pregnant, she's probably also wondering if some of that crazy is going to affect the baby. I almost wonder about that myself."

Tate nodded. Avery had told him about his mother's obsession with keeping stacks of Bibles in each room to ward off demons. Other than that little quirk, the woman was as nice as they come, to hear Avery tell it.

"When I came to your mama's place, I figured you'd just gotten drunk and flipped your lid," Avery said.

"That's exactly what it was."

"You really think so? Maybe I'd believe that if you didn't wake up puking a bunch of grey junk into the toilet bowl." Avery got up out of his chair and paced back and forth in the little space between the coffee table and the TV. "I know what it looks like when a man has too much liquor and loses his cookies. That's miles away from what you were doing, so don't even look at me like that."

"You didn't say a word about this until now? I puke up a bunch of…" Tate held up his hands, lost for words.

"It's called ectoplasm," Avery said. "Physical evidence of contact with the other side. I found that on the internet."

"I puke up a bunch of *ectoplasm*, and you just now decide to tell me about it? Come on, man. I can't believe that."

"Hell, I didn't want to believe it myself. I'm right where you are now. I put it out of my head, convinced myself that it wasn't real. Then I saw that thing in George Young's garage. And the dreams started." He stopped pacing. "Now I see you, looking like you hadn't slept in days, and I wonder what sort of dreams you're having."

Tate didn't feel much like discussing his dreams. "So I haven't been sleeping much. That doesn't prove anything."

"Look," Avery continued, "I know you hate the guy, but I think you need to have a talk with George Young. And that constable from Edgewood."

"What does Ray McFettridge have to do with this?"

Avery laughed, but there was no humor in it. "Man, you really are in the dark, aren't you?"

"What's my mom mixed up in?"

"Look, I told you about the shit that's going on around here, and you don't want to believe me. Why don't you find her and ask her yourself?"

Tate stood. "So it's like that now, huh?"

"Yeah, it's like that. We're friends and all, but I got a kid on the way and a girl that I need to do right by. This paranormal, supernatural shit, I don't want nothing to do with it. I've seen enough. I understand you got to deal with it, your mama being involved and all, but I just can't help you." Avery looked like he was on the verge of tears. It was hard seeing him like that, so Tate just turned and walked out the door.

Chapter Forty-Seven: Ray

It was early when Ray pulled into George's driveway. But George and Myrna were already hard at it. They were loading boxes from the garage into the backseat and trunk of George's car. But a quick glance into the open garage told Ray that they'd barely made a dent.

"Going to need that dumpster again, aren't you?" Ray said as he and Stephanie climbed out of his truck.

George finished wrestling a box into the jam-packed trunk then stood up and leaned from one side to the other, stretching out his back. Myrna stood at his side. She still looked tired, but not nearly as bad as she had yesterday.

"I've left that Horton character three voice mails and haven't heard one peep back. Guess he isn't a fan of repeat business," George said. "There's one other place that does haul off service, but they can't get out here today. I didn't think, given our circumstances, that it was wise to wait." He kicked at the ground and sighed. "Do you think we did the right thing getting Myrna's house cleared out first? Most of Kathy's stuff is here, after all."

"That house of hers, it was a vortex of psychic energy," Stephanie said. "Kathy was leeching off all that free-floating mojo. Just like I said yesterday."

"But are you *sure*?" George insisted.

Ray looked at Stephanie. She shrugged. She'd been doing that an awful lot lately, as if he was now the expert. A few hours scratching at the Ouija board and suddenly he knew everything? Hell, he wished that was true. Maybe then he'd have some sort of clue about whether or not his plan had a snowball's chance in hell of working out.

"Guess it's good thing I have my truck." Ray pointed over his shoulder. "So, we just loading up and making runs out to the landfill?"

"Myrna's Crown Victoria has plenty of space. Between her car, mine, and your truck, we ought to be able to make good progress," George said. "And who knows, maybe Horton will finally return my call. But I just can't see sitting around on our hands and waiting for him."

"Well, let's get to it then." Ray hitched up his jeans and walked toward the garage.

The first box he grabbed might as well have been a pot of boiling water. He slid it from the top of a stack of similar boxes and had nearly turned around before the burning sensation registered with his nerve endings. Pain flared in his hands then raced up his arms. It was full-blown agony during the few seconds before he dropped the box. His eyes filled with tears. His head felt like a helium balloon trying to pull loose from his neck. The hard floor of the garage jarred his tailbone as he sat down heavily.

If he lost consciousness, it was only for a moment, long enough for the others to swarm around him and start asking him if he was okay. By that time, the pain was mostly gone, although his palms felt prickly, like both hands had gone to sleep.

"Hey, maybe you shouldn't get up," George said as Ray got to his feet.

"I'm okay," Ray said even as he clutched the other man's shoulder for support. Stephanie attached herself to his side and helped him out of the garage. He sat down on the hood of George's car and wiped a hand across his forehead. He looked around at the trio of concerned faces staring back at him and tried to force a smile. "Really, y'all, I'm fine. Just got a little scare there. Don't want it to be said that I'm not willing to do my share of the work, but I don't think I can handle any of those boxes in there."

George and Myrna turned their concerned gazes on Stephanie, who cleared her throat and explained, "I guess that confirms some of what we thought might be going on. It was probably just more of the shock he got back at the bookstore when he picked up those paperbacks."

"I'd say it wasn't as bad as that, but yeah, that's what it felt like," Ray said.

"You think it's wise being so close to all this?" George nodded in the direction of the garage. "I thought you were having a heart attack back there."

Ray looked down at his hands. The tingling was starting to fade. "You know, I think you're right. A couple aspirin and a nap might help. I hate to bail out on all this work, but I'm not much use if I fall out every time I touch one of those boxes. But I reckon y'all will need my truck. Think I can borrow a car from someone?"

"You can take mine," Myrna said. "Just let me get my keys out of my purse."

Ray had never been much of a liar, but he was fairly sure they'd bought his story about the aspirin and the nap. Well, maybe not Stephanie. She'd given him one of those looks when Myrna handed over the car keys. It was a look that said *I hope you know what you're doing.* She'd followed up the look with one of her patented half-shrugs and watched him drive away.

He'd known since yesterday that he'd need some time alone in Myrna's house to make this work. He hadn't expected an excuse to just jump into his lap and spare him the ordeal of dreaming one up. It looked as though things were starting to fall into place.

Whatever was hanging around in the house couldn't show itself in broad daylight while all that clean-up was going on. But Ray had a feeling it would come out and play if he was alone in the house, even if all the shit they'd pulled out of there was in the landfill. He suspected that it didn't make a damn bit of difference if both houses were cleaned out top to bottom. That was just too easy.

He parked in Myrna's driveway and looked at the house. From the outside, you'd never know that some sinister supernatural force had been hard at work inside the walls. But Ray suspected that was just how it was with the whole world. There was always some force operating just outside of human understanding, hovering in the spaces most people couldn't look into. He'd known this for a fact most of his life, even if he'd trained himself to ignore it. Ignorance was probably not only blissful for most people, but necessary. It made it possible for most people to sleep at night.

He walked onto the porch and took a quick look over his shoulder. There were no nosy neighbors watching him. So far, his luck was holding. It took him a few tries to find the right key, and then he was inside. The house seemed huge now that it was mostly empty. Very little of the furniture had been salvageable. A single chair and an empty bookshelf were all that remained in the living room. The dining room table was still intact, but only two of the chairs hadn't been reduced to splinters. One chair sat at each end of the table now, and looking at them filled Ray with a strange loneliness.

He moved into what Myrna had called the TV room, only now there was no TV in it. Myrna's boxy old set had gone into the dumpster, its screen having been smashed in by Kathy's furious ghost. The couch was still there, although its upholstery was slashed here and there as if the world's biggest housecat had been using it as a scratching post.

Ray wandered through the house, climbing the stairs to the second floor and marveling at how clean the place looked. All the while, he revisited his talk with Monmouth. According to him, there was no actual spell or incantation for summoning entities. It was merely a matter of the talent possessed by the person doing the summoning. As Stephanie was fond of pointing out, you either had the talent or you didn't.

What was it Monmouth had said?

A matter of reaching out with the psychic self, that's all an incantation really is. It was Frasier who was always so insistent that we put in references to a medium's gibberish, although we knew that such nonsense was only for show.

Ray had been plenty pissed off. All that pompous ass could offer in the way of advice was to focus and hope for the best?

The secret is to focus your energy here, Monmouth had said, tapping the middle of Ray's forehead. *You've heard of the psychic third eye? There's some truth to it. When you are ready, close your eyes, and focus your energy on your third eye. When it opens, you'll either see the entity you seek or you will not.*

Ray had a few choice words for that. One of them was "fucking" and another was "bullshit." The others were just placeholders.

Monmouth didn't seem too bothered by that. He'd just sat back down by the fireplace.

When that unseen eye opens, it does more than see, chap. It also illuminates.

And that was it. The oily bastard had ushered him out the door, and Ray had snapped awake back in the world of the living.

Ray plodded back downstairs and into the TV room. He flopped down on the couch and shifted around until he was comfortable. He closed his eyes and relaxed. He concentrated on his breathing, taking deep breaths and exhaling slowly. And then, shoving every thought from his mind, he focused.

The shriek that tore him out of his trance was like an icepick in Ray's ears. It rose in pitch and volume until he was sure that his eardrums—along with every window in the house—would burst. When he opened

Brad Carter | 325

his eyes, it appeared at first as though night had fallen, that he'd slept the day away on Myrna's couch. But then he realized that the darkness was the effect of thousands of whirling shadows crammed into the room. They whipped around, sliding over the walls, ceiling, and floor, leaving vapor trails that dissolved in mildew-scented wisps. Ray wanted to throw his hands in front of his face, but something held him motionless.

From the center of this shadowy vortex stepped a woman. Long black streams of liquid slid off her limbs as she crossed the room. The streams became slid from her body as she moved until she stood completely naked in front of Ray. He recognized her, of course. George had shown him a photograph of his dead wife Kathy. The photo was old, taken before they were married, and in it, Kathy had been a smiling, bright-eyed woman, her face framed by a beautiful mass of dark brown hair. This woman was hollow-eyed and expressionless. While she was far from the rat-faced monstrosity that the deputy had described, her vacant face and pallid complexion were just as disturbing. To Ray, she looked like a corpse.

"You're just a man," she said. "This is a surprise. When I was called, I expected it to be the other. Instead, I find just a man."

"The other?" Ray asked, straining against the invisible bonds that held him.

"You'd have me explain myself?" She laughed. It was unsettling, laughter coming from that expressionless face, that slack mouth.

"Why are you doing this?" Ray's muscles burned from the effort, but as far as he could tell, his mouth was the only part of him that was free to move.

Kathy reached out one pale hand, holding out her palm in front of Ray's face. She spread her fingers, each of them tipped with a nail like a hooked claw. "And now, you die."

Ray squeezed his eyes shut, waiting for the razor touch of those claws. His vision went dark for a moment then returned. Although his eyes were shut so tight that the muscles in his cheeks ached, Ray could still see. Only now, the room was no longer filled with shadows. In fact, the room was gone altogether, the wood paneled walls and beige carpet replaced by a stark white space completely devoid of furniture. And the woman standing before him no longer looked dead. She looked not only alive, but frightened out of her wits. Her arms were crossed in front of her breasts, her thighs pressed together in an attempt at modesty. She shivered.

There was a shrieking in the distance, as if the window-rattling cry from moments ago was carrying on miles away.

"No, don't open your eyes," Kathy said, clapping a hand over Ray's face. "It'll see us. It'll kill you."

Ray kept his eyes closed, but he went right on seeing everything. Maybe that Monmouth wasn't so full of hot air after all.

"What is it that might see us?" Ray asked. He wished he had something to offer her, a blanket to wrap around her or a jacket to drape over her shoulders.

Kathy shook her head. "I don't know. Something ancient and really, really bad. Something evil." She wrapped her arms tighter. "One second I was laying down in my bed and the next, there was this bright light. I could feel myself drifting towards it, like floating on a raft in the ocean. It was almost nice. But then something cold and dark grabbed me and pulled me back."

Ray stood awkwardly, freed from the invisible bonds that held him on the couch. He wanted to put his arms around her, but didn't know how she might interpret it. Ghost or not, the woman was in her birthday suit. "What does it want?"

"I was sick. I know that," Kathy said. "It saw my sickness and knew that it could use me. It wasn't a brain tumor that killed me."

"But George, he said that the doctors…"

"It may have looked like a brain tumor. Maybe it even *was* a brain tumor. But that was just a symptom. That thing…it's what killed me. It got inside and grew until it killed me."

Ray shook his head. "I don't understand. You said it grabbed you after you…" He let that one hang.

"After I died, you mean? It's okay. It's not like you can offend me with it…I know I'm dead… yeah, that's when it took over. But that wasn't the first time I'd seen it. Back when I was a freshman in college, just a kid really, I tried to kill myself. Took a boatload of pills, cut my wrists open, and got in bed. And then there was darkness. But there was something else, something so dark that I could see it, even in that pitch black. I could feel it trying to crawl inside me. It was in my mouth, in my…" She kept one arm over her breasts and dropped the other so that her hand covered her pubic area. "My neighbor discovered me and called 911. They pumped my stomach, stitched up my wrists. I thought the

Brad Carter | 327

thing I'd seen, that I'd felt…I thought it was just a nightmare brought on by the pills. But when my parents brought me back home to Wisconsin, I was different. Whatever that thing had done to me had changed me."

Ray looked around the room. He wished there was something to sit on. "You started buying things. Hoarding them."

"It was a compulsion. If I stopped, I had nightmares. It drove a wedge between me and everyone I knew. My friends, my family. George was the only one who could get close, and in the end, it drove him away too. I hated it, but I couldn't stop. And the whole time, it was inside me, waiting until it was strong enough to take over."

"A friend of mine had the same problem. This house we're in…" Ray paused looking around at the bright, unadorned space. "The house we *were* in was packed full of stuff. We cleaned it out, hoping that we could get rid of you. Well, of this thing that's using you, anyhow. Guess it didn't work, huh?"

"Having it inside me, I know what it thinks. I can hear its thoughts." Kathy shuddered, as if disgusted at the idea. "It thinks of itself as some ancient god. Whether it is or not, I don't know. My gut tells me that it's not."

Ray nodded. "Let me guess. *Xax-Ghuzuul.*"

Kathy's eyes went wide as saucers. "Yeah. How did you know?"

"Something I read somewhere. But never mind that. If you know what it thinks, you know how to kill it, right?"

She nodded. "I think I do."

The shrieking that had been carrying on in the background seemed to draw closer. Ray's eyelids itched. He thought they might fly open of their own accord.

"Well, how?" he asked, clapping a hand over his eyes.

"Kill me." Kathy's voice was little more than a whisper. She moved her arms to her sides and tipped her chin up. "If you kill me here, while it's still out there in your world, I don't think it can keep using me to hurt people."

"That doesn't make sense."

But Ray knew that it made as much sense as anything else that had happened in his life lately. Here, behind the veil, who knew what was possible?

"I'm already dead. You can't hurt me, not really," Kathy said. "I want you to understand something: I want this to be over. I've had to stand by helpless while this thing torments people. I watched it kill that poor man. I watched my own hands tear his throat out, and I couldn't do a thing to stop it. I've been able to keep it in check. It almost killed this black guy in a garage. I'm not sure how much longer I can hold it back."

"I just don't know," Ray said. "I don't think I can do it."

"Now, don't get me wrong. I don't want to die." She set her mouth, putting on a brave face. She tipped her chin up, presenting her neck. "But it has to be done. The longer this thing hangs around in your world, the stronger it will get. Don't ask me how I know that, but I do. It's been in my head so long. I just want it gone. Please."

Ray took a deep breath. He thought of being stuck by Steven Lovelace's side during his rampage. He remembered the feeling of utter helplessness as he watched that human monster revel in violence. But he couldn't imagine how it would have felt to be forced to share a body with him, to see through Lovelace's eyes as he cut and stabbed and hacked.

"Tell George that I love him and want him to be happy. Tell him that I never wanted any of this." She leaned her head back farther. "Now do it before you lose your nerve."

"I'll try to make it quick."

Ray wrapped his hands around Kathy's throat. She closed her eyes as he squeezed. At first she simply stood there, but as the seconds slipped by and the pressure on her throat grew, she began to shake. Her hands squeezed into fists and beat on her thighs. Horrible wet, gagging sounds pushed through her throat. Ray turned his head, but he forced his hands to keep squeezing.

And then, after what seemed to Ray to be an eternity, her body went limp. She slid out of his grip and fell to the floor. Breathing heavily, tears streaming out of his eyes, Ray sat down beside her.

"What now?" he asked her still body.

She stared back at him with dead, glassy eyes. Then the muscles beneath her face began to twitch. It was so subtle at first that Ray wasn't sure he'd seen it at all. But the movements became stronger, violent even. With a sound like branches snapping underfoot, the bones in Kathy's face twisted, reshaping themselves into something more animal than human.

"Grotesque, is it not?" The voice behind Ray was unmistakable. Those smooth, cultured tones could only belong to Connor Monmouth.

Ray looked at him for a moment but found himself unable to turn away from Kathy for longer than that. The popping and cracking of her bones was a percussion section with no rhythm. Her shoulders dislocated, and her arms lengthened. Her hands hooked into claws. Between her breasts, her sternum pressed forward like the keel of a ship.

Monmouth clapped a hand on Ray's back. "Well done, old chap. It looks like the bugger is well and truly snared. Now, if you'll be so good as to help me drag her back to my study, we'll put an end to this nasty business."

"And just how do we get there?"

Monmouth snapped his fingers, and a door appeared in the wall in front of them. "Suppose I lift the shoulders and you take the legs. Or would you prefer it the other way 'round?"

When the door opened directly into Monmouth's cozy sitting room, Ray was hardly surprised. Sure, why not? He was walking around with his eyes shut tight, yet he could see everything. He was carrying the deformed, half-alive body of a woman he'd just strangled. And he was doing all of this in some land-of-the-dead limbo. So why shouldn't a door appear out of nowhere and open into an English occultist's hideaway? Perfectly natural.

They carried Kathy's body into Monmouth's secret room behind the bookshelves. As soon as they set foot in the room, the specimens in the display cases commenced howling and beating their wings. Ray's stomach heaved. When Monmouth directed him to drop Kathy's body in the middle of the room, he doubled over, clutching at his gut.

"They do make a glorious noise, do they not?" Monmouth said as he crouched over the body.

Ray clapped his hands over his ears to block out the din. He fell to his knees then slumped over. He laid his head on the carpet, praying that this would all be over soon. But he was helpless to look away from the grisly proceedings in front of him.

Monmouth was busy waving his hands over the body. His mouth worked furiously, but Ray couldn't make out a single word. He watched as Monmouth reached inside his smoking jacket and withdrew an ornate silver dagger. The occultist held the knife aloft, his eyes rolled up into his head as he jabbered. He plunged the dagger down, burying it to the hilt in Kathy's belly. Her arms and legs flopped around in feeble spasms, and her misshapen mouth lolled open, but she seemed incapable of much more.

All at once, the room went silent except for the wet sound of Monmouth hacking a long trench in Kathy's abdomen. When he'd made a slit from just below her navel to the bottom of her ribcage, he tossed the knife aside. It thumped down on the carpet inches from Ray's face.

"Beg your pardon, old chap." Monmouth rubbed his hands together over the body. Droplets of blood flew from them. "I quite say that you look a big worse for the wear, but don't worry, we'll be done soon enough."

He turned his attention back to Kathy's corpse. Drawing in a deep breath, he plunged his hands into her slit abdomen. He hummed a happy tune as his fingers squelched through her innards. Ray's nausea reached a crescendo, and he vomited onto the floor.

"Just a moment more," Monmouth sang. "Then you can open your eyes and be on your way. The morsel I'm after is in here somewhere. A tiny cocoon that will become a beautiful butterfly is buried in these entrails."

Ray opened his mouth to tell him to hurry up, but all that came out was a startled cry as something that felt like a sledgehammer punched through Ray's shoulder. His eyes flew open in shock. Monmouth screamed, but the sound was distant and fading. Ray's lungs filled with air so hot that he was sure they would melt. He clenched his stomach muscles, trying to forcefully expel the air from his lungs, but it went right on filling him until he passed out.

Chapter Forty-Eight: Tate

Tate had been up since before sunrise. He hadn't been able to find his mother yet, so he figured he might as well put in some time at the station. He had no idea if the rumor mill had started cranking into overdrive about his recent absence, but he intended to see that no one got any dumbass ideas about him no longer being fit for the office of sheriff. Maybe he'd cracked a little bit under the strain of the last few weeks, but he *was* human. So he made a quick appearance, staying just long enough to let everyone know he was back in the game. Then he got one of the cruisers from the lot and set out, determined to find his mother.

He tried her cell phone and it went straight to voice mail. He didn't leave a message. Even if she'd found her phone in that trash heap she lived in, she might be avoiding him. After their last meeting, he wouldn't be shocked. And besides, she was shacked up with George Young—couldn't be much doubt about that now—and the smartass writer probably turned her even more against him. He sighed. This was going to take a lot of sorting out.

For the first time since Percy Flannigan turned up dead, Tate was in luck. He figured he'd spend the morning driving all over creation trying to catch sight of his mom's car, but there it was in her driveway. Maybe she'd gotten tired of her new boyfriend and had come home for a break. Or, worse, maybe Young was in there with her. Tate shuddered at the possibilities that scenario might entail.

He parked the cruiser by the curb and crossed the lawn, coaching himself as he went.

Stay calm, stay reasonable. Don't let her talk you around in circles.

Mounting the porch, he wondered how calm he could remain if Young answered the door. Even as sheriff, he couldn't just strong-arm the guy out of there and shoot him on the front lawn. Things were never that simple, Tate supposed.

He rang the doorbell and stood there running through his opening speech in his head.

Look, Mom, I know that we've had some disagreements lately, but I think if we can just sit down and talk...

He was preparing to ring again when he heard it. The noise had probably been going on since he'd stepped onto the porch, but he'd been so lost in his own thoughts that he hadn't noticed. It sounded like a fight was going on in there. There was a sound like a strangled moan followed by a heavy thump. Tate's heart nearly jumped into his throat. He took a couple hurried steps back, bent his knees slightly, and kicked the door. If this had been one of the cop movies he loved so much, the door would have jumped off its hinges with a satisfying sound of splintering wood. But in the real world, the sheriff of Gayler County didn't have enough weight behind the blow to do much more than make a loud bang. It took him three more tries to break the lock out of the door frame. And when it happened, his forward momentum carried him over the threshold and spilled him onto the floor.

He popped up quick, drawing his gun and edging toward the source of the noise. It was coming from the TV room. Tate paused.

That moaning was coming from the room with the big couch in it. What if his mother and Young were fooling around in there? The thought brought with it a mental image that made him shudder. As he shook his head to clear away that awful picture, he noticed for the first time since crashing through the entryway that the house was almost completely cleaned out. From his vantage point in the hallway, he could see into the front room and around the corner into part of the kitchen. They were not only tidy, they were nearly empty. It even looked like the carpet had been cleaned. He glanced to his left and saw that the stairs were likewise free of clutter. Just what the hell was going on here?

Tate raised his gun, took a quiet breath, and sprang around the corner into the TV room. The strange tableau that greeted him was enough to make him blink his eyes a few times to make sure that it wasn't some hallucination brought on by stress.

Ray McFettridge stood in the center of the room. He appeared to be doing some herky-jerky dance with a woman who didn't have a stitch of clothing on. They spun around, and Tate saw that Ray's hands were clutched tight around the woman's throat. They pressed nose to nose. She gurgled and moaned and wheezed, her hands clenched into fists and beating on her thighs. Ray's eyes were closed tight, and veins stood out on his neck.

"Jesus Christ, what the hell is going on in here?" Tate holstered his weapon and ran into the room, hollering for Ray to let the woman go. If Ray heard him, he gave no indication.

It was immediately clear to Tate that all the shouting in the world wasn't going to defuse this thing, whatever the hell it was. His next tactic was trying to insinuate himself between Ray and the woman. This strategy fell flat as well. If he'd had a crowbar, he might have been able to pry them apart, but short of that, they weren't going to budge. The same was true of Ray's grip on the woman's neck. If Tate had a pair of bolt cutters, he could have snipped the constable's fingers off, but that was probably the only way he could loosen them up.

Time was a concern. He had no idea how long this had been going on, but that woman was bound to be getting close to passing out at the very least. She might even be getting close to death, for all Tate knew. It was time for drastic measures.

He took three steps back and unclipped the Taser from his belt. He had no idea if the woman could even hear him, but he figured he ought to give her some warning. "Ma'am, you will receive a shock momentarily. I apologize."

He aimed for the center of Ray's back, but the electrode barbs went high and bit into his shoulder instead. Ray and his dance partner jerked around for a moment then crashed to the floor. Ray pitched straight forward, pancaking the poor woman as he fell. Tate edged forward cautiously, ready to pull the trigger again if Ray wasn't down for the count. He planted his foot on Ray's side to roll him over.

"Awful sorry about that, Ray. I don't know what was going on here, but…"

His next words caught in his throat, snagged up on his startled breath. The naked woman was gone, vanished as if she'd never been there at all.

Tate had simply had enough. He was sleep deprived and pissed off and he wanted some answers. He hauled Ray onto the couch and slapped him awake. While the constable squirmed and mumbled his way back to consciousness, Tate stood with his hand on his holstered pistol. The implied threat was the least he could do.

Ray looked up at him with bleary, confused eyes.

"I figure there's some compelling reason you can give me for not hauling your ass in right now," Tate said. "So start talking. Fair warning, though. I catch a tiny whiff of bullshit, I'll slap the bracelets on you and toss you in a cell, constable or not."

"What?" Ray looked like a blackout drunk who'd just woken up in a strange place.

"I'll tell you what," Tate snapped. "You're in my mother's house. That's breaking and entering, just for starters. And when I entered the room, you were involved in an altercation with some woman. So add attempted murder to the list."

Ray reached his left arm across his chest and winced as he rubbed at his shoulder. "I think you've got the wrong idea. Your mother let me borrow her car. She knows I have keys to the house."

"She also know you were trying to kill a woman in her TV room?"

"Look around. You see a woman in here?"

Rage boiled up in Tate's belly. "Don't you dare sass me, Ray. I want to know what the hell is going on."

Ray held up his hands. "Just calm down. I think we'd better call your mom. I'm going to reach into my pocket and get my phone. Don't shoot me or anything."

"Good luck getting ahold of her. She lost her cell phone."

"I bet George still has his," Ray said.

Tate thought his head might explode. Under the circumstances, that might just be merciful.

Brad Carter | 335

Chapter Forty-Nine: Stephanie

The scrawny sheriff made all four of them sit on the couch. While they sat there, packed shoulder to shoulder, he stood in front of them with his hand resting on his gun. Like he might just decide to shoot them if their answers weren't good enough. His body language was pure swagger, but his eyes were full of confusion.

Myrna did most of the talking. That was good. She was his mother, and if anyone could talk him down, it had to be her. And Stephanie had to admit that the woman had a gentle, soothing way about her as she explained things.

"Son, I don't know what you've got against him, but George is a good man. He's the reason that I finally got this house cleaned up," Myrna said.

The sheriff snorted. "Cleaned up? Mom, it's been cleaned *out*. Your TV's gone. All the furniture in the front room is gone. What else did he take?"

"He didn't *take* anything. I told you, some of the stuff was just old and needed to go. I want to start fresh."

Stephanie thought the woman's explanation was pretty plausible: she'd gotten close with George and didn't want her son to know about it. As a gesture of goodwill, George had persuaded her to clean up the house. And George had agreed to get rid of all the things that had belonged to his wife.

"That still doesn't explain what Ray is doing over here," the sheriff said.

"He was helping out," Myrna said, her voice full of patience and sincerity. "I met his cousin Stephanie at the flea market, and we hit it off. It was her idea to pitch in and help with the house."

Stephanie nodded as earnestly as she could manage. "My cousin had a headache and needed to lie down somewhere quiet. We were making an awful lot of noise at George's house, so he came over here."

The sheriff narrowed his eyes. "Then what about the rest?"

Myrna sighed. "The naked woman you said Ray was dancing with?"

"He was strangling her, Mom."

"Son, look around. There's no naked woman in here. And if Ray fell over on her after you zapped him, how could she have possibly gotten out without you noticing? Be reasonable. You've been under a lot of strain lately with this murder case. You've just gotten a little out of sorts, that's all."

The sheriff stood there fuming. Stephanie could practically taste the anger boiling off him. He jabbed his finger at George. "My mother is an adult and can make her own decisions about who she dates. But that doesn't mean I have to like it. You've got my full attention now, understand? Be on your best behavior, because I'll be watching." He moved the finger in Ray's direction. "And we'll just see about this come election time. I'm not sure what the hell you're into, but I aim to find out. And when I do, you can bet your bottom dollar each and every one of your constituents will too." Finally, he pointed at Stephanie. "You're a long way from Memphis. I was you, I'd watch my step. Come to it, might be time for you to think about heading back home."

He crossed his arms over his chest. Stephanie supposed that he was staring them down, so she dropped her gaze to the floor, hoping to look sufficiently cowed.

Myrna cleared her throat. "Tate, honey, you look terrible. I don't know what's wrong, but you need to get some sleep. Have you been eating?"

It was such a motherly thing to say that Stephanie had to bite her lip to keep from laughing. The sheriff didn't seem the least bit amused.

"If y'all don't mind, I'd like to talk to my mother alone," he said. The tone in his voice said that he didn't give a shit if they minded or not.

George paced back and forth on the porch, pausing now and then to throw worried looks at the house.

"You're going to wear a rut in this porch if you don't give it a rest," Stephanie said.

She sat in one of a pair of wicker chairs. Ray sat in the other. He still looked pale and a bit sick, but that wasn't surprising. He hadn't gone into much detail, but once they'd been kicked out by the sheriff, Ray let it slip that the woman he'd locked horns with was Kathy.

"I had Myrna's keys, so I just let myself in," Ray had said. "I just wanted to get a feel for the place without all the distractions. I didn't think it would happen so fast."

Beyond that, he'd been pretty vague. He'd been back behind the veil; that much was apparent. Most of the texts agreed that those little trips could really take it out of a person, and Ray looked like he'd gone ten rounds with the boogeyman. He was sweaty, and the dark circles under his eyes looked just as bad as those the sheriff was sporting. Of course, Ray had also just been electrocuted by that same sheriff. That could explain some of his space-case stupor.

Stephanie gave up trying to get George to sit still and turned her attention back to Ray. "So, it's done?"

Ray snapped back into focus. He looked over at George for a moment then back at her. He nodded. "I think so. I did what Monmouth wanted me to do."

"So you're not sure or what?"

"I can't be sure about anything, but I think we'll be okay. I think…"

He trailed off again, his face going slack. Then he sprang from his chair, leaned over the edge of the porch and vomited onto the grass. There seemed to be way more coming out of him than was normal, but he brought it up without any gagging or gasping. When he finally finished, he slumped back into the chair. His head lolled over onto his shoulder, and his eyes closed slowly. Stephanie's heart jumped. She was sure he was dead. But then he started to snore. His mouth hung partly open, and a trickle of drool ran out.

George stopped pacing long enough to ask, "Is he going to be okay?"

"Well, I can't really say, George. He just finished fighting it out with your wife's ghost and then your future son-in-law saw fit to shock the shit out of him for his trouble." The hostility in her tone was unwarranted and she knew it. But she was scared and didn't know how else to react, so she went on. "I'm sorry for the minor interruption in your love life, I really am. But I think Ray here has had enough. Think you can help me get him into the truck?"

"Sure, anything you need," George said, suitably chastened. "What should I tell the sheriff when he comes out?"

Stephanie sneered. "Tell him we had better things to do than wait on him to come out here and make more idle threats. Now, get over here and give me a hand."

Ray wasn't as zombified as he'd been while he did his wandering behind the veil, but he wasn't exactly a chatterbox, either. Stephanie had to drag information out of him. All she really learned during the whole ride home—she drove; no way was he getting behind the wheel in that state—was that he'd somehow gotten Kathy's ghost to manifest in the flesh then strangled her to death and deposited her spiritual essence behind the veil where it belonged. Of course, those were mostly Stephanie's words. Ray seemed incapable of speaking more than a sentence or two. Just in case he was interested, she told him about how they'd hauled the boxes in George's garage over to the landfill. Ray just nodded.

It was the dinner hour when they arrived at Ray's house, but neither of them felt much like eating. Ray went straight to his bedroom without any sort of preamble. Stephanie heard the shower in the master bathroom start running. She went to the kitchen and got a Coke from the fridge, wishing there was some whiskey or rum to mix into it. Hell, at this point, she'd even settle for some vodka, which she thought tasted like lighter fluid. But there wasn't a drop of booze in the house. So she settled into a chair at the kitchen table and nursed her soda while she looked out at the backyard.

Something wasn't right. She didn't need any supernatural psychic gift to tell that. The old Chambers intuition was in full swing, telling her that Ray was being less than truthful about what had happened. George may have taken his assurances about Kathy being gone at face value, but Stephanie knew that there was more to it. Nothing could be that easy.

Chapter Fifty: Myrna

George handed over a check to the man who'd just finished repairing the front door and told him to have a nice day. Then he ducked inside, closing the new door behind him.

"Looks solid to me." He smiled at Myrna. "I think even your son the sheriff might have a time busting this one down."

She held out her hand. "Come with me, okay?"

"I'd follow you anywhere."

She led him up the newly cleared stairs.

"Are you sure this is a good idea?" he asked. "Your son seemed pretty angry. I bet he'll be keeping an eye on my house. He'll know if I don't come home."

Myrna paused at the top of the stairs, turning to face him. "I can't be alone. Not tonight."

"Then why here? Why not go back to the motel?" He stood one step down, and it was enough of a difference that they could look at each other eye-to-eye.

"Because I want you to be here when I wake up in the morning. I want you to be with me when I tell my baby boy goodbye." Myrna's voice caught on the last syllable, and she thought for a moment that she might cry. But no tears came. Instead, she smiled and tugged on George's hand so he'd come up one more stair. Then she put her arms around him and laid her head on his chest.

"It's just one room," he said, stroking her hair. "You don't have to jump into this right away. There will be time."

She pulled back and looked up at him. "You let go of Kathy today."

"I let go of Kathy a long time ago. What happened today…" He took a breath and let it out slowly. "What happened today was something else. Whatever that thing was that Ray dealt with, it wasn't Kathy. I have to believe that, otherwise…" He let that thought hang in the air.

"But it made me realize something," Myrna said. "They don't belong here. Kathy, the grey people, my baby boy. As much as I want to hold onto him, he's not a part of this world anymore. Tate was angry, and I'm sure he didn't mean some of the things he said. But he was right when he said that I had to let Dale go. It's selfish of me to hold onto him like this."

George glanced at the closed door of Dale's room. "You seemed so definite yesterday when you said that you wouldn't get rid of his things. I just don't want you to rush into something you'll immediately regret."

"You make it sound like I'm scrubbing every trace of him from my life. It's not like that. I'll keep all the macaroni art and handprint turkeys he made for me in kindergarten. I have his baby books and scrapbooks with all his Cub Scout badges and pictures of his little league teams. But the baseball cards and comic books and model airplanes and action figures and clothes…they're things I can let go. They're things I *need* to let go. He can live on in my memories, but it's cruel to force him to live on as a ghost."

"As long as you're sure," George said.

She led him the few steps down the hallway to Dale's room. She hesitated on the threshold.

"Well, maybe we can wait until morning. One more night won't hurt anything," she said.

Chapter Fifty-One: Ray

The alarm clock beside the bed told Ray that he'd been out for hours. It was half past midnight when he jumped abruptly from sleep to full-on wakefulness. He was lying naked on top of the blankets, which were damp and warm beneath him. He must have come straight out of the shower and flopped down on the bed. It was a strange thing to do, but then he'd been pretty out of it. In fact, as he sat up and swung his legs over the side of the bed, he couldn't really remember much about what had happened during the afternoon. He'd been at George's place, helping to clear things out of the garage. Then he'd gone to Myrna's to see if he couldn't do some reconnaissance work with Kathy's ghost. Then…nothing. He crinkled his brow and searched his memory, but came up empty.

What the hell, he hadn't had a full-on blackout since his heavy drinking days. The feeling wasn't something he'd missed since then.

He staggered into the bathroom and splashed some cold water on his face. As he came up for air, scrubbing at his cheeks with a hand towel, he caught a glimpse of himself in the mirror and nearly screamed. His knees buckled, and he pitched forward, grabbing the counter just in time to keep his face from smacking into the mirror. He closed his eyes, telling himself that when he opened them, the image staring back at him would be his normal face. But when he looked again, what he saw was far from normal.

Half of his face had been twisted into monstrous deformity. It was as if his skull had been split down the vertical axis, and one half had been grafted onto something dredged up from a backwoods sideshow. If he turned to the right, and looked out of his left eye, the image in the mirror was good old Ray. A little pale and haggard looking, but still Ray McFettridge and no mistaking it. But if he turned the opposite way and looked with his right eye, he saw something that a carnie barker might have called the Amazing Rat Woman.

On that sideshow half of his face, his lips were plump and red, but they were pulled into a permanent sneer. His nostril was pushed back so far that it appeared to be a black hole in the center of his face. His right eye was a beady black marble that had drifted almost to the side of his head. Even the hair on his right side was different. His cropped grey had been replaced by thick brown locks so dark they were nearly black. They spilled over his shoulder.

Horrified, Ray looked down at his chest. The patch of hair that covered his sternum was half gone, replaced on one side by a breast capped with a distended red-brown nipple. His right hand flew up to his throat and clamped down tight. The long nails at the fingertips dug into his neck, and rivulets of blood ran down onto his chest.

"Mine now. Shouldn't have interfered, little man."

The voice certainly came from Ray's throat, but it sounded nothing like him. He tried to answer it, to spit back some defiance. The thought was there in his mind, but he was unable to give voice to it. He turned his energy toward removing the claws digging into his neck. He strained and bore down, but couldn't budge a single finger. His left arm, the one that was unaffected, flopped around uselessly.

"Blame the lawman," the alien voice told his reflection. "Had he not interrupted, that fucking Englishman would have me pinned to the wall of his torture chamber. Good thing for me he was quick on the draw."

Ray remembered his mother's warning, that visiting the other side left him open to all sorts of nasty things.

"You should have listened to her," the voice continued. "The writer's bitch wife was mine, and you thought to take her from me. Now, you're mine. Fair trade. And so nice to be inside something living again."

The hand released his throat abruptly. It traveled over both sides of his torso, spreading the blood in nonsense patterns like a child's finger painting. The jagged nails scraped lightly against his skin.

"You will do everything I desire." The voice was little more than a whisper.

As if to demonstrate the truth of that statement, the claw tipped hand rose and formed a fist. The index finger extended and turned around to point directly at Ray's left eye. With agonizing slowness, the finger moved forward. Ray tried to blink, but couldn't manage even that. Tears streamed down his cheek as the nail pressed against his eyeball. The pain was white hot intense, and it raced through his skull. Laughter hiccupped from his throat.

"Mine. All mine."

The nail broke through the surface with a squishy pop. The finger rooted around as gobs of viscous fluid dripped to the counter. It felt like the finger was probing to the back of Ray's skull.

"Be still. Submit. The pain will stop if you just give in."

The finger pressed in further, the jagged nail seeming to scrape across his brain. Agony far beyond any Ray had ever known flared through his body. He wanted to scream that he'd do anything to make it stop. If only the pain would go away, he'd let this thing kill him and be done with it.

"Oh, you will die, that much is certain. But not yet. We have work to do."

Getting dressed was awkward with half of his body nearly useless. His arm and leg moved, but they did so sluggishly, slower than their fellows. But the operation was successful. Ray was still too frightened to examine his body further and didn't turn on any lights in the bedroom as he dressed. He chose a t-shirt and jeans from a basket of laundry he hadn't bothered to fold. If buttoning and zipping his jeans with only one fully functioning hand was difficult, tying his shoelaces was impossible. He settled for a pair of flip-flops instead. His shuffling gait, like a drunk version of Boris Karloff's Mummy walk, was slow and ridiculous, but at least the pain in his skull had faded.

He moved down the hall, his numb left arm flung out for balance. With each step, his coordination increased. And Ray's control of his own body ebbed away. When he reached the living room, he couldn't force limbs to respond to the simplest commands. He was a passenger in his own body.

"Stop right there, Ray." Stephanie stepped out of the kitchen and into the living room. She held Ray's gun in her outstretched hands. "I knew something wasn't right when you came back."

Ray turned around to face her and watched as she recoiled at his appearance. The voice that came out of Ray's mouth was a mockery of his own tone and timbre. "Shoot, then. You can damage this vessel, but you can't kill me. You're too weak. You might as well be deaf, dumb, and blind, you silly bitch."

"Ray, I know you're in there somewhere," she said, taking a hesitant step backwards. "You have to try to get control."

"Too late for that. I have him now."

Ray felt the impact of two slugs, followed by a rush of pain that was quickly extinguished. Stephanie squeezed the trigger again and again, but the remaining bullets went wide of their target. Ray heard the lamp behind him shatter. Then he felt his body march forward, more assured in its movement than it had been.

"No, no, no!" he screamed.

Although his voice rang out in his head loud enough to cause his eardrums to ache, he could tell that no sound issued from his throat. He was as powerless and invisible as he had been when he floated in the company of Steven Lovelace and his two followers. And he found that he was just as helpless to escape. He couldn't even turn away from the events that unfolded in front of him.

He saw his new right hand draw back and take a swipe across Stephanie's face. The black claws at the tips of the fingers opened a quartet of gashes in her cheek. The claw on the index finger caught on her lip for an agonizing moment before tearing free. Ray saw his unchanged left hand close on Stephanie's neck, his thumb pressing down hard on her throat. His right hand joined in, clamping down hard enough to crush his cousin's windpipe. She battered his sides with her fists and drove her knee into his crotch with desperate force. Ray hardly felt it. She stared up at him with wide, unbelieving eyes.

Ray went on screaming until he thought his head would burst, but his hands continued to do their terrible work until Stephanie stopped struggling. Her limp body slid through his hands and thumped down on the floor, covered in dark, sticky blood. Even then, he was unable to look away.

"Cunt." The single syllable came out of his throat like he was hacking up a wad of phlegm.

In the silent moment that followed, Ray found that although he knew himself to be crying, there were no tears issuing from his remaining eye. He turned and walked to the front door, the flip-flops popping against his heels.

Driving was much easier than walking. Since his right leg was unaffected by the slowness and uncertainty that claimed its counterpart, working the pedals was simple enough. He tried to force his hands to jerk the steering wheel. He tried to make his foot stomp on the brake. Not only were these efforts entirely futile, the thing inside him raised his finger and jabbed it into his ruined eye, bringing a fresh wave of agony. It was the worst injustice: he could feel everything but was powerless to respond, while the thing inside him seemed immune to pain but was in complete control of his body.

The truck pulled over to the side of the road.

"Continue to fight me and I'll make it much worse," his voice croaked. He stared at himself in the rearview mirror for a moment. He could feel his unnatural right hand creep across his thigh and unzip his pants. The hand reached inside and clamped down on his scrotum, squeezing until Ray was sure something would burst. A sharpened nail dug into the soft flesh. He screamed and blubbered soundlessly until the hand withdrew.

"We are going to become fast friends," his voice said. "This flesh and blood body is so much nicer than my last vessel. I'd almost forgotten how delicious pain could be."

The truck pulled back onto the road. The vehicle seemed to drive itself, taking a right at the end of the gravel road and heading for the paved county roads and Barlow. Ray wasn't surprised. He hoped that George and Myrna had gone back to the motel. If they were out of the house, maybe this thing wouldn't be able to find them. Maybe, given time, he could talk it down, make it see reason. Stephanie said he had power beyond what he thought possible. Thinking of his cousin brought him up short. He remembered her wide eyes going blank as he'd strangled the life from her.

"They did not leave the house," his voice said, answering the question he hadn't spoken aloud. "I can feel them there."

Ray felt his own lips pull into a smile.

His voice continued, "Yes, I can hear it all, every thought that slips out of your soft brain. I was old before the first slimy thing crawled from the sea and struggled to force air into its body, so don't believe for one moment that you can defy me."

What are you? Ray thought. *Are you really Xax-Ghuzuul?*

"There was a time when that name could invoke my presence. But that time was long, long ago."

So, if you're some sort of god, why even bother with us little people? Aren't we beneath you?

The truck rumbled on for a minute, and Ray figured that his puppeteer was no longer in the mood to answer questions. But then his voice spoke again.

"Gods require sacrifice. We require death. It is the food that we digest. For thousands of years, I have starved behind the veil. But now I am free to walk this world once more, and I shall grow strong again. I'll glut myself on pain and suffering and death. And I have chosen this man and woman to start my feast."

Ray forced himself to laugh. *Bullshit. You're no god. Kathy told me all about you. She said you're just some peon demon with a jumped-up ego who thinks he's an ancient god. Like a kid playing dress-up. If you were really such hot unholy shit, you wouldn't have needed Kathy's ghost to walk around on this side of the veil, and you wouldn't need my body now. You're just small potatoes with an outsized ego.*

"A peon demon who has absolute control over you. You'd do well to remember that. Insult me again and you'll know how it feels to have your manhood torn off and fed to you."

Ray relaxed into silence. He forced himself to take the mental equivalent of a deep breath and scrubbed all thoughts from his mind. It was no easy task. Trying to swat each thought down only seemed to cause another to pop up, like playing some mental game of Whack-a-Mole. But the drive to Barlow wasn't a short one if a driver stuck to the back roads, and so far, the truck hadn't gone near the interstate. He still had time to figure it out.

Although he couldn't close his eyes or plug his ears, he could focus on the sound of the wind blowing past the truck. One of the windows must have been open a crack, and the air whistled through as they sped over the cracked and potholed asphalt. Like the white noise of ocean waves, the sound of the air and the truck's engine ebbed and flowed but was always there. Ray focused on it, losing himself in the steady drone. Gradually, the pain faded away, and the claustrophobic sensation of being locked inside his unresponsive body dwindled to mild discomfort and then to nothing at all. He drifted, numb and alone.

When the disconnect came, it did so with a sound like the tearing of fabric. Whether it was actually audible or an invention of Ray's subconscious, he couldn't know. What he *did* know was that one second, he was inside his ruined and transformed body, and the next, he was outside it, floating in the truck's cab. His fellow passenger twitched and pulled a face like a person about to sneeze. It lifted its right shoulder in a half-shrug.

Ray felt the same sense of disorientation he'd experienced years ago when he'd slipped into Steven Lovelace's van, but this time it was tinged with calm determination rather than fear. And this time, he made no attempt to escape. He intended to see this through to the end.

The truck rolled on.

The thing from behind the veil made no attempt to hide itself. It parked the truck right in Myrna's driveway. It slid out of the vehicle, not even bothering to close the door behind it. Ray sailed out alongside it, and saw that the transformation of his body was ongoing. Since he'd withdrawn, his ribcage appeared to have shrunken, the sternum now thrust so far forward that it strained at the t-shirt covering it. The breast that had sprung up on the right side was pushed almost into the armpit. And the face had continued to twist and reshape. Ray figured that within minutes his own body would be unrecognizable. The thing swatted at him like an annoyed picnicker trying to disperse a cloud of gnats. But its hands couldn't close on Ray's insubstantial form.

He left the thing behind, passing through the door effortlessly. He didn't pause to consider how he accomplished the feat. Instead, he flew up the stairway and into Myrna's bedroom. George and Myrna were there, lying close together under a single sheet. Ray paused, hovering around the edge of the bed. He hadn't given any thought to this part. In truth, he'd never really expected that he could successfully disengage from his body. He hadn't let himself get to the part about waking up two people who couldn't hear or see him. He fluttered about the room frantically, trying to make some sort of noise. But it was no good. His physical presence was either nonexistent or so close to it that he couldn't physically interact with his environment.

He drifted out of the room and hovered at the top of the stairs. There was a faint scratching at the front door as the thing tried to work its way inside. It was probably a matter of time before its patience shattered and it smashed through the door.

Ray spun around in frustration, and fixed his gaze on the door to Dale Wilson's room. An idea formed in his mind.

Chapter Fifty-Two: Chris

The neighborhood was nice. Big, old houses with wide lawns. Trees whose long limbs canopied the street. Chris shook his head. It just showed how insidious the forces of cosmic chaos really were. Even in these tasteful houses could lurk a hoard of junk that defied all human logic and decency. Sure, the lady who owned the house had cleaned the place out, but Chris no longer nurtured the hope that people could change their ways. Once infected by the disease of chaos, the prognosis was never good. No doubt this woman was only hitting the "Reset" button, shifting her stash of junk to another agent of chaos so that she'd have room to amass even more useless stuff. There was only one cure for this disease, and it was the cure Chris had given to his own brother: a swift end. But this time, there would be more than a simple death. It was time for a grand declaration. He was ready to serve notice to the people of this dirty little town that a cleansing fire had come.

Chris crouched in the bushes at the side of the house. He'd approached from the next street over and had cut through two neighboring backyards. So far, everything was quiet and going according to plan. A faint smile played across his lips. At long last, things were coming together.

He pressed against the wall of the house and peeked around the corner. There was a truck parked in the driveway, so he knew that the guilty party was home. No doubt she needed such a vehicle to haul her garage sale purchases home. The thought pulled his mouth into a sneer. He couldn't see the front porch from his vantage point, but he could see the faint glow of a light that must have been near the front door. That was enough for Chris to make up his mind to go in through the back of the house. One nosy night owl neighbor could spoil the whole thing. There would be plenty of time later to announce his arrival, but for now, stealth was key.

The strength of the Golden Knight coursed through him. He hefted his two-gallon jug of gasoline in one hand and his wind chime in the other as he moved through the shrubbery towards the back yard. His pocket bulged with the box of matches he'd found in a drawer in the pederast's kitchen. He crept slowly, wanting to enjoy the anticipation. It was delicious.

There was no lock in the latch on the wooden privacy fence surrounding the backyard. The gate opened without as much as a squeak from the hinges. The yard was a simple square of grass. No ostentation in the form of bird feeders or ornamental gardening. There was a small concrete patio with a picnic table, and a stack of folding lawn chairs leaned against the house. But that was it. In the days before his full awakening, Chris might have paused to consider the possibility that he was making a mistake in targeting this woman. But now he knew of his own infallibility. He'd merged with the Golden Knight, and there was no longer room for doubt.

The door was locked securely, but the window only a few feet away was not. He used one end of his wind chime to pry the screen loose and slid the window open. It went up without a fuss. He put his wind chime through his belt so that it dangled on his hip as if in a scabbard. It was a nice feeling, strong and manly. He tossed the gas can inside. He grasped the window sill, boosted himself up, and wriggled through, landing on a battered and torn sofa. The room was dusty, but, apart from the couch, it was also completely empty. He stood up and glanced around, trying to envision the place as it must have been before the woman had filled a dumpster with her collection of junk. It must have been a horrifying mess. But the woman's mess-making days were soon to be behind her.

Chris uncapped the gas can and upended it over the couch. Eye-watering fumes filled the room as the liquid soaked into the torn cushions. He walked out of the room, dribbling a line of gas behind him as he went. There was a stairway to his right, and he poured the remainder of the gas at its foot. It was perfect. Once he'd started the cleansing fire, he'd dash upstairs and incapacitate the woman. By the time he'd finished, the house would be ablaze, and he would simply stroll out the front door. The purifying flames would dance around him, but they would not burn him, for he was filled with a holy fire that burned hotter than any other. It would be a glorious scene, worthy of the Golden Knight himself.

He set the empty gas can down quietly and took the box of matches from his pocket. The time had come. The match rasped across the side of the box and leapt to bright life. He dropped it into the wet stream at

350 | ONLY THINGS

his feet and watched as a thin line of blue and yellow fire whispered down the hallway and into the room at the back of the house. There was a faint *whoompf* as the sofa caught fire. Chris nodded, his chest swollen with pride. He slipped the wind chime out of his belt and mounted the stairs. There was a sound from the direction of the room with the couch. It sounded like something had just thumped down on the floor.

Chapter Fifty-Three: The Conjoined

It seemed like years ago that they all sat in George's living room, laying their cards on the table about the weirdness that had crept into their lives. Back then, Myrna had talked about the Kathy thing attacking her son's ghost. She'd said that it had forced itself into his mouth and taken complete possession of him.

"It spoke with his voice and everything," she'd said. "I'm not even sure it actually happened or if it was just a dream. It seemed awful real, but who knows?"

Then Stephanie had said something about the merging of two forms to create strength. Ray couldn't remember. There'd been so much information dumped into his brain lately that some of it was bound to have slopped out over the edge. Still, she'd said something along those lines, he was sure of it.

He drifted into Dale's room, a plan of sorts taking shape in his mind. It was last-ditch, desperate, Hail Mary type shit, but Ray's window of opportunity for doing anything was quickly narrowing. He had to try *something*.

He used Stephanie's telephone strategy to summon Myrna's dead son. As calmly as he could manage—which wasn't all that calm now that he could hear footsteps on the stairs—he envisioned the old rotary dial job he'd had when he and Emma had moved into their first place. It had been a bright red desk model that they'd jokingly referred to as the Batphone. He dialed 3253, the numbers corresponding to the letters in Dale's name. The phone rang twice.

"Hello?"

Ray turned and looked for the source of the voice. A young man sat on the bed. He wore a pair of battered and stained blue jeans, a sleeveless t-shirt, and a perplexed expression. His skin tone was washed out and grey, as if he was an image lifted out of some old movie.

"You Dale?" Ray asked.

"I sure am. But since this is my room and you're the one who brought me here, don't you think you should be the one introducing yourself?"

"You can see me?"

"No, but most people can't see me, so I guess it's not so weird. Hear you loud and clear, though," Dale shrugged. "I was floating around in the dark, just sort of sleeping, and your voice was like an alarm clock. So, you mind telling me who you are? Not that I'm not grateful to be back or anything."

Ray floated close to him. "I'm a friend of your mother, and she's in a lot of danger. I wish there was time to explain, but I need you to open your mouth."

"Open my mouth?"

The slow, heavy footsteps on the stairs stopped. The thing was at the top of the stairs, Ray thought. Probably sniffing around, trying to decide which door to barge through.

"If it wasn't life or death, I wouldn't ask," Ray said. "Something is coming up those stairs to kill your mother, and I think I might know a way to stop it."

"I'm listening."

"Remember that shadow that got inside you and used you like some kind of puppet to frighten your mother?"

"Hard to forget," Dale said.

"I think there was something to that. Like the combination of two spirits—or whatever you call them—merged to make something more solid, something with physical strength. You see what I'm getting at?"

Dale considered, but only for a second or two. Then he opened his mouth like he was in the dentist's chair waiting on the drill to start, and Ray plunged in.

There was a moment of complete darkness and silence as Ray settled into his new body, then his senses came awake. Something like flesh—something almost as solid, anyhow—coalesced around him. He jumped up from his seat on the bed and nearly fell flat on his face. If it hadn't been for a waist-high stack of comic book boxes, he'd have gone down. It took a moment to regain his equilibrium before he threw open the door and stepped into the hallway.

There was shouting from Myrna's bedroom, a voice that Ray didn't recognize.

Brad Carter | 353

For a panicked instant, he was sure he was too late. He saw the thing wearing his old body lumber off the top stair and into Myrna's room. He heard a shriek of something like mingled rage and pain. At the same moment, his newly returned sense of smell registered the pungent stink of smoke. He looked to his left and saw smoke drifting up the stairway.

"Don't just stand there!" Dale's voice screamed inside his head.

Ray's paralysis broke, and he ran. But the bedroom door slammed shut just as he reached it.

Chapter Fifty-Four: Chris

Chris had fought down the urge to go to work as soon as he entered the room. Soon enough, the house's smoke alarms would go off, and the two lovers would awaken. Realization would dawn on them as they met his stern, unyielding gaze. And finally, they would know that judgment had been passed. He stood at the foot of the bed and watched their peaceful slumber. One would hardly know, just looking at them, that they were agents of a cosmic force that could be the undoing of the species.

A minute went by, and still no squawking of smoke alarms. Sure, there were no basic safety precautions in this house. Just as Julian had scorned smoke alarms, this woman had chosen to disregard her own safety. Some people didn't just deserve a painful death, they were begging for one. And if they were begging, Chris was happy to oblige.

He raised his wind chime and took a deep breath. "I am the cleansing fire, and I have come to purge the world of filth and disorder!"

The two lovers started awake. The man clutched the woman protectively while also making some vaguely defensive gesture. Chris almost laughed at how pathetic they looked. The man sputtered something indignant, and Chris let him have a taste of the wind chime. He aimed for the old codger's head, but the guy was quick for someone who'd just woken up, and he dodged at the last possible instant. The blow landed on his shoulder instead, and the guy made a grab for the wind chime. Chris pulled his weapon back, but the movement caused him to jerk forward and bark his shin on the bedframe. The wind chime flew out of his hand.

As he looked around frantically for his weapon, he saw the horror that slouched through the doorway. The door slammed shut behind it with a sound like a thunderclap.

"A little privacy for this dance," the thing said in a low growl.

Chris tried to bellow his rage at the interruption. But he found his throat dry. Maybe it was the smoke that was starting to drift in. Surely the cleansing fire within him would allow no fear.

The creature—for surely it wasn't human—was the embodiment of ugliness and deformity. It was neither androgynous nor hermaphroditic, but Chris could see elements of both sexes present in its anatomy. Its face was a mishmash of features, as if some deranged god had pieced it together from scraps of dead bodies. Fear slithered into Chris' guts. There was something in the abomination that he recognized. Some distant, half-remembered trauma swam through his memory.

"Go away," Chris whispered. He squatted down, patting around on the carpet for his wind chime. His fingers closed on the smooth metal, but it was little comfort.

The creature cocked its head to one side and drew in a long, hissing breath through its wide, flat nose. "You have something in you that I've smelled before. Something from the darkness behind the veil."

"I am the cleansing fire, the Golden Knight of Perfection." Chris sprung up from his crouch. He swung his weapon, but the creature dodged the blow.

The creature made a hacking grunt that could have been laughter. "I remember you now. Another would-be *Xax-Ghuzuul*. You slipped through the hole in the veil that I made. The pilot fish to my shark. Buried yourself in that boy that was in the hospital. That weak, shattered boy that I'd passed over. So tell me, are you content with my leavings?"

A flash of white light burst across Chris' vision, so sudden and hot that he was sure his eyeballs would burst. He flailed about blindly, crashing into a dresser. In the aftermath of the lightning strike, he saw a series of images. No, not just images. These were memories drawn from the thing inside him. The Golden Knight of Perfection. The Cleansing Fire. At last, its true self bubbled up to the surface for Chris to see. And what he saw was far from the dream of a dragon-slaying hero wielding a sword of fire.

Two shadowy forms, dark enough to stand out even against the blackness of their surroundings. Both of them were crawling toward a distant pinprick of light, a star against the vast darkness. On and on they went, through the murk, the bright spot in the distance becoming larger as they neared it. Occasionally, the larger form would turn and lash out at the small follower. And they would fight.

The creature made the guttural laughing sound again. "You see it now for the first time, its true face."

Chris shook his head, as if he could clear away the nightmare images and make his vision return. But the images continued to unreel before him.

As they grappled, their shadows coalesced into shapes. The smaller form became a man dressed in warrior garb and swinging a sword. The larger form became a giant rat who slashed at the small warrior with razor claws and serrated incisors. The rat maimed and mutilated the warrior, and left him for dead.

The creature was close enough now that Chris could smell its rotten breath. "Persistent little bastard, you are. I told you then that the world only needed one *Xax-Ghuzuul*."

"There were always two faces of the god..." Even as he said it, Chris had no idea what his words meant. "You wouldn't share."

The pinprick of light had grown into a small doorway. The rat wriggled through, thrashing its massive hindquarters to propel itself forward. The warrior crept up cautiously and peered through the bright hole into a hospital ward. He watched as the rat pushed his bulk down the throat of a young woman who lay asleep with an IV plugged into one arm. The warrior jumped through the doorway, scurrying into the adjacent room, where a young man lay in a state similar to his neighbor. The warrior stared at the young man's mouth, which hung slightly ajar.

Chris screamed as he recognized the face as his own.

His vision cleared, snapping back into focus. The creature drew back one arm and swiped at Chris' face. Its claws raked a trio of gashes across his forehead. Chris' head snapped back, and he saw that the man and woman had slid out of their bed. They were backed into a corner between the bed and a window that looked out into the backyard. The woman pressed against the man's shoulder as he looked back and forth from the scene in front of him to the window. Clearly, he was calculating the risk of jumping. There was a banging on the door like something was trying to beat its way inside. Smoke trickled in under the door.

Everything had gone to hell. The power of the Golden Knight had ebbed away to nothing. That deep, reassuring baritone which had guided him these past weeks was silent. The quiet strength the Golden Knight had radiated had been replaced by a steady whine of knee-knocking fear. Chris was alone. The presence inside him had burrowed so deep that it was lost.

He struggled to his feet and swung his wind chime. The blow landed on the creature's deformed ribcage with a meaty *thunk*. It laughed, baring a pair of massive incisors that sprouted from black, bleeding gums. And then it was on him, slashing and biting and ripping. It grabbed his head between two leathery hands and slammed it down on the floor. There was a sound like wood splintering, and Chris wasn't sure whether the bedroom door had just broken away from its frame or if his skull had shattered.

Chapter Fifty-Five: The Heroes

Ray threw Dale's body against the door, hammering away with his shoulder at the solid wood surface. Dale seemed to finally sense the true danger his mother was in, and he was screaming away inside Ray's head for him to put his weight into it and break the damn door down before whatever was inside killed his mother.

"Jesus, listen to the racket in there," Dale said as Ray threw his shoulder into the door.

If this had been a newer house, they'd have busted the thing right out of the frame after a couple tries. But these older houses were built by folks who meant it, and although there was a little give with this blow, the door was still stuck. Dale kept on talking. Maybe he thought he was helping, like a basketball coach screaming at his team from the sideline. But all he was accomplishing was making Ray's head hurt.

Or making his own head hurt, Ray supposed. Hell, the whole thing was confusing. As soon as Ray had gotten into this body, he felt a jolt of power. Dale had been in tip top shape when he died, and this re-animated form was no different. All the old aches and pains were gone. Ray realized just how much he'd become accustomed to bad joints, sore spots, and all the other shit that went along with being an old timer. Now, he felt young and strong. Hell, from a certain point of view, he *was* young and strong. After all, no matter how loud Dale could scream inside his head, it was Ray who was in the driver's seat.

The smoke that had been creeping from downstairs was now billowing. Grey clouds hung on the ceiling. Ray crashed into the door again. This time the frame buckled, and there was the gunshot sound of solid wood breaking. He stepped back like a place kicker lining up a field goal then kicked just below the doorknob. The door swung open.

Ray stepped into the room. The sight that greeted him was strange enough to freeze him in his tracks for a moment. His old body—now so deformed that he hardly recognized it as anything other than some creature—was engaged in the business of beating a man to death. It gripped the poor fellow's head in its hands, smashing it onto the floor. The face and skull had been reduced to a pulpy red mass that defied recognition. For a horrible second, Ray thought the victim might be George. Then he saw the author huddled into the far corner, his arms thrown protectively around Myrna.

The creature looked up from its work, noticing Ray for the first time. It snorted as it rose from its haunches. "The one that got away. You are a slippery little thing."

"Dale!" Myrna tore herself away from George.

"Myrna, no, stay back," Ray said.

George grabbed her, reeling her back into his arms.

A smile of recognition spread across the creature's face as it looked at Ray. "I wondered where you'd gone."

"Dale!" Myrna reached out, straining to get away.

The creature's eyes cut sideways, looking at Myrna. A grey tongue flicked out of its mouth and slopped saliva across its lips. For something so bulky and strangely proportioned, it moved lightning quick, reaching out with its left arm and dragging Myrna out of George's grasp. Her feet left the ground as it flung her across the room. She hit the wall near the bathroom and slid down, collapsing on the floor.

The scream of rage that tore itself out of Ray's throat did so in stereo. Dale's voice and his own bellowed as Ray charged the creature. In the split second before his shoulder plowed into the thing's misshapen torso, Ray wondered if Dale had ever played football. If not, the boy was about to learn the proper way to tackle. He slammed the creature into the dresser, and although it was one of those solid-looking antique pieces, it caved right in.

Down they went, clutching at one another like wild animals. Ray got a finger into the creature's mouth, trying for a fish hook. The jaws clamped together and snipped off the digit. Claws dug into his sides, pushing right through the skin. Ray could feel them curling around his ribs. His mouth flooded with hot blood.

"Goddamn it, George, run!" Ray screamed through the pain. The words came out gurgling and wet. "Get Myrna and get out of here! Now!"

He'd managed to work his maimed hand back around the creature's face. He pressed his thumb into its black eye. It howled as he dug in, pushing until the eyeball burst. The claws withdrew from Ray's ribs as the creature pawed at its face. In the brief moment before it renewed its assault blindly, Ray saw George throw Myrna over his shoulder and charge out into the smoke-filled hallway.

"Let's finish this," Ray said, unsure if he was speaking to the creature or to Dale. Either way, they both seemed to agree.

He wedged his right forearm under the creature's chin and slammed his left fist into its ribcage. The thing thrashed away from him and headed for the door, guided by some sightless sense of direction. Ray's legs were numb in places and screaming agony in others. But he managed to throw himself on top of the creature and wrestle it back to the floor. They landed in the hallway, only a few feet from the top of the stairway. Through the smoke, Ray could see a pair of firefighters ushering George and Myrna out of the house.

The creature raged and spat and screamed. It struggled and twisted beneath him. But Ray held on.

"Thrash around all you like. We're not going anywhere," he said.

Chapter Fifty-Six: Tate

Tate was debating with himself whether he should try some of the sleeping pills he'd picked up at the Rexall. He didn't much care for the idea of doing drugs, but he sure as hell wasn't looking forward to another marathon of nightmares. He took a long, hot shower, thinking that it might help relax him. Then he got the sleeping medicine out and started wondering if he could go through with it. He had the pills out and was staring down at the little blister pack when his phone rang.

As soon as he answered, Avery started in, spitting out a crazed jumble of words in a panicked voice. Tate didn't catch every single syllable, but he got enough to know that he was going to be wading into deep shit very shortly. The way Avery told it, the whole thing had been like a line of dominoes falling. First a 911 call had come in from someone claiming to be related to Constable McFettridge in Edgewood. Her story, which she croaked out in a voice that was barely audible, was that the constable had flipped his lid and tried to kill her. For some reason that she couldn't explain, he was headed to Barlow to kill two people: George Young and Tate's mother. By the time a car got to Myrna's house, the place was completely engulfed in flames.

Tate didn't wait for Avery to get any further. He stomped into his shoes and ran for the front door.

They had the hoses going full blast by the time he got there. It looked like the county's entire fleet of emergency vehicles had shown up. Bart Stilwell was working crowd control, keeping the concerned and curious alike on the other side of the street. Avery was nearby, leaning against one of the cruisers and watching the blaze. He stood up at Tate's approach.

"They got both of them out," the deputy said. "Your mama and George Young. Straight to the hospital, but they seemed like they were going to be just fine. Some smoke inhalation, maybe."

Tate's heart fell to the pit of his stomach as he looked back at the house. He was no expert, but he knew the place was a total loss. It didn't really matter. The whole state could burn down for all he cared, as long as his mom was okay. He slumped against the car and tried to regain his composure before going off to chase the ambulance. Last thing he needed was to flip his truck taking a curve too tight and wind up as his mom's neighbor in the hospital.

"You have any idea who else was in there with them?" Avery asked, wincing as a blast of heat blew out one of the second story windows.

Tate shook his head. "Someone else was in there?"

"They got here and pulled your mama and her friend out of the house quick. Guy I talked to said Young was going down the stairs with your mama over his shoulder, beating on the fire with a blanket in his other hand. They got out easy, you think about it. But all the firefighters that went in after that said they heard voices coming from upstairs."

Tate went on shaking his head. "Voices?"

"Said it sounded like a couple other people…"

The rest of Avery's reply was lost in the noise of more windows shattering. Two firefighters ran out of the front door, waving their arms and shouting. A moment later, another figure emerged. It was a hulking, stoop-shouldered person engulfed in flame. If he didn't know better, Tate might have thought it was a gorilla rather than a person.

"Jesus Christ, there was someone else!" Tate shouted.

As soon as the words were out of his mouth, another fiery figure stumbled out of the doorway. This one was a normally proportioned man. He staggered around, his burning arms flung out at its sides for balance. Then, like one of the professional wrestlers Tate had watched as a kid, he jumped on the back of the other and dragged it back into the burning house. As the two burning shapes did their strange backwards dance, the smaller figure turned his head and looked back at the people gathered in the yard. He raised his arm and waved. He seemed to look right at Tate. The two figures disappeared as the porch collapsed in a fiery heap.

Tate fell to his knees, staring at the house. What he'd glimpsed in that instant was impossible.

Avery squatted beside him. "You okay, man?"

Tate nodded, unable to speak. Even if he could, what would he say? That in the moments before the porch collapsed, he'd seen his dead brother wave at him, smiling as he dragged some burning gorilla back into the house? How could he even begin to explain?

"Did you see them?" he asked.

Avery made a face. "See who?"

"The two people on the porch."

"No, I didn't see nobody on the porch. But you better get along if you want to catch up to your mama." Avery rose and reached down, offering his hand to help Tate up. "If you don't think too much about things, it's a lot easier."

Epilogue: Chicken, Biscuits, and Peace on Earth

Tate had wanted to cook his mom and George a meal, but his limited ability in the kitchen forced him to settle for some fried chicken and biscuits from the Colonel. He whipped up his own mashed potatoes, a feat that aroused in him a small swelling of pride. He figured that qualified the meal as half-homemade, anyhow.

He told his mom and George that it wasn't exactly a demonstration of culinary skill, but everything had to start somewhere.

"You said a mouthful there," George said as he squeezed some honey from the plastic bear onto his biscuit. "Taking that big first step can be an ordeal, but it gets easier with practice."

"We still talking about cooking?" Tate asked.

"If you like."

Tate took another piece of chicken from the bucket then asked how the search for a new house was coming. Since his mom's place was a blackened heap of ashes and George's house held nothing but bad memories, the two of them had been looking for a new place to move into. He knew there were other things—more important things—they could talk about. For instance, how the coroner had taken Tate aside and told him that there was absolutely no way that Stephanie could have made that 911 call, that her throat had been completely crushed. And maybe they could even talk about why Ray's body had never been found, and that the only bones pulled from the house's ashes belonged to some large, unidentified animal. Or maybe how the last two firefighters out of the house had tendered their resignations the morning after the fire, refusing to give any concrete reasons for their departure.

Instead, they discussed the summer heat and humidity. They debated whether or not the new Starbucks would take hold in downtown Barlow. Small, inconsequential things. And Tate supposed that was just fine.

Later, when they'd had their fill of chicken and biscuits, and after they'd eaten slices of Sara Lee pound cake with whipped cream on top, Myrna scooped up all the dishes and headed for the sink.

"I'll take care of this," she said. "Why don't you boys go sit on the porch?"

Tate wished he hadn't decided to show off with the potatoes and corn. Then they could have eaten off paper plates, and his mom never would have had this opportunity to throw him and George together. But he was stuck now.

"That sounds fine," George said.

Tate took his glass of iced tea and led the way to the porch. He unfolded a pair of lawn chairs from the stack by the door and sat down. George lowered himself into the other, and the two men looked out at the insects swarming the streetlights.

"Like the extended stay hotel? I hear there's free breakfast," Tate said after a moment's silence.

"It's not bad. Bed's a little soft for my taste, but the breakfast is good. But it'll be nice to get into a house. A hotel is pretty impersonal."

Tate let another moment of silence creep in. Frogs croaked their night songs in the distance. He cleared his throat. "They haven't found Ray McFettridge's body. And I suspect they never will."

"They won't," George said. "Ray's long gone."

"And I'm not about to ask how it is you can sound so sure about that. I used to think that I wanted to know all the answers to everything. That's probably what got me into law enforcement. But now I know better. There's some things I'm better off not knowing."

"That's one hell of a philosophical statement."

Tate shrugged. "It's how it is. Maybe someday, you and Mom can sit down and explain all this to me, but right now, I'm okay with just leaving things as they are."

"If that's the way you want it. Probably for the best, if you don't mind me saying."

"Thing is, officially, Stephanie Chambers' murder is still on Ray. I don't like that one bit. Everything about it points right at him, a whole pile of physical and circumstantial evidence. But something about it just doesn't figure. Ray as a murderer? That just doesn't sit right." Tate paused, thinking about Stephanie's phone call and how it apparently was made after she expired. Then he put that thought out of his mind. Avery was right. It was better to not even think about some things at all. He took a drink of his iced tea and went on. "Listen, I think it's best we put the past behind us. Start fresh, you understand. It looks like Mom's set on having you around, and that means…"

"That you're stuck with me?" George laughed.

Tate felt a bit of heat creep into his cheeks, but he laughed too. "Guess that came out wrong."

"Don't worry about it."

Myrna joined them on the porch, unfolding a chair and placing it between the two men.

"It's nice out here," she said. "Cooling off now that the sun's down."

They sat in silence, each of them looking at a different part of the darkness.

Epilogue Two: The Apprentice

The two moths in the killing jar beat their wings furiously as they attacked one another. If Stephanie looked closely, she could just make out their faces. One looked disconcertingly human, with the strong jawline and flowing hair of a comic book hero. The other was the twitching, beady-eyed face of a rat.

She turned to Monmouth, who smiled at her in that inscrutable way that she'd come to hate already in the few days she'd known him. "How long will they go on like that?"

"Who knows? Some go on for quite some time before they accept the inevitable. But tell me, why do you look so troubled? They're monsters," Monmouth said.

"I'm just worried that Ray, or some part of him at least, is still in there."

Monmouth's smile betrayed nothing. He took her arm and led her back into his study. "It will be nice having you around. This place is decidedly lacking a feminine touch."

"Don't get any funny ideas." Stephanie tugged free of his hand. She sat down in one of the antique leather chairs by the fireplace. "I'm not here to play hanky-panky."

"Charming." Monmouth sat down, crossing his legs and placing his hands in his lap. "So, tell me, if you're not here for a romp, where would you like to begin?"

"At the beginning," Stephanie said. "I want to learn everything."

Monmouth raised his eyebrows. "And why not? We have all the time in the world. It's one of many advantages of being dead."

A Preview of Brad Carter's
SATURDAY NIGHT OF THE LIVING DEAD

Chapter 1
Opening Credits

My headache graduated from dull pounding to full-on ferocious migraine as the two black-suited thugs dragged me out of the backseat of the car. They each grabbed an arm and ushered me towards the nondescript office building. My feet were heavy and half asleep, and I scuffed the toes of my shoes as I struggled to keep up. We passed through two sets of automatic doors and into a lobby that contained a bored looking security guard behind a small desk, two badly wilted fichus trees, and a No Smoking sign. The guard was leafing through a battered issue of *Field and Stream*, and he looked up long enough to nod at the two suits. If he even noticed my presence, he gave no indication. He blew out a long breath through his walrus mustache and went back to his reading.

Our awkward trio took a short trip down a hallway and paused in front of an elevator.

The plastic zip tie securing my hands in front of him chafed at my wrists, but I kept it to myself. The two muscle-bound giants flanking me looked about as likely to break bones as offer any type of comfort, so I didn't complain. I just suffered in silence while we waited for the elevator.

For what must have been the thousandth time since my return to the world of the living, I wondered just what the hell was going on. No one had spoken a word to me or shown me any identification. And to my shame, I had just gone along with it. Not that I'd had much choice. One minute, I was walking across a field strewn with debris and bodies, and the next I was coming to in the back of some spotlessly clean car, bracketed by two black-suited thugs. When I woke up in this world of lesions and contusions, I had no idea how long I'd been out, who I was with, and where my friends were. Confusion blurred my memories. Trying to get a fix on the details of the last twenty-four hours was like viewing a scene shot through one too many layers of gauze. I was sure of just one thing: that I was scared.

For the first time since the whole night had gone to hell, the horror of everything was catching up with me. Not just the adrenaline-tingle of plain old fear, but a sledgehammer blow of pure, pants-shitting horror. The sum of the night's events was just too much to contemplate without being overcome with terror, so I settled for letting myself get carried forward by the unfolding events like a jellyfish pulled this way and that by a strong riptide. It wasn't much of a plan, and it didn't say much for my courage, but it was all I had.

The riptide carried me into an elevator, up three floors, and into a room that was alive with the sickly glow and buzz of failing fluorescent tube lighting. Like so many things I'd experienced in the last twenty-four hours, it was like something out of a movie. This was the room where the unorthodox and reckless cop shouted an interrogation at the arch criminal terrorizing the city or some such bullshit. A plain table with a chair on either side, plain walls, and not much else.

"Have a seat," one of the black suits said. "Someone will be with you shortly."

I almost laughed at the casual tone and delivery. It was like the guy was showing me to a table at Applebee's (or, God help me, Rowdy's) rather than a seat at an interrogation table. But I was afraid if I started laughing I might not be able to stop, that I might go on cackling madly until my voice box ruptured. The two suits left the room, the metal door closing behind them with an ominous thud. I sat on one of the plain aluminum folding chairs.

There was no clock on the wall, and my watch wasn't on my wrist anymore, so I had no idea how much time passed before the door opened again. The man who entered was short, with a slight paunch and thinning brown hair combed across his shiny scalp. Like the meatheads, he wore a dark suit and tie. But this guy wore it less like a secret agent from some clandestine government spy squad and more like a mid-level bureaucrat. I could see him in the back office of the DMV, discussing statistical data or something like that. He hardly looked at me as he sat at the table, instead fiddling with the briefcase in his lap. He withdrew a couple thick manila file folders and a digital recorder.

Finally, he looked up and gave me a weak smile. He pushed his glasses up on his nose and said, "My name is Clarke. That's Clarke with an 'e' in case you're wondering."

"Pleased to meet you." I showed him my zip-tie bound hands. "I'd shake your hand, but..."

Clarke frowned. "Oh, good heavens. These young guys, they've seen too many movies." He dug around in his briefcase and came out with a small pocketknife, which he used to saw through the plastic ties. "There you go. I'd apologize, but I doubt it would matter much to you. Suppose we just get down to it instead?"

"It doesn't seem to me that I have much choice in the matter."

Clarke clicked on his recorder and placed it in the center of the table. "Agent Jamison Clarke, access number 8913 dash Z. Interview subject is Ryan Parker" He nodded at me. "Mr. Parker, I'd like for you in your own words to describe the events leading up to the occurrences of the past twenty-four hours in Edgewood, Arkansas. Details are important, so if you would, please be specific."

That was it. There was something in this little man's officious attitude and prissy voice that set me off. The intimidation I'd felt in the presence of the two secret agent types earlier was gone. While those two were menacing and mysterious, this Clarke was more like a meter maid. His air of petty authority blew the top off my well of reserved outrage.

"If you would, please go fuck yourself," I jabbed a finger at him. "I don't know where I am or where you've taken my friends. And I've yet to see any kind of identification. On whose authority am I being held here? Miranda rights, the Geneva Convention, due process, habeas fucking corpus...you guys ever hear of any of that shit?"

Clarke's mouth puckered at the outburst. "You're not being held against your will, Mr. Parker. You are, of course, free to go at any time. But I would suggest that you stay."

I sneered. "Would you now?"

"Walk out that door and a call will be placed to local and state police departments concerning your whereabouts and possible involvement in tonight's..." Clarke waggled his fingers in the air as if plucking from them the proper words. "Tonight's events. I guarantee that they'll hold you on their authority. That is, they'll hold you for as long as it takes for them to realize that they're way out of their depth. Then, the federal agencies will take over. FBI, Homeland Security, all those departments which aren't exactly known for giving the benefit of the doubt."

"Fuck you. Really." I extended my middle finger.

Clarke continued, undeterred. "I can show you my driver's license, but that's the extent of identification that I carry. The agency that employs me is not the kind that issues ID badges and such. More to the point, this agency has no name. It's easier for certain members of the government to deny the existence of something when it has no name. And believe me when I say that the handful of people in Washington who redirect funding our way want all the plausible deniability they can get when it comes to this agency." Clarke laughed, as if at some private joke. "As for your friends, they are elsewhere in this building, in rooms much like this one. They are participating in interviews of their own, possibly giving the interviewer a hard time just as you are. Nobody on your side of the table ever wants to make this easy."

I took a deep breath, let it out. "With Carrie, I can promise you she's giving someone an even harder time. And they've probably had to sedate J.P."

"Ms. Wilderbach and Mr. Kendrick did seem to be quite a handful. But given the circumstances, I can't say I blame them. I can't really blame you either, now that I think of it." Clarke's little smile returned. "We got off on the wrong foot. I'm working on my people skills all the time, but I see that I'm not quite there yet. My wife is on my back about it constantly. She says I need to learn to relate to people, show empathy, that sort of thing. She's probably right. In my defense, this job really does take it out of you. Not much of an excuse, I'm afraid, but it's the best I can do. How about some coffee?" He looked me up and down, getting a good eyeful of the disgusting rags I was wearing. "And I bet I can rustle up some fresh clothes. How would that be?"

Without waiting for an answer, Clarke got up and left the room.

***

The coffee was bad, but I'd consumed worse over the years. I figured that in a situation like this—when you're feeling wrung out and ragged from battling a legion of monsters and being held captive by some secret government agency—even the worst cup of mud in the world was a luxury. The clothes were dark grey hospital scrubs, normally the kind of thing I wouldn't wear, but I wasn't in a position to be picky. I imagined that my old clothes would probably be incinerated.

Clarke sipped his coffee and sighed contentedly. "Coffee makes everything better, am I right?"

"Whatever you say."

"Now, Mr. Parker," Clarke said, putting his cup on the table. "You are the owner of the property on County Road 412. Correct?"

"You know I'm the owner. I can't think of any other reason I'd even be here." I swallowed down another mouthful of coffee. It was good and hot, but it didn't exactly improve my outlook. "Are the questions all going to be this simple? We might be here until next week. How about you tell me what the fuck it was that happened last night? Pardon me for going out on a limb here, but you seem to be taking all of this awful calmly. So calmly, in fact, that I bet you can explain a lot more about it than I can. Am I wrong? Or do you just always take weird shit in stride?"

Clarke's poker face smile remained. "As a member of this agency, I've seen stranger."

Now it was my turn to smile. "Oh really? On a scale of weirdness, what would you rate this one? Give me a one-to-ten."

He thought it over for a second. "I'd say it was a solid six. Maybe six and a half."

"Bullshit. You can't be serious."

"I'm absolutely serious." Clarke nodded. "We specialize in situations such as yours."

I laughed at that one. "You know, after what I've been through, I'm inclined to believe anything. So shoot, Agent Clarke. What do you want to know?"

"Mary Claire Lawson. Start there."

Now it was my turn to think things over. "What does she have to do with your government investigation?"

"Humor me."

I stared into the middle distance for a moment, gathering my thoughts. I rubbed my sore wrists. And I answered honestly. "She was, in a lot of ways, the love of my life. Before and after she died."

Clarke fidgeted for a moment in his chair then settled down. "And you came to Edgewood for her funeral?"

"That's right."